SPARKS LIKE STARS

ALSO BY NADIA HASHIMI

A House Without Windows
When the Moon Is Low
The Pearl That Broke Its Shell

FOR YOUNG READERS
One Half from the East
The Sky at Our Feet

Sparks

LIKE

Stars

A NOVEL

Nadia Hashimi

WILLIAM MORROW
An Imprint of HarperCollins*Publishers*

SPARKS LIKE STARS. Copyright © 2021 by Nadia Hashimi. All rights reserved. Printed in the United States of America. No part of this book may be used or reproduced in any manner whatsoever without written permission except in the case of brief quotations embodied in critical articles and reviews. For information, address HarperCollins Publishers, 195 Broadway, New York, NY 10007.

HarperCollins books may be purchased for educational, business, or sales promotional use. For information, please email the Special Markets Department at SPsales@harpercollins.com.

FIRST EDITION

Designed by Kyle O'Brien

Library of Congress Cataloging-in-Publication Data has been applied for.

ISBN 978-0-06-300828-1 (hardcover)
ISBN 978-0-06-305716-6 (international edition)

21 22 23 24 25   LSC   10 9 8 7 6 5 4 3 2 1

For Amin, my eternal flame

Sparks Like Stars

PROLOGUE

UNTIL NOW, MY HISTORY HAS REMAINED BURIED IN ME THE WAY ancient civilizations are hidden beneath layers of earth and new life. But people insist on digging into the past, poking at relics of yesterday to marvel at the simplicity of extinct creatures. We display the evidence of our superiority in glass cases, housed in grand buildings sometimes half a world away from where they were found.

In London, I saw the Elgin Marbles, lifted from the Parthenon, the Gweagal Shield stolen from Aboriginal Australians, and the brilliant Koh-i-Noor diamond. In the language of my childhood, Koh-i-Noor means Mountain of Light, a name that obscures the diamond's dark history.

But I cannot be too critical. Not while I have my own plundered treasure in a box, far from where it was unearthed. How it came to be with me is the story that I have never wholly told, not to the woman who helped me flee a country on fire, not to the woman who raised me as an American, and not to the man I almost loved.

Were it not for the day my buried life appeared before me unannounced,

I might have kept it all hidden forever. And I might not have asked those questions I'd stifled to preserve this unexamined life.

What are you? I have been asked as I pay for my coffee, as I check out a book at the library, as I explain to my last patient of the day how I will remove the tumor growing inside him. As if I am a species, not a person. People throw identities at me and look to see if one will stick: Greek, Italian, Lebanese, Argentinian, Eastern European. I trigger a railroad switch and divert their questions away from crates of ammunition and streams of pity and preserve for myself the first and only peaceful decade of my life.

But untold histories live in shallow graves. Some nights, the cold wakes me and I find I've clawed my way out from under the covers. I count the stars to catch my breath.

Once upon a time, a little girl with velvet ribbons in her hair crouched deep in the belly of a palace, tucked behind copper pots and urns and cartons heavy with treasures of a lost world. Each time she was shaken by the urge to scream, she plunged her teeth into the soft flesh of her forearm. She knew only that she should remain perfectly silent and prayed no one would hear the thin echo of the song her father would sing when he found her awake well past her bedtime.

> *While I slumber, you are open-eyed*
> *I am naïve but you are ever wise*

Because of him—in spite of him—she did not wail in the dark.

Meters above her, soldiers wandered, some solemnly and others less so, through the warren of hallways. Walls were marked with crimson splatters—the fingerprints of revolution. A general, feeling presidential, slid into a plush Victorian sofa and traced the curves of its lacquered arms. His chest puffed to think that people would soon come to appreciate the sacrifices he'd made tonight for the greater good. He stood and walked across a hand-knotted burgundy carpet, delicate white flowers laced through an elephant's foot motif. He checked the sole of his left boot, then his right. He needn't have worried, though. An Afghan carpet, perhaps by design, conceals blood just as well as it conceals spilled tea.

The city, a halo around the palace, waited on an announcement from the president to explain the sight of Sukhoi jets and the sound of gunfire. American diplomats stationed in Kabul, some still fuzzy from cocktails, wondered what bizarre conflict had befallen their peaceful and exotic post. One silver-haired American woman, teetering from the effects of a stubby cigarette she'd purchased off a hippie couple, tried to touch the paper airplanes that soared over her head. She applauded the flash of fireworks, as Americans do.

Never, that little girl in the palace knew with brutal certainty, had any child in history been more alone.

On that night, giants were felled. A dizzying void swallowed all that had once been. But the trembling little girl could not succumb. She would be brave because her father had once told her that the world lived within her. That her bones were made of mountains. That rivers coursed through her veins. That her heartbeat was the sound of a thousand pounding hooves. That her eyes glittered with the light of a starry sky.

I am that girl, and this is my story.

PART I

April 1978

CHAPTER 1

A STRING OF VEHICLES PULLED INTO THE CIRCULAR PALACE driveway, disappearing one by one as their engines and headlights cut off. I watched silhouettes emerge and approach the main entrance of the palace.

"Neelab, they're here," I whispered.

"How many cars?"

"Fifteen, maybe. It's too dark out. Hard to tell."

"We're going to have to go soon," Neelab warned.

Mother must have seen the cars approach too. Her voice echoed from down the hall. The palace buzzed as it did on those special occasions when its grandest rooms filled with the most important guests.

"Sitara! Where are you?"

I could not hide my disappointment. I looked at Neelab, sitting on the floor with her knees drawn to her chest. The lamplight cast a yellow glow on her cheeks.

"It's a weekend," I groaned.

"They want all the little children in bed when they open that box downstairs," Neelab said, repeating what her mother had told her. "You might as well go to her before she finds you."

But surrender had never been my style.

"What about you? I bet your mother is looking for you too."

Neelab shook her head.

"No way. I'm a young woman now. The rules have changed."

This amused me. "You're barely a full year older than me. And you'd have to wear heels to look me in the eye."

"Go ahead and tease, but if I wanted to, I could throw on one of my dresses and join them downstairs and no one would say a thing," Neelab declared, arms folded across her chest. I loved her too much to point out to her how flat it still was.

"Is Neelab with you?" Mother called, as if she'd forgotten that Neelab and I had been inseparable since I had learned to walk. "It's past time for her to turn in too."

Neelab avoided my eyes then. She hated to be wrong almost as much as I relished being right.

My best friend and I had ducked into the presidential library so I could thumb through a text I'd discovered last week. *The Book of Fixed Stars* was written a thousand years ago by an astronomer named al-Sufi. Like me, he'd been fascinated by constellations, stories written in a pen of light. I'd drawn the velvet curtains so I could match the constellations on the page with the stars of the night sky. One by one, I found them and marveled that time hadn't stolen a single flickering gem.

"I'm here, Madar," I replied, glancing at the pages splayed before me. Al-Sufi had sketched the serpentine tail of Draco, a fork-tongued dragon, circling Ursa Minor. I had read, but had yet to confirm through observation, that it was visible all year long from Kabul's latitude.

Our months were named after constellations, and soon it would be the month of Saur, or Taurus. I drew lines between stars and saw the bull's swordlike horns piercing the sky. The hairs on the back of my neck prickled to picture the giant beast leaping down from the heavens and galloping on this land.

Mother poked her head between the French doors of the library.

"There you are. It's getting late, girls," she chided, gently. "Sitara, I need you to stay with your brother so I can go downstairs. They're serving dinner soon, and it won't look right if I'm not at your father's side."

"But Kaka Daoud told us we could—"

The man I called Uncle Daoud was Neelab's grandfather. For the past five years, he also happened to be the president of Afghanistan, and he granted us almost unlimited access to the presidential library with its irresistible floor-to-ceiling bookshelves.

In truth, there was no blood relation between my father and President Daoud, but our families were so close that Neelab and I had been raised as cousins. My father was the president's most trusted adviser. We often stayed overnight in the palace, especially when the president hosted evening functions. Neelab and I would find a corner of the palace to hide in on those nights and talk until we fell asleep, the sound of music streaming up from the garden. We exchanged secrets that bound us together more profoundly than blood would have. Neelab knew of the time I had taken one of my mother's pearl rings and traded it with a classmate for a doll with eyelids that opened and closed. And only I knew that General Jamshid's pimply-faced son had penned a love note to Neelab, song lyrics on a sheet of lined notebook paper.

Over the years Neelab, her brother Rostam, and I had explored every square foot of Arg, the name for the presidential palace. We would walk the perimeter, summoning moments from history and inserting ourselves into them. While Neelab and I fired imaginary bullets from our fingertips, Rostam pretended to be an invader trespassing the deep trench that was now filled in with green grass.

We conjured the silky voices of the king's concubines in the building that was once a harem, then popped into the structure once used for army barracks and marched, high-kneed and saluting. Rostam read stories of Genghis Khan's conquests in this land while we sat in a vacant turret, our eyes tracing the sawtooth mountains that guarded Kabul like palace walls.

If we could have moved through time, we would have visited every decade of Arg's history to see how accurate we'd been in reenacting the signing of treaties, the betrayal of trusts, the never-ending fight for our country's independence from foreign invasion.

One day we sat in a copse of trees in the orchard with one of Boba's history books. Rostam had watched me thumbing through the pages in search of a conflict or period we had yet to stage.

"Whoever wrote this must have gone through his days with his eyes closed!" I'd said as I slammed the book closed and searched the spine for the author's name.

"Here we go. And what's wrong with this one?" Rostam had asked, one eyebrow raised. Neelab had been lying on the grass, one leg crossed over the other. She rolled onto her side and propped her head on her hand.

"Think of all the people in the palace," I'd said, waving at the grand buildings in the distance. "Are there only men in there? Or in Kabul?"

"What are you getting at?" Rostam asked.

"There are no women in the book," Neelab had said, taking pleasure in explaining to her older brother something so obvious.

"Be reasonable. You cannot blame the book," Rostam had argued. "Men are the kings and advisers, the warriors and the explorers. They make decisions and execute plans and make history. The books are a record of that. Last week, I picked the 1842 defeat of the British, remember? Both of you had to play the parts of men or you would have had no roles at all."

It was one of our best performances because we did not simply revisit the Afghans driving the British and the sepoys out of the country. We re-created the tea parties and Shakespearean plays performed by British officers and their wives just before the fighting began. We used every word of English we'd learned from our tutors.

"Sitara will explain to you now," Neelab said as she adjusted the imaginary top hat on her head and waddled parallel to a row of shrubs. She was channeling the stodgy, bespectacled British emissary with aspirations to colonize Afghanistan.

"Rostam," I'd said, with the impatience of an overworked teacher, "a British poet warned soldiers they were better off dead than facing the wrath of Afghan women. If you think women are not creatures of action, you've got pumpkin seeds for brains."

Rostam did not apologize, nor did he become indignant. But I know that he heard me, because he never excluded women from history again.

"YOU CAN RETURN TO THE LIBRARY TOMORROW," MY MOTHER offered. "But this is an important night, and I need your help. Faheem's been terrified of sleeping alone lately. You don't want him to wake up and find himself alone, do you?"

"It's not fair. I always have to look after him," I protested.

"Better not complain. I'd rather look after sweet Faheem than have Rostam looking after me," Neelab said with a shrug.

Now that Rostam was thirteen years old, he didn't want to be seen playing with girls. That suited my mother just fine, since soon people would read much more into our time together, ignoring the fact that we'd been playmates all our lives.

Even Neelab would suggest that she and I could become real sisters if I could just stomach marrying her brother. I hated when she made those comments, but more because I had started to look at Rostam a little differently. He didn't carry himself like a child anymore. I missed his company and wondered if that meant I liked him more than I should.

Though I shared every little thought with Neelab, I kept this one to myself.

"Girls, girls," Madar admonished.

I released the curtain from its tasseled tieback and, sighing loudly enough for her to hear, slid the Arabic book back into its place between other Dari, English, and Cyrillic titles. I understood just how awful it was to be gripped by fears, even irrational ones. My fear of the dark drew me to the twinkle of stars.

"I'm having a hard time keeping my eyes open anyway," Neelab said. "Sweet dreams, Sitara. Good night, Auntie."

"Good night, Neelab. Get some rest. Sitara will be up bright and early looking for you."

Neelab circled her arms around my mother's waist and squeezed before slipping into the hall.

I turned away then so Neelab wouldn't give us away with a pert smile. Once she'd left, my mother turned her attention to me.

"Let's hurry. You know," Mother whispered conspiratorially, "your Kaka Daoud can't butter his bread without your father's input."

"And Boba can't butter his bread without yours. Maybe you should have an office next to Kaka Daoud's as well."

Mother beamed, her smile the finishing touch on her elegant appearance. She wore a navy blue dress, belted at her trim waist. The hem fell just past her knees and the sleeves flared slightly at the wrists. My father had purchased the material, a delicate brocade, during his most recent trip to Lebanon. The design was my mother's own, though the stitching had been done by the same seamstress who had made her wedding dress and every other gown she owned. She'd paired her shift with tan slingback heels and a simple necklace, a calligraphy of Allah in eighteen-karat gold. She had her hair pulled back in a twist and had softly teased her crown to add an extra inch of height. I touched my mother's face, marveling at the way her hazel eyes shone from beneath the inky liner she'd used on her eyelids. Was it envy, vanity, or just a surfeit of love to want to be as beautiful as one's mother?

"Sitara, what is it?" my mother asked. She smoothed her hair, betraying a flash of insecurity. "Is something wrong?"

"No, Madar-*jan*. Not at all. I was just thinking."

"About what?" she asked.

I stole a kiss from my mother's cheek. According to my father, the Qur'an teaches us that heaven lies at the feet of mothers. I roamed the palace feeling anchored by my mother's presence nearby.

"When are we going home?" I asked, missing the indulgent mornings when Faheem and I would sit on our parents' laps in our pajamas. We came to the palace too often to feel like guests, but that still did not make our room here feel like home. "I think Faheem's grown homesick."

"After the weekend," my mother assured me. "Your father's been so tied up in meetings the past few weeks, but things will get better soon."

"Is it very bad?" I asked. The meetings had been getting longer and longer for a time. Then they became very short, and some ended with the slamming of a door and feet pounding down a hall.

Mother cupped my face in her hands.

"Everything will be fine. Tonight is about celebrating our country's past with people important for our country's future."

"The Russians will be here?"

"And the Americans, the Indians, and the French too. And maybe some others."

"But our tutor taught us that the Americans and Russians do not like one another. Will there not be fighting?"

"No, my love," Mother replied, smoothing my hair. "Food and art are very capable peacekeepers. And besides, they should know better than to have their schoolyard scuffle in our home. Our people have seen enough. We finally have the peace we deserve."

I knew the history to which she was alluding. I could recite Afghanistan's record of fighting off conquerors and knew that every changing of the guard came with turbulence. Most people in my world adored President Daoud Khan. But out in the public gardens one day, I had heard a man singing a popular song. He'd replaced the lyrics with ones that haunted me and lodged in a corner of my brain with the power of rhyme:

> *My brother turned martyr by your dark night,*
> *Sleep lightly, dear President, sleep light.*

"Perhaps I should join the event? I might be able to write about it for the newspaper," I suggested in my most erudite voice.

Mother pursed her lips.

At the end of the last school year, our principal had announced a writing contest for the graduating eighth-graders in our school.

How can the people of Afghanistan best celebrate our nation's Independence Day?

Though I was only in the fourth-year class and not much of a writer, my brain churned with discussions I'd had with my parents over dinner about the three times Afghans had to fight off the British. I penned an essay that began with a verse by the British poet Rudyard Kipling.

> *When you're wounded and left on Afghanistan's plains,*
> *And the women come out to cut up what remains,*
> *Jest roll to your rifle and blow out your brains*
> *An' go to your Gawd like a soldier.*

The world read Kipling's poem, I explained, and saw Afghan women as butchers, whereas these women were defending their homes and families from invaders. Afghans could best celebrate Independence Day by recording our history in our own words.

I had slipped my carefully written paper into the principal's box. On the final day of classes, the principal called me into her office. I was terrified that a teacher had reported me for daydreaming or poor pen-manship.

Ask your parents to pick up this Thursday's newspaper, Sitara. Your essay won the contest and will run in the paper.

My father came home with half a dozen copies, and my parents beamed to see my byline. President Daoud even joked that I might have a place in his cabinet before I graduated from school.

"It's far too late for you to be up," Mother said. "Ask your father for a personal debriefing another day. He'll certainly oblige."

I could tell from the tone of her voice that she would not be swayed.

"I'm too tired anyway. Go on and have fun. I'll rest with Faheem now."

My mother closed the doors of the library behind us and followed me into our guest room across the hall, a room I could find with my eyes closed from anywhere in the palace. I knew the wallpaper patterns by heart, including where the paper was starting to lift at the corners. I knew how many bulbs were in each chandelier and which windows to open to invite a fragrant breeze.

Our own home on the other side of the Kabul River was a fraction of the palace in size but warmer in every way that mattered. I shared a bedroom with my brother, an arrangement that suited me fine. Because I was seven years older than him, I was usually responsible for him when Madar was tied up in the kitchen or with guests.

I changed into the pajamas my mother had laid out for me. Faheem's small foot tapped against the mattress in a steady, restless rhythm. Sliding into the low bed and kissing his temple, I pulled the bedsheet over my shoulder and lay facing Faheem. His legs grew still, and he exhaled deeply.

"Sleep well, my sweets."

"Good night, Madar-*jan*."

I feigned a yawn, careful not to overdo it. I listened to the fading click of her heels, imagining her moving down the hallway, past my father's office and Kaka Daoud's office. The president's living quarters were on the opposite side of the second floor. That was where Neelab slept, so there was little chance of bumping into her in the middle of the night by accident.

Before she'd left the room, I heard my mother whisper one word of thanks under her breath—*shukur*.

My mother was ever grateful. People who had suffered generally were. When my parents were first married, my father was one of eighteen students granted a scholarship to study engineering in the United States in a place called Oklahoma. A handful of universities wanted Afghans to study engineering and agriculture so they could go back and work alongside the American companies building dams and towns in Afghanistan.

I wished I knew more about Oklahoma, but they never spoke much about their time there. I only knew that the land was so flat that they thought the sun could take a seat on the horizon. Roads seemed to stretch into forever, and the city looked like it could swallow Kabul whole. Though few people they met in town could have found Afghanistan on a map, they were friendly. One neighbor welcomed them with a pie and a jar of pork sausages that my father passed along to an American classmate. He immersed himself in his studies, determined to become valuable to Afghanistan's future. Though my mother wasn't there for her studies, she learned to drive and became fluent in English by taking classes at a library and watching television shows and repeating the lines aloud.

She also gave birth to my sister, who lived and died before I took my first breath. Everything I knew of my sister fit in the palm of my hand: one photograph of my mother holding her swaddled in a blanket and one of her propped on my father's knee, an American birth certificate, and a beaded silver bracelet with an evil eye charm.

The charm had failed to protect her, though. Shortly after my parents returned to Afghanistan and introduced my sister to cooing aunts and uncles, she was struck by an unrelenting fever. She was gone in a matter of days, leaving my parents' arms empty and their hearts broken.

I wish I could have seen my two daughters side by side, Boba sometimes said. *But she will never be far from our thoughts. I have picked a star in the night sky and imagine that is her in the heavens, forever our light.*

With a kind of magic I didn't fully appreciate as a child, my parents spun grief into gratitude. I knew my mother was thinking of my long-gone sister as she watched Faheem nestle close to me. We were, she never tired of telling us, the greatest comforts God could have given her. Being a child, I took this to mean we had suffered our allotted tragedy.

By the time I was ten years old, I did not curl in my father's arms or seek kisses from my mother for every scrape as often as I had the year before. I did not chase their affections, believing that they, like sands in the desert, existed in infinite supply.

CHAPTER 2

WHEN I COULD NO LONGER HEAR MY MOTHER'S FOOTSTEPS, I brought my hand out from under the bedsheet and tickled the tip of Faheem's nose. He did not stir. I peeled back the sheet and slid one foot, then the other onto the floor. Faheem did not wake even as I tiptoed across the room and opened the door just wide enough to slip through. I stepped past the library and rounded the corner of the hallway, the clanging of aluminum pots and lids growing louder. To my left was a narrow set of stairs that led to the rear of a bustling kitchen as the palace staff prepared to serve dinner for the dignitaries. I continued down the hallway, my path dimly lit by small sconces.

At the sound of approaching footsteps, I froze. I held my breath and listened. I heard what sounded like a door close at the far end of the hall. When I was sure footsteps were not approaching, I put one foot in front of the other, stepping with my heel first. I'd not moved three steps when I paused again.

This time I was certain I'd heard something.

I pressed my spine against the wall and looked left and right, already knowing there was nowhere to hide here. My heart thumped loudly.

I inched farther along until I reached an arched cutout. Tucked into its rounded space was a half-moon table draped in embroidered silk. Atop the table was a vase of pale green onyx.

I paused, debating the chances of running into someone if I made a dash for the end of the hallway.

That's when I felt someone—or something—grab my ankle. I gasped and fell forward. My arm grazed the table and braced my fall. I rolled onto my back and saw the vase teeter perilously on the table's edge before coming to rest. Relieved, I looked to my left.

"Neelab!"

Crouched between the legs of the table was Neelab, with a bright and mischievous grin. She'd pulled the table cover to the side.

"You little sneak!" I hissed. "You nearly killed me!"

"Danger lurks around every corner," Neelab whispered ominously. She emerged slowly from her secret nook, unfolding her lanky limbs.

I forgave her for scaring me and vowed to find an even better hiding spot for our next round. We crept quietly to the end of the hallway. A curved staircase led to the downstairs banquet room, and just to the side of the arched entrance was a serving station. With our backs pressed against the wall in the darkened stairway, we could stay out of sight and still have a pretty good view of the festivities.

The serving station boasted an array of glass bottles that I knew were not meant for children. My father did drink on occasion. It seemed to make him more playful, like the version of him that would crawl on the floor with Faheem and me. But I'd also seen some of his friends become terribly angry after a couple of glasses. At a party two months ago, one general scolded me for not greeting him formally. When I saw him vomiting in the bushes later that evening, I raced to the upstairs room where all the children had gathered, even waking the ones who had drifted to sleep. I brought them outside with the promise of Russian chocolates if they helped me surprise a general in need of cheer.

The man was still hunched over with a handkerchief to his mouth when the little gang I'd assembled greeted him with a loud salute, their flat hands raised to their foreheads.

My father only pretended to chastise me for that one.

I spotted my mother on the far end of the room. She was standing with Neelab's mother and grandmother, the first lady, as they spoke to a few foreign women. They could have been posing for a magazine cover with their small purses tucked primly under their arms, pleated skirts falling just below their knees, and tortoiseshell hair clips. I continued to scan the room.

"I see your grandfather," I whispered. "But where's the box?"

Surely the box wouldn't be far from the president. I kept my eyes on Kaka Daoud, who stood beneath a wide tapestry depicting a team of *buzkashi* players on horses. The horses, thick-veined and muscular, seemed ready to leap out of the fabric. The players wore sheepskin coats and stretched their hands to the ground to capture the goat carcass and score a point. One player, a whip between his teeth, had the carcass in one hand and red reins in the other.

The president, a solidly built man with a high forehead, wore a simple black suit. He seemed to be looking at the floor, frowning, as he listened to a military officer I did not recognize. The officer, in an olive jacket with brass buttons, looked flustered. His hands moved frantically as he spoke, one of them landing on the president's arm.

I hadn't noticed my father approaching, and yet there he was, leaning in to whisper something in Daoud Khan's ear. He issued a polite nod to the military officer and with a hand on the president's back, guided him toward a Russian dignitary. His slim frame made the president's paunch more prominent, and I found myself wishing our president would at least pull his shoulders back.

My father said something that made the Russian pivot so that both men stood with their backs to the rest of the room. I could see only slivers of their faces. Their stiff postures and firmly planted feet reminded me of ceramic dolls.

Their formation broke with handshakes and grim expressions. My father's eyes followed the Russian man as he walked past the row of chafing dishes and exited the room. I had no idea what the men were discussing. I was more taken by the way my father always seemed to rearrange people and ideas with a meaningful look, a raised eyebrow, a tapping finger—and he wasn't even president.

In the privacy of our home, when he was nothing more than our father, he had nicknames for me. I was his jewel, his doll, his butterfly. When I grew too big to be bounced on his knee, he would still treat me to ice cream. He would return from abroad with presents—nesting dolls from Kiev, a sandalwood jewelry box from Delhi, a hand-painted bowl from Istanbul—that made me hungry to see this great world with my own eyes. For Faheem, who was still too young to understand why Boba was gone for a week at a time, he brought a plastic revolver and a model jet. The best part was that he took the time to wrap the gifts in newspaper, giving us a few more seconds of delicious suspense.

Maybe that was why I sensed the energies shift downstairs. I noted that a cluster of guests had gathered around a high-topped marble table in the center of the room, necks craned and ears cocked.

"The box," I said.

Neelab nodded in agreement.

Someone clinked a fork against a glass, and the buzz quieted. President Daoud peered at a wooden crate set on the table. The Russian man he'd been speaking with earlier extended his arms toward the guests and encouraged them to clear space. People obliged and took a half-step backward.

"We have waited so long for this moment," a bald man announced.

"Which minister is he?" Neelab asked.

"He's from the Department of Very Important Matters," I said.

"Oh, right—the one that will handle your punishment when you get us in trouble tonight," she replied. Then the minister began speaking.

"This is a sampling of the treasures excavated from the ancient city of Ai-Khanoum over the past twelve years. Imagine it, my friends, a great civilization found under layers of earth! Tonight we say our sincerest thanks to the Russians and to the French for retrieving this history. Tonight, the future of Afghanistan meets its gilded past."

Ai-Khanoum, in the northern part of the country, was one of the farthest reaches of an ancient Greek kingdom. I'd been reading so much about the constellations and the myths associated with the Greek gods that I'd gotten Neelab interested as well. We tried to guess at what treasures might have been left behind centuries ago.

The room stirred with polite applause, the clinking of glasses, and celebratory drags on cigarettes.

The minister picked up a crowbar that had been placed next to the crate and placed it in the hands of the Russian.

"Finally!" Neelab said, squeezing my arm softly. We'd waited a month for this crate to arrive and then another week for these thirty people—a mix of Afghan, French, Russian, and American nationals—to gather for the revealing of what lay inside. My mother and father were now standing side by side, speaking with foreigners I didn't recognize.

"I bet they pull out a sculpture of a bull. Taurus, right? Or what was the one you found today, a dragon?" Neelab whispered to me.

"Shh! I can't hear what the Russian is saying."

The Russian spoke in halting Dari, his accent so thick that I could barely make out his meaning.

". . . These pieces of old Afghanistan . . . a new home in the Kabul Museum . . . all that remains of a civilization . . ."

A hum of approval moved through the room, while I sat back with my arms folded. How could a kingdom capable of erecting cities in far-off lands be reduced to a few trinkets in a crate?

I wanted to get a closer look.

The Russian man lifted a velvet-lined box into the circle and opened it. He pulled back a square of fabric and tilted the container, arms extended above his shoulders and the heads of the guests so everyone could see its contents. When he swiveled slowly and by degrees to the right, I nearly slipped down the steps, struggling to get a better view.

It was a gold ring with inset teardrops of turquoise and garnet. The stones were nearly the size of my fingernails and easily seen even from a distance. The room thrummed with wonder.

"Centuries . . . centuries old . . . beautiful Bactrian gold," the Russian explained. "Proof of the long history between Greeks and Afghanistan."

"And of the longer relationship between women and jewelry!" shouted a jovial voice. My mother laughed. The mood was bubbly. Even the president's usually stoic face had lightened.

The Russian continued retrieving items from the crate. He held up coins, a bone figurine, and a small statue. My father and President Daoud slipped away from the festivities, coming together to stand side by side beneath the tapestry with half-emptied glasses in their hands.

I couldn't take my eyes off the image of them with their backs to that woven *buzkashi* scene. The two men who loomed tall as mountains in my world were suddenly dwarfed by rearing stallions and their whip-clutching riders, a stampede ready to storm this very room.

CHAPTER 3

ARG WAS GUARDED BY A HANDFUL OF SOLDIERS WHO WERE meant to be seen, not heard. I once asked my father if they had ever considered replacing the soldiers with uniforms on sticks. My father pondered my ridiculous questions with the same attention that he gave my more earnest ones. He would narrow his eyes and turn my words into an image in his head, an X-ray revealing the carefully aligned bones of my reasoning. I stood inches taller in his presence. And for a child to feel grand in the storied, soaring halls of Arg was no small feat.

Because the soldiers were present, we found ways to turn them into props for our play. To engage in some amateur espionage, Neelab and I tracked their movements and assigned each one a secret code name. The soldier with green eyes we called Sabzi, or spinach. When we were his only audience, he would make his eyes cross and pinch his nose as if he'd just smelled a foul odor. Our parents and all the other adults in the palace only ever saw a solemn face on him.

The other soldiers were too fearful of being reprimanded to risk a moment of lightness. We gave them even more teasing names, perhaps out of spite. The guard who was forever squinting we named Kishmish, because his entire face took on a wrinkled appearance when he looked at anything farther than his outstretched arm. A soldier who sniffled with allergies we called Darya, for his nose seemed to run like a river. Shair, or Sham, was a soldier who always stood straight and silent as a candle. Perhaps the most disciplined of the soldiers, he was quickest to click his heels together in salute. Rostam, on the rare afternoons when he was not with his private tutor, did a most perfect impression of Shair's deep and deferential voice.

The day after the party, Neelab and I were still anxious for a closer look at the velvet-wrapped treasures from Ai-Khanoum. I was certain we could find the collection, but a thorough search of the palace had left us exhausted and empty-handed. Over a breakfast of fried eggs and tomatoes, Neelab suggested we ask Boba to open the crate for us. I cringed at admitting defeat, but I knew the relics would soon be moved to the museum and I would lose my chance to see them up close. We planned to soften up Boba by emphasizing our keen interest in this newly discovered piece of Afghan history. I studied my parents' interests and habits and knew that if I could tug at our mutual love for history, I could get Boba to break some rules too.

We raced down a hallway bathed in morning light. Arg sat on eighty-three glorious acres in the heart of Kabul. With its many buildings and open green spaces, it was a city within a city with stories upon stories. Neelab's grandfather had become the country's first president by self-declaration, ending the rule of the king, his own cousin, while the monarch visited Europe. But the deeper story, true or not, was that people were planning on ending the king's life as well as his rule, so Neelab's grandfather had done him a favor.

"Do you think he will let us hold it in our hands?" Neelab asked, biting her lip.

"Yes, but only if we don't tell a soul about it."

A man's voice interrupted our chatter.

"Don't tell a soul about what?"

We whirled around to see who had overheard us. It was Sham, or Shair, which made sense. No one else could have approached us so noiselessly.

"A sparrow," I replied swiftly. Any pause would have suggested I was lying, so I blurted out the character from the nursery rhyme about a sparrow served for dinner. The verse had been trapped in my mind since morning. I'd watched my mother hold Faheem's hand in her own and trace circles in his palm, bending in each of his fingers and turning them into characters of the song:

> Lilly lilly the little pond
> Where algae grew round and round
> And caused a slick that in a wink
> Slipped a sparrow who'd come to drink
> This finger took him
> This finger cooked him
> This finger put him on a plate
> This finger sat down and ate
> And when little pinky asked, to be fair
> Auntie, Auntie, where's my share?
> In the pot, she said short and sly.
> But the pot is empty, was his reply.
> Then it must be in the cat's belly round.
> But the cat is nowhere to be found.
> Here he is! Meow Meow Meow Meow!

With the cat's meows, Madar's fingers would tickle at Faheem's sides and he would fall into a fit of laughter. Sometimes afflicted by delighted hiccups, he would stick his palm out and beg for another round.

"A sparrow?" Shair repeated.

"Yes, you must have heard of them. They are winged creatures who live in the trees," I explained. Neelab lowered her face to hide her smirk.

My snarky reply barely seemed to draw a reaction, and I thought perhaps Shair was tolerating my mischief because of my mother.

My mother couldn't stand keeping aloof from the people who guarded over us. She made small talk with all the soldiers. She knew the names of their wives and parents. She remembered where their families were from and always made a point to draw some line of connection—a common high school or a relative who had descended from the same province. She stopped when she spoke to the soldiers, instead of speaking only in passing. It took just a couple of seconds to look a person in the eye and give them the respect they were due, she insisted.

But they are just soldiers, I'd once said to my mother.

We are all soldiers of some kind was her obscure reply.

I had walked away instead of persisting. I didn't wear a uniform or carry a rifle over my shoulder. I hadn't sworn to protect the nation or the president. But I kept these arguments to myself because I was certain my mother would otherwise launch into the many ways in which I could improve my character. And sometimes I wanted to revel in my imperfections.

One day I watched my mother fold a pile of clothes I'd outgrown. She'd used a length of satin ribbon to tie them into a neat bundle, which she then delivered to Shair when we arrived at the palace. As we walked to the parlor where Neelab's mother awaited us, I asked Madar why a soldier would need girl's clothes.

Shaking her head, she told me that Shair had three children, including a daughter two years younger than me.

Clothes look better on children than in drawers, she'd said.

Impossible as it seemed, I tried to imagine Shair as a father. I wondered if he stood on guard in his home as he did here in the palace. I shared this thought with Neelab and then hunched over to salute tiny, imaginary children with a sour expression on my face. Neelab had laughed so hard that she snorted, which led to both of us doubling over.

"I thought you were leaving today. Has your mother not asked you to ready yourself?" Shair asked. I'd never heard him string so many words together. "Perhaps she is looking for you."

"No," I replied. "We're staying with my father. He and the president have had much to discuss."

Shair looked stymied, as if he were trying to translate words into a language he didn't speak.

"Are you all right?" Neelab asked. She had my mother's heart. She sensed uneasiness in others and felt an urgency to do something about it. But Shair did not look at her. He cleared his throat and waved us off without another word.

"The candle is not at his brightest today, is he?" I murmured as we hastily walked down the hallway. Neelab shook her head.

When we were far enough away, I turned to see if Shair was still watching us. Backlit by the sunlight that fell through the windows behind him, he had both hands on his hips. Face to face, I'd felt comfortable enough to speak freely with him, but from this distance, his dark silhouette quickened my step.

Neelab pulled on my arm.

"He's just doing his job. If he didn't scold us, someone would scold him. And much more severely."

She was right. During a parade, Neelab and I had stood shoulder to shoulder, watching rows of soldiers march in sync past the president and his family. To the public's eye, the formations were perfect. Men in uniform were propelled to synchrony by a drumbeat, by stripes and stars on breast pockets and tasseled epaulets. We watched the pomp of our country's military with pride that day.

The very next week, Neelab and I snuck away from dinner and slipped into the former harem of King Habibullah. Decades after the king's assassination, his killer had still not been identified. There was an abundance of suspects: his son who then assumed the throne, an English spy, a disgruntled peasant. The harem had once been home to forty women, all of them vying for the king's attentions. I was convinced that we could find some hidden message or overlooked clue confirming that one of his concubines had had a hand in arranging his end.

But instead of solving the mystery of the murdered king, we stumbled upon a general glaring at a soldier accused of accepting a bribe. The soldier stood with his arms at his sides, his lip trembling. He denied the charge, first in a bold voice and then, as the general barked his contempt for liars, in a whimper.

From behind two columns wide enough to hide our presence, we watched the general's hand slice through the air and clap violently against the soldier's cheek. The sound reverberated against the walls of the two-storied room. We ducked our heads as if afraid to be struck by the ricocheting sound.

I wondered if Shair had ever been reprimanded so brutally. If I were more like my mother, I might have found a reason to ask him. It was odd, I realized, not to know anything about the men who were tasked with defending us against all the rest of the world.

But I did not give it more thought. With the carelessness of children, we continued our quest, followed by the ghosts of kings and concubines, of roosters and soldiers, of all the many pompous creatures who strutted with pride just before their fall.

CHAPTER 4

A FEW PACES BEFORE REACHING MY FATHER'S OFFICE, WE SLOWED to catch our breath and compose ourselves. I stole a glance through the glass door and saw Boba in his usual position—a pen pinched between his fingers, poised as if to strike the page before him. He didn't even notice when we opened the door.

"Boba," I said softly.

My father looked up, eyebrows raised.

"Girls! What good fortune brings you my way this morning?"

The office had just enough space for a wooden desk and two chairs. There was a curio behind his seat with book spines running the length of each shelf. On one wall was a trio of black-and-white photographs of uniformed men. A picture of our family sat on his desk, facing him. In the picture, I held Faheem while our parents sat on either side of us. Faheem looked ready to wriggle out of my arms, and I looked terrified of dropping him.

"We've finished our homework for the week and returned our books to the library. How is your work going?" I asked, easing into the true purpose of our visit. Boba leaned back in his chair. He seemed more intrigued than annoyed by our interruption.

"I might have better luck flying a kite in a box," he replied with a sigh. He lowered his eyeglasses. "Where are your brothers?"

"Rostam is trying to train the white pigeons in the garden to do flips and loops, and Faheem is watching him."

"And do you girls think he will be successful in this bold mission?" my father asked.

Neelab shook her head.

"Faheem told him to give up," she said. "Everyone knows the pigeons who call Arg home cannot be trained."

"Wise observation, Neelab-*jan*. Now, I can't imagine you two came here to discuss the temperament of pigeons."

Since my father respected straight talk, I placed both my hands on his desk and looked him in the eye.

"Boba, we want to see the treasures from Ai-Khanoum! You all kept the party off-limits to us, and now they're going to be shipped off to the museum."

"I see," Boba said. He set his pen down gingerly and moved a glossy magazine aside so he could rest his elbows on the desk. "First of all, what do you girls know about Ai-Khanoum?"

"It was an old city in the north of Afghanistan when it was a kingdom of Greeks and Afghans, nestled at the crossing of two rivers," Neelab recited dutifully.

"And King Zahir Shah stumbled upon it during a hunting trip," I added.

"I was getting to that," Neelab insisted, shooting me a look. She derived just as much pleasure from impressing my father as I did. I pressed my lips together and nodded, a silent apology.

Boba reached into his vest pocket and extracted his silver pocket watch with the image of a horse's head on the case. The watch was a gift from my mother, one she had hoped would inspire him to come home from his work at a reasonable hour. He pursed his lips and rapped his fingers on his desk.

"Let's go," Boba said, rising from his chair. "You two have just as much right as anyone else to see what's left of the great kingdom."

We followed my father down the narrow stairs that led to the kitchen. We walked past the cook and his two assistants. The sweet smell of chopped cilantro mixed with the sting of diced onions. One of the assistants wiped his eyes with his shirtsleeve, then brought his knife back to the marble cutting board. My father greeted them all by name. They paused in their work and issued cheerful replies, the chef putting a hand over his heart in a show of respect.

"Through here, girls."

On the opposite side of the kitchen was a narrow hallway that ended with a door. My father opened the door and pulled at a chain that hung from the ceiling. I hesitated. We had ventured all over the palace and its gardens, even entering areas forbidden to others when soldiers had their backs turned. But intrepid as we were, we had never been below the palace. It was uncomfortably dark and had far too many hidden corners.

"The basement lighting isn't great, so watch your step." He looked over his shoulder at me and touched my head. If he sensed my nervousness, he did not acknowledge it. I glanced back at Neelab, whose hand gripped the banister as she strained to see ahead.

"You go first," she whispered awkwardly. "Since it was your idea."

Neelab was a year older than me, but she was not nearly as bold. Sensing a chance to outdo her, I pulled my shoulders back and followed Boba.

We couldn't see much under the weak light of a single bulb. We descended the plank steps slowly. Each footfall elicited a creak of protest. At the bottom of the stairs, the expansive basement was cordoned off into sections with heavy braided ropes and folding dividers. To the left were stacks of cardboard boxes. A few feet away, enormous aluminum cooking pots and frying pans were haphazardly arranged on a metal rack. I spotted two old Russian radios on an end table. To my right, stacks of framed paintings leaned against the wall, along with mirrors and a few rolled-up carpets. I stayed close to my father and kept an eye on the lopsided boxes, which seemed ready to shape-shift in the thin light.

Behind the stacks of kitchen supplies and a divider painted in green and gold, Boba led us toward a narrow alcove. I could almost touch both sides of it with my outstretched arms. Another rolled carpet, thick as a tree trunk, was propped against the far corner of the space, and a stack of wooden crates sat opposite it.

"I know you won't run off talking about this, but I still want you both to promise to be discreet about what you're going to see. Look away, girls."

My father must have felt my stare over his shoulder, but he said nothing. I couldn't look away without knowing what I was looking away from. I watched as Boba pressed his hand against the wall until his fingers caught on a small latch. He turned the latch clockwise, and we heard a soft click. With a pull, the lower part of the wall suddenly became a door. Inside was a hollow space and a second door with a metal handle and three dials with numbers from 1 to 99. The dials were inches apart from one another and arranged in a triangular configuration. Boba turned the dial to the left first, slowly adjusting the knob until the notch above it pointed to 63. Then he set the top dial to 27. Once he'd spun the bottom dial to a number hidden behind his jacket sleeve, he pulled the handle downward. Between the sheets of metal, the teeth of the cams clicked into alignment and released the hasp.

Neelab and I both jumped at the heavy footsteps overhead.

"You weren't scared of the kitchen staff a moment ago. No need to be scared of them now," Boba chided without looking up.

With a quiet pop, the door opened, and Neelab and I peered into the dark interior of the enormous safe. It was almost as tall as me. My father stepped into it with his back hunched and retrieved the same crate we'd seen at the party. Neelab grabbed my hand, an electric thrill passing through our intertwined fingers as Boba lifted the top off the crate and pulled out the first velvet-lined box.

One by one, he showed us pieces we'd not been able to see the night before. His penlight illuminated a plaster medallion, an intaglio, and a collection of bronze coins. He let us bring our faces close enough to them that I saw grains of sand on their surfaces and could trace the curves made by third-century carving tools.

"The archaeologists found the remains of a royal palace in Ai-Khanoum, a building with tall columns, storerooms, a library, pools, and fountains. It was home to architects and doctors, tradesmen and politicians. Think of how long ago this was and how much those people had managed to build."

I recognized the box that held the ring well before my father opened the clasp. This was the only piece we'd glimpsed last night. Neelab let out a dainty *ooh*. My best friend was the kind of daughter mothers wanted, one who would wear prim dresses and pearls. She could sit for hours without making a peep and didn't go home with muddy knees, as I did.

While Neelab was mesmerized by the gold and the stones, I was stunned by the ring's ability to outlive anyone who had worn it.

"This piece is exquisite," Boba admired. The turquoise shone richly against the lustrous gold. "Just imagine that two thousand years ago, a craftsman made this ring by hand with nothing more than a hammer and a flame. The design comes from Greece, but the gold and turquoise are Afghan. Such intricate settings. As if the craftsman knew his work would become evidence of a lost civilization."

"Maybe he did know," I suggested.

"It's unlikely. People cannot imagine their civilization will not endure forever. Pride is blinding."

"Why will this all be put into the museum? Why not display it here in the palace?" Neelab asked.

"Because it's part of Afghanistan's history and history belongs to the people."

As I watched my father pack the boxes away and slide the top back on the crate, one question nagged at me.

"What brought the end of Ai-Khanoum, Boba?"

My father gave the crate one quick tap with the heel of his fist.

"Didn't invaders come at them from the East?" Neelab asked.

Boba straightened his back and looked at us, the slanted light of the bulb reflecting off his lenses.

"Yes. But if it hadn't been invaders from the East, it would have been invaders from the West," he explained. "Our land seems to attract the most restless men. Every single one looking to make a name for himself, no matter the price."

Boba shut the safe and gave each of the three dials one quick spin. He sealed off the compartment again, and we retraced our steps back up the stairs, floorboards again creaking and groaning. Once we were in the kitchen, my father kissed the top of my head and touched Neelab's chin.

"*Sahib!*" a soldier called out from the doorway. He pulled his feet together and drew his shoulders back.

"Yes, what is it?"

"The president is asking for you. Urgently, sir."

My father nodded.

"History lesson is over for now, girls," Boba said with a wan smile. His eyes looked heavy with shadows, even in the bright light of the kitchen. There were lines etched into his forehead and a heaviness in his step. It occurred to me that I'd not seen my father sleep in days. "Promise you'll stay out of trouble."

We nodded obediently and drifted into the gardens to look for our brothers. The high walls of the palace gave the illusion of privacy, even when there were probably a hundred people spread over the eighty-three acres of grounds and buildings. As we walked, I let my fanned fingers graze over the shrubs and took in the bright scent of the orange trees. One rosebush had gone into early bloom, and Neelab, an amateur botanist, wanted to touch the velvety petals.

Uniformed soldiers were posted beneath an arched portico of Dilkhusha, my favorite building in all of the palace. The soaring wooden doors creaked open, and President Daoud Khan emerged. With their faces partially hidden by olive-colored caps and their pant legs tucked into thick-soled boots, the soldiers stood at attention. The president, flanked by three advisers, walked with his hands clasped behind him and his body angled forward, as if a strong wind blew at his back. He walked a few meters away from the palace before turning on his heel and pacing in the opposite direction.

Neelab and I crouched down. Shrouded from view by the dense rosebushes, we watched and listened.

"Sir, give the word and I'll order the soldiers to round up the prisoners and do away with them tonight."

Neelab's face went slack, her eyes fixed on her grandfather. I held her elbow because she looked like she might topple over.

"So another crop of white flags will grow out of the earth?" a second adviser barked. "Creating martyrs out of dissidents is like taking a blade to an itch."

My father emerged from a side door and joined the conversation that had clearly been going on for days.

"Respectfully, we are in the very quandary I predicted when the construction of the prison began. We build large schools in hopes they will fill with children. We build grand *masjids* in hopes they will fill with believers. We built Pol-e-charkhi, a prison large enough to fit thousands of people. Did we really intend for those cells to sit vacant?"

"We don't have time for philosophy," one adviser retorted. "What's to be done? Moscow says if we allow them to increase and gather, those fingers become a fist."

The president stopped abruptly, clapping his hands against the sides of his legs. Neelab and I flinched at the sound.

"No one kills a single prisoner without my word!" he declared.

"Moscow will not be pleased if—"

"We did not wrest free of the British to be ruled by Moscow," my father insisted.

"Enough!" Daoud Khan roared.

The adviser lowered his head and relaxed his shoulders. I'd never seen the president's jowls quiver with anger. By the expression on Neelab's face, I doubted she had either.

"He is right. Moscow has mistaken our hospitality and gratitude for weakness. I am not under their control. This nation is not under their control!" he grumbled. "The Politburo needs to take a step back or they will put us all in danger."

Neelab motioned for us to leave. As she turned, she let out a yelp. Two scarlet drops slid down her forearm from where a thorn had pierced her skin. Knowing the sight of blood made her light-headed, I quickly pressed the hem of my black shirt to her arm. When I lifted my shirt from her arm, the blood was gone.

But Neelab did not look relieved. Instead, she looked betrayed by the soft blooms.

"Come," I said to distract her. "Let us find the boys."

We spotted our mothers at the fountain. Faheem was pitched over the circular concrete edge, his hand splashing in the bubbling water and a bare foot dangling in the air. I heard my brother's corkscrew laughter, the giggles that rose and fell and drew more attention than the *muezzin's azaan* at prayer time.

The palace had been desperate for lightness lately. The walls seemed to be bending inward. Neelab stared at the fountain.

"Sitara," she started quietly. "Do you think the people of Ai-Khanoum escaped? Or do you think they were buried with all those treasures?"

I'd known Neelab so long, it was as if our lives were plaited together. Sometimes I imagined she was God's way of making amends for reclaiming my older sister before I could meet her. I could tell from the lilt of her voice that Neelab was terrified. We were fluent in the cutting conversations of politics, but what we'd just heard chilled us both.

"It was a long time ago, Neelab. Maybe they went back to Greece or went searching for some other land," I offered. She was not assuaged by my theory.

"There must have been children in Ai-Khanoum," Neelab said somberly.

I found myself saying things I didn't even believe because I wanted to rally her spirits.

"I didn't see any toys or small rings in the crate. I bet they were too busy carving stone into columns to think of having children."

Neelab looked skeptical.

"Come," I said brightly, pulling at her hand. "Let's sneak up on our mothers. With all the wives and foreigners present last night, maybe we'll catch a bit of juicy gossip."

We stepped forward in synchrony, as we always had, except that I dared to look back. The wooden doors were once again closed. The president, his advisers, and their tall shadows had all disappeared and the garden was once again serene.

Faheem was crouched behind a wheelbarrow in a game of hide-and-seek, his flattened palms pressed over his eyes, his chestnut hair catching the afternoon sun. A note of glee escaped his parted lips.

"Where is my little boy? Wherever might he be?" my mother sang out. But her voice was tinged with melancholy. Perhaps she was lamenting, as all parents do, the truth my brother had yet to learn—that closing his eyes would not make him invisible to those determined to find him.

CHAPTER 5

April 27, 1978

AFTER THAT DAY IT WAS AS IF THE PALACE WAS A PURSE AND SOMEone had pulled its strings. Arg became a dark and suffocating chamber. I overheard my parents debate whether it would be best for us to leave. But then a commander increased the number of armored tanks stationed outside the palace's high walls and the bolstered security reassured Boba.

President Daoud's family had been sequestered in the sunroom of Dilkhusha. When I heard someone call Rostam's name across the lawn, I wondered if my friends had tried to slip away and pay me a visit. Hours later, there was still no sign of them. I huffed to think I had to wait for the storm to pass before I could rejoin Neelab and Rostam.

My mother gave me little room to wander, ordering me to stay close by. I felt like a prisoner in a place that had always been my playground. We were still across from the presidential library, so I could at least find an escape on those rich shelves.

My mother kept mainly to the bedroom with my brother. Faheem had been complaining of a stomachache since the night before. She'd been spooning warm fennel tea into his mouth while he tried to bury his face in his chest. I was seven years old when he was born. I remember curling myself around Madar's growing belly and feeling my brother's sharp kicks. Excited as I was to meet this new sibling, I also worried that he might siphon off all my parents' attentions.

But once he was born, I was so smitten by his tiny fingers and powdery smell that I didn't resent him one bit. And Madar's lap somehow had room for both of us, the curious anatomy of a mother's love.

I would press my head to her chest and hear the rhythmic thumping of her heart, as if a clock sat caged in her chest. I listened for it anytime I lay next to her, pushing away gnawing thoughts of hearts subject to the limits of time.

At noon, the hilltop cannon boomed as it always did. Though the morning had dragged, the hour had still snuck up on me. I was starting to feel hungry and wondered if I should help prepare something for Madar and Faheem. My father was tied up in discussions that didn't seem to be going anywhere because he still hadn't emerged with any good news.

I peeked into the bedroom and saw that my mother had fallen asleep curled around Faheem. Not wanting to wake them, I walked softly toward the kitchen. I stopped when I heard the familiar voices of the kitchen staff speaking in panicked whispers.

"You can't be serious! Why would they do this?"

"I just saw it with my own eyes. Those tanks outside have just turned their guns on the palace. We are under siege!"

I walked into the kitchen.

"Why would the tanks point their guns at us?" I asked. "And what do you mean we're under siege?"

The two men had their hands on the counter, their faces grim. They were unfazed that I'd overheard their conversation.

"Find your mother, little girl," one man said, barely looking at me. "Stay with her. This is not a time for play."

Startled by the edge in his voice, I left without asking for food. I wanted to report to my mother what I had just learned and gauge her reaction. I wanted even more to find my father. He would be able to fix whatever it was that had gone so terribly wrong. Though I couldn't name it, I had a sense that something ominous was happening.

I shook my mother's shoulder. Her eyes were still heavy with sleep, since she hadn't gotten much the night before. But once I had unloaded the news on her, she blinked away the haze. She made me repeat what I'd said and promise that I had not misheard. She composed herself and reassured me, but I'd already seen the flash of panic on her face.

"Everything will be fine. I must find your father," she said, blinking rapidly.

As if summoned, Boba appeared in the doorway. He was unshaven and sullen, his sleeves rolled up.

"Sulaiman—" my mother said.

My father squeezed my shoulder and walked across the room, sinking into the chair as if he were carrying his weight in stones.

"The winds have changed direction," he said.

"Speak clearly," my mother said, her voice trembling.

I sat by Faheem, whose stomach seemed to have settled just as the rest of the palace was beginning to retch. I had my arms around him and my chin on his head when I heard what sounded like coins rattling in a giant tin can.

"Get down!" my mother shrieked. In one swift move, she and my father grabbed us, covering our bodies with their own. We crouched on the floor, the four of us, paralyzed. Even Faheem seemed too stunned to cry. After a few moments, the gunfire ceased and we peeled away from one another. The room was untouched. We were unharmed, though I didn't feel intact.

My father stood and went into the hallway.

"I see one of the guards," he said, looking back at my mother. "Let me find out what's happening."

"But, Sulaiman!"

I saw hesitation in my father, and it made him almost unrecognizable. He cupped his hand around his forehead as if his thoughts might otherwise swirl out of his skull. He shook his head and knelt in front of us.

"We will find a peaceful end to this situation. We must."

My mother groaned softly, for she knew what that meant. Any and all talks happened with my father's mediation.

Not long after Father left our room, I heard a horrific sound. The sky threatened to split as jets flew low over the palace, spraying artillery on the grounds. I couldn't hear my own shrieks through the explosions. We stayed put, too nervous to move. My father returned to us, whispering to my mother that a faction of the army had indeed turned on the president.

The conversations I'd overheard in the last two weeks echoed in my head. Grievances and doubts abounded, from the families of the political prisoners to the university students. Some thought President Daoud's visit to the United States had turned him into a pawn of the Americans. Others demanded that he take an even stronger stand against Moscow. And away from the stoic first lady's ears, women debated whether the president had too much pride to see the regime through the unrest.

Boba had spoken sharply with President Daoud.

You won't fix this problem by culling dissidents, he had warned. *The Americans hold our right hand, the Soviets our left. Mark my words, neither will let go of its grip even if they see us torn to shreds.*

Kaka Daoud, Boba, and the circle of advisers stayed locked in a wood-paneled conference room. The kitchen was deserted, though I doubt anyone had much of an appetite anyway. Day stretched into night. Boba lumbered back to our room at a late hour, his eyes bloodshot. He smelled of tea, alcohol, and cigarette smoke.

"Boba, are they going to hurt us?" I asked, doing my best not to cry. I could not stop my chin from quivering.

"No, no, my darling girl," Boba replied, his voice a low rasp. "They are our own people. Just as quickly as they turned left, they can turn right. All will be fine."

My mother's eyeliner smudged as she wiped away tears before they reached her cheeks. I caught her mouthing prayers, her knuckles blanched as she held my father's hand. We remained knotted together in one small room. Terrified and exhausted, the dozens of people contained in the palace by mutinous soldiers drifted to sleep in tufted chairs, in four-poster beds, and with their backs up against embossed wallpaper.

I looked for small signs that we were not facing the end of the world, holding on tight to my freshly spun theory that if the sun and moon kept their rituals, my world would remain intact.

Perhaps it was a need to confirm the existence of the moon that woke me from my fitful slumber that night. It might have been my peculiar dream. I'd been back in the palace gardens watching my father play hide-and-seek with President Daoud, and Neelab was high-stepping into the fountain to toss Ai-Khanoum coins into the water.

Whatever the cause, I woke abruptly. I tried to go back to sleep but couldn't keep my eyes closed. I was thirsty too.

Faheem shifted next to me. I held my breath, not wanting to wake him. He made a short, tranquil hum before his breathing fell into a somnolent rhythm. I wanted to touch his face but when my fingers neared his cheek, the dark line of his eyelashes fluttered, and I pulled away.

My eyes adjusted to the dark, and I could make out the shapes of the furniture. I sat up. My mother was asleep in the bed just a few feet away. My father sat upright in the chair, snoring softly with his glasses in his hand. To see him resting brought me relief.

Boba often found me awake, reading, when I was meant to be asleep.

Instead of becoming angry, he would tuck me in and sing a song by Ahmad Zahir, the wild-haired crooner enchanting the radio waves and house parties.

> *While I slumber, you are open-eyed*
> *I am naïve but you are ever wise*
> *I lie in rest, and yet you travail*
> *Your glimmering love set to prevail.*
> *When the clouds in the sky break away*
> *Wink, my Star, and light the day*

Boba had an important job to do, my mother would explain as she knelt at our bedside, rubbing Faheem's back and stroking my hair. She'd looked weary too, and maybe that was because her job was no less vital than his.

Now my mother lay on her side, her hands tucked under her face. Her chest rose and fell like waves rippling across a lake. She looked beautiful even in her sleep—her perfectly straight nose, her round eyes, her hair in dark rivulets. The pendant she wore, the golden name of God, dangled in the hollow between her collarbones.

I put both feet on the floor and tiptoed to the door.

I stepped quietly into the hallway and came face to face with the French doors of the library. Moonlight fell through the window. I entered the room and walked over to the bookshelf to touch the spines of the president's books, some linen, some glossy, until I pulled out *The Book of Fixed Stars* and turned to the page I had bookmarked. I walked with it to the window, trying to glean a story from the scattered stars.

It was the month of Taurus, so I searched the sky for the mythical bull. But a noise on the lawn drew my attention to a cluster of uniformed soldiers. An army truck, its headlights dark, rolled into the long driveway that led to the main palace's entrance. At the sound of footsteps in the hallway behind me, my stomach contracted. I pressed my back to the window and wondered who, besides me, was sleepless.

As I listened, I heard more than one set of footsteps. They started and stopped in unison. I held my breath, wondering if I was foolish to be afraid. These could be soldiers who guarded the palace day in and day out. Surely, they could overpower the handful of bad apples who had turned against us.

A series of sharp pops erupted, crackling through the night. I looked outside and saw soldiers dashing toward the palace. My palms were sweaty. Maybe the soldiers had come to tell the president of some breaking news. Surely, they would wake Boba too. If my parents woke to find me missing, they would worry. I took a couple of steps toward the library door.

There was a sudden explosion of gunshots, shrieks and shouts, and slamming doors. More gunshots rang through the palace halls. I ducked behind the curtain, pressing my back to the window. My throat swelled with a trapped scream.

I peeked out from behind the curtain. I had closed the door to our bedroom behind me and for a merciful split second, I was convinced that would be enough, that I had hidden my family from danger.

But I hadn't.

The door to the bedroom flew open across the hall. I caught sight of my father—his shirt untucked and his glasses askew. I wanted to call his name, but I was frozen where I stood.

As soon as Boba stepped fully into the hallway, it looked like someone shoved him by one shoulder, then the other. The sound of gunfire registered a second later, and I watched my father's body slump to the floor like a rag doll.

I understood immediately that he was gone. I looked back at the open bedroom door and saw my mother pressed against the far wall of the room, directly opposite me. Our eyes met. I signaled my mother to hide, to run, to find a way to escape the monster that was about to enter our room.

The air was thick as a storm cloud.

My mother let out a mournful groan. Her voice slipped into the hallway, past my father's body, and settled, like a breath, in my ear. Mother swaddled Faheem with her body, her fingers covering his eyes. She tilted her head and looked at me longingly, lovingly, even as two looming silhouettes stepped into the frame and she recognized that this was not a night of mercy.

Madar, I tried to cry as children and the silver-haired do when they face the sharp end of the world. If heaven lies at a mother's feet, what hope is there in her absence?

Madar, the summoning of a salve, the singing of a lamentation.

CHAPTER 6

April 28, 1978

I DARED NOT PEEK OUT FROM BEHIND THE CURTAIN. HIDDEN FROM view, I grasped at every possibility that kept my family alive. Surely someone—anyone—was rushing them to a hospital where they would be stitched up and restored. I prayed for white gauze and syringes and the able hands of doctors. But these hopes were flimsy as soap bubbles, especially as voices I did not recognize echoed through the hallways unchallenged.

When I was four years old, I'd been awakened one night by my mother's shouts. A burglar had crept onto the roof of our Kabul home and sent a vase crashing as he'd slipped into our home through a window. When he fled, my father gave chase, leaping from rooftop to rooftop. He caught the man on the roof of a home one block away. At least, that's how I remembered it.

It was as likely that he'd chased the man down the street as it was that he had catapulted across the homes of our neighbors while they slept. Regardless, this was my memory of the night, and it became part of how I saw my father. It was the reason I believed my father could and would protect us from any danger. I remember when he walked me to school I would watch his shadow stretch long ahead of us and believe it was the shape of truth. To me, day or night, Boba was larger than life.

That was why I could not comprehend why I'd seen Boba buckle as he had. I expected him to appear in the window at any moment and pull me onto the roof of the building to escape. I peeked at the clock on the wall. After three hours of standing, the muscles of my legs burned. Still, I stood as straight as I could, trying to keep my body hidden in the small sanctuary behind the curtain and out of view to anyone looking up from outside.

Where was everyone? Why hadn't President Daoud exploded onto the scene with loyal troops to round up the murderers? I listened hard and eventually heard the boom of President Daoud's voice rise from somewhere deep in the palace.

Traitors!

I couldn't make out any other words.

I felt unmoored and wanted badly to slide down and give myself over to the floor. The moon still glowed bright, but in an hour or so the rising sun would turn the horizon pink.

I listened to the movement of boots, the thud of thick soles on fine carpets. I heard orders barked and loud grunts of exertion. I dared not peek. I only looked down at the darkened carpet beneath my feet and waited for the stench of my urine to lead the soldiers to me.

They moved up and down the length of the hall, going in and out of rooms. I closed my eyes tight, though what I saw with my eyes shut was more terrifying than what I saw when I kept them open.

Footsteps entered the library slowly. I heard a man's breathing, the sharp intake of air through flared nostrils. I was working up the nerve to smash my elbow into the window and take my chances leaping to the ground when the curtain snapped back. I found myself face to face with a soldier—or, more precisely, the unblinking eye of a Kalashnikov. I closed my eyes shut and quaked.

I do not know how much time passed this way, with my existence dependent on one finger curled against a trigger.

At some point, I opened my eyes.

The rifle's tip quavered but stayed trained on me. I dared to look past the barrel to the trembling arms that held it up. I saw a man, panting, his red-rimmed eyes bulging. He looked over his shoulder and back at me.

He wiped his palm on the thigh of his pants.

"You must go!" he hissed, nudging my arm with the rifle's barrel. I jolted when the warm metal touched my skin. "Go!"

He wiped the sweat from his brow.

I whispered a prayer, looking past him at the emptied bedroom across the hall. My eyes fell to the darkened floor.

"I want to be with them."

The soldier went to the doorway, looked down the hall, and then returned to me. He grabbed my arm and walked me out of the library with the end of his rifle pressed between my shoulder blades.

I walked, not daring to look at him.

I heard footsteps and the murmur of voices coming from the direction of the president's quarters.

Neelab? I forced my best friend out of my thoughts and focused on taking quiet steps.

"You can't hide. There's nowhere to go," he said, his breath hot and rancid in my ear.

Would he let me hide?

Beneath the hallway table. In the kitchen cabinets with the gallons of cooking oil. In the bathroom with the painting of the bird on its wall. Behind the bar in the banquet room. All my ideas were terrible.

Then I remembered the basement.

My pace quickened.

"Where?" he asked.

I made my way to the narrow staircase that led to the kitchen. I stepped carefully and the soldier followed.

Judging by the opening and shutting of cabinets and drawers, there were at least two men in the kitchen.

I pointed at the kitchen and then down. The soldier walked around me, lowered his weapon, and plodded down the steps. He moved heavily across the kitchen tiles.

I couldn't make out what he said. I wondered if I should run back down the hall instead of trying to get to the basement.

"All clear. This floor too. There's nothing more to do here."

"Yes. That's why the commander asked me to get you. Some changes to your assignments, maybe."

I flinched at an explosive sound—a cabinet door slammed shut.

I squatted in the stairwell, my hands over my ears when I was grabbed by the arm and jerked into an empty kitchen. Fingers pressed into the bones of my forearm.

"Go!" he commanded, and I hurried toward the basement door.

I slipped into the pitch-black basement, my legs shaking. The door behind me closed shut before I'd made it down even two steps. I found the banister and felt for each plank with my toes before taking another step. When my feet touched the cold floor of the basement, the door above opened again. I ducked just as a white light skittered down the steps. A flashlight.

I picked it up and clicked it off.

"That was me tripping over your mess," I heard the soldier holler. "Are we ready to clear out or not?"

It was Shair's voice. I was certain. It had been his face behind that rifle.

"A lot messier than it needed to be," he added.

Keys jangled.

"We have a lot to move before daybreak. You can drive."

Shair stood at the top of the stairs, clutching in his sweat-slick palm a ring of keys and the dangerous secret of my existence.

CHAPTER 7

April 28, 1978

JUST EIGHTEEN MONTHS EARLIER, I'D HAD MY FIRST ENCOUNTER with death. My grandmother lay in a coffin, gray-lipped and wrapped so tightly in a sheet of white muslin that it would have suffocated her if she had still had breath in her body.

While Boba heaved a shovelful of dirt on the lowered coffin, Madar-*jan* whispered in my ear that my grandmother would be welcomed into the gardens of heaven. I found it hard to reconcile that ascending destiny with the coffin interred under two meters of earth. I'd watched my grandmother tend to her plants, pruning one stem at a time and checking the soil's moisture with a finger. Like her plants, she bloomed with the sun and wouldn't even draw the curtains in her home. How could this dark hole be her path to heaven?

Nonetheless, I chose to believe in the hope my mother offered so that I didn't despair at the thought of my grandmother in eternal darkness.

The first time I heard footsteps approaching the basement door, I held my breath and prayed that I could wrap my arms around my mother again in those celestial gardens. But the footsteps retreated and left behind a deepening silence, one that summoned the soft echoes of my father's voice.

That look in your eye when you know you are right, you remind me so very much of the legendary Malalai and her battle cries. Half-dead men defeated the British because of her. Afghanistan's secret weapon has always been her women.

But, Boba, I'm just a girl.

What a thing to say! As if a girl is made of lesser materials. Have you forgotten the words of Rumi? You are not a drop in the ocean. You are the entire ocean in a drop.

I had never truly given myself over to those words until this moment.

The thought of the ocean inside me, with its infinite drops, ran through me like a charge. My existence was integral to the universe.

What was Malalai's battle cry, Boba? I asked the silence. My father's voice replied.

> *Young loves, give your youth to this battle and be proud*
> *Or by God you'll live with shame as your shroud!*

I hurt to think of the afternoon when Boba had brought me to this space, wanting to show me the treasures of a lost world. I crept deeper into the alcove, wanting to touch the crates he'd touched again. I wished Neelab could be here with me now, so we could at least hold on to each other. My fingers trembling, I opened the latch just as Boba had done. I ducked into the black hole and pulled the secret door closed behind me.

It had occurred to me at some point in the last few hours that the absence of gunshots might not mean the killing had ceased—it could mean that there was no one left to kill. I was devastated. I was also furious at Shair. Had he fired the shots that killed my family? That he had saved me by bringing me down here did nothing to dampen my rage.

The three knobs of the safe pressed into my spine. I pushed back in frustration. I thought of Ai-Khanoum, where a whole civilization disappeared beneath the ground.

No, I told myself. *I will not let these people disappear me.*

My fingers curled around the flashlight Shair had thrown to me. I clicked it on and pressed the light against the palm of my hand, making it glow pink. I turned to face the safe and shone the light on the dials.

I had seen the combination, hadn't I?

The dials felt heavy. I twirled the one on the left first, slowly. I stared at the numbers, willing the combination to rise from the ashes. I twirled again and closed my eyes.

I saw Neelab and the nervous anticipation on her face when Boba had revealed the safe to us. Her nose had crinkled with glee. I felt her fingers wrapped around my arm, a friendly and excited squeeze. I heard her voice then, distant and fleeting.

Of course you remember, Sitara. You never forget a detail.

When I opened my eyes, I gave the dial one more twirl and landed on 63. Then I fixed my attention on the second dial, tapping the knob as if to ask for help.

Twenty-seven.

With the light in my left hand, I rotated the top dial until I heard a soft click.

I was missing only the last number—the one that had been hidden from view by my father's arm. I had never seen this number.

I pressed my forehead against the metal door of the safe. It was a number between 1 and 100. I turned the dial to 1 and tried the handle, but it didn't give way. I moved the dial to 2 and tried again. Another tick forward to 3.

At 33, the locks released and the handle relented. I took a deep breath, then inched backward to give the door room to open. If it groaned this loudly when Boba opened it, I had not noticed. For now, it seemed that no one on the floor above me had noticed either. I swept the flashlight across the safe and peered inside.

I opened one small crate at a time. I touched the plaster of a miniature bust and the gold of a multistranded necklace. What would happen to these pieces? What would happen to me? Surrounded by these precious survivors, I wondered if I could plot an escape. I replaced every treasure in its lined box with care—all the treasures but one.

I slid the turquoise and garnet ring onto my left hand, touching the hammered metal of the band and the smooth surface of the stones. It twirled loosely around my finger. I turned the ring so that the stones were tucked into my palm and made a fist to keep it from slipping off.

It was quiet upstairs, and that quiet emboldened me. I had just crept out of the alcove when I heard the basement door open. I slipped backward, my feet shuffling in a panic. I was barely in the alcove by the time they were in the basement, close enough that I could smell the smoke and sweat on their uniforms.

"Bring that old radio upstairs. I think I can get it working again," said one of the soldiers.

"Yes, sir."

When their footsteps drew near, I silenced my screams by biting into the heel of my hand and digging my fingernails into the thin flesh of my knee.

"What about this carpet?"

"Maybe. Unroll it and see if it's worth carrying upstairs or if it's down here out of sight for a reason."

At that moment, the entire palace rocked once more. I fell onto my side, and a yelp escaped my throat. Thankfully, the soldiers had shouted even louder, and in a flash they ushered one another back up the stairs.

A second boom rattled the walls. I tucked my head between my knees believing the entire palace was about to come crashing down on me.

I crawled out of the alcove once more. The soldiers were gone. The radio was gone. The unfurled carpet was covered in plaster and bits of paint.

A year before, on my birthday, our house had rattled with the force of an earthquake. I had been half awake when my mother grabbed me by the hand, Faheem on her hip, and pulled us out of the house.

Outside is safer, she'd hollered.

Madar-*jan.* From the night of the coup on, I would forever wonder if the look in her eyes in that final moment had been love or fear.

I heard crashing overhead and imagined pots, chairs, and chandeliers falling to the floor. A tower of stacked boxes in the basement toppled over, glass broke somewhere. My hands flew to my head instinctively.

This was not an earthquake. Earthquakes did not smell of gunpowder, sweat, and blood. This would not cease until the entire palace was destroyed.

The will to live is strongest in those who have a reason to live, something to save. I should have had none, and yet I refused to go quietly. I can only imagine it was because my parents had insisted that their every hope for the future lived in me.

I climbed the stairs, the air growing thicker with smoke as I neared the door. I opened it slowly and a sliver of hazy light fell on my face. Hearing no voices in the kitchen, I entered. I looked over at the stairs that led to the upper level and felt my throat tighten again. The floor was littered with upturned pots and broken plates. A light fixture dangled precariously overhead.

I took one step and a sharp pain made me pull my foot back. I balanced with one hand on a wall and lifted my foot. A triangle of glass poked out of my sole like a shark fin.

Leaning against the wall, I shut my eyes tight and pulled the shard out with one swift motion. Hearing shouts nearby, I pressed on. I hobbled into the long hallway and looked from one apocalypse to another as I passed each room. A shattered Chinese vase. Toppled dining chairs. A jagged, zipperlike crack on the ceiling. A parlor door dangling on a hinge. The badly splintered door to the president's office with three gaping holes in it.

I peered into the parlor that had been Neelab's favorite hiding place for games. An emerald-green settee was hacked in two. One leg had broken off the marble coffee table, making it look like the table had taken a nosedive into the carpet. A painting lay facedown on the floor.

Through this parlor, I could get to the south side of the palace, where high shrubs offered some cover. I dashed to the open window, throwing one leg over the ledge and then the other. The palace air, thick with destruction and sin, dissipated as I exited. Straining to see through the red smoke, I found a single star. It was all the light I needed to find my way.

I walked, sidestepping, with my back to the palace wall. If I could get to the road, I would somehow find refuge in Kabul.

But as I turned the corner, the twinkle of that star exploded into a blinding beam of light. Fingers dug into my arm, and a hand clapped over my mouth before I could shout. I tried to wrest free but stopped when I saw the subtle glint of metal, a revolver on a hip.

A gun. All I had to do was reach out and grab it.

What if Malalai had not been crying out to revive the battered soldiers? What if she had been shouting those words to ready herself for battle?

A chorus of voices erupted.

We are all soldiers of some kind. My mother's voice summoned a crescendo of the drumbeat in my chest.

Go to your Gawd like a soldier.

You are the entire ocean in a drop.

The luminous laughter of an angelic little boy.

Sitara's going to set you straight now.

Voices rose and collided in my head, drowning out the sizzle of burning grass and furniture and the distant rumble of tanks.

I filled my lungs with the smoky night air and made a single commitment to neither live nor die as a coward.

CHAPTER 8

April 28, 1978

"ACT LIKE YOU ARE ASLEEP," SHAIR WHISPERED. BUT SLEEP WASN'T really what he wanted me to feign.

Every muscle of my body tensed as he carried me away from the palace, moving so briskly and anxiously that twice I thought I would fall to the ground. I turned my head away from his chest and the stench of sin.

He dropped me onto the floorboard of a car and tossed an old wool blanket over me—one that stank of cigarette smoke and exhaust fumes. I lifted a corner of the blanket, but the air in the car was just as stifling. Shair shifted gears, and we passed beneath the looming portico of the palace.

When I was sure we had turned onto the road, I threw the blanket off my head.

"Was it you?" I asked, my voice as gravelly as the road.

He did not answer.

"Was it you?" I repeated, louder.

I saw his jaw clench. The car bounced as he raced over a pothole, slamming my shoulder against the backseat.

"Did you kill them?" I moaned, trying to push myself to sitting.

"Get down!" he snarled. I heard a click, the unmistakable cocking of a pistol. I obeyed, slipping back to the floor of the car.

This was a side of Shair I'd never seen—one that, perhaps, had not existed just a week ago.

"You must be quiet. Be very quiet!"

As he steered away from the palace, the sharp smell of smoke did not fade. I pictured all of Kabul in shambles, the whole world ending abruptly.

With every turn, I eyed the handle of the door, preparing for the moment when I could leap from the car and tumble out. But the car never slowed, and when it did stop, Shair hopped out and opened the back door before I could get my bearings.

I tried to spring past him, but he caught me with one arm and hissed that I'd be making a big mistake if I didn't obey.

Once he'd confirmed there were no onlookers, he pulled me into the stairwell of one of the apartment buildings. I recognized the apartment complex and felt my chest swell with hope. I had an uncle who lived nearby. I just needed to get to him. Moonlight cast eerie shadows on the concrete landings. He opened the door on the third floor and pushed me into an apartment, much to the surprise of the woman inside.

"Wha-what is this?" she asked, bewildered.

"No one" was his curt reply.

The woman blinked slowly, as if her eyes were adjusting to a dark space. She looked at my gashed foot, which was tracking blood onto the carpet.

"He's a killer!" I shouted. Shair and I glared at each other for a beat, nostrils flaring. He took a step, looming over me.

"Why is she calling you a killer?" she demanded.

"She's a child of misfortune," he declared, looking at me. "And she *will* be quiet."

"Misfortune? Do you mean she's an orphan?"

I was not an orphan. *I have a mother and a father,* I wanted to say, but my tongue knotted in my mouth.

The woman crouched in front of me, trying to make sense of the situation.

"My God," she said as she looked me over, her face aghast. She raised her hand to touch me, but gasped when I slapped her hand away.

"Tahera, stitch her foot. Then wash and feed her. She should sleep."

"Stitch her foot? I'm not a doctor! You can't expect me to—"

Shair pulled the apartment door closed behind him and brought the conversation to an abrupt end. Tahera ran to the balcony and stared into the street, muttering frantically. She spun around and, as if she'd hoped I would have disappeared when she had her back to me, cursed.

She snatched a newspaper off the table and placed it beneath my foot to catch the blood.

"Be still. What is your name?" she asked as she knelt before me.

I did not answer.

"Come," she said, motioning for me to rise with her. "Here is the washroom. I'll bring you clothes."

Either out of exhaustion or because her posture reminded me of my mother in prayer, I did not try to run from her.

"Please. Let me go," I said in a low whisper. My father's brother lived two buildings away, as did my mother's cousin. If I could just get my bearings, I was sure I could find them. I could even find a few other familiar homes across town if I could just get free.

Tahera's eyes fell upon the ring on my finger. I folded my arms and hid my hand from view.

"I cannot do that," she said haltingly.

I followed her to the bathroom, walking on the ball of my foot only. I caught a glimpse of myself in the bathroom mirror. I looked like a feral

animal, fresh from an alley fight. My hair was greasy and matted with
flakes of plaster. My clothes were soiled and stiff. My lips were cracked
and scabbed. I bent my knee and saw the split flesh on the sole of my
foot. The two edges like a gaping mouth, with bits of dirt and flakes of
glass embedded in the wound. No wonder it sent shocks of pain up my
leg to walk on it.

I moved mechanically. Tahera used a pitcher to pour tepid water over
me. My scraped cheek burned. A collage of bruises appeared on my arms.
My foot had started to bleed again. Brown water pooled at my feet before
disappearing down the drain.

Tahera dressed me, looking away anytime I looked at her. I followed
her back to the living room and sat upright on a cushion on the floor
while she retrieved a basket from the closet in the hallway. She stared at
its contents and then at my foot.

"Don't touch my foot," I hissed, drawing it toward me protectively.

"I don't want to," she said, her voice so close to breaking that I almost
pitied her. "But it is badly cut. You can barely stand on it."

Shair had warned Tahera to keep the apartment lights off. She placed
a candle so close to my foot that I could feel its warmth on my skin.
With a pair of stainless steel tweezers in her trembling hand, she plucked
debris from my wound. I buried my face in a cushion, reeling from a pain
I hadn't felt until now.

It took Tahera a dozen attempts before she was able to thread the
needle. I watched her bring the needle to my foot and exhale through
tight lips. She blinked rapidly and readjusted the candle. I sobbed stupidly. It was just flesh, after all.

I jerked when the needle pricked my skin. Tahera held on to my ankle
with one hand. Shair must not have gone far because he appeared then and
quickly assessed the situation. When he knelt beside me, Tahera offered the
needle to him, but he rejected it with a quick shake of his head. Instead, his
hand wrapped around my ankle like a vise and held my foot to the floor.

I kicked with my free foot and managed to hit the square of his jaw. Tahera gasped. He cursed under his breath, his hands turning into fists. I braced myself for a retaliatory blow.

"If you're going to sew, then do it," I said to Tahera, sticking my foot out toward her. I would not show fear. "But I don't want his hands anywhere near me."

Tahera held the quivering needle against my skin for so long I thought she might put it down and leave my foot open. Then she inhaled sharply, and I felt the sting as it pierced my skin. I bit my lip and counted twelve passes of the needle, the tip dulling with each plunge. White bursts of light flashed behind my closed lids.

When it was over, Tahera tore a pillowcase into strips and used them to bandage my foot. She pulled a blanket over me and retreated into their bedroom, looking exhausted and desperate to get away.

Shair sat in a chair, guarding over me. Determined not to fall asleep in his presence, I sat upright and stared at the compartments of the wall unit opposite me. I pinched my palm or my arm when I felt my eyelids growing heavy. When I heard Shair's breathing grow long and deep, I slid a glass ashtray off the end table next to me and felt its weight in my hand before I tucked it under my thigh. Was it heavy enough to knock him out?

Time would tell.

Eventually, exhaustion won and I fell asleep as well. When I opened my eyes, Tahera was once again kneeling at my side. Three children stood behind her. There was a boy who looked around Rostam's age and a girl who appeared a few years younger than me. I recognized her dress, a purple frock with a satin sash. I would have worn it for another year if my mother hadn't insisted that it had become inappropriately short. I wanted to rip it off this girl's body. The youngest was a toddler the same height as Faheem. I sat up sharply, keeping the blanket pulled to my chin.

Shair emerged from the kitchen with a cigarette dangling from the corner of his mouth. Beneath the blanket, I felt around for the ashtray but found nothing. I looked up and saw it in Shair's hand. He tapped his cigarette so firmly against the ashtray's curved edge that ashes scattered into the air.

Shair cleared his throat and summoned his children. He spelled out simple rules for them. No one was to mention me outside the home, nor were they to ask me any questions. They would not entertain any of my requests, nor would they approach me.

As her husband spoke, Tahera brought me a plate of bread and a cup of tea.

"Eat something," she said.

I did not budge.

Tahera lifted the blanket to get a look at my foot. I grabbed fistfuls of wool in my hands, not wanting to be on display. Tahera pointed to the ring on my finger.

"What is that?" she whispered.

When she reached for my hand, I jerked back. The cup of tea she'd set beside me toppled, the tea disappearing into the carpet.

"Tahera!" Shair said sharply. "Don't touch a thing on her."

Tahera's face flushed as if her husband had just called her a grave robber. She pulled her shoulders back indignantly and scowled at her husband.

"This is temporary," Shair said. It was unclear if he was speaking to me or his wife or all of us in the room. "All you have to do is stay quiet."

Over the next few days, I made several attempts at escape. I bolted for the balcony and for the front door. I tiptoed from the living room at night and waited for moments of distraction in the daylight. Each attempt succeeded only in inciting an argument between Tahera and Shair. Sometimes my attempts led to my being bound at the wrists for hours.

With each passing day, the soldier looked more haggard. Tahera remained tepid with me, sometimes kind but more often looking at me as if I'd robbed her of something. The apartment being a modest one, I was privy to most conversations between them. Shair railed at his own brothers for calling him a godless Communist. Tahera worried about her cousin whose loose tongue and political opinions might get him killed under this new regime. The radio announcer declared that the Communist Party would be installing a new government, one that would do more than pay lip service to the Afghan people.

I turned Shair's name over in my mind. *Shair* meant "lion." Neelab and I had called him a candle when he was, instead, a deadly jungle beast.

Sham. Shair. These two names said together became a new conjoined word, *sham-shair*, which meant sword. Feeling like I'd been sliced apart, this new name made more sense than anything I'd endured in the last days.

The children heeded their father's warnings and eyed me from a generous distance. After the first couple of days, even Tahera seemed to set up a perimeter. The one time I'd called out to my mother in a half-asleep state, I'd woken to find Tahera inching backward, as if afraid the word *Madar* would settle on her like cigarette smoke on a wool vest.

"Shair, you must be honest with me," she'd whispered to her husband late that night when the children had gone to bed. I could make out their figures in the kitchen, where a single candle glowed. "What will happen to us if this girl is found in our home?"

Shair rose to his feet. He opened a cabinet and reached between the jars of sugar and corn flour. He withdrew the revolver, turned it over in his palm, and tucked it into his waistband.

"Let's hope we never find out."

CHAPTER 9

I WOKE TO THE SOUND OF SHOUTING. THE SOLDIER'S LANKY SON stood on the far end of the living room, pointing a finger at me. He called for his mother, his face pinched with revulsion. I looked down and saw a red stain on the cushion where I'd been sleeping. I felt a wetness between my legs.

"What have you done?" I shouted, rising to my feet. I retreated and pressed my back against the wall, certain that I had been stabbed in my sleep.

"Hush! No one has done anything to you," Tahera said wearily. She lowered her voice. "You are no longer a child. Women bleed every month. It is a sickness we must bear."

She handed me a rag and underwear, then closed the bathroom door. She did not tell me where the blood came from or why.

Shair's son kept his distance from me after that day, looking at me like I was a stray dog who'd brought fleas into their home. But his eyes lingered on me while I ate, when I closed my eyes, and when I asked for permission to use the bathroom. I hid my face most of the time, feeling awash with a shame I didn't know was possible.

Day after day, Shair's daughter emerged from the bedroom wearing clothes I recognized—an orange corduroy skirt, a striped top, denim pants. I seethed to recall how carefully my mother had tied the bundle for Shair to take home.

"Did you do something terrible?" she asked me one day, her voice a whisper. "Why is my father punishing you?"

"Because he's a monster!" I shouted, unable to stomach her looking down at me while wearing the clothes I'd just recently outgrown. She stayed far away from me after that.

Though my spirits were decaying, my body was recuperating. The stitched gash on my foot looked better. My abrasions were healing, and the bruises on my forearms, from where I'd bitten myself silent, had faded into yellow halos. Tahera tended to my wounds, sometimes making idle conversation to fill the void.

"The woman next door has such terrible taste in music. One of these days I'm going to remind her that she's not the only person living in this building."

"My mother was never afraid to speak her mind," I replied gruffly.

Tahera only blinked in response. She hastily tied a bandage and disappeared into the kitchen, stopping her cooking and cleaning from time to time to look at me.

Only the youngest child interacted freely with me, and I almost wished he didn't. He broke my heart and saved me all at once. He would sit beside me and offer me whatever food he was eating—bread, raisins, milk. Sometimes he and I fell asleep together on the living room cushions, and I would wake expecting to see my brother's face.

Tahera would scold the baby if he lingered around me, but she did little to keep him away. Sometimes she seemed glad to have him preoccupied with the strange girl in the living room. Sometimes she lied to Shair about where the baby had played all day.

When it was time for meals, the family would sit cross-legged around a vinyl tablecloth spread across the living room floor. The baby was tucked beside his mother, eating morsels of rice and spinach from her fingers. The older children shot sidelong glances my way. Shair and his wife exchanged only a few words at a time, their thoughts bottled in my presence.

My place was in the corner of the room with a bowl of food separated for me. I had little appetite and probably ate more from the baby's hands than I did at mealtimes.

I stared at the balcony and thought of the distance between this apartment and the ground. Even if I were brave enough to jump, I knew Shair would snatch me by my shirt or hair before I could get my second leg over the railing.

From behind a gauzy curtain, I stared into the windows of other apartments. I looked down at the street and a small field where boys would gather to play soccer. Kabul, from what I could see and sense, had not been decimated. I heard car horns, songs on the radio, and children shouting. There was a distinct absence of gunfire, of wailing. I could not understand why it seemed that only my world had come to a screeching halt.

"My uncle lives in that building there. I want to go to him," I said for the thousandth time.

The room went silent. The children looked from their mother to their father. Shair chewed his food, unfazed. Tahera held a piece of bread in front of her mouth, as if she'd forgotten what to do next.

"I will scream. I will scream so loud that the whole neighborhood will hear me," I threatened, my voice rising. Tahera's bread fell from her fingers.

"Hush, child," she pleaded.

"I'm not a child anymore, remember?" I bit back. "As if that matters. Look at him. He is a grown man and cannot answer when I ask him if he killed my family. Do you not care to ask what happened to the woman who sent the clothes your daughter wears? Do you not care to ask him why I'm alone? Do you not care to know who lies beside you at night?"

Because I was glaring at Tahera, the thunderous clap of Shair's hand across my face stunned me. I held my burning cheek.

Tahera burst into tears. The teenage boy's eyes went wide, and the daughter and toddler pulled closer to their mother.

Tahera began mumbling under her breath, rocking back and forth as if in prayer.

"Your uncle," Shair said, standing over me, "stopped by a vizier's office yesterday. He offered his help to the new government. How stupid of you to think he would take you in and risk being thrown in jail."

My uncle. As the eldest brother, he'd never forgiven my father for disagreeing with his politics. Would he really shelter me if he'd shut my father out?

"Shair, we cannot go on this way. You have to do something," Tahera declared. "I have not stepped outside this apartment for a moment since she's been here."

"I know that!" Shair roared. He hurled the ashtray against the wall. At the sound of glass breaking, I ran to the balcony and burst outside as if the entire apartment were consumed in flames.

"Help me! He killed my family! Please help—"

A hand clapped over my mouth. In a flash, I was yanked back into the apartment. Shair pinned me against the wall by my shoulders, leaning in so close I could see the wild squiggle of blood vessels in his eyes.

"What if she tries something like that again?" Tahera cried.

"Then I'll shove her over myself and we'll be done," Shair swore, looking straight at me. "I've told you not to bother asking pointless questions. Ponder this instead, if you're so smart. What would happen to anyone foolish enough to take you in?"

I pressed my lips together in defiance.

Shair's nostrils flared. His breaths were short, compressed.

"Let me read you something," he said. He retrieved a folded piece of newspaper from the breast pocket of his olive-colored uniform. He unfolded it and began reciting names.

"Fareed Agha. Mirwais Khan." He paused between names, watching my face to confirm I recognized the names. "Abdullah Raheem."

These were my father's friends, the men I had called "uncle." The people who patted me on the head and marveled at how tall I'd grown. The men who slipped brightly wrapped candies into my palm on holidays and told me to treat myself to ice cream.

"All these men have taken positions in the new government."

I winced.

"There are other names that do not make it into the newspapers. Those are the ones who have disappeared," Shair said plainly, as if it all made perfect sense. He released his hold on me.

I crumpled to the floor.

When night fell, I stared out the window at the pointy nose of Taurus until my eyelids grew heavy. Shair took his place sitting guard over me. Kabul was in a deep slumber when I woke to Shair slapping a stretch of duct tape over my mouth. I tried to scream, to kick and claw, but stopped when I saw that he had his pistol pointed at me again.

"Not a sound," he warned.

Tahera surely heard my struggle. I imagined her on the other side of the bedroom door, wringing her hands.

Shair wrapped a shawl over my head and shoulders and led me out of the apartment. Despite my limp, he moved us quickly and silently through the building's stairwell and then, checking to make sure no one was around, pushed me headfirst into the familiar smell of stale cigarettes and gasoline. This time, though, he shoved me into the passenger seat of the car. He walked around and slid into the driver's seat, tucking the gun beneath his thigh.

My stomach sank when he pulled away from the austere apartment complex. He drove in silence until we reached the Ministry of the Interior, which I recognized despite the damage it had suffered. Here, finally, was evidence that something horrible had happened.

"Do you see?" he said, pushing the back of my head so my forehead pressed against the window. I said nothing. He pulled his hand away and drove west to show me more pockmarked buildings. Then he drove toward the barricaded road that led to Arg, and my heart nearly stopped. A cluster of soldiers guarded its entrance. He drove out of the city, down a lonely road. A dust-colored compound that seemed to stretch forever came into view.

It was Pol-e-charkhi prison.

"You see this place? The president did us a favor when he built this place. Now we have somewhere to put his people."

The tips of machine guns poked out from guard towers along the compound's perimeter.

Shair spun the steering wheel. His driving was erratic. I stayed close to the passenger door and waited for the right moment to throw myself from the car. He made a hard left and circled through one of the city's roundabouts, stopping the car beneath a waving PDPA banner.

He glared at me and I understood. It didn't matter how many buildings stood unharmed. It didn't matter that a hole had not opened in the earth or sky. Everything had changed. Everyone had changed.

Shair grabbed me by the nape of my neck and pulled my head toward the windshield, forcing me to look outside. He jabbed at the glass, smudging it with fingerprints.

"Anyone you thought was your friend or family before will slam their door in your face or risk the same happening to them. Your people are gone. Your Kabul is gone."

His rage swelled and swelled until it spilled out the lowered windows and swirled around the car like a sandstorm. He took the gun out from under his leg and held it loosely between his hands. The air grew thin, as if the oxygen had been siphoned out of the car.

"Your Kabul is gone," he repeated.

Then, Shair crumpled. He buried his face in his hands. The vanishing of the lion terrified me more than his anger. I knew I had to get out. I pulled on the door handle, but it was locked. I pounded on the glass and rattled the handle, desperate to escape before Shair did whatever it was he had planned for tonight.

"Child," he said mournfully. "I have no choice. I never did."

CHAPTER 10

SHAIR DIDN'T KILL ME. INSTEAD, HE DROVE ME TO THE FAR END of Chicken Street, where we sat in his car, the engine and lights shut off. I'd been in many of these shops with my mother but had never seen them dark and shuttered. When I peeled the tape from my mouth, Shair did not protest. He leaned back in his seat, and we sat in silence until an hour passed and he sat up sharply.

"Get out," he said, opening his own door and coming around to my side. I followed him out of the car to a dark niche between two shops.

At the sound of footsteps, Shair poked his head out. He hissed at me to keep my back pressed against the wall. Conscious of the revolver in his hand, I obeyed.

"What are we doing here?" I asked, growing impatient enough to test him.

Shair did not answer.

When I thought my legs might give out, he pulled at me.

"Walk behind me," he growled. He kept a hand on the sleeve of my shirt. I considered breaking away but was duly terrified of being stopped by a bullet in my back. His pace was brisk. We were closing in on two women a few meters ahead of us.

"Don't hurt them," I whispered to him. "Please!"

The women stood in front of a door, one reaching into her purse. As we approached, she whirled around.

"*Salaam*, who are you?" she said, loudly enough that a sleeping stray yelped in protest. She had stepped, protectively, in front of the other woman. She clenched her right hand in a fist with keys pointing out from between her fingers like tiny blades.

From behind Shair, I examined the two of them. The one who had turned her hand into a claw appeared close in age to my mother. The woman behind her was a good bit older, with thick wooden bangles that clacked on her thin wrist. She looked confused until her gaze fell upon the revolver Shair held at his side.

"What do you think you're doing?" the older woman shouted in English, stepping between the younger woman and Shair. They hadn't even noticed me.

"Mother, let me handle this," the other woman said, her voice controlled and firm. She never took her eyes off Shair's face, not even when she pulled her mother back by her sleeve.

Shair looked from one to the other, then took a single step to his left. The women's eyes fell on me.

"You help girl," Shair said in halting English. "Kabul dangerous."

He was going to leave me with them. Shair disappeared into the night, his footfalls like raindrops on a roof.

You help girl. Kabul dangerous.

Their eyes rolled over me slowly, as if there were some message to decipher in the gray T-shirt and trousers I was wearing, a boy's outfit that hung loosely on my frame. I didn't realize my hands were balled into fists until I saw their eyes flicker at them. Still, I kept them tight and ready.

"Wait! Who are you? Is this your daughter?" The younger woman whispered loudly down the street. But Shair had disappeared into the dark, like a candle flame extinguished between two fingers. I heard the familiar sound of his car rumbling to life one street over.

Daughter. Before our tutor, my father had taught me the English words for family members, marveling at how close their words were to ours. Daughter—*dokhtar.* Mother—*madar.* Father—*padar.* Brother—*braadar.* In the most precious names, he said, the differences between East and West dissolved.

"Isn't that bizarre!" the older woman said. "He didn't even take our handbags!"

They looked from me to the darkness as if they weren't sure what else might emerge from the night.

"Hello," the younger woman said to me in English. She spoke cautiously. "My name is Antonia. What is your name?"

I did not answer.

She said more, but my heart was pounding so hard that I couldn't hear her words, much less try to understand them. She motioned to the doorway behind her, placed a hand on her chest, and then pointed to the window of her apartment. I heard her say *khaana*, home, and *chai*. I looked at the shop behind her and saw the stairs that led to the apartment above it.

I turned to look at the neighborhood. A turbaned man pushed an empty wooden cart past the far end of the street. A taxi sped by without stopping. There were very few people walking around that night. I wondered if there were people who knew me or my father. I wondered if I should take my chances and make a run for a familiar home, maybe even my own home.

Before I could give it another thought, two men in military uniform rounded the corner. I inhaled sharply and flattened myself against the shop window. The American women swiveled to follow my gaze. In a flash, the woman named Antonia ushered me through a door and up a flight of stairs. I was inside an apartment above a bakery before I could resist.

In the living room, the woman shut the windows and drew the curtains. She instructed the older woman to go to the kitchen and bring juice for me while she peered out the window. I had never heard someone order an elder so brusquely, but the older woman seemed glad for the instruction.

"I'll fetch us some juice!" she announced, then crossed the room in sprightly steps. A moment later, she emerged from the kitchen with a bottle of mango nectar and an empty glass. She filled the glass with thick, orange juice.

I did not take it. My father told me that butchers place a sugar cube in the mouths of lambs before they are slaughtered. I would not be an ignorant lamb.

"Have a sip at least. You look a bit wilted," she said gently.

I looked at my feet.

"You're absolutely right," she said, as if I'd just admonished her. "Let's give you a moment to breathe first. Not to mention you probably don't understand a word coming out of my mouth."

But I did understand most if not everything she said, thanks to the practice I'd had with my parents and lessons from my tutor.

The woman placed the glass on the coffee table and took a seat on the sofa. She pointed to the armchair, but I remained standing, keeping my body as close to the apartment door as possible.

The younger woman, Antonia, was still at the window, looking left and right. I knew she was looking for Shair. I hoped he was gone for good but couldn't be sure. Satisfied that there was nothing to see, she took a seat beside the older woman.

"Okay, okay. Let's start with some basics," she said. "I'm Antonia."

"You can call her Nia, if that's easier. I used to call her that when she was just a little girl," the older woman interjected cheerily. Nia was a lot easier for me to pronounce. Even in my head, I couldn't make the syllables of her full name roll out smoothly.

"And this is Tilly, my mother," Antonia said.

They behaved nothing like any mother and daughter I'd ever seen.

"What is your name?" the woman named Tilly asked, her eyes wide and childlike. Her fingers toyed with the fuchsia scarf that hung around her neck. Then her expression soured and she turned to her daughter. "Oh, I can't do anything but speak to her in English! Can't you ask her in Afghani?"

"Dari," her daughter corrected softly. She was doing a fair job of pretending not to look at my nails bitten to the quick and the half-healed bruises and scrapes on my body.

"Fine, in Dari then. And ask her if she—"

"Mother, please!" Antonia said, and Tilly blinked tightly and pressed a fingertip to her lips.

"*Nam-e-shoma chee ast?*" Antonia asked stiffly. Her Dari surprised me, and not just because she'd addressed me with the formal *you*, a kind of respect that was never given a child. Though she had only asked my name, I did not answer.

Her mother suggested a few more questions to ask, her eyes darting from me to her daughter.

"Mother, can you leave this to me, please?"

Tilly nodded. She had her elbows on her knees, and though she was thin, her movements were so jaunty that she could have been mistaken for a child.

"You are safe here. I want to help you," Antonia continued in Dari. "Was that man your father?"

"What did you ask her?" Tilly whispered.

"If that man was her father."

"The man with the gun?" Tilly balked. "That was certainly not her father. They have completely opposite energies."

Antonia blinked slowly.

I remained silent, still unsure what to make of the entire situation. I was away from Shair but now in the hands of foreigners.

The older woman pursed her lips and let out a long whistle. She said something about Afghanistan being a very exciting but strange country. Antonia stood and disappeared into an adjoining room. A moment later, she emerged with sheets, a blanket, and a pillow, all of which she set on the far end of the sofa. Then she went to the kitchen and brought back a collection of offerings—two slices of buttered bread, a bowl of pistachios, an apple, and a foil-wrapped chocolate. She placed the tray next to the untouched cup of mango juice.

"Will you call the police?" Tilly asked her daughter.

With her eyes on me, Antonia shook her head.

"No," she said pointedly. "I will not call the police. I will not call anyone until I know how to best keep this child safe."

I was relieved to hear her say this and hoped she was speaking truthfully. I'd been poisoned against trusting anyone in a uniform and didn't know if I'd ever recover from that.

The women took off their shoes and tucked them into a closet along with their jackets. They changed into pajamas and took turns using the bathroom. Antonia filled a cup of water for her mother.

Then, without barricading any doors or standing guard over me, they slipped into the bedroom and left the door half open. I heard a click and the room went dark. Thankfully, Antonia had left a small lamp on at the far end of the living room so I could still see my surroundings. The silence grew long, and I convinced myself the women had fallen asleep.

I stared at the food left out for me and felt my stomach knot with hunger.

I wished I could look to my parents for guidance. With a nod, a slow blink, or a slight lowering of the eyebrows, they would remind me to offer a polite *salaam* or signal that I could accept a lemony *Vzletnaya* candy from a general. I longed for even a wordless cue now.

Should I?

I searched the silence for a reply but heard none. My stomach growled

loudly, and I decided I needed to quiet it. I took in all the food that had
been left for me, starting with the juice and finishing with the chocolate.
I left only the pistachios because I couldn't crack a shell without thinking
of the evenings spent listening to my father tell me stories of the far corners of the world as he slid salted green nuts into my eager palm.

Madar, Padar. Please find a way to speak to me.

What would become of me in this apartment? Though I was not
trapped here at gunpoint, I still felt like a caged animal. I heard my father
singing along to a song on the radio, looking at me in a way that told me
he wished I could feel the Sufi lyrics the way he did.

> *Why in prison do you choose to reside,*
> *When the door to freedom is open wide?*

Did that mean walking out the door of this apartment? I was too frightened of the unknown to do that.

I tiptoed to the bookshelf, which had only a small stack of books, a
mug full of pens, and some folders and booklets. Curious, I took a closer
look. The booklet had a picture of a carriage on it with a single word
written in large font across the page—*Oklahoma*.

I blinked hard. I felt my mother's breath on the top of my head, my
father's hands on my shoulders. Could it be that they'd found a way to
signal me from beyond?

I thought of the mother and daughter sleeping a few feet from me,
who had taken me in at gunpoint. If I was going to survive, I would have
to begin trusting someone.

"My name is Sitara," I whispered, my voice as thin as the gauzy curtain that separated me from a roiling Kabul.

CHAPTER 11

ANTONIA BEGAN TIPTOEING AROUND THE BEDROOM AT FIRST morning light. I could sense her looking into the living room and did my best not to stir. In the next forty minutes, she appeared in the door frame and retreated again at least three times. At her fourth pass, I sat up and pulled the blanket around me like a shawl. I'd trapped her in her bedroom long enough.

She entered the living room and kept her voice hushed.

"I hope you slept well," she said, making just brief eye contact with me before stepping into the bathroom. That suited me just fine.

Tilly emerged from the bedroom, plopped down next to me on the sofa, and touched my hair.

"Good morning," she said softly. "Did your head dance with dreams?"

This woman had a funny way of speaking.

A walkie-talkie on the table whirred with static and then a voice I couldn't understand. Antonia popped out of the bathroom, a toothbrush in one hand. She brought the device to her ear and issued a brief reply before returning to the bathroom. I heard running water and gargling.

That morning Antonia seemed too busy doing three things at once

to ask me any questions. I watched her button her pants while she discussed lunch options with Tilly. The walkie-talkie buzzed to life twice
more, and each time she fired off concise responses without pausing her
reading or slicing or pulling the curtain back to peer at the street below.

"Don't call him until I get into the office. It won't pay to get ahead
of ourselves."

And just a few moments later, with a hand on her hip:

"I've already got a write-up. Why does George always seem compelled to do work that's already been done?"

When she realized I was watching her, Nia moved to the kitchen and
lowered her voice. I listened for signs of danger but heard only the clink
of glasses and crumpling of paper. Needing the bathroom, I rose. On my
way there, I glanced into the kitchen and saw Nia folding and refolding a
dishrag while she held a phone to her ear.

When I returned to the sofa, I sat there, fixed as a cushion, until Nia
came and sat on the coffee table, one leg crossed over the other.

"I work at the American embassy," she explained. "I must go there
today, but I will come back very quickly. Do you understand?"

Tilly popped her head out of the bedroom. She had on a pink bra
and turquoise palazzo pants.

"You're not seriously thinking of leaving, are you?" she asked Nia,
her hands on her hips.

I tried to understand why Shair had left me with a woman from the
American embassy. Was he using me for some sort of a plot?

"I've got to, Mother," Antonia replied. She slipped on a blazer and
walked toward the door. She paused for a beat, looked down at my hand,
and then turned to me. "The man who brought you here. Do you know
his name?"

I tucked my hand behind me and did not reply. I'd been wearing the
ring with the stones tucked in my palm, but the glint of the band was
hard to hide.

Antonia smiled as if to tell me she wasn't upset by all that I would not share with her. I could see she didn't want to leave.

"I will come back very soon. You will be fine here. My mother likes to talk," Antonia said softly. "But you don't have to—"

"Go if you have to go," Tilly said, charging across the room in her bra and pants to shoo Nia out the door. "I can almost guarantee we won't burn the place down while you're out."

TILLY PUT ON A SHIRT AND WENT TO WORK IN THE KITCHEN. SHE cut orange slices into circles and triangles and arranged the shapes on a plate to create a face, complete with rinds for eyebrows and buckteeth made of two square crackers. I looked up at Tilly in confusion, which seemed to delight her. She shook her shoulders and twirled on her heels.

She sat down beside me and sucked on an orange wedge. Then she placed one hand over her chest and repeated her name slowly and deliberately. I looked at her splayed fingers, her perfectly round nails, and the pale brown spots on the back of her hand.

"Tilly," she said one final time. "Like 'silly,' but with a 't.'"

She might as well have handed me a wrench. What was I to do with this name? Never in my life had I addressed an elder by her first name. My parents would have been mortified.

Music blared in the street. I looked at the window. In the daylight, the curtain did little to hide the unbroken sky. The air carried the faint scent of charred wood and gunpowder. I wondered if Tilly smelled it too, or if the red smoke I'd breathed in that night would stay with me forever.

I hadn't seen a single familiar face since the night of the attack. I decided to make a list of all the people I knew. The soldier had said I had no family left. But even if that were true, there were other people. I had teachers and neighbors. There was the seamstress who took in my mother's dresses. If I could get to one of them—

That's where I hit a wall. Tahera had looked at me as if I were a live grenade. What if Shair was right and I was a danger to others too?

I rested my throbbing head on a pillow.

I must have fallen asleep because when I woke, the room was silent and Tilly was gone. An empty teacup sat on the coffee table. The thought of being alone in this apartment brought me no comfort. I stepped quietly, slowly, to peer into the bedroom. A yellow quilt covered the bed. There was a single photograph on the dresser, a black-and-white of Antonia, standing in the backseat of an open jeep with her arms folded across her chest and her head tilted back in laughter. The jeep was surrounded by untamed shrubs and a few trees. Antonia wasn't looking at the camera. She was looking at the two men to the right of her, men with dark skin and loudly patterned shawls covering their torsos. One held a large water jug over his shoulder, and both looked quite pleased to be having their picture taken. There was a second photograph of Antonia shaking hands with a man in a suit. They stood in front of a simple palace with tall columns and an American flag flying from the center of its roof.

I walked down the narrow hallway. The bathroom was empty. Two meters away, I saw a set of steps. I tiptoed toward them and saw that the stairs led up to a half-open door through which sunlight fell.

I followed the light, hungry for fresh air and the sun's warmth on my face. I pushed the door open and saw Tilly sitting on a vinyl folding chair. She had her back to the door and her feet propped up on a stack of books and magazines. She'd pulled up her wide pant legs and was sunning the crepelike skin of her thighs. A plume of white smoke drifted upward from her head.

I walked toward her and saw that she held a stumpy cigarette between two fingers of her right hand. She greeted me with a languid smile.

"Isn't this an amazing sky," she said, stretching her arms out as if to embrace the air around her. Tilly's silver hair and pale green eyes reminded me of a watercolor painting. She touched the tip of her cigarette to the arm of the chair to extinguish it. She held out a plate with wafers.

I took one and sat cross-legged on the concrete of the roof to keep out of view.

Tilly closed her eyes, drinking in the sun's glow. From the shops below, I heard the tinkling of door chimes and echoes of bargaining. For two weeks, I'd not walked farther than the length of a room. My legs felt unsure of themselves, weak. I stretched them out in front of me.

I thought Tilly had fallen asleep, so when she spoke, her voice startled me and caused me to sit up straight.

"You were limping," she said. "What happened to your foot?"

I tried to hide my foot from her. She shook her head, disappointed.

Tahera's stitches had pulled the edges of my wound together so tightly that the flesh had formed a lumpy ridge. I tried not to walk in the presence of Tilly or Nia, not wanting to draw attention.

"Maybe not today," she said, turning to me. "But it will get better. And I'm not just talking about your foot. A foot is just a foot after all. I don't know what happened to you, but I can see it was beastly, whatever it was. It *will* get better."

She settled back into her chair and gazed at the cloudless sky.

"What does an old woman know—that's probably what you're thinking. I know this old woman isn't always right. I was never known for making sensible decisions. You can ask Nia and she'll be the first to agree. But I also know that children are very, very good at taking life's lemons and making lemonade. I left Nia with plenty of lemons," Tilly said wistfully. She pumped her small fist in the air. "And just look at her now!"

I didn't understand what lemons had to do with anything, but I did understand she was telling me to trust her daughter. I wasn't ready to do that because her daughter worked for a government and at the moment anything connected to governments made my palms sweat.

"I haven't been here long. I flew in just a few weeks ago. Antonia was so surprised to see me, maybe even more surprised than we were to see you," she exclaimed. "But I missed her. She's a good person with a great big heart. And the way she knows how to work with all kinds of people—oh—it's . . . it's alchemy! She didn't get that from me, though I did give her a love for the stage and stories. Her father, he was the one who really paid attention to her. He worked for a newspaper. Started reading articles to her before she could walk. Brilliant man though he was . . . well, it's not right to speak ill of the dead. But he was a bit . . ."

Tilly folded her arms and made a serious face. It took a great effort to follow her words, and even then I was sure there was much I was missing. Still, it was a welcome distraction.

"My point is that she'll do anything she can to help you—to make sure she figures out the problem and gets you to exactly where you need to be. Do you believe in kismet?"

At first, I didn't recognize the word.

"Kismet. Fate. Destiny written in the sand," she said, twirling a finger in the air. "What will be will be. Have you heard of Marlene Dietrich? I'm sure you haven't. You're far too young."

Qismat. I understood then, though I had no idea what or who she was talking about.

Tilly rose to her feet so effortlessly that she might have been pulled up by an imaginary thread. She began to strut across the roof of the building, leading with one pointed toe and humming a rising and falling melody. She danced her fingers around her calves then up the length of her leg in a movement so sultry, I almost looked away. She circled the small rooftop as a seductive dancer would, rolling her hips with each step and holding the edge of an invisible veil to her face.

"Aren't I lovely?" she said, batting her eyes and tracing her torso. She turned her head to the side and pulled her shoulders back, aiming her breasts at the sun. She placed one hand on her lower back and the other behind her tilted head. She slid her left foot so far in front of her right foot that I feared she would fall to the ground.

I'd never seen an adult behave in such a way.

"You smiled!" she said accusingly, playfully. "The lady of the moonlight has done her job then."

She slinked, catlike, back to her chair and collapsed with a heavy breath before turning to face me. There was a resolve in her expression, a faith that looked big enough to hold the both of us.

"If you ever feel like talking, you should know I'm very good at listening. I know it doesn't seem like I would be, but I am," Tilly said, her voice bright with mischief. I couldn't follow what she said after that. Like her dancing, her talking spun her in different directions and consumed much energy. She let out a long sigh, leaned over to me, and concluded with: "Pardon my French."

If she'd been speaking French, I hadn't realized. I let my hair fall forward to hide the unbidden tears that streaked my cheeks. I hadn't meant to smile. I prayed God would forgive me for that moment of lightness. I prayed my family would forgive me. I was so angry at myself.

And yet, I wanted Tilly to keep talking because Tilly drowned out the perilous thoughts in my head.

I had spent the last two weeks struggling to metabolize the hard truth that my sister Aryana and I had traded places. While I was alone for the first time in my life, she was no longer a solitary twinkle in the night sky.

Kismet. *Qismat.* My story, written in the sand.

Tilly traced the rim of her glass with a finger. Her eyes weren't just green. They were all the colors of an old world, unburied, with flecks of gold and copper. She looked impervious, as if she'd never had a bad day in her life. She moved as if she didn't know her age.

Though Antonia and Tilly were nothing alike, these two women did something I'd not seen strangers do before. When most adults looked at the world, children blurred and fell away. But Tilly and Nia looked at me as if the rest of the world had fallen away and I was the only person left standing.

Sometimes it's when people are silent that you hear them most clearly, Boba had told me.

In the silences, Antonia had made me a bed and given me space to breathe. And as I sat beside Tilly, she looked over at me with misty eyes that crinkled in the corners.

I squeezed my eyes shut tight and tried to picture Boba's face.

If I was going to survive this *qismat* alone, I needed to trust someone, but I wasn't sure I was ready to trust Antonia.

I twirled the stolen ring on my finger and traced the chiseled faces of the gemstones. The kingdom of Ai-Khanoum, Lady Moon, had been buried twice—once where it had been erected and a second time in the basement of Arg.

The ring had become a talisman for me, a key to my survival. Against the scarred pink of my palm, the red of the garnet deepened. It was the color of the carpet upon which I'd read stories, the color of my father's wool sweater, the color of pooled blood. The turquoise body was smooth as the inside of my mother's wrist. It was the color of heaven-bound minarets with veins the color of shattered evil eyes.

I had the ancient world wrapped around my finger even as the modern world I lived in curled its cruel fingers tighter around my throat.

CHAPTER 12

TWO DAYS LATER, I EMERGED FROM THE BATHROOM, MY FACE still damp. I'd been hot since morning and tried splashing water on my face to cool down. I found Antonia sitting at the small dining table in the corner of the living room, with her ear pressed to the radio. She had the volume so low that I'd not heard it until I opened the door. As soon as she saw me, Antonia shut the radio off.

"What do they say?" I asked, wishing I could open the window for some air. Antonia paused before turning around. The day before I'd said a few simple phrases. *Good morning. No thank you.* She did not press for more, which I appreciated.

"There's too much static. More noise than talking," Antonia said, shaking her head. She'd come home for lunch and, presumably, to check on me. "And most of it can't be trusted anyway. All is quiet today, it seems."

She stood and began to pack her bag to return to the embassy. Once she left, I hopped over to the radio and turned it back on. Tilly looked like she might stop me, but then slid onto the sofa instead to observe. I adjusted the dial until the announcer's voice came through clearly.

His tone was solemn, authoritative. The People's Democratic Party of Afghanistan, as the official ruling party, would continue to work on behalf of the people to improve infrastructure, resist imperialism, and bring prosperity to all Afghans. Qualified individuals had been appointed to key ministry positions. The party was unified and strong and fully supported by the people of Kabul. The nation's future never looked as bright as it did in this moment. I could neither stomach listening to it nor bring myself to turn it off.

The sound reminded me of home and the way my father always had his ear to the ground. He knew most of the announcers personally and would sometimes call them if he thought they hadn't covered all sides of an issue. These were rarely short conversations. My father had taught me to recognize and see through propaganda, to be suspicious of every statement that did not allow room for debate or question.

Your Khala Meena is a good example of propaganda. She swears no woman or man in Kabul has ever cooked a better fried eggplant or sautéed squash. And when she says her cooking puts that of your other aunts to shame, what do I always tell her?

I need to taste it to believe it, I had said. Truly, Khala Meena had not a flicker of humility in the kitchen. She would look pointedly at her guests as they ate, collecting praise as if it were a dinner tax.

Let people serve you information, he had said mischievously, *but never let them serve you your opinion.*

I listened to the radio for another hour but heard no mention of the coup or those who had been killed. The empty talk made my head ache and must have put me to sleep because I woke to hear Antonia's sharp whispering in the next room.

"The news, Mom? I said this morning it wasn't good for her to listen to it."

"I'm not a jailer, Nia. I believe in freedom of speech," Tilly said defensively.

"This isn't about freedom of speech," Antonia replied.

"I beg your pardon. Freedom to hear speech," Tilly retorted.

They entered the living room, which seemed to shrink when they were both in it. This mother and daughter couldn't even move around the apartment without bumping into each other. My eyelids were heavy and thoughts slow. I'd not slept much the last two nights, and what had started as an itch on my foot had turned into a dull throbbing.

Tilly noticed me fidgeting and sat beside me on the sofa.

"Her foot doesn't look good," Tilly said, inspecting my wound with her hands clasped behind her back.

That morning I'd seen yellow pus oozing from the wound. The skin around it had grown hot and tender. Nia came to look for herself and immediately sat down.

"Damn," Nia sighed. "It's infected. She needs antibiotics."

"Can't you take her to a hospital?"

"No," I said, my head filled with Shair's warnings that nowhere in Kabul was safe for me anymore. "No hospital!"

Antonia chewed her lip.

"Come on, honey. You know all the important people in town. The minister of this and the new head of that. You must know a doctor who can see her," Tilly coaxed.

I looked up, alarmed.

Which important people in town did Antonia know? And why was she meeting with the new regime? Even Afghan schoolchildren knew foreign spies wandered among us, passing themselves off as businessmen or teachers in order to gather information for their colonizing governments. I had a terrible thought then. What if Nia was a spy? What if they were both spies?

What did they want from me? My heart pounded. I rose, wincing as my right foot touched the ground, and considered running down the steps and asking for help from the bakery owner downstairs. I could slip out the door right now and head into the street, or I could make a run for the rooftop. Neither seemed like a viable path to safety. Feeling defenseless, I hopped and slid to the kitchen and slowly opened drawer after drawer until I found a paring knife. I spun around to see Antonia staring at me.

"Sweetheart, what are you doing with that knife?" she asked.

What was I doing with the knife?

I started to set the knife down but stopped when I saw her eyes dart over to the opposite counter. Was she looking for a bigger knife? Had I been duped by them?

"Please, sit down. Let's talk," Antonia said.

"What are you two—" Tilly said, appearing in the doorway of the kitchen. She froze when she saw the blade in my hand. "Oh, holy hell. Put the knife down unless you're planning on attacking an orange."

"Why you take me?" I asked. "Are you *jasoos*?"

"*Jasoos*? What's *jasoos*? Nia, does she think you're Jesus?" she asked her daughter. Then she turned to me, exasperated. "She's not Jesus! She can't even step into a church without breaking out in hives."

"Listen to me. No, I am not *jasoos*," Antonia swore, her palms up. "I work at the American embassy. I'm here representing America as a diplomat. I help to build . . . teach English. I took you in because that man said you were not safe in Kabul. I brought you here to keep you safe."

"Which is exactly what Jesus would do," Tilly added.

My hands trembled. I looked from one woman to the other, knowing my life depended on my ability to make the right decision, to remember everything my mother and father had taught me, to think of them without breaking in two, to know when to run and when to stay, to know how much of myself I would have to shed to carry on. My foot was on fire. With my ears buzzing as loud as jet engines, it was hard to see or hear my own thoughts.

Maybe Boba had been wrong about me. Maybe Malalai's warrior blood did not course through my veins.

I fell to the floor in a dead faint.

CHAPTER 13

I WOKE WITH A GROAN, STIFF-LIMBED AND GROGGY. AS I BLINKED, my vision came into slow focus. I saw a dresser, its drawers marked with scrapes so deep they left the wood's pale flesh exposed. A lapis pendant dangled from the two carved spires at the top of the mirror. Sunlight fell on the blue stone with veins of white mineral. A medicine bottle sat at the end of the dresser.

I peeled the blanket off and listened to the soft pad of footsteps in the hall and Tilly's hushed voice. Otherwise, it was oddly silent. In the way Boba never realized just how loud the television was until my mother would shut it off, I hadn't understood the volume of the thrumming in my head until it was no more.

A change of clothes sat on the edge of the bed—a shirt, pants, and even underwear in my size. The clothes on me were damp with sweat. I hid behind the door and fumbled to put them on hastily. I opened the door a sliver, then a little more.

"Well, look who woke up on the right side of the bed today!" Tilly exclaimed when I limped out of the bedroom. I had to look up to meet her eyes.

Wearing a green linen dress, Tilly stood on the seat of the armchair holding a stapled stack of papers. A string of multicolored beads hung around her waist. Her hair, the color of rain clouds, was pinned at the back of her head. The boxy shape of the dress and its square neckline echoed the angles of her body, the horizontals of her collarbones and shoulders, the verticals of her nose and legs. My eyes lingered on the plush pink slippers on her feet.

"Before you come any farther, do you have any weapons on you?" she asked, holding a hand up to halt my entry. Antonia emerged from the kitchen, looking relieved.

My neck flushed with embarrassment.

"Good," she said, waving me over so that I could help her descend from the chair. "Now, time to get some food into your tummy or those antibiotics might give you a bellyache. There'll be more time for rehearsal later. And now that you're feeling more like yourself, do you think you could at least tell us your name?"

"Sitara," I said.

"Sitara," Tilly repeated.

For the next few days, I was cared for like a most precious patient. Antonia checked my wound often and took my temperature. With me, their voices were light as birdsong. With each other, their conversations were often clipped and punctuated with facial expressions that needed no translation.

While Antonia's work pulled her from the apartment, Tilly went only as far as the shops downstairs. Coming back with a melon or a bottle of orange soda, she would reenact her conversations with the store owners and talk about how the women in the market reminded her of Cleopatra. Tilly talked about Antonia too. She told me that her daughter had once set a man's broken arm after he'd fallen off the back of a truck in Turkey. Tilly brushed my hair and brought me plates of food she insisted would help clear the poisons from my body. She sang to me and read aloud from a book about a woman who'd fallen in love with a man who rode around town on horseback.

My wound improved. Red faded to pink. The yellow fluid dried out. I still walked gingerly, but came closer to planting my foot solidly on the floor.

Tilly started calling me Star, the English cognate of my name. I spoke only a handful of words and, even then, only to answer their questions. But silence is a heavy coat, and I found myself desperate to shed the weight.

One night I stood in the doorway of the kitchen watching Antonia dry the dinner dishes. She turned just briefly to smile at me before putting the plates into the cabinet and rubbing the silverware dry. The drawer slid shut with a quiet thump. Antonia folded the towel in half, hung it from the rim of the sink, and stepped into the living room. Then she sat cross-legged on the floor and motioned for me to join her. I positioned myself, as I always did, so that I could both see and reach the apartment door. Tilly, wearing earrings made of iridescent glass beads that dangled from her lobes, sat on the armchair.

"You are safe here," Antonia said twice, first in English and then in Dari. She had changed out of her work clothes and into a pair of soft cotton pants and a plaid shirt. Strands of hair that had fallen loose from her ponytail framed her face and gave her a youthful appearance. "And if you trust me, I will do anything I can to help you. Do you understand?"

More and more, I was beginning to see that Antonia was like my father in her work: she was a peacekeeper, and a most trusted adviser. In the conversations I overheard, I could see that the embassy depended on her. If she was in such command over the phone, certainly she must be one of the most important officials in the embassy.

Like a critical director on a movie set, Tilly gave a subtle nod for me to continue.

"Yes. I am okay here," I said slowly, clumsily.

"Okay. That's good," Antonia replied.

I took a deep breath, then put forth my big request.

"I want to go to my house, please."

"Your house?" Antonia repeated, treading carefully. "Where is your house?"

My mind raced as I second-guessed my own plan. Did I really dare reveal where my family had lived? Every clue could help people figure out my identity, and I was still not certain that was a wise move.

Antonia began naming neighborhoods. When she named the quiet neighborhood at the base of a mountain, my foot began to tap out a nervous rhythm.

"That's good. Your house is not very far from here."

But a house is like a watermelon rind, important only because it holds a sweet and tender fruit.

"Tell me about your family," Antonia said carefully, gently.

My eyes fell to the floor.

"My family . . . my family is in Arg when . . . only me . . ."

I felt more like a girl confessing a crime than recounting one, my face hidden in my hands. Antonia placed a gentle hand on my forearm.

"I am sorry. I am so, so sorry."

And then she said nothing, though she looked like she was holding back a thousand questions. Instead, she rose and went to the kitchen, returning with a glass of water.

"What is your father's name?" she asked gently. Her Dari, mercifully, was rooted in the present tense and stole nothing from me.

"Sulaiman Zamani," I said, his name swelling in the room until it filled every corner.

Antonia repeated his name, her head tilted to the side as if she were trying to dislodge a memory.

"Was he in the president's cabinet? And was he working with the

French and the Kabul Museum on the antiquities collection? I was at the Ai-Khanoum—"

Antonia froze. She glanced quickly at my hands, which were clasped in my lap, the ring rotated so that my fingers only partially hid the stones.

"Oh," she said, startled.

I tucked my hands under a throw pillow.

"You know him?" I asked. Tilly looked at her daughter, her eyes mirroring the hope in mine.

Antonia nodded. She'd met my father on at least three occasions and remembered him as a very thoughtful and articulate man.

I wanted to hear her talk more about my father, but she wanted me to continue.

"My m-m-mother," I stammered.

I told her about my family with words that fell heartbreakingly flat. They were so much more than their names would imply, but it was all I had for now. I resurrected them in this small way, in this safe space with Antonia and Tilly listening intently. I moved back and forth in time, from the harrowing moments of the coup to the halcyon days that preceded it.

And though I trembled and stammered as I talked about them, it did not kill me, as I had feared it might.

"Your father studied in America, didn't he?"

I nodded.

"Where were you born?"

"Here," I said. "Only my sister born there."

"Your sister?" Antonia repeated, then waited for me to explain. I told her about my sister's brief life, captured in a shoebox of mementos. Then I told her about Neelab, who had been like a sister to me, and Rostam, my friend. I told her that the president's family had been in another area of Arg that day. I wanted to believe Neelab and Rostam were still alive somewhere.

"The soldiers," I said. "They change to bad. Everything change."

To call it "change" felt like a pale version of the truth, but I didn't know words like "betrayal," "treason," or "mutiny" then.

"People do terrible things for power," Antonia admitted. "What about the soldier who brought you here? Did you know him?"

Shair. I told her everything about him—how he hadn't bothered to warn us about the coup and might have shot my family. I told her about him dragging me out of the palace and trapping me in his apartment, with his family gawking at me.

"You brave, brave girl," Tilly said, her voice gritty and low. Her chin quivered slightly as she spoke. "To think what you've been through. And yet here you sit, strong as stone."

Antonia touched her fingertips to my knees.

"I don't know how, but I will help you," she vowed, and I wanted desperately to believe her. "I will not let anyone else hurt you, and I don't know how but we will find a way to make this better."

"Oh, for heaven's sake, Nia. You start by putting your arms around the girl!" Tilly said through tears. She crossed the room and crouched next to me, wincing as she bent her knees. She smelled of oranges and cinnamon and the stubby cigarettes she smoked but also faintly musty—a scent I couldn't name.

The phone rang. Antonia ignored it. She slid back, making room for Tilly to pull me into an embrace. She sat against the wall with her knees pulled to her chest, perhaps pondering the unkeepable promises she'd just made.

Tilly pulled away for a moment, her cotton shirt darkened by my tears.

"It's an inside-out world, isn't it? Sometimes the world turns inside out and we're in the center and it's oh so dark and we think we will never, ever see the sun again," Tilly whispered, cupping her hands together. Her voice rising feverishly. "But it won't stay that way because little girls can turn the world outside in again and keep it spinning and spinning. My little Nia knows it. Oh, come here, you sweet thing."

She pulled me close again, a tangle of aches and pains and regrets.

We rocked together as a predestined pairing. Like two lines of a couplet. Like two edges of a jagged wound. Like a lost mother and a found child.

CHAPTER 14

"HARD TO BELIEVE IT WAS THREE WEEKS AGO TODAY. I WAS RIGHT here on this roof, not knowing what I was seeing. Nia kept calling, 'Get off the roof, Mom,'" Tilly said, imitating Nia's voice. She gazed at the sky. "I saw it all, but I didn't know what my eyes were seeing. And to think . . ."

Her words drifted off. I imagined her on this roof while Sukhoi jets crossed the skies above the palace, firing upon us.

I sat cross-legged beside her with my notebook on my lap, as had become my routine. I'd been scribbling details of my life, bits of conversations with my parents and Faheem's habits, afraid I would lose the private moments we had shared. Without asking what I was writing, Antonia had come home with a new notebook, sliding it across the table as casually as if she were passing a napkin. Grateful, I filled the lined pages for hours at a time, though the effort often left me drained and freshly devastated.

In a few minutes, Tilly fell asleep in the folding chair. She slept often and deeply, probably because she moved with the energy of a twister while she was awake. She groaned softly in her sleep, her neck at an awkward angle. I took the fuchsia shawl off her lap, balled it up, and placed it under her head.

I walked to the edge of the roof. I saw mountains in the distance, saw the staggered rooftops of the next block. I resented the throngs of people who moved through the day as if what had transpired three weeks ago had been nothing more than a movie. Voices, taut with sorrow, floated over from a nearby apartment.

"*His mother takes food to the prison every day. They won't even tell her if he's dead or alive.*"

"*Doesn't your husband know someone in the army? Can't he ask him?*"

"*And what if he tells his superiors that I've asked? These animals will disappear him in the middle of the——*"

"*Shh!*"

A window slammed shut. Maybe people weren't as unaffected as I thought. Kabul was turning into a city of eavesdroppers, liars, and skeptics. People spied on people they believed to be spies.

I opened the door to return to the living room. Antonia had her back to me, the telephone receiver pressed to her ear. On the dining table was a short stack of manila folders. She didn't notice that I'd entered.

"With all due respect, please don't ask me what my women's *intuition* is telling me," Antonia said, throwing a hand in the air with exasperation. "I work off *information*, not intuition. We've got files on most of the new people in charge. We need to establish relationships with them now. Moscow has wanted everyone else out of their way for a long time."

Her voice softened then, becoming the assuaging tone she used with me.

"I know he was your friend, sir. I know you lost many friends that night. We all did. But at this time, we've got to separate our personal feelings from our professional obligations. We can't make emotional decisions."

I walked to the couch and lifted the corner pillow. I found the pale green tin Antonia had given me to hold the ring. I didn't want to take it off, but she warned me that it was too fragile to be worn. She stuffed a handkerchief in the canister and watched as I placed the ring inside. I checked on the ring often, as if it might suddenly vanish.

Antonia spun around, suddenly aware of my presence. She bit her lip and pressed her hand to her forehead.

"Maybe it's best we discuss this in person," she said when her eyes met mine.

Nia said goodbye and cradled the receiver. She offered a thin smile and beckoned for me to join her.

"Star, come sit with me on the couch. It's past time to get those stitches out."

We sat together on the couch, my foot on Nia's lap. She held my foot with both her hands, rubbing my heel gently and nodding.

"The infection has cleared up. It's looking much better."

"You are like doctor," I said, which made Nia laugh.

"Hardly. I've just spent a good amount of time in places where there weren't many."

Nia brought a pair of scissors, tweezers, and a roll of gauze from the bathroom. New, pink skin had grown over much of the thread Tahera had used to close the wound on my foot. Nia snipped some threads easily, but had to nudge the tweezers into the flesh to free the rest. I bit my lower lip and looked away.

"What was Tilly doing upstairs?" she asked.

"She is sleeping," I replied. "She is very tired."

Nia shook her head.

"I've got to pick up some vitamins or something on my way home from the embassy," she muttered. "She's thinking about who knows what and forgets to eat."

"She is like you," I said.

I must have caught Antonia off guard. She pressed her lips into a thin smile and returned her attention to the stubborn, buried threads in my foot.

I looked toward the entryway and saw Nia's bag by the door. Every time Nia left, my heart pounded. I worried about what might happen if she didn't return or if someone showed up at her door. What Shair had said to me made more sense now than it had on that dark night. This was not my home anymore. I could go nowhere. I could seek no one. And I certainly couldn't stay in this apartment forever.

"The soldier," Antonia began, as if she'd read my mind, "I'm afraid he is right. I am working on options. The longer we wait, the more chance there is for people to learn that you're here. People are afraid to talk about the coup for fear they'll end up in jail. You are a witness to that night, Sitara."

Her delicate phrasing did not cloud the danger she was communicating.

"I think we can get you to America," she said. She rubbed my heel firmly, which helped to distract from the soreness around the edges of the wound.

America.

I'd once asked my parents if they would ever want to live in America again. I'd heard from them about highways wide enough for three cars to travel in the same direction side by side, grocery stores with so many varieties of breakfast cereal that it warranted its own aisle, and university campuses with people from all over the world. My father had laughed and told me about a town in the south, Lashkargah, where Americans lived. *Now they want to live here,* he'd said.

What would happen to me in America? To think of going there without my family was a bitter prospect. How was I to survive on my own? Would I be sent to an orphanage?

"It might not be forever," she said, seeing my crestfallen face. "But for some time, until we can find your family. And until we can be sure Kabul is safe for you."

Antonia set the scissors on the coffee table. I pulled my foot to me, seeing holes where the needle had pierced through my skin and pink lines where the thread had pulled my skin together. I could almost smell the bitter smoke that had enveloped Arg the night of the coup.

"I will go," I said.

Antonia nodded.

"Okay. I just need to figure out exactly how to get you there without taking any chances. I have an idea, but it means we'll need to talk about your sister."

My sister? As if the living were helpless, Antonia was turning to the dead. It was almost laughable.

I'd once overheard a distant relative complain at a family party that promotion to a higher rank didn't seem to be his fate. He had been a soldier for years but had nothing pinned to his chest to show for it.

Padar, I'd asked my father as he carried me to bed late that night, *why would Allah not give him a better fate?*

Though I was heavy-lidded and yawning at the time, his reply remains clear in my memory.

Allah does not deliver your fate fully formed, my father had said. *It is up to you to shape it. But fate doesn't bend easily. Think of a blacksmith bending a rod. He cannot, without daring to hold the rod to fire.*

I was beginning to understand what it meant to hold my fate in my hands, and to know that I'd have to withstand fire if I wanted to bend it toward survival.

Chapter 15

"WITH YOUR SISTER'S AMERICAN BIRTH CERTIFICATE, WE COULD get you out of the country and into the United States," Nia said. "But that means I have to find a way into your home."

I knew exactly what that meant and immediately took out pen and paper to begin sketching out a plan for the two of us to go to my house and try to retrieve the certificate. The sight of an American woman with an Afghan child, though, would bring dangerous attention.

"You can wear *chadori*," I proposed. "You do not talk. Only I am talking. We walk fast and come fast."

"I cannot let you go there. It's best if I go alone," she insisted.

"I'll go with her," Tilly offered, stirring a lump of sugar in her tea. Her eyelids were dusted with a glittery blue powder to match her dress. "I wandered all over the city when I got here, and it wasn't a problem at all."

"And made a few friends along the way, didn't you?" Antonia replied glibly.

Tilly slurped her tea loudly, her brightened eyelids fluttering over the rim as she ignored her daughter's comment.

"I know my home. I can find everything. You go alone, you will come back with nothing," I warned. Antonia paced the living room, one hand on her hip.

"Fine," she said. "But we'll need to move carefully so we're not noticed. Do you think you can do that?"

As planned, Antonia purchased a blue *chadori* from the market. Tilly ran her fingers over the mesh window and draped the supple fabric over her arm.

"Nia, do you remember the costume I wore in that production of *The Glass Menagerie?*"

"How could I forget? I sat through twenty-four performances," Antonia said dryly.

"Twenty-four sold-out performances," Tilly corrected.

The following day I wore one of the dresses Antonia had bought for me from the same secondhand shop my mother used to frequent. Antonia pulled her hair back, then loosened it and retied it. In the cover story I'd devised, Antonia would play the part of an Afghan woman too modest to show her face in public or speak to strange men. Since I was a child, I would speak for her.

"It's a marvelous plan, Nia," Tilly said, nodding her head in approval. "One that requires a bit of performance even in the absence of dialogue. Girls, forget you're acting. Be who you say you are and you'll have the audience wrapped around your dainty little fingers."

"Are you okay?" Antonia asked me. I tensed, realizing fear was a contagion and that Nia and I were at risk of infecting each other with it. I stood and put my hand on the doorknob, hoping bravery was just as transmissible.

Tilly squeezed us both and kissed our cheeks. She stood in the doorway to see us off.

"You'll both be spectacular!" she said, as if we were headed off to our first day of school.

I kept my gaze up but my head lowered. At the end of Chicken Street,

Antonia whispered to me to slow down. My foot had been healing rapidly, and I was moving faster than Antonia could. As I watched her feet catch on the long hem of the *chadori*, I was reminded of a joke my mother had once made.

The longer the chadori, the less likely people are to trip and fall, she said. I had looked confused. *Not the woman wearing the chadori,* she clarified, *but the perverted men who gawk at women's ankles.*

It felt impossible to be moving through Kabul in the crystalline light of day without my mother or father. I expected everyone around me to be able to tell I was an orphan, as if it were written across my forehead. Uniforms set my nerves afire, and there seemed to be soldiers everywhere. I had lost faith in so much around me in those weeks, barely trusting the ground to hold as I walked over it.

And I felt oddly like a traitor, as if I had no right to be walking through the streets after what had happened to my family.

I waved down a taxi and had him deposit us at an intersection just a few blocks from my home. We would walk the rest of the way. I wore a headscarf to keep me at least partially disguised from neighbors and anyone else who might recognize me. We took slow, measured steps until my house came into view.

And then I froze.

It was as if I'd stepped back in time. President Daoud's white Toyota was parked outside our home. For a moment, I believed Kaka Daoud was in our living room, perhaps discussing an important matter with my father. But when a soldier stepped out of the car and lit a cigarette, I whirled around and buried my face in the blue pleats of Antonia's *chadori*.

Antonia urged me to breathe.

We were three houses away.

"I want to go home," I told Antonia.

"Absolutely. We can catch a taxi on the next street," she replied. "Let's go home and rethink our options."

What were they doing in my home anyway? Were they touching my father's suits or books? My mother's hairbrush? Had they trampled on Faheem's toys with their bloody boots? What if they had destroyed the photographs I'd come to collect?

"My home," I said.

I could not see Antonia and could barely hear her over the crash of thoughts in my head. I wanted to stand in the kitchen where my mother cooked noodle soup with red beans and chickpeas, in the living room where my father checked my homework, and in my parents' bedroom where I taught Faheem the sport of hiding our father's briefcase to keep him from going to work.

I had my hands on our privacy wall when Antonia grabbed me. I tried to wriggle out of her grip.

"What's going on here?" a voice boomed.

The smoking soldier stood over us, a nub of a cigarette dangling from his lip. He had his hands on his hips, just inches away from a revolver.

Antonia held my hand tightly. She remained slightly hunched and raised a hand under her *chadori*, as if to beg forgiveness.

"Have you lost your mind, little girl?"

"I have not," I said defiantly, though my actions suggested otherwise.

"If you haven't," he said in that condescending tone adults use to make children see the wrong of their ways, "then why make your poor mother run after you like that?"

The door of our home opened then, and another man emerged. From the epaulets on his shoulders and the cap on his head, I knew this was someone of rank, an officer. He cleared his throat. The soldier crouched before me whirled around to face his superior.

My breath caught in my throat. I recognized the man, a general I'd seen in my father's company. I hid my face in Antonia's *chadori*. Her arms circled tightly around me.

"This is not playtime," he snapped at the soldier.

"Forgive me, sir, but I was not—"

"Let's go!" The general commanded the soldier to go to the car. I held my breath, waiting for him to recognize me. Antonia, without loosening her hold on me, whirled around and started to march us back toward the corner of the street. Her *chadori* swung wide enough to veil my terror-stricken face.

The car door closed and the engine grumbled to life. We kept walking, Antonia maintaining an even pace. I heard the motor approach us and sensed the car slowing down.

"*Khanum,* one moment," the general said, calling on Antonia to pause. As I stood between Antonia and the privacy walls of the homes, I regretted that I'd ever left her Chicken Street apartment. "Do you live on this street?"

Antonia shook her head slowly and then took another step forward.

"Then what are you doing here?" he asked, enunciating his words so there was no chance for us to misunderstand.

If Boba were alive, I thought to myself, *he would be demanding you answer that very same question.*

But I'd gotten us into this mess, and I had to get us out.

"My mother is a midwife. She was called upon to visit a woman in need," I said, keeping myself behind the drape of Antonia's *chadori.*

My heart beat a thousand times before he spoke again.

"You are too young to be seeing new life enter this world."

"If I am not too young to witness death, then surely I am not too young to witness life." The words were out of my mouth before I could talk sense into myself. Antonia's hand squeezed mine tightly, in panic or anger.

"So you have witnessed the fragility of life. Did it not frighten you to come close to *marg?*" the general asked, his arm resting on the open window of the car door.

It was an odd time for my mind to realize that the name of the palace, Arg, rhymed with the Dari word for death, *marg*. How convenient, I thought, for poets who might one day pen a verse about the night the blood of patriots soaked the carpets and splattered the halls of the citadel.

"Hakim," the general said without looking at the soldier in the driver's seat, a soldier so eager to please his superior that he had forgotten to close his mouth. The general rested his hand on the outside of the car door, his fingers tapping against the white metal. On his pinky finger was a ring I recognized as my father's. "Does this little girl not look like someone we know?"

CHAPTER 16

I KNELT BEHIND THE BEDROOM DOOR, OBEYING TILLY'S INSTRUC-tion to remain out of sight. With my eye pressed to the keyhole, I managed to catch a small glimpse of the man and woman who had settled into the sofa at her invitation. The golden-haired man's name was Indigo. He wore a thin brown jacket and flared blue jeans. His gray paisley scarf was knotted at his neck, with its long end hanging over his chest like an elephant's trunk. The woman with Indigo was named Patricia. She had round-rimmed glasses and fine brown hair she wore in a long braid. Patricia sat hip to hip next to Indigo, so I guessed she was his wife.

I heard cupboard doors opening and closing as Tilly told them they absolutely had to try the salty cookies from the bakery downstairs.

"Salty cookies?" the woman asked.

"They're like biscuits—but not at all like biscuits—sprinkled with black sesame seeds. They're flaky and bizarre and you'll love them," Tilly promised as she pushed a plate toward the two visitors.

Antonia walked into the apartment then. She'd been on edge ever since the general had stopped us on my street. His driver, Hakim, had shrugged and motioned to the dashboard clock that they were going to be late.

Farewell, then, the general had said with a wave. *Bring healthy, patriotic Afghan children into this world, good ladies.*

It was clear from Antonia's stiff greeting that she had not been expecting visitors. Tilly made the introductions in a voice as light and cheery as a red balloon.

"I'm sorry, but Tilly didn't mention she'd be having anyone over," Antonia said sharply.

"Aren't surprises grand?" Tilly exclaimed. "Now, look what I've gotten them to try for the first time. Why break bread together when you can break cookies?"

Antonia looked over at the bedroom door. If she spotted my eyeball, she did not react to it.

"He was in the middle of a story," Tilly explained. "So they buy the camels?"

"So, like I was saying, these three German fellas buy four camels off this Afghani man," Indigo said. "They each get one to ride, and then the fourth is there to carry their load. They're a mini-caravan, lumbering across the desert with shadows ten times their real size. They go about twenty miles that day and then set up camp. One of the fellas is smart enough to tie up the camels' feet so they won't wander off."

"Germans are meticulous," Tilly commented.

"Morning comes. These three Germans wake up, stretch, and go out to check on their camels, and lo and behold, the camels have vanished. But they're clever Germans who just had a good night's rest, especially since they didn't have to go the last twenty miles on foot. So they start following the hoofprints in the sand and—get this—all four camels had trekked the twenty miles back to their owner."

"A tourist scam like no other," the woman added brightly, as if something about the scam pleased her.

"It's a true story. My friend met one of the Germans. That Afghani man made a killing off those camels every single time some soft-footed overlanders passed through."

"Afghan," Antonia corrected. "The people are called Afghan. Afghani is the currency."

"Funny money," Tilly said. "Not that 'dollar' makes all that much sense, come to think of it."

"Where are you from, Indigo?" Antonia asked.

"Ohio, both of us. We were running in the same circles for a couple of years before we got together. Patricia's brother was one of the students shot at Kent State. Lucky he got away with just a hole in his leg. A whole lot of Americans died to keep the Communists out of Vietnam."

My father had told me about the United States fighting in Vietnam. I remember how he had to spin the globe to get from America to the far end of Asia.

"Twenty years we'd been stuck in Ohio. Almost our whole lives. Patricia and I wanted to get out and breathe. We hopped on the trail in Istanbul six months ago. Went through Turkey and Iran and then into Afghanistan. Reading. Eating. Partaking. We were supposed to be in Pakistan by now to celebrate my birthday, but we just keep straying off course."

"Actually, there is no course," Patricia said. "Have you read Siddhartha? Amazing, really."

"A couple years back. It is very good," Antonia replied and then swiftly redirected the conversation. "I'm surprised the coup didn't scare you off. What made you stay?"

"That was wild, wasn't it?" Indigo exclaimed. Though I couldn't see their faces, I saw Patricia lean into him. "A bunch of our friends headed out a couple days after it happened. Honestly, I didn't know what was going on. Thought they might be holding some military parade or something."

"Antonia's interested to know when you're planning on leaving and how," Tilly inserted, her tone soothing. "She works for the embassy, so they're always keeping tabs on Americans here. For safety reasons, of course."

"Yeah," Indigo said, drawing out the word and running his fingers through the silk of his hair. "I've been around long enough. I don't think that's all there is to it."

"Mother, can we have a word, please?" Antonia said, rising from her seat.

"We won't be long," Tilly said, as they stepped into the bedroom. Antonia looked at me, then turned to her mother.

"What were you thinking, bringing a couple of hippies here?" she whispered with her back to the door.

"You said we need to get Star out of the country without the wrong Afghans finding out. These people can do that," she explained.

"These people. What exactly have you been doing with these people?"

"What does that have to do with anything?" Tilly asked.

"This is so like you to do this," Antonia muttered. "I told you I'm working on a plan with my contacts, people who understand the situation, not with some free spirits who help you get high."

"You need to get her out of the country now. You said yourself that your people refuse to take a child with family here. And if her uncle is one of the bad guys now—"

"The bad guys?"

"Yes, the bad guys!" Tilly said, shooting me an apologetic look. Until now, they'd had these conversations when they thought I couldn't hear them.

"And who are the good guys, Mother?" Nia asked. She sat on the corner of her bed.

"Aren't we the good guys? You and your friends at the embassy?"

Nia said nothing. She stared at the wedge of comforter between her legs. Tilly cupped my face in her hands. Her fingers felt cool and soft against my face. She said something about leaving the guests alone too long and returned to the living room. Nia stood and followed her.

I went back to the door so I wouldn't miss a word. Antonia let out a long, slow breath and leaned forward in her seat.

"There is a person who needs to leave Afghanistan," Antonia said, finally breaking the prickly silence. "Quietly."

I heard the sofa creak and the man clear his throat.

"Is that why you invited us over?" he asked.

"What route are you planning on taking to get to Pakistan?"

"What does 'quietly' mean?" he asked.

Antonia didn't reply.

"Are you asking me to smuggle someone out of the country?" Then he laughed, a staccato laugh with sharp inhales. "That's the craziest proposition I've ever heard, and I've heard some crazy stuff. I'm out to see the world, not the inside of an Afghan prison."

"Indigo, it's a delicate matter," Tilly added. "Do you remember the first conversation we had? You found me walking along the Kabul River and stopped me to tell me how much I reminded you of your grandmother."

"Thought you might shoot me on the spot."

"I was just short a gun and a bullet. But then you told me about your grandmother. About what a hero she was. How she'd practically walked through fire to rescue her two children from a burning house."

"It's true," Patricia agreed. "She really did save two kids."

"Indigo, have you ever wondered what you would do if you'd been there?"

Indigo didn't reply.

"Things are fiery here. There's a child here that needs saving. And when you have a chance to save a child, you don't overthink it. Heroes just do it, like your grandmother did, and that's why you were walking along the Kabul River talking to strangers about her."

"Whoa, a child?" Indigo exclaimed. He shook his head and raised both palms in protest. "An actual child? No, thanks."

"Indigo, let's just hear them out," Patricia said gently.

"You know what? Here's what I think we should do. Let's just forget we had this conversation," Antonia said.

"Forgotten," Indigo insisted. "We're definitely not looking for this kind of trouble."

"This isn't trouble," Tilly said. "How could you call a child trouble?"

Indigo stood then, and Patricia rose with him. Antonia walked to the door, ready to see them out. It might have ended there. They might all have walked away from that living room if Patricia hadn't put her hand on Indigo's shoulder.

"Baby, remember what you read to me in Bamiyan when we slept under that great Buddha?" she asked. "The bright light of seeking can blind a person from finding anything at all. We're not looking. We're *finding*."

I cracked the door open a hair in time to watch Indigo fall back into his seat with the weight of stones.

CHAPTER 17

"THE SOLDIER WHO BROUGHT YOU HERE," ANTONIA SAID, AS SHE took slow strides across the living room. "I knew I'd seen him before. He was guarding the new minister of education. I had a meeting with him just after the coup and that man—you say his name is Shair?—was standing outside the office. I'd forgotten until this morning. I sat down to call the minister and that's when I made the connection."

"So that's how he knew you!" Tilly exclaimed. She was sewing buttons onto a caramel-colored suede vest with fringes, a costume for the upcoming performance of a musical called *Oklahoma!* that Antonia and her colleagues were putting on.

"Must be. And it wasn't a bad idea. Star is safer with us than anywhere else right now. He must have followed me to this apartment," Antonia explained.

"I hate him," I said, though these words were inadequate.

"I understand that completely. But he got you out of the palace, and he may be able to help us get you out of the country."

"No!" I cried. "I will not go with him!"

"Of course not! I would not do that to you," Antonia said, crouching before me, pleading with me to trust her. Her hair fell forward, framing her face. "I only want him to help us get the birth certificate from your home. I think he can do that this week, on the night of the *Oklahoma!* performance."

Tilly began humming, her eyes half closed.

"We've invited people from the other embassies, from the colleges, and from the new government. It's a bizarre time for a show, but I'm hopeful we can use it to our advantage."

I'd found the script for *Oklahoma!* before I realized Antonia was leading a production here in Kabul. I found it odd that people from the embassy would spend their free time singing and dancing on a stage for all the Foreign Service officers and Afghan notables to see. I could not imagine my father or his colleagues doing any such thing and most especially not in the wake of a coup. Americans were not fazed by much, I gathered.

"Tell us your plan, Nia," Tilly sang out. She held out the vest and admired her handiwork. "We've got to be in on it to make it work."

Antonia kept her eyes on me, even as Tilly slipped into the vest and buttoned it up. She moved side to side, the suede fringes swinging.

"I'm going to schedule another meeting with the minister. If the same soldier—Shair—is on guard duty again, I'm going to press him to get the birth certificate for us the night of the show. That's the night the general won't be there. He's already confirmed he's coming to the show."

I glared at Antonia.

"I know you don't want him in your home, but you saw what happened last time," Antonia said plainly. "There's no other way. Now tell me exactly where the birth certificate might be."

I told her about my mother's nightstand and the hidden drawer, the thin compartment between the top drawer and the top of the nightstand. She handed me a yellow notepad and asked me to draw a map of our home. My first attempt was a mess of lines. It looked nothing like a home. The second attempt was worse. I crumpled the paper and pressed the tip of the pen to a fresh page, biting my lip as I tried to stop my hand from shaking.

Antonia watched over my shoulder.

I drew the straightest line I could, and then another. I drew a series of parallel lines to mark the stairs and made a big X in the square representing my parents' bedroom. I slid the pad across the table.

"This is good," Antonia said, studying the page. She folded the paper and tucked it between the pages of her notebook.

"Mother, I need to talk to you about the night of the performance," she said.

"What is it now?" Tilly asked.

"We can't leave her alone here, and I need to be at the show. I'm going to have someone else play your part. I need you to be with Star that night."

"Why wouldn't we bring her to the show?" Tilly asked, flummoxed. "Surely you've heard of the brilliance of hiding in plain sight."

"Mother, please," Antonia said.

"I can have someone I know come and stay here with her," Tilly suggested, but Antonia refused.

"I will not trust her to anyone else."

"You're right," Tilly said brightly. "Just tell my castmates that I'm terribly sorry to have let them down. And tell the ambassador too. He's been telling folks that the show will have an actual star onstage. Did you know the Chinese ambassador is coming to see me specifically?"

"I shouldn't be surprised you'd be this way," Nia said. "Nothing's changed."

Tilly inhaled sharply.

"I can stay alone," I said. "You say this is two and half hour. It is not too long. I stay here and sleep."

I'd been alone in the apartment for brief periods, when Antonia was at work and Tilly stepped out to pick up groceries or replenish her supply of cigarettes. The apartment had become a safe house for me.

Antonia tapped the eraser end of a pencil against the tabletop in a precise rhythm, three quick taps and two slow taps, a debate in beats. Tilly had rested her case and didn't feel the need to say another word. They bickered so much that they could do it in silence now. An hour later, Nia offered a plan. Tilly would participate in her small role, then excuse herself early and return to the apartment.

Antonia was gone the next two nights for dress rehearsals. Tilly stayed with me, flipping through the script and complaining about the instant coffee Antonia had brought home. She filled the long days telling me stories she likely wouldn't have told in her daughter's presence. She told me about the time Antonia had trapped a squirrel in a shoebox, and how she'd once kicked a fourth-grade classmate between the legs for trying to kiss her.

"I used to watch her play outside her school from across the street. I loved to see her jumping rope or sitting on benches with her friends," Tilly said, pouring piping hot tea into a cup. "She could play alone and be just as happy as when she was in a crowd. I wasn't around much when she was little. I had shows up and down the coast and spent more time on buses than a bus driver."

"But she was with you?"

"No, she was home with her father. He was a very good father. He used to love seeing me onstage, but then complained that the stage was the only place he could see me. He kept it up for a long time, caring for Antonia all alone. Until one day he didn't wake up. Nia got herself dressed and walked to school. She came home and tried to wake him up again. She dressed and fed herself for two days before she broke down in tears while a teacher read a story to the class. That teacher stayed with her while they sent people to the house."

"What happened?"

"It was a heart attack that killed him. Antonia was a couple years younger than you are now. When I came home, I found two trays of food

she'd made for her father. She'd even fed the cat and brought in the mail."
Steam swirled above Tilly's cup, misting her eyes. "She was a strong girl,
just like you. She was alone. I think that's why she has such empathy for
you. She sees herself in you."

"What is empathy?" I asked.

"Oh, how can I describe empathy," Tilly pondered, then stood up
sharply. She extracted a tube of lipstick from her bag and drew a frowning face on her cheek. She pointed to the frown, her face pinched with
sorrow. "Do you see this? Now come give me a hug."

I wrapped my arms around Tilly and our faces met, cheek to cheek.
Then she opened a compact and pointed to the faint frown face on my
cheek.

"That," she said, her voice breaking as we both stared at the pigment
I'd absorbed from her, "is empathy."

Tilly baffled me in many ways but she also could sound like clarity
itself.

"Why is Nia angry with you?" I asked.

Tilly closed her eyes. There were tiny black smudges on her eyelids
and just below her eyes.

"I nursed Nia until she was three years old. You had to see it. I would
slip backstage between scenes, and there she would be, ready to jump into
my arms. Lights, camera, breasts! I couldn't figure out how to make her
stop. She didn't really need it. She was eating hamburgers with pickles
by then, for heaven's sake. So one day I sprinkled cayenne pepper on my
nipples and—"

She scowled. Tilly was a kaleidoscope of emotions, spinning and
transforming constantly.

"God gives people children without confirming their credentials first.
I wasn't good at doing all the things she needed me to do. I wasn't there
to help her or the person she loved most in the world. I've flown around
the world to be with her now, but that doesn't change what I was then."

Tilly raised her arms, maybe to see if she could take flight again. Then she let them flop to her sides and sighed.

"It's a messy business, having children. Parents are supposed to be wise and worthy and selfless, and really, it's the other way around. Most of the time you can get away with the masquerade and it feels great. But then you walk off the stage and into the daylight, and suddenly the whole world can see it was all bad makeup and props," Tilly said, tears sliding down her cheeks, wetting the pain she'd drawn on her face.

By some dark magic, I watched Tilly shrink with sorrow and grow with love. She grew distant even as she drew me in, and my own cheeks became slick with tears as I thought of how much love I'd lost.

CHAPTER 18

THE NIGHT OF THE MUSICAL, I LISTENED TO ANTONIA ADDRESS last-minute urgent calls for black paint, a wooden bucket, and a ten-gallon hat and reassure a nervous cast member who was deeply afraid she would forget all her lines at curtain call.

I watched Tilly dab cream onto her face, dust powder onto her nose and cheeks, and draw a brown pencil along her lower eyelid. She pulled her skin taut at her temples and cursed at the wrinkles that reappeared when she let go. She applied the same red lipstick she'd used to teach me about empathy and blew a kiss at the mirror. She was as heavily painted as an Afghan bride on her wedding day.

"Stage lights make it look like you're not wearing any makeup at all," she explained. "If it's not bold, it's a waste of time."

I wondered if I could attend the show without being noticed. Besides my father, most men wouldn't deign to lower their gaze to meet mine. So many adults treated me as if I were a canary in a cage, expecting me to chirp and flutter when they tapped on the bars and wanting me to be still and silent when they turned their backs.

Tilly, fully made up and with her costume draped over her arm, stood by the door. Antonia went through the apartment drawing the curtains. She reminded me to stay away from the windows and declared the rooftop off-limits as well.

"Okay, okay. I will not go to the *baam*," I promised. Tilly looked alarmed.

"The bomb?" she asked, unaware that the Dari word for "roof" is pronounced the same as the English word for a large explosive.

"The roof," Antonia said, clarifying. We stumbled upon these confusions daily in our bilingual conversations, filling the gaps with whatever was within reach.

I locked the door behind them, as ordered, and gave them enough time to make it down the street before I peeked out the window and confirmed that they had turned the corner. Shuttered storefronts left the street quiet and dark.

To the sound of the ticking clock, I changed into a shirt and pants and tied my hair back. I knotted a headscarf under my chin and buckled my shoes with trembling fingers. Running through my checklist, I placed a lemon and a piece of bread in a plastic bag and took one deep, steadying breath before entering Chicken Street.

I rehearsed my story in my mind. Like Antonia, I'd spent the last two days rehearsing for tonight, practicing lines from a script of my own creation. As I'd hoped, most people did not notice me or the lemon bouncing against my hip. Even stray dogs were too disinterested to uncurl themselves as I passed.

When I spotted a police officer on the corner, I went down a side street and came back on the other side of him. This added minutes to my route, but I was determined to be smart, not hasty. Like a mouse in the dark, I moved through the clay labyrinth of Kabul.

And it worked.

I stood at the end of my block, looking for signs of movement inside my home. This time there was no car parked outside. None of the neighbors were outside either. There was an unseasonable bite in the air, a chill that seemed to have driven everyone into their homes and out of their yards.

I walked in measured steps toward my house, the second from the last on this block, passing a row of homes connected by rooftops and hidden by privacy walls that partitioned yards and ran the length of the block.

I was close enough to see the latch of our front gate, the latch that had been loose for about a year. Even if the gate was locked from the inside, it gave way if the door was pushed up and in at the same time.

I was twenty feet from the gate when a soldier ambled around the corner. My foot seemed to hover in the air until I could force it back to the ground and keep walking. The soldier and I were headed straight for each other, a face-off. I could barely breathe.

To my horror, the soldier stopped directly in front of my home and, with movements fit for a stage, arranged his feet and shoulders into a guard's posture.

I did not slow my step, my thoughts racing as I passed him in front of our gate. Saying a quick prayer, I stopped at the door to our neighbor's home, the one just after ours. I placed my hand on their latch and pushed. The gate yielded and swung inward with a jarring creak.

Once inside their yard, I pressed my back against the thick trunk of their walnut tree. When I was confident no one inside had heard the gate open, I tiptoed closer to the house. A window glowed from behind a lace curtain. A radio announcer reported on another day bursting with progress in the hands of a regime dedicated to uplifting the people.

I slipped around the corner and stayed lower than the rosebushes abutting the house. I was halfway across the yard but by no means in the clear. I needed to climb over the shared wall that separated this house from mine. I eyed the chicken coop positioned against the wall to see if I could climb on top of it without collapsing the structure.

As if to protest my plans, there was a burst of clucking and fluttering of feathers.

"Ashraf! Turn that radio down or you won't hear me. Did you not feed the chickens today? You can't expect eggs from hungry hens."

Ashraf never fed the hens. I'd heard this very argument a thousand nights from my bedroom.

"I think I know what killed our rooster," Ashraf grumbled loudly.

"What is that supposed to mean?"

The radio announcer's voice faded. I stepped closer to the coop and tore the bread I'd brought into pieces, stuffing the chunks through the mesh. The hens began to peck at the ground, their squawks turning into a low, contented clucking. I wasted no time, hoisting myself onto the roof of the chicken coop. The plywood bowed slightly with my weight.

I reached up, curled my fingers around the lip of the wall, and pulled with all my might. The past weeks spent fidgeting in an apartment and picking at food had weakened me. Breathless and terrified that the neighbors would discover me, I tried to pull myself up.

Behind me, a door clanged.

With my forearms scraping against the wall and my foot slipping twice, I gave one more heave and managed to swing my leg over. I eyed the steep drop beneath me as I dangled myself into our empty yard, but before I could think about it too much, I lost my grip and fell to the ground. The impact shot up through my ankles, and I curled into a ball, stifling a groan.

On the other side of the wall, Ashraf cursed the chickens.

Our home was dark and strangely intimidating. I concentrated on my mission as I walked past my mother's flower beds and a stone birdbath and slipped in through the back door.

As Antonia had suspected, marauders had gone through our belongings. The floor was littered with splayed books, cigarette stubs, and sofa cushions. It smelled nothing like home.

I stood before the shelves that ran half the length of our living room, the rows of books that were as much a part of my father as his left arm. My mother had organized her literature collection in the order in which she'd read the books. She'd explained her reasoning to me once, her fingers running across the spines.

I can retrace my steps this way, the stories that became part of me before I was a mother and those I read with you in my arms.

Voices carried in on an evening breeze sent me pounding up the stairs and into my parents' bedroom. I closed the door behind me and held my breath until I was certain no one had entered the house.

But when I turned around, what I saw felt like a punch in the stomach. The plastic bag fell from my hand and the lemon rolled out.

Their bedroom had been ransacked. Dresser drawers gaped open, and clothes were strewn across the bed. My mother's jewelry box, a lacquered piece my father had brought from India, had been looted. Their cream and navy comforter lay crumpled on the floor and even the bed itself looked askew.

Though it had been nearly a month since the coup, I would not have been surprised to find their bodies in that room. It looked like they'd been killed a second time. I wanted to leave and never come back. I wanted to clean everything up. I wanted to pack everything in this house and take it with me. I wanted to hurt the people who had done this. I wanted to curl up in my parents' bed.

But I knew I couldn't stay here. I might suffocate if I did. I went to my mother's nightstand and pushed on both sides. I rattled the table until the secret compartment slid open, and found the bundle of papers held together with a rubber band. I put it in my bag with clammy hands.

I opened the door to my mother's armoire. Her carefully curated wardrobe, the pieces she'd discovered in secondhand shops, the ones she'd sewn by her own hand, inspired by European designs, and the blouses my father had wrapped with tissue paper and given to her—they were all gone. Only a pair of jeans remained, tossed to the floor.

I looked up and saw the leather cover of a bound photo album. Even on my tiptoes, I could not reach it. I brought over the chair from my mother's vanity table and stood on it. My fingers touched the edge of the album, pushing it backward and nearly out of reach. I groaned and stretched my body until my calves and shoulder could go no farther.

I did not give up. One millimeter at a time, I pulled the book to the lip of the shelf and ducked when it tumbled onto my head. Photographs slipped out of the plastic sheaths and spilled out onto the floor. I scrambled to gather them. Even as my fingers worked, I caught glimpses of my parents' faces, of my brother's dewy eyes, and felt a knot grow in my throat. I would have sat down and had a storm of a cry then were it not for the voices I heard.

There was no mistaking their proximity this time, though I couldn't tell where they were coming from or where they were going. I scrambled to grab a handful of photos and collect the bag I'd brought.

The front gate was a trap, given the soldier stationed there. I had to leave through Ashraf's yard again, but there was no coop for me to climb on our side of the yard. Escaping meant following in my father's footsteps the night he'd chased a burglar from our home. In a flash, I was on the balcony, pushing off the railings and planting my elbows on the flat roof. I hoisted myself up, one knee at a time, panting so loudly that I expected the neighborhood lights to turn on.

Hunched, I crept across the roof toward Ashraf's home next door. Ashraf's voice boomed from below. Had he heard my footsteps? Or had my weight sent plaster flakes scattering from their ceiling onto their heads? I crept along the perimeter of the house to reach the far end.

I dangled myself from the edge, palms sweaty. I landed with a thud on the balls of my feet and one outstretched wrist. The pain moved from bone to bone, firing across my rib cage.

Had Ashraf's wife looked outside, surely she would have thought a corpse had dropped from the sky. But she'd not noticed, and after a few moments I pulled myself to stand. My legs wobbled slightly. I steeled myself behind the walnut tree before stepping back into the street.

The soldier cleared his throat. I prepared to run. As I walked past him I realized he was leaning against the wall with his eyes closed. He did not stir.

I walked back toward the apartment with the same measured pace, keeping my eyes on the ground. I was a mere two streets away from Chicken Street when a police officer stopped me.

"Hey, little girl," he called out. I pretended not to hear, but he called out again, quickening his step to catch up to me. I felt a tap on my shoulder. "Are you deaf?"

"I'm so sorry," I replied, my voice sounding shrill to my own ear. The photographs bulged conspicuously in the back pocket of my pants. I prayed he wouldn't notice. "I must not have been paying attention."

"It is late for you to be wandering about alone."

"You are so right. I would much rather be in bed."

"Where is your home? I want to see that you get there."

I had prepared for this. Now it was time to test my cover.

"It is very brave of you to offer, kind officer."

"Brave?" he asked, confused.

I nodded emphatically.

"No one wants to come to my house anymore. That's why I'm out this late in the evening. If it were not a most serious emergency, I would not have been sent out for a lemon."

I pulled the lemon out of the bag and held it delicately, as if it might hatch.

"A lemon?"

My throat was so dry I thought my words might not make it out.

"My family home has been cursed by a *djinn*. Terrible things have been happening to our friends and family within a day of leaving our home. We found a *jaadugar* to lift the curse. We had everything she needed except for the lemon."

His hands went to his hips.

"So, I must be getting home before . . ." I shook my head forlornly. I dropped the lemon back into the bag that held my bundle of papers and trained my eyes on the ground.

"Your home is close by?" he asked hopefully.

"Yes, sir. Just around the corner and halfway down the block."

He looked down the street, craning his neck.

"Run along then. I'll watch after you."

I walked away with measured paces, my legs twitching to break into a run. I dared not turn around until I'd made it around the next corner. I nearly tripped over a sleeping dog, stumbling to stay on my feet, before making it back to Chicken Street and seeing that the lights were still off.

I pounded up the stairs and found the door as I'd left it: with a folded piece of paper blocking the lock.

I sank onto the sofa, the bag still in my hand. When my breathing started to slow, I took out the bundle of folded papers. The rubber band snapped, and they fell loose onto my lap. I sifted through them until I found the one I needed.

CERTIFICATE OF LIVE BIRTH
STATE OF OKLAHOMA—DEPARTMENT OF HEALTH
STATE FILE NO: 135-55-027484

My mother's name was in one box, my father's name in another. There was an address that meant nothing to me, a home I'd never lived in. My sister had weighed six pounds and ten ounces, born two years before me in an America I'd never seen.

The paper had long, angled signatures with loops and crosses. It bore a blue stamp and an emblem, a five-point star in a circle.

Aryana Zamani.

Sister in the sky, I thought with fresh tears streaming down my face, *how is it possible that you are all I have at this moment?*

CHAPTER 19

ANTONIA PACED THE APARTMENT WEARING A BUTTON-DOWN shirt with a ruffled collar, her skirt billowing with every turn. The skirt was so long that it gave the impression she was floating.

"I just can't believe you would do something so . . . so . . . dangerous. Anything could have happened to you out there!"

"I should have stayed," Tilly muttered, wiggling out of her vest. A button popped and skittered across the floor. Tilly didn't bother to reach for it, tossing her vest onto the coffee table. "Why didn't I stay?"

The success of my mission did little to comfort them.

They'd stared as I'd spread the documents across the living room table like a hand of cards—my sister's American birth certificate, my Afghan birth certificate, and Faheem's as well, my mother's high school diploma, and the deed to the home in my father's name.

The photographs told the story of us. My mother in a white veil, her lips painted a deep red, her eyes bashful and lowered. In another photo, my father balanced Faheem on one knee while I planted a kiss on top of my brother's head. I could still feel his feathery baby hair tickling my lips.

My grandmother perched proudly on a chair on a patch of grass, with my mother sitting at her feet, her legs tucked under her and her eyes hidden behind round sunglasses. She wore a summery dress with capped sleeves and a loose bow at the collar.

It hurt to look at them. It hurt more to look away.

"You could have been taken. You might have been seen," Antonia said, rising out of her seat and moving to the window. She pulled the curtain back and looked both ways down the street.

"I am careful. No person follow me."

"Did you speak with anyone?" Antonia asked.

When I did not answer immediately, Antonia sat in front of me.

"Tell me," she said gravely.

I recounted the exchange with the police officer, confirming that he'd not asked my name or followed me back to the apartment. I had passed undetected, careful to make an extra loop before walking down Chicken Street just to be sure no one had tracked my steps.

"You are a clever fox!" Tilly exclaimed.

Antonia shook her head, then reached for Aryana's birth certificate, handling the paper with the kind of care reserved for artifacts.

In the morning, I changed into a pair of Levi's jeans, a red pullover, and a navy blue baseball cap.

"What do you think?" Nia asked her mother.

"Aren't you going to draw some stars and stripes on her?" Tilly asked.

Antonia ignored her.

"I think it works. Now, I just need a few more days and I think I'll have a plan for how we leave."

Tilly looked at her daughter, cockeyed.

"What do you mean by that? We have a plan already. Indigo and Patricia are our plan."

Antonia shook her head.

"It's not safe. They have two other passengers I've not vetted. Hell, I haven't even properly vetted those two. I haven't seen their car. What if it stalls on the road?"

"Speaking of stalling," Tilly grumbled.

Antonia's eyes lighted on me like a butterfly on a bloom.

Antonia reminded me of my father, steadfast and diligent. I wondered if Antonia's cautious nature would keep us in this apartment a bit too long. I thought of Faheem hiding in plain view, his hands over his eyes. I was not a child. I knew this apartment wouldn't cloak my existence forever.

Tilly stirred a spoonful of instant coffee into a cup of boiling water and sat down with her novel. She watched as Antonia scribbled in her notebook and made calls from the rooftop.

"Why can't you have a boyfriend in the CIA?" Tilly asked under her breath.

That evening I listened to the slow song of the *azaan* and tried my best to feel inspired. The *muezzin*'s voice seemed more beseeching than coaxing, a mournful melody. Though I didn't rise, I cupped my hands together under the blanket and prayed for God to keep me safe, to grant my family entry to the gardens of heaven, and to forgive me for resenting Him as much as I did.

If faith was a life raft, mine was riddled with holes.

I had nearly fallen asleep when I heard their hushed voices.

"Can you even imagine what will happen if people find out an American from the embassy snuck an Afghan girl out of the country with a couple of hippies? Let me work out a better way."

"Please don't hate the idea because it's mine, Nia," Tilly said. She sounded nothing like the woman who had danced, with rolling hips, across the rooftop or the woman who belted out songs from musicals. Tilly sounded more like the woman she was when her lipstick had faded, when she slept with her mouth half open, or when the lift of her leafy cigarettes had spun its way out of her bloodstream. She was a different woman at night, when the lavender scent of her perfume dissipated, when she smelled elemental and organic, like the musk of fallen leaves.

"Mom, this isn't about me or you. It's about her," Antonia insisted.

"Maybe that's true," Tilly said, sounding exhausted and unsure. "But I also know you don't trust my judgment. And I can't blame you for that. If I thought apologizing would do any good—"

Tilly's voice broke.

"I can't do this now, Mom," Antonia said, a hitch in her voice. "We can't do this now. Let's take care of this girl and leave that one be. We're fine, I promise."

I heard sniffles. A throat cleared. A deep sigh. A chorus of discomfiture.

WHEN I OPENED MY EYES IN THE MORNING, ANTONIA WAS AT the breakfast table sipping coffee.

"Sitara," she said, rising to sit at the end of the sofa. She gave my ankle a light squeeze. "I need you to trust me. I'm going to get you out of here safely. It may take a few more days to figure it out, but we will do this."

I nodded because it was all I could do.

When Antonia had gone, Tilly wrapped her arms around me. She brushed strands of hair from my temple.

"Let's wash up and get dressed," Tilly suggested. "We need some sunlight."

I did as she suggested, slipping into the corduroy pants and pullover Antonia had bought for me. I brushed my hair slowly, thinking I needed to take control of the situation. My sister's birth certificate was on the bookshelf. I knew my way around Kabul's streets. I was still a child but old enough to move through the city undetected.

You must take a step, before you ask God to bless your journey, my father used to tell me. If I wanted God to protect me, I needed to do my part. When I thought of slipping away from Antonia and Tilly and taking that step on my own, I felt a tug at my heart stronger than I would have expected. We were not related by blood, though looking at the rift between mother and daughter, I didn't know if that mattered much.

And yet I did not feel out of place in this apartment. Tilly had become like a grandmother to me, the two of us fused by the weight of the world around us.

"Let's take in this gorgeous morning before it disappears," she announced. She'd changed into a lilac tunic with straight-leg navy pants. She wore a necklace of knitted flowers, pouty petals surrounding silver beaded centers. We climbed the stairs to the rooftop. I stretched my legs and let the air fill my lungs. We'd been outside only a few moments when my stomach began to growl. Both Tilly and I often forgot to eat. I hadn't had anything for breakfast and wondered if she was hungry. Tilly snored lightly, lulled to sleep by a reaffirming sun.

There were hard-boiled eggs in the fridge and some bread left over from the night before. I would fix her a plate too.

I walked down the stairs and through the apartment door. I walked through the living room and into the narrow kitchen. I was pulling two plates from the cabinet when I heard a door open behind me.

Had Antonia come back already?

I stepped out of the kitchen and found myself face to face with a man who smiled oddly at the sight of me, as if his search was over and he'd found what he'd come looking for.

But I hadn't expected to be found. The second his hand touched my shoulder, the scream I'd stifled since the night of the coup erupted from my throat, loud enough to stir the sullen martyrs in their graves.

CHAPTER 20

INDIGO WAS LUCKY I HADN'T REACHED FOR THE PARING KNIFE again. He stared at the shards of the ceramic plate I'd dropped and shook his head.

Tilly! I'm a friend of Tilly's, he'd stammered when I started to shout. *Didn't you hear me knock?*

He and Patricia had decided to leave a day ahead of schedule, he told Tilly when she came down the stairs. He didn't want to leave without checking in. Tilly had looked at me.

"What do you say, Star? What is your heart telling you?" she asked, looking equally ready to head out the door with Indigo or climb back up the stairs and resume her morning nap under the sun.

I looked at this man Nia wasn't willing to trust and wondered if she was right. He was gulping down a glass of water Tilly had handed him. He looked too scared to be scary.

Antonia wanted time to figure out the perfect plan. She wanted to work with people she knew, but I was worried about the people she knew. She was at the ministries and arranging meetings with the very people who had organized the coup. What if one of her contacts told them about me? Aware that there was no such thing as a perfect plan, I said resolutely, "It is time to go."

Tilly cleared her throat and told Indigo we needed a few moments to gather our things. She brought the duffel bag to me and scrawled a note to Antonia. We didn't discuss it. We left as if we'd been expecting Indigo to appear, as if we were headed out of town for a holiday.

Indigo promised to get us to Islamabad. He said it wouldn't be hard to find the U.S. embassy once we were there. After that, he said, we would be on our own. Tilly nodded.

Stepping out of the apartment, I wondered if I was making the right decision. Tilly looked more relieved than nervous. The van smelled of cigarettes and stale bedsheets. The woman next to me eyed me with excitement, though she pretended to be looking at something outside my window.

"Her name is Patricia," Tilly said, pointing at her. She put her hand over mine. "My gosh, you're still shaking. Indigo must have given you quite a fright back there."

Kabul grew small as we rolled south, down a road I'd traveled with my family. We were joined by another couple. They were all overlanders, as I later learned they were called—Americans and Europeans trekking along a meandering trail from Turkey to as far as Goa, in western India. They stopped in Iran, Lebanon, Afghanistan, and Kashmir along the way, dipping into the local culture and the local weed. They picnicked by lakes and bought embroidered scarves to carry back home. They haggled halfheartedly, amusing artisans and shop owners.

The other couple in the van knew nothing about my situation and thought I was Tilly's grandchild, half-Afghan and half-American and very wary of strangers. We were on our way to Islamabad, Tilly said, because she was in urgent need of specialized medical care for a blood disease. I thought it was a brilliant cover story. Between Tilly's bony wrists and my honey-colored hair and green-speckled eyes, we each looked our parts.

Patricia chatted with the other woman, whose hair and eyes made me wonder if she'd been painted by the same palate of colors as the sky. Both women looked a few years younger than Antonia, but that might have been because they carried backpacks instead of dossiers. Indigo sat in the driver's seat, while a man with a half-folded map and a small booklet on his lap sat in the passenger seat, his right foot resting on the dashboard.

"Map, check. *Eastern Bound*, check," he said, flapping the two together.

"Ah, the infamous guidebook!" Tilly asked. "May I see it?"

"Sure," he said, reaching over the seat. "Worth every penny. Covers the trail from Istanbul to Kathmandu. Told us to stuff ourselves in Turkey and not expect good food again until we reached Kabul. That was pretty good advice. What do you say, friends?"

"My God, that bathhouse in Turkey!" Patricia's friend groaned. "The harem? What was it called?"

"Hamam!" Patricia laughed. "I don't think these people have public harems!"

"Did you see concubines there?" Tilly asked. "I've always wondered what it might be like to be a concubine."

"You haven't lived," the woman said, "until you've had a decade's worth of dead skin scrubbed off you by an enormous woman wearing red underwear."

"You loved it. You told me it was the best birthday gift you've ever gotten," her boyfriend insisted.

"I've thought very seriously about leaving you for that woman," she said, eyes wide and devilish.

Tilly took the booklet from him and began to flip through it. I looked over her shoulder, catching bits and pieces. Indigo's friend lit a cigarette with the car's lighter and slipped a cassette into the player. Tilly started to hum and sway.

While I didn't recognize the song, the smoke took me home, to rambunctious nights when aunts, uncles, and friends gathered for food and music. My aunt would play a tambourine while her husband sat cross-legged in front of a harmonium, air moving in and out of the bellows, sending vibrations through the reeds. My father's fingers would tap a rhythm on a *tabla,* the heel of his palm thumping a bass beat. They were all amateurs. They weren't literate in chords or sharps and flats but they made the house thrum until the early hours of the morning.

My mother always brought a dish of *mantu* to these gatherings. I might have been five years old when she first allowed me to help fill the dumplings. I would dip my finger into a bowl of water, wetting the four sides of the square dough. Next, a spoonful of minced onions and beef went into the middle. Then I would pinch the corners together, sealing the dumpling into a perfect point. Placed side by side in a round steamer, they looked like the beaks of nested baby birds peering skyward. My mother did not like to cook, but with this one dish she made every couple of months, she had created quite a reputation for herself.

Be smart with your efforts, she'd told me once.

I had always been my father's spirited girl, the child who had grown up in the halls of the palace. But the absence of my family made me re-consider who I was. If it hadn't been for my father's outstretched arms, perhaps I never would have dared to leap from the sofa cushions. If it hadn't been for my mother's applause, I might not have dared to dance in our living room. I only moved as boldly through the world as I had because I knew they would catch me, no matter how far I fell.

Without them, I might be nothing more than a coward.

But maybe, I thought, if I could manage to feign bravery in this moment, then I could feign bravery at another moment. And maybe if I feigned bravery enough, I could grow into it.

The road ahead snaked between mountains, like a necklace disap-pearing into a bosom. Tilly lifted her hand and squinted against the sun's glare. I closed my eyes, my eyelids transforming the sunlight into a thousand colors, bursting and flashing like fireworks only I could see. I wondered how many times my father had traveled this road without us, accompanying President Daoud Khan or other senior cabinet members on official trips. He'd always brought back treats from his travels. I may not have been able to recognize the cities by sight, but knew them by taste. Moscow was bits of wafer or pralines hidden in small cocoa bricks. Paghman, with its crisp mountain water, tasted like snowflakes on my tongue. Kandahar popped sweetly between my teeth, releasing the juice of pomegranates. Jalalabad made my cheeks pucker with its tart oranges. My mother would slice the rinds into strands, steaming them into a yellow rice with bright green pistachios and moon-white almond slivers.

I pictured my mother's back over the stove, steam floating to her face as she lifted the pot's cover. It was all so vivid, so real. I felt the familiar lump in my throat again.

"My goodness," Tilly exclaimed. "We couldn't possibly be . . . Are we taking that road?"

I didn't have to look to know what had caused her alarm. The tortuous road we were on, an asphalt gift from the West German government, was not for the faint of heart.

On our right was the jagged face of the mountain, its peak hidden from view. Boulders perched precariously on the mountain's visage, freckled with orange wildflowers and patches of yellow-green grasses. On our left was a drop so sheer it might have been a fall off the far edge of the earth. Cars moved in both directions on this winding road, signaling one another with a wave or a honk of the horn.

A dark shape crossed the sky, flapped twice, and swooped over the van. I couldn't tell if it was a buzzard or an eagle or if a piece of the mountain had broken off and the great sky had conspired to keep it from falling.

The ascent sent a tickle through the passengers. Patricia knelt on her seat, her face pressed against the glass. The air thinned. I felt the rev of the engine through my feet. Indigo's friend reached over and turned up the volume on the radio. The singer was a man, his voice a high-pitched daydream. The overlanders joined the chorus, which was the one line of the song I could make out.

Ohhhh, I just want to be your everything!

"Slow down, babe," Patricia cajoled. "This road is pretty wild."

"I'm gonna get us there."

Indigo's eyes met mine in the rearview mirror. Patricia must have noticed too. Her hand went to Indigo's shoulder and stayed there as she whispered into his ear.

I looked away, feeling like an interloper.

Just as Patricia looked back and smiled beatifically at me, a truck approached head-on. The lorry weaved slightly, the ropes straining to keep its bundled cargo in place. The truck's horn bleated, breaking through the ballad. Indigo yelled and jerked the steering wheel to the right. The van tilted, its tires lifting off the road just enough to make my stomach rise and fall. Tilly howled, her hand flying across my chest to secure me. My head bounced against the back of Patricia's empty seat.

Metal and glass crunched against the unforgiving mountain.

I touched my head, blinking to clear the confusion. Patricia lay, face-down, in the small space in the middle of the van. Indigo yelled her name as he fumbled with his seat belt. The two men and the other woman scrambled to reach her, their limbs knotting the hollow of the van.

I feared, very seriously, that Patricia was dead, even as they called her name. Before the coup, death had been a plaything. My friends and I had laughed and joked about it. We'd made it part of our imagined stories. But I hadn't believed in it because I hadn't really seen it. If the sun rises every day, it is hard to imagine that it is not promised.

But now that I'd seen death, I knew it was a thing with teeth.

I buried my head in Tilly's shoulder, not wanting to watch as Patricia's friends pulled her onto the seat. Even when I heard her groan, I still did not dare look. From the floor of the van, she cursed at Indigo, which made him breathe a sigh of relief.

"You really scared me there. Oh, Patty, you scared me bad."

My eyes were still clamped shut, my face pressed into the small space beneath Tilly's collarbone.

Tilly.

I thought back to the night she'd knelt on the floor of Antonia's apartment, rocking me as if I were hers. And the way her arm had sprung to keep me from flying out of my seat.

Why wasn't that arm curled around me now?

"Tilly?" I said, looking up at her. A scarlet line trickled from above her left eyebrow, where the skin had split apart. Her eyes fluttered slightly.

"Tilly!" I called again, stupidly. I grabbed her by the shoulders.

The sun's rays fell directly on Tilly's head, her silver hair shimmering. I pressed my cheek to Tilly's. It was because of me that she sat in the cradle of mountains, bleeding.

"Forgive me," I whispered in Dari.

I turned my head to look out the window and saw the flighted creature, observer or omen, soaring above us with wings in full salute.

CHAPTER 21

TILLY, LEANING AGAINST THE MOUNTAINSIDE, SWORE SHE WAS fine. She let Patricia's friend press a tissue to her forehead, and the bleeding stopped within a few minutes. She puffed out her cheeks and rolled her eyes, giving me a squeeze when it did not elicit a laugh from me.

"I'm fine now, really."

The wound looked ugly, but far from fatal. Someone pulled a bandage out of a backpack and hid the gash under it. I wondered if it would need stitches or antibiotics. I didn't want her head to look like my foot.

Indigo, Patricia, and their friends examined the front of the van and decided its injuries were not fatal either. One headlight had shattered, but it was still daylight and the other would be enough to light the road at night. The hood of the van had tented in slightly, making it impossible to open. But the engine rumbled to life, much to Indigo's relief. Cars continued to come blazing along the road, and Indigo signaled everyone to get back into the van.

"We're like bowling pins out here," he said, trying to make light of the situation. No one laughed, not even nervously.

We continued our journey without music, without much talking.

The van and the explorers within it had been jolted, the chemistry altered.

We emerged from the mountain pass and saw the sprawling city of Jalalabad stretch out before us. I did not know these streets or buildings. I had only experienced this city as a carefree child, following my parents.

The city was home to a few points of interest that my father had pointed out. Mausoleums of kings, a Hindu temple, and a medical school that one of my father's cousins had attended. My father wanted me to become a doctor too and even used my interest in the stars to convince me medicine was my destiny.

I've told you about Ibn Sina, the astronomer. He was also the father of modern medicine. From here to Europe, physicians used his text to treat disease and save lives.

He was a genius, Padar. My teachers have assured me I am not.

Why do you need teachers to tell you what you are? Have I not told you about the falling girl?

Tell me again, I had insisted, because his explanations were adventures.

If Ibn Sina were here, he would tell you to imagine yourself as a falling girl. You are suspended in air, clouds so thick you cannot see. Your limbs are spread wide and touch no surface. Nothing reaches you. Nothing touches you. And yet you know you exist. How is that possible?

I had not wanted to disappoint him, but I wasn't sure I understood Ibn Sina's philosophical ponderings. I had closed my eyes, playing the part of a girl floating through space. I existed because I was here to say so. Even in suspension, I could think and breathe and be me.

You need no one to confirm you. You are everything you believe yourself to be.

We crossed a bridge, drove down tree-lined streets and past rows of homes. We stopped on a busy street. Though we'd traveled only a couple of hours, the temperature was much warmer than in Kabul. Indigo and his friend left for a few minutes, then returned with a bag of oranges and freshly baked bread. A few minutes later, Tilly had a heap of orange peels on her lap. With fingers and chins sticky with citrus juice, we could breathe a little easier. Indigo's friend snapped a couple of photographs of the kiosks on the side of the road. Patricia and her friend posed half-heartedly for a picture before we got back into the car.

We circled through a roundabout, crossed the eastern end of the city, and continued along the highway that would take us to Pakistan. Signs of a border checkpoint appeared. Indigo wiped his brow with the back of his hand.

"Border coming up. Everybody got what you need?" Indigo asked, trying to sound casual.

Tilly rifled through her handbag. She pulled out her passport and the birth certificate. She searched some more, muttering to herself.

"Is everything okay?" Patricia asked sweetly, rubbing her shoulder. She'd pulled the neck of her top down earlier and shown us the faint bloom of bruises across her upper arm.

"I can't seem to find my granddaughter's passport. This is just ter-rible," Tilly lamented. "I could have sworn I put it in my bag. I left it on the kitchen table so I wouldn't miss it. Sweetheart, did I give it to you?"

She looked at me, a hand to her temple. I shook my head and pre-tended to look around our feet, as if it might have been dropped.

"What should we do?" the other American woman asked.

"I don't think they'll make a big deal. Let's just tell them we're Amer-icans," her boyfriend suggested.

No one wanted to turn back. Getting me across the border without a passport required trying our luck with the border patrol officers or con-cealing me in the van and trying to slip me through. Indigo, Patricia, and the other overlander couple argued the risks of each option. Tilly stayed out of the debate, wringing her hands and nattering to herself about how she really needed to get to that doctor in Islamabad. I pressed myself close to my forgetful grandmother. It didn't take much acting for me to look like her anxious grandchild.

In the end, in a decision made by no one person, the back of the van was opened. Bags were removed and I was instructed to lie down in the trunk, the narrow space behind the last row of seats. I had to steady my breathing going in, as I was reminded of being shoved into the back of Shair's car. We were just a small stretch of road away from the border. Tilly stroked my head and kissed my cheek before they buried me under bags.

"This just feels a little crazy," the man said to Indigo.

"It won't be for more than a few minutes. What's crazy is that a piece of paper could be so important."

"If we end up in an Afghan prison . . ."

"It'll be a step up from your apartment back home," Indigo said, finishing his friend's sentence.

A nervous snort. A throat cleared. I lay curled on my side, feeling every bump in the road. After a few moments, the car slowed and I heard the radio turn on. Indigo greeted someone, his voice bright as the Jalalabad sun.

I listened carefully and tried to imagine what was happening. I heard no shouting or panic. Footsteps moved around the car, approaching the trunk door. I held my breath, praying my legs or head were not visible between the duffel bags and backpacks.

"Hey, hey, American!" an accented voice called out. My mind flashed with visions of palace guards, uniforms that belied allegiance.

There were two loud thumps against the back of the van. Indigo shouted something.

If I had to run, I would run. If I had to fight, I would fight. The drum in my chest beat insistently. My head twirled with a strange kind of vertigo, as if I were falling from the sky.

CHAPTER 22

"OH, INDIGO. YOU LOOK LIKE YOU'RE GOING TO LOSE YOUR lunch," Tilly chided, giving his shoulder a squeeze. "Did you think we wouldn't make it into Pakistan?"

The overlanders looked exhausted, as if the five hours we'd spent together since Kabul had been more like five years.

In truth, it was the five minutes we'd spent at the border that had really sapped their strength. I'd heard Tilly at the rear of the van talking about needing some fresh air. She described the van careening into the side of the mountain. I thought I heard a tremble in her voice. Her voice was so close, inches away. She said she had a terrible headache and hoped to see a doctor as soon as they crossed into Pakistan.

How kind of you, she'd said. *How did you know I was thirsty?*

I could imagine the soldiers looking at her silver hair, the Band-Aid on her forehead. Any self-respecting Afghan man wouldn't keep a withering elder on her feet for long or badger her with questions. Even I wanted to offer her a chair.

The van rumbled along in silence. I avoided looking at the others, feeling like I caused a whole lot of trouble everywhere I went.

Indigo parked the van across the street from the American embassy, a long brick building two stories high. We stood under a plane tree on a street with gated embassies on either side of this compound. Cars and people moved in both directions on the tree-lined road. The embassy was bordered by a brick wall. Police officers who looked to be Pakistani guarded the gray metal gate at the entrance, and an American flag was hoisted high a few meters behind the gate.

"When you doubt what kind of person you are, come back to this moment," Tilly said to Indigo and Patricia. She spoke as if she were a coach, sending her battered players into the final quarter. "This precious girl is out of danger because you came for her. This is who you really are."

Patricia wrapped her arms around Tilly and me and squeezed us tight. The gesture surprised me. She smelled of talc and incense, smoke and flowers, and with my face buried in the soft cotton of her tunic, I was a shade embarrassed once I realized I was clinging to her. I let go and stood at Tilly's side.

The other couple looked relieved to see us go, waving to us from inside the van. They were going to spend a week in Islamabad and maybe venture into the countryside. Indigo needed to get the vehicle fixed before they went back to Kabul and retraced their steps to Turkey. Patricia's eyes misted when she talked about going home to the United States.

"You're one tough cookie," Indigo said as he gave Tilly a hug.

"So are you!" Tilly cheered. "Be proud of yourselves. The Himalayas didn't kill us. So go and *live*. And don't forget to hug your mothers. For God's sake, please hug your mothers."

This woman who didn't know the Himalayas from the Hindu Kush kept me from feeling utterly lost and alone. I couldn't understand why Antonia didn't feel the same way about Tilly. Here she stood, on a tree-lined street in Islamabad, making these two couples laugh, even as their stomachs likely still fluttered to think of how close they'd come to plunging into a chasm or being tossed into a dank prison cell.

But they hadn't, and she wanted them to remember that.

"Now Star and I are off to get her passport sorted. Farewell, friends," Tilly said, taking my hand and nodding in the direction of the embassy.

I watched the van pull away, Patricia's hand waving from the open window. We were on our own and ready to set Antonia's plan into motion. Tilly dug a tissue out of her bag and pressed it to her nose. I gave her hand a squeeze to remind her she wasn't alone.

Police officers with bright badges stood on the curb just outside the embassy and watched as we approached. I had to will my feet to move toward them, remind myself that I was far from Kabul. I might as well have been crossing a raging river. Every step felt treacherous.

We saw the police officer's mouth move. His words melted into the drone of traffic behind us. I dared not look him in the eye. I held on tightly to Tilly and kept my eye on the flurry of people moving in all directions.

Tilly exchanged a few words with them and showed her passport. In a moment, we passed through the front gates and were escorted by a police officer into a brick building. Inside, three soldiers stood on guard with rifles on their shoulders, their eyes hidden behind sunglasses. I could tell from their faces and the flags stitched onto their uniforms that they were Americans. A soldier sitting behind a desk took Tilly's passport and my sister's birth certificate and examined them front and back. Then he nodded at the bandage on Tilly's forehead.

"Ma'am, have you had that looked at?" he asked.

"This is a scratch. We have more urgent matters to deal with," Tilly announced. "My daughter, Antonia Shephard, is a Foreign Service officer at the Kabul embassy. She's contacted some folks here about our predicament. We need some help with documentation."

The soldier considered her for a moment and made a phone call before walking us down a long hallway. He carried Tilly's bag for her while I kept mine slung over my shoulder, the bulk of it pressed against my belly. We were led into another room, a sparse office with a desk and two chairs. Tilly pulled a packet of crackers out of her bag, and though I had no appetite, I ate them to quell my roiling stomach. Being inside a government building in plain view had me rattled.

"They're calling Antonia," she whispered in my ear. "She'll sort it all out."

I watched faces, too nervous to understand the English. It felt like they were talking at double speed, and most of it flew over my head. A woman set a small glass bottle of apple juice in front of me and offered Tilly a fresh bandage. Tilly thanked her but, when she had gone, muttered that we had "bigger fish to fry."

"Fish?" I whispered, puzzled. But Tilly's attention was on the man who had just entered the office, his hand extended. He had wavy brown hair and square-framed glasses. Tilly shook his hand.

"Good to meet you," she said. "I hope they've briefed you on our passport situation already. Do you know my daughter, Antonia?"

He started to speak, then looked at me and paused.

"Could we step into the hallway?" he asked Tilly, extending his arm toward the door.

"If that's where good news is best delivered, then certainly," she said. Tilly looked at me and I nodded. She touched my shoulder before she exited the room. They stood just outside the door, where I could still see her listen and nod and point at something in the distance. I looked at the expression on the man's face. If he was one of Antonia's friends, why did he seem so wary of us?

I touched my hip, feeling for the lump beneath the fabric of my pants. Just before we left Antonia's apartment with Indigo, I'd locked myself in the bathroom to use the small sewing kit in her medicine cabinet. My mother had taught me to sew buttons onto shirts, and in the bathroom I managed, without too much difficulty, to stitch the ring into the pocket of my pants. It felt routine now, corrupting my parents' teachings so that I could find ways to survive in their absence.

I had thought about leaving the ring behind, placing it on the shelf of the medicine cabinet for Antonia to find. She likely would have taken it to the Kabul Museum. I didn't know if any of the Ai-Khanoum pieces had made it there or if they were still trapped in the basement of Arg. But this ring had become a talisman for me. As if this loop of ancient gold held together boulders instead of gems, the ring prevented me from feeling untethered, vulnerable to any rogue wind.

I stood and looked out the office window. Tilly and the man were out of view. I could make out the shapes of people moving down the hall, and some passed close enough that I could see the shiny buttons of a blouse or the geometry of a man in a jacket. There were hardly any soldiers in sight in this part of the embassy, and those I saw didn't seem to be carrying a weapon. People moved purposefully, but breezily.

The door opened and Tilly stepped back into the room, her lips thin and her shoulders pulled back. She tucked the envelope with my birth certificate back into her handbag. The man next to her had an expression equally grave on his face, his hands deep in his pockets.

"Aryana, honey, we're going to spend the night in town. This gentleman, Mr. Harris, has been kind enough to find us a hotel close by so we won't have to go far. By tomorrow," Tilly said, turning her pointed attention to the man beside her, "Mr. Harris is going to have a shiny passport ready for you. He understands how eager we are to get you home."

I, the reluctant liar, nodded and pretended my name was Aryana.

Parents generally slip when calling their children's names. My parents had even confused my brother and me when calling us to come in from the yard. Neelab's mother had once called the names of her own five sisters, Rostam, and a sister-in-law before she managed to summon her daughter's name.

But my parents had never called me Aryana because her name was never said casually. Her name was preceded and followed by words of prayer, by eyes blinking back tears, and by heavy sighs. But now, because of me, my sister's name was being spoken plainly and without a whiff of commemoration.

"I will do everything I can," the man said sternly, "but you're well aware of the challenges. I'm hoping to have some answers for you and . . . Aryana . . . soon."

May your spirit live in light, dear sister, I said under my breath.

"Absolutely. We'll be here in the morning. It's a date," Tilly said. She tucked a folded piece of paper into her purse. With our two bags in tow, we retraced our steps. The same soldier escorted us to the front door, signaling to the Pakistani officers guarding the front gate to let us out. Tilly hailed a taxicab and handed the driver the slip of paper with the address of the hotel.

I was quiet in the car, thinking of how fate could be decided by a bullet or a birth certificate, by a stamp or a stampede. I was still falling and feeling in the pit of my stomach that my landing would not come softly. I sensed an electricity in the streets around us, a loose wire. My stomach clenched when a man in a red T-shirt and dark jeans stepped in front of our car at a red light and looked past our driver, to see his passengers.

Within a few moments, the yellow taxi slipped out of the serene neighborhood of embassies, each with a unique flag hoisted high on its front lawn and each with a unique reason for planting itself on foreign soil. This cast of banners were lifted into the air like the raised hands of diligent students in a roll call. Of politicians casting self-serving votes. Or of righteous witnesses preparing to testify.

CHAPTER 23

WHEN, AFTER TWO HOURS OF TRYING, TILLY FINALLY GOT through to Antonia, she sank back into her chair with relief. We were exhausted from the day's journey and the hours spent at the embassy.

"Nia, thank goodness. Where have you been?" she asked, her back resting against the velvet of the armchair.

"Where have *I* been? Mom, did you really just ask that?" I could hear the bewilderment in her voice from where I stood. I didn't bother pretending I wasn't listening.

"Sweetheart, we didn't mean to give you a scare. Indigo stopped by, and we had to make a quick decision. You had way too much on your shoulders already. But we can hash all that out later when we're in the same country. Meanwhile, the folks at the embassy here have an obvious love for formalities. Do you have any friends at the Canadian embassy? Just in case."

I couldn't make out Antonia's response, and Tilly did not reveal any details after she cradled the phone.

"Is your head better?" I asked as we slipped into the twin beds.

"Much better," Tilly said brightly, so I believed her and fell into a hopeful slumber.

I woke to a sky of dusty rose. Our window looked out on an empty school with a small soccer field and a playground with swings. If Neelab had been with me, we would have found a way to steal a few moments there, pitching our bodies forward and kicking our legs to lift ourselves into the sky.

"Star," Tilly said. I turned to face her. She was sitting up in bed, a pillow propped behind her. "How did you sleep, dear?"

"Fine," I replied before my thoughts turned to last night's conversation. "Will they give me passport here today?"

"Nia thinks they will, but that it might take some time."

"She is angry with us?" I asked. It did matter to me how Antonia felt.

"No," Tilly scoffed. "She's angry with me. That has nothing to do with you. It's me. It's always been me."

Tilly reached for a tissue on the nightstand. She pinched the tip of her nose with it, sniffling.

"I must be allergic to something in the air."

The air was different here. Islamabad smelled of industry and incense. I'd stared out the window on the short ride to the hotel, watching people move through streets and shops with bags swinging at their sides, some dressed in tunics and some in shirts and slacks. This was a different city, but one that pulsed at Kabul's pace.

We ate a quick breakfast of boiled eggs and bread at the hotel. Tilly gathered salt crystals on her fingertip then touched the tip of her tongue.

"Antonia wants to join us, but she can't leave Kabul for another two days. I'd much rather travel with her, but I was also hoping we could be on a plane to the U.S. before then."

I hated feeling like a burden.

Every Ramadan, my parents paid the local *masjid* to feed families less fortunate than our own. One day as I walked with Boba to the *masjid*, our conversation circled around the meaning of the holiday.

A man holds his empty hand out for help. Another man wears thick gold rings on every finger and has a brick of gold in the palm of his hand. Which man struggles more to bear the weight of his outstretched hand?

I thought I'd understood his meaning then, but I didn't really understand it until now.

"She must do too much for me," I said.

Tilly shook her head, vehemently.

"Never think that. Not for one moment. You don't know my daughter as well as you should. Nia only does what Nia wants to do. Do you know why she's working in Kabul?"

I shook my head. Tilly dabbed at her nose.

"Every few months, I get a letter from Kabul. Nia doesn't tell me much about herself. She never has. But she writes to me about the people she's met. When her driver came to pick me up from the airport, I felt I knew him already because she had written to me about this gentleman who did beautiful pencil drawings of birds. She told me about students from the university who would bring her dried mulberries and practice their English with her. Or the factory owner who asked if she was related to Elvis Presley." Tilly let out a laugh.

"Maybe it was those letters that made me get on a plane and follow her to the other side of the world. I don't know. But I do know that if I hadn't been here, I would have gotten a letter from her about the night the bravest girl in all the world showed up at her door."

I made a new promise in that moment. I would find a way to show my gratitude to these two women even if I couldn't imagine being capable of offering anything to anyone.

We returned to the embassy. Tilly waved at the officers in front of the gate and announced that we had been told to return. She smiled impatiently, as if she wouldn't tolerate being asked to wait. The officer spoke to someone on a walkie-talkie, then led us back into the same building we'd entered the day before. It was morning, and the embassy whirred with activity. More people were moving through its hallways than the previous afternoon.

We were led into a room by the same man and offered the same seats. He stepped out and returned with two cups of mango juice and a small plate of biscuits, which I could decline thanks to the hearty breakfast we'd just had at the hotel. I didn't want to accept their offering if they were going to tell us they could do nothing for me.

Moments later, Mr. Harris entered the room. "Tilly, as I discussed with you yesterday, this is a complicated matter and will take time to sort out, officially and unofficially. The birth certificate is helpful, and certainly there are extenuating circumstances involved. But we don't have anything documenting parental permission to travel. It's just not that simple."

"Mr. Harris, Leo, our friend and compatriot. My daughter has spoken very highly of you. She said you are relentless and righteous. Now, are you telling me that my very smart daughter is wrong?"

"Ma'am," Leo said, shaking his head, "Antonia is the best we have. We were together in Morocco, and I would never want to be on the other side of an argument with her."

Leo knew my story or a closer version of it than we'd ever revealed to anyone else. Antonia had shared some details with him yesterday, enough that he felt compelled to help even if he didn't know how.

"If we issue a passport from here, you may get questioned at the airport. Pakistani immigration is going to raise an eyebrow to see the two of you traveling together, and the last thing we need is to draw attention. There are some people who think we don't know how to mind our own business," he said, making sure his voice was not audible from the hallway.

"The longer we stay here, the more time there is to catch attention.

We need to get moving," Tilly said, as if Leo were holding her up from getting to a doctor's appointment. Leo let out a deep breath and ran his fingers through his hair.

"That's not how it works at all," he said, barely hiding his frustration. "I'm going to have to step out for a bit."

Whether some other matter needed his attention or he simply wanted to exit the conversation, I was not sure. Tilly gave me a nod and let her shoulders fall. I wondered how much of her confidence was real and how much was an act.

The sound of the clock on the wall ticking filled the room and chipped away at our patience. Two hours passed. I tried not to feel anxious, but the skin on my arms had become prickly, my hairs standing on end. I told myself to breathe, to remember that we were in the American embassy, which was almost like being in the United States itself.

Tilly stood before a large map of the world on the wall, tracing the borders of Afghanistan and its surrounding countries.

"I didn't know Afghanistan touches China," she observed.

If Tilly had much to learn about Afghanistan, I also had much to learn about America. One night I had sat on the balcony with Antonia as she studied the script for the show the Americans were putting on. I asked her to explain the story to me. At first she said it was a love story, but then, after chewing her lip for a second, she amended her description.

"Two love stories," she'd said. "Set in a time long ago, the beginning of a new state in America—Oklahoma. At that time, it was Indian country."

"We have Indian people in Afghanistan too. And a Hindu temple," I replied.

"Not that kind of Indian," she'd explained, and then went on to tell me that the people who lived in America before Europeans settled there were called Indians too, and that American cowboys had ventured into that land to grow America.

Surely there must have been a war. No people gave their land up without a fight. While I wondered why people would sing and dance about war, she sighed and explained that it was really a story about a woman choosing a husband.

"You are not married?" I'd asked. There was no trace of a man in Antonia's apartment. I didn't know any women her age who were not married with children. She was a beautiful woman, and I could not imagine why no one had courted her.

Antonia had shaken her head.

"I don't think I could be someone's other half. I move from country to country. Men don't like it when their wives aren't home to greet them," she'd explained. "I suppose that's why they used to make women resign from the service if they got married."

I had never thought of my parents as two halves. I saw them as two individual wholes, but also as a single organism that lived and breathed for me. And maybe because of me. It almost seemed as if I'd brought them to life instead of the other way around.

I jumped when the swirling sound of a siren began, drowning out whatever it was that Tilly was trying to say to me. Flashing lights, red as the smoke that engulfed the palace the night of the coup, poured into the room and cast ghostly shadows on Tilly's face and on the map of the world.

Yet again, I hadn't seen the danger coming.

The door of the office was flung open, and two soldiers stepped in, faces half hidden by helmets and fingers poised on triggers.

CHAPTER 24

IN THE CRADLE OF MY FATHER'S LAP, I LEARNED THE HISTORY OF Afghanistan. Boba told these stories in the way the voice on the radio would tell stories, giving each historical figure a distinct voice, a posture, and a weakness. One night he would tell me of the day Alexander of Greece fell madly in love with an Afghan woman, Rukhshana. The next night he would tell me about Genghis Khan from China, who organized his Mongol army into units of ten. Ten multiplied into a thousand, which was how, some theorized, his descendants, the ethnic Hazara, got their name.

Love and war are two ends of a single rope, Boba told me once. Poetry comes from the tangling of the two. Deep into the night, high in the hills, warriors would gather around fires, strumming lutes and singing songs about love as old as the mountains, with their swords tucked under one leg.

Even in peacetime?

Of course! For a warrior, peacetime is only the prelude to war.

The Marines ushered us down a maze of hallways. Everywhere I looked, people were closing windows, stuffing papers into folders, and moving toward the innermost parts of this massive building.

"Will someone please tell us what is happening!" Tilly shouted.

"We must hide," I said. I squeezed Tilly's hand, my eyes skittering from the soldiers running beside us to the walls and windows around us, looking to see which would fail us first.

We moved as a cluster, feet shuffling in disunity. We stood in a room with a long table at its center when we heard a series of booms. Tilly held me so close that I felt the rise and fall of her chest. Her breaths were short and shallow, quickening every time we heard artillery fire break through the near-silence. People around us offered reassurances.

"Everything will be fine. We're behind brick walls and a metal gate. The police will get them under control."

"He's right. Their backup is probably just arriving now."

My parents had been just as confident.

I could hear shouts coming from outside, a cacophony of anger. How far into the streets did this go? I thought of Antonia, sitting at a desk in the embassy back in Kabul. I wondered if she and her colleagues were under attack also.

"What's happening?" Tilly asked the woman standing next to us. She was fiddling with a walkie-talkie, trying to secure a connection to someone outside.

"Protests. Just some students probably. Some people don't want us here," she said. But the shouts seemed to be getting louder, and the smell of smoke wafted into the room.

I would not let anything happen to Tilly. If there was anything I could do to keep her alive, I would do it. The tissue in her hand had turned to pulp. We were moving, back into the hallway and up a flight of stairs. I took Tilly's bag and held her arm steady as she navigated the steps, the crush of people around us becoming unnerved by the riotous sounds.

We pressed into a vault, a small room lined with filing cabinets and cardboard boxes, and the Marines shut a heavy double door behind us.

For the second time in my short life, I was caught in a storm. Updates came sporadically and did little to soothe us. A clamoring mass of bodies had collapsed a segment of wall and then climbed over the bricks, bent rebar, and crumbled mortar to reach the outside of the embassy. They had set fire to the building, and the heat was seeping into the vault. Some said it was an attempt to smoke us out. Others shook their heads and said the guards were fully capable of managing a protest.

"Everything's going to be fine," Tilly said to me. She said it more times than I could count. I felt for the ring sewn into my pocket and touched it nervously.

The doors to the vault opened momentarily, and an American soldier with a gunshot wound was brought in. The woman at his side was pressing down on his wound. Her calls for a doctor went unanswered.

I jumped when I heard something pounding on metal behind me. On the far end of the room was a narrow hallway and a ladder that led to a hatch door. The hatch bent inward, cratered with the force of each insistent blow. The soldiers stood poised to fire, barely blinking. Sweat collected on foreheads.

Then the banging stopped.

In the fifth hour, Tilly began to cry so quietly that I might have missed it. I don't think anyone else noticed. I leaned in closer to her. The room was starting to melt, the oxygen sponged up by eighty pairs of lungs and a simmering fire just outside the walls. When I lifted my foot, the sole of my shoe stuck to the melting vinyl of the tile floor. A patch of carpet caught fire. I heard a soft pop and fizz as a man drained a can of soda onto the burning rug.

The shouts and pops slowed, but the fumes worsened—smoke and vinegar. My chest tightened, as if all the people in this room were pushing against my rib cage. But Tilly was in worse shape. She vomited into a paper bag, all color drained from her face, then slid to the floor with her head between her knees. I knelt beside her, my clothes sticking to my skin.

The room was nearly silent, as if people couldn't find words important enough to justify using what little air remained in the vault.

"We cannot stay here," I said to no one in particular. Tilly was past the point of putting on a show of confidence for me. Surely the adults in the room would have come to this conclusion even if I'd not said a word. The walkie-talkies offered nothing but static. The room was hazy with smoke. No one was coming to save us, and we had only one soldier guarding the vault from the outside.

"We have to get to the roof," the woman with the walkie-talkie declared. The hallway, opaque with smoke, was certain death. Two soldiers worked the bowed hatch, muscling to turn the wheel against an unseen force. They pried it open just enough for a current of air to swirl through the vault. The opening, a waning moon, offered little view of the outside world.

The soldier couldn't get more than a shoulder out.

"It's jammed from the outside." He plunged his arm into the gap. The soldiers switched places. The woman with the walkie-talkie climbed the ladder and took her turn. She came back down the ladder, ruddy and breathless.

I dropped Tilly's hand and pushed my way through the huddled bodies. Tilly called out after me, but her voice was low and hoarse. I stepped past American men and women in damp shirts. The whole room would perish if we didn't get that hatch open.

I put my foot on the bottom rung of the ladder and felt a stabbing pain so acute that I wondered if the wound had torn open again. Hearing my yelp, the soldier put his hands on my shoulders to pull me down. I wrested away from him, climbing and climbing without knowing what lay on the other side of the hatch.

"Be careful," a voice called after me. "Don't let go."

Bending my body into the shape of a crescent moon, I slipped out of the vault and onto the roof of the building. Grunting, I managed to free the piece of rebar that had been locking the outside latch.

"It is open!" I called into the space. I pulled and the soldiers pushed. The door flipped open, and one by one the Americans joined me on the roof. The embassy grounds were charred, smoke billowing up from buildings, flames licking at every window. I felt as if I were standing on the roof of Arg, watching the palace go up in flames.

I knelt by the opening of the hatch door, waiting for Tilly to emerge. She came out coughing, her face glistening with moisture and her hair wild.

"Tilly! You are okay," I said dumbly, all my words caught up in the smoke.

To evacuate, we needed to get to the ground, but we were on the roof of the highest building in the compound, a blazing fire on our heels. I was terrified but not alone. Eighty Americans ran across the rooftop with me, jumping four feet to the searing roof of the second building and then another twelve feet down to the roof of the auditorium.

The Americans helped me get Tilly from one building to another, one man easing her down while another readied to receive her. I saw the glint of a ladder propped against the side of the building, the flicker of red lights beyond a cluster of trees. Shouts in a language that sounded simultaneously foreign and familiar.

I crossed scorched earth for the second time in my life, unsure if it would be my spirit or my knees to buckle first. Unsure which fire would shape my destiny and which would burn me. Unsure if what I was running toward was any better than what I was running from.

CHAPTER 25

"ARE YOU LEAVING TOO, LEO?" TILLY SAID, RUBBING OFF BITS OF adhesive from the crook of her arm. It was three in the morning, and we were in Leo's home, a three-bedroom apartment in a quiet neighborhood. He had insisted on bringing us back here, though it was obvious he was responsible for most of the other people in the mission. We'd been taken directly to the hospital, where doctors and nurses had sorted through the exhausted and injured. Tilly had been laid out on a stretcher with crisp white sheets that turned her paler. They'd inserted a needle into her arm and dripped clear fluids into her veins. She'd now removed the gauze and tape, but the adhesive clung to her papery skin.

"We're evacuating all non-essential staff. I'm staying on."

Leo looked exhausted. He'd been taken to the British embassy while we went to the hospital. At some point in the middle of the night, the army declared the streets safe for travel. The Americans were rounded up and divided into groups. Leo made sure Tilly and I were among the twenty people taken to his home. Leo's wife, unfazed by the swell of people in their living room, had turned their modest space into a shelter. She distributed saltines, mandarin oranges, clothing, and cups of water.

People sat shoulder to shoulder on the sofa and on the living room floor, knees bent and heads resting against the wall.

Leo stepped away for a few moments, returning with wet hair and a fresh set of clothes on. He took a seat in the living room next to the phone. The calls didn't let up.

"I'm sorry, which press did you say you were with?" Leo asked, squinting to hear the response come across the line. "Right, right, okay."

I listened to him recount the events of the night. But he didn't answer all the questions he was asked. Time and again, I heard him say he could not offer official comment.

Leo sat with his knees angled outward, tapping a pencil against the table.

"How are all these people getting home?" Tilly asked.

I pressed an orange peel to my nose to combat the smell of smoke emanating from my hair and clothes.

"Pan Am is diverting a flight from Delhi. They're coming here in a few hours, and we'll get everyone home. The Pakistani army is going to escort us there," he explained.

"Get us on that flight, Leo," Tilly said, with just a flicker of the fire she'd had a day earlier.

Leo looked at Tilly with consternation. He lowered his voice, glancing around to see if anyone was listening in.

"We haven't had the birth certificate verified yet," he reminded her. "Without the documentation—"

"Documentation!" Tilly coughed. She was sweating, her cheeks flushed. She pinched her nose with a tissue. "Do you even hear yourself? Just a few hours ago, this girl saved the lives of every person in that vault, and you are hung up on a piece of paper. A piece of paper!"

I felt for the ring in my pocket, traced its now-familiar edges. If I was honest, part of me was afraid of getting on a plane and leaving this continent. And if I was completely honest, all of me was afraid of what would happen if I were to make it to America. Those two fears radiated through me at unique wavelengths.

But twice now I'd walked through fire. And I knew from the night of the coup that I had to keep moving, to continue taking steps in the hopes that God would bless my path. As I approached him, Leo eyed me warily.

In Dari, the word for witness, *shahid*, and the word for martyr, *shaheed*, differ by only a vowel. They are two leaves, splitting from a common stalk, catching light and rain at different angles. With a slight reshaping of lips, I could go from witness to martyr. Indeed, it felt as if the world around me was calling me by those two names and waiting to see to which I would answer.

"Your name is Leo," I said. "In the stars, this is the name of the lion."

Shair, the shameful soldier, had also been named after the king of the jungle, the ultimate beast. How many hopeful parents around the world had named their sons with such optimism, only to commit them to a lifetime of disappointment?

"Are you a lion?" I asked Leo.

Leo straightened his shoulders. He looked into my eyes for the first time since I'd met him. The pencil fell from his fingers and landed with a light clink on the glass table.

AS THE PLANE LIFTED OFF FROM THE RUNWAY, MY CHEEKS WERE wet with tears. I felt a buoyancy in my bones, as well as a heaviness in my chest. My father had brought me bits and pieces of the world from his many trips. He'd promised we would one day fly together to places he had shown me on a globe so I could collect my own treasures. My first flight was supposed to bring me closer to him. Though my parents were gone, I still felt like a traitor to be leaving them behind.

The airplane took on altitude, the engine rumbling beneath us, gears shifting. We bobbled through a veil of clouds, and Tilly's hand stayed on mine until we were above the fray. Her face looked flushed, and thin beads of sweat persisted on her hairline. Her staccato breaths unsettled me. She sounded as if she was trying not to cry.

A solemn silence permeated the plane as all who had just evaded death ascended into the heavens. With my eyes on the bright blue sky outside the window, I drifted to sleep, losing track of time and place. I didn't know if I was falling or flying, if I would soar or sink. All I knew was that nothing would ever be the same again. I had new hollows and edges and curves and knots. I let my head fall against the seat and prayed for wings.

CHAPTER 26

"WHEN WE GET THERE," TILLY EXPLAINED, "WE'LL TELL THEM you're going to stay with me. Antonia will come soon. Once they meet you, once they see how brave and bright you are, they will do all they can to help you."

I did not know who "they" were, but hoped they would be as kind as Antonia and Tilly. Tilly sensed my discomfort and brushed my hair away from my face and squeezed my hand. She looked at me the way my grandmother did when she was still alive.

Tilly pulled a small booklet out of her purse and offered it to me as a way to pass the time. It was the travel guide, *Eastern Bound*, that she'd taken from Indigo's friend. I flipped through the sections, each devoted to a country. Chapters began with ink drawings of a bearded man with a turban on his head. In Turkey the cartoon man held a bow between his hands. In Iran he sat perched on a rearing horse, and in Afghanistan he sat in profile, the tip of a long-necked water pipe between his lips. The pages were decorated with childish flowers, leaves of five fingers, and miniature buses with clouds of smoke trailing behind them.

I pointed at words I didn't recognize and asked Tilly what they meant.

"Nymphs and satyrs are just people drunk on themselves," she said. "You're destined to be a sober goddess, which is infinitely better."

Tilly fished one of the magazines out of the seat pocket and offered it to me instead. I flipped through it until I saw her eyes close. Then I took out my notebook and, as I often did, jotted down what Tilly had said so I could try to make sense of it later. My notes ran back and forth in time, jumping from what I remembered to what I still had to figure out. The flight attendant brought me apple juice, which I gulped down before drifting back to sleep.

We were halfway across the Atlantic when Tilly began moaning. She was sniffling and blowing her nose, using a handful of crumpled tissues she had stuffed into her pocket. It looked like lifting her hand to her face caused her pain. Allergies, she had said. The flight attendant brought a small box of tissues, a shadow of concern behind her smile.

"Ma'am, is there anything I can get you?"

"Do you have anything for a headache?" she replied.

The flight attendant went to check and returned with a small bottle that rattled as she handed it to Tilly.

"Lucky for you, the pilot gets killer migraines."

"Not that lucky," Tilly said softly, with long spaces between her words. She'd grown pale again.

Her headache did not improve. She couldn't get comfortable. I got out of my seat and asked the flight attendant for water with ice. The plane was dark then, with the window shades pulled down as we flew through a night sky. I walked back to my seat, almost losing my balance when the plane jostled slightly.

When I returned to the seat, I stopped short.

"Tilly!" I shouted.

Tilly was slumped on her side, her body convulsing as if controlled by a *djinn*. Her back stiffened and her limbs moved with a quick, jerking rhythm. I held her shoulders, feeling the turbulence in her body.

"No! No! *Leave her!!*" I shouted at the *djinn* to let her go. I wanted to call for help, but all the English I knew had flittered away like napkins caught in a gust of wind.

People around me slowly started to stir. Perhaps they thought I was a child having a tantrum or reliving the siege.

One meek overhead light clicked on, and then another. A man peered over his seat and, with one glimpse of Tilly's face, began shouting. *Emergency*, I heard him call. In a flurry of movement, I was pushed aside. I could barely see past the tangle of people who had gathered, some to help and some to see what could possibly have made this day even worse.

The flight attendant asked if any doctors were aboard the plane. No one answered. There was a retired nurse and a man whose sister had epilepsy. They laid Tilly down in the aisle of the airplane, turned her on her side, and searched through the first aid box for anything remotely helpful. There was nothing.

I stood and watched, feeling useless.

When Tilly stopped seizing, I let out a breath I didn't know I'd been holding. She was alive. Soon, I told myself, she would speak to me and remind me that Antonia could handle anything and that I had nothing to worry about.

I waited for her to speak again.

Her breaths were slower, ragged.

She slept, moaning slightly. When the flight attendant and a man sitting one row behind us tried to move her back into the seat, Tilly grimaced. Her hand went up to her neck, and I thought she'd injured it when she'd been slumped over, her head lolling. As the plane descended and tiny homes and ribbons of highway became visible, I called Tilly's name. Whether she heard me, I do not know.

The captain ordered everyone, including me, to stay seated until Tilly could be lifted onto the stretcher on the tarmac. Two men in uniforms hoisted the gurney into the back of an ambulance.

"I will go with her," I insisted. But they shook their heads. I panicked, pulled away from them, and chased after the twirling red lights, dwarfed by a cavalry of planes. Fingers pressed into my arms hard, then harder, when I shouted in protest.

Tilly and I had come so far. We had been through so much. She had made promises to me, and I clung to them even as I watched her disappear.

CHAPTER 27

THE END OF ONE DAY IS THE START OF ANOTHER.

"This is temporary," they said to me, these people without names. They sat me in a stark room and entered only to deliver bad news. It was not the welcome Tilly had promised.

Blurred by exhaustion and a flight across time zones, I couldn't tell if the man who entered now was the same one who had walked in earlier. There were no clocks on the wall or windows to the outside world. A man in a button-down shirt brought me bread, a dense circle of dough with a sprinkling of black seeds on top. The bread had been sliced in two and a creamy white spread oozed out from between the two halves. I pushed it away, my appetite spoiled every time I thought of Tilly, pale and breathless.

With my hands beneath the table, I felt for the ring stitched into my pocket. I prayed they would not search me. This ring and I, twin survivors, were the last vestiges of our respective empires.

When two men entered the room together, I pushed my chair back and readied myself for anything. They had plastic-covered badges clipped to their shirt pockets, but I couldn't steady my thoughts enough to read what was written on them. One had a mustache and sideburns that looked like lamb's wool. He held a clipboard in his left hand. The other man was clean-cut, not a hair out of place.

"Where is Tilly?" I asked. The solitude had given me enough time to formulate fears and questions and to translate the latter into English. "I want to go to Tilly."

One man sighed with exasperation. The other scratched his head and sat in the metal chair facing me.

"Sorry, but that's not possible right now. She was very sick and needed to see a doctor right away," he said, his words patronizing and slow. "We want to ask you a few questions first."

They started by asking me my name. *Aryana Zamani,* I told them. When they asked my date of birth, I told them the day, month, and year recorded on my sister's birth certificate. Then they asked for the names of my parents. I took in a long, deep breath and wondered if I was saying too much or not enough.

Once we get home, Tilly had said, as if I were returning to America instead of fleeing there for the first time, *we're going to tell people your true story. You will have nothing to hide there. We will keep you safe.*

Antonia had agreed, even as she'd chewed her lip and looked for holes in our strategy. And there were plenty of holes to be found in the plan we'd concocted to get me from Kabul to the United States. But alternatives were scarce and even more dangerous, which was why I'd landed in a room as white and threatening as an avalanche.

"Did you know anything about the embassy attack in Islamabad?"

"We were there," I said.

He was going to ask another question, but his colleague elbowed him and shook his head.

"May we?" the mustached man asked, pointing to my bag. It sat beneath the table, the strap of the bag looped around my foot as if it might otherwise drift away.

My small duffel bag held all I had: two pairs of clothing that Antonia had purchased for me, my notebook, the frayed copy of *Eastern Bound*, and the handful of photos I'd gathered from my parents' bedroom.

"It is my bag," I said, to explain why they should not be allowed to go poking through it.

"Yes, your bag," they replied. *Cheshm safed*, I wanted to shout. To call someone white-eyed was to imply that their eyes could not see reason or decency. It was a phrase my father reserved for the most brazen politicians.

"No." I shook my head. The two men looked at each other, one raised an eyebrow. Their eyes drifted to the floor as I nudged the bag under my chair with my foot. I folded my arms across my chest.

With a shrug, they decided to leave the issue of the bag and resume the questioning. They had taken my birth certificate before they'd brought me to this room and now placed it on the table before me.

"Is this yours?" the mustached man asked.

I nodded.

"Look," the other added, "you understand us, right? So here's what you need to know. That nice lady who brought you here is going to be in a whole lot of trouble if you don't start answering our questions. You may just be a kid, but we need to know who you are and why you've come here. If you don't talk, that lady is going to jail instead of the hospital."

The mustached man's eyes flashed to his colleague for a split second and then returned to me. He did not contradict his colleague.

My heart sank to think of what Tilly had gone through on my account. From being quarantined with me in Antonia's apartment to the accident on the road to Jalalabad and being trapped in the vault of the embassy, this woman I did not know had stood by me as steadfastly as any grandmother. Already I owed her my whole heart. I could not bear to think they would punish her for her kindness, not when she was so very ill.

"This is my paper," I said plainly, pointing at the birth certificate. "My mother and father name is here."

"So you were born here. How long did you live here?"

"Two years," I said, feeling inadequate.

They started over, asking again the same questions that I'd not answered before. Little by little, my reluctance gave way and I gave them our address in Kabul, told them what my father did, and said that my grandparents were not living. The mustached man began making notes on his clipboard. I answered everything with the fewest possible words, both because of my limited English and because I did not want to give them any more information than I needed to.

You'll need to keep it simple, Antonia had said to me on the phone in Islamabad. *Tell them the truth, as much of the truth as you can bear to tell. They need to understand what you went through so that they can understand how important it is for you to stay.*

But my name is not the truth, I'd replied.

My father had such disdain for liars and cheats. *The corruption of an entire nation begins with one lie,* I'd heard him say.

But Antonia had seen it differently.

The truths you will tell are far bigger and much more important than this one small change.

I'd wished with all my heart that Boba and Antonia could have debated this directly.

The men asked my grade in school, and I felt a hole in my story. I worried, as unaccustomed liars do. If I told them I was in fifth grade, my age would not have matched. But what if I told them I'd been in year seven? Could they contact my school? I imagined my principal on the phone with these men, informing them that no child named Aryana Zamani had ever sat in her classrooms.

I saw just how easily they would suss out my lies. I sat on my hands to stop them from trembling.

Tell them the truth, Antonia had said. Boba had said the same.

And that's what I did. When I named Arg, they looked as if they'd never heard of the place, so I had to explain to them that it was the presidential palace. When I said President Daoud Khan's name, one of the men asked me how to spell it. His colleague elbowed him and motioned for him to write down my story. I continued to relate the events of the coup, just as I had with Antonia and Tilly. As I told these two men that my family had been killed before my eyes, I was surprised to find that I could speak of that moment without collapsing to the floor. I worried briefly that I wasn't grieving enough. It was hard to measure, since I'd been grieving alone.

I sniffled, wiping my nose on the back of my hand. One of the men got up and looked around, then handed me a napkin. I thanked him.

And then I continued until I had told them all the big truths about the night Shair delivered me to Antonia at gunpoint, about Tilly and me crossing the border into Pakistan, and how I'd helped us escape from a hatch door to the roof of the Islamabad embassy.

Pages of notes later, the official looked at his partner, and I could see that whether I told them I'd been in fifth grade or seventh grade or what the principal of the school might say did not matter to them one bit. I had given them details about a coup, details no child could have imagined. Antonia was right. The big truths obscured the little lies. I drank the water they'd brought for me and hoped they would lead me out of this room soon.

"You heard anything about a military coup over there?" one man said.

"Let's just keep in mind, she's a kid. Last night Ella told me she saw a three-legged deer baking cupcakes in our backyard," his colleague replied.

"Now I go to Tilly," I said, wanting nothing more than to confirm with my own eyes that she had a doctor at her side.

"No," the clean-shaven man said, looking at the birth certificate again. He turned it over and held it up to the light, as if it were a gem and he was assessing its clarity. "That's not how this works. You do tell a mighty story, but we've got to do some homework now. You're going to be going somewhere else until we can figure out what's what."

CHAPTER 28

ONCE UPON A TIME IN KABUL, I STOOD AT THE FAR END OF MY block and spotted four boys gathered in a circle. These boys had been troublesome in the past. They pestered younger children and made a sport of kicking a ball against a neighbor's gate and then hiding around the corner. I walked toward them, wanting to see what had captured their attention.

The boys had crowded around a stray dog, one with tawny fur and dark-rimmed eyes. The boys had tied a rope around his hind leg and were taking turns poking at his prominent ribs and hunched shoulders with a long stick. The dog yapped and whimpered, gnawing at the rope.

Leave him alone! I'd hollered at them.

The stick passed from hand to hand. The boys either hadn't heard me or chose to ignore me. As I stepped closer, I noticed that one of the dog's front paws was deformed. It was shorter than the others, not quite reaching the ground. Given the shape he was in, it was a wonder he was still putting up a fight.

The dog managed to kick up a small tornado of dust as he struggled against the pull of the rope and the boys orbiting his misery.

I shouldered my way through the ring and took the stick out of one boy's unsuspecting hand. I snapped it in half and then snapped those pieces in half again. A boy holding the rope stepped toward me.

What do you think you're doing, stupid? he demanded.

How can you call me stupid with a face like that? I fired back, with all the drama of a Bollywood hero. *What incredible hunters you are to have captured a lame dog! God save you all, future heroes of our country.*

I coiled the rope around my hand.

A boy in an untucked shirt and threadbare jeans made a go for the rope, clawing at my forearm. I pulled sharply away, but when I turned my back to him, he reached over my shoulder, then under my elbow. I stomped on his foot, and he let out a howl. I stomped on his other foot. His friends snickered to see him hopping backward. After two hops, he fell onto his backside. I hurdled one last jeer as he crawled away.

If your father asks about your scraped knees, be sure to tell him you were fighting with a girl!

The boys departed, leaving me and the dewy-eyed dog in the street. Or I thought it was just the two of us until I heard slow and steady clapping. I whirled around and saw Boba standing in the doorway of our house. How much had he seen?

Boba crouched down to get a better look at the dog's sores. His lower lip had been torn and one of his nails snapped back. Boba clucked his tongue against the roof of his mouth in pity.

People are God's cruelest creations. They'll step on the smallest of backs to feel an inch taller.

Boba, are you angry? I asked.

Very, he answered. *And disappointed.*

I bit my lip, nervous.

I came out because I heard the ruckus. I saw you stomp on that boy's foot. That was disappointing.

Because I shouldn't have confronted them?

Because you didn't need your father's help, he said, rising to his feet. *Now, let's set this poor dog free.*

As if offended by the conversation, the dog growled. I took a step back, shocked. The dog shook his head and bared his yellowed teeth.

But I helped him, I said, feeling betrayed.

Boba took the rope from my hand and held the dog at arm's length.

Don't expect him to bow at your feet because you saved him today. He's saved himself every other day of his life.

As I was shuttled from one office to another, from one curious stranger to another, I couldn't help but feel like that stray dog. Men and women asked me a hundred recycled questions, prodding me like a nine-year-old boy wielding a stick. I had no escape. I spent the first night in a room at the airport where I was alone for such long periods of time that I feared I might have been forgotten.

The morning started with more questions from the same man who had seemed most doubtful about my story.

"Please, I want to see Tilly. Please," I begged.

By the next afternoon, I was in a car.

"Where we go?" I asked the woman escorting me out of the building. She had a large leather bag hanging on her shoulder, bulging with papers and a notebook. She too had a name badge clipped to her sweater. ANN, it read. CHILD PROTECTIVE SERVICES. Documents were so important to Americans, it seemed, that they pinned them to their clothing for all the world to see.

"We're going to a hospital," Ann replied, and my spirits soared. Finally, I would be with Tilly. I was eager to see how much she'd recovered since I'd watched her being loaded into the ambulance, her skin mottled.

A dark blue sign surrounded by trees and small plants announced the hospital. Ann drove the car right into a multistory building just for cars. It was the first time I'd seen a parking garage, and I was stunned by its size.

The hospital was a sprawling building next door to the parking garage, connected by a concrete path. We entered the building and went down a maze of hallways until we reached a clinic. Ann handed a sheet of paper to the receptionist, a woman with a blouse so low-cut I could see the crests of her breasts. She read the paper and spoke to someone on the phone before agreeing to lead me to a room in the back.

"They bring Tilly here?" I asked Ann. "I can see Tilly now?"

Ann looked perplexed, like she didn't know how to answer my simple question.

"Yes, but no."

"Why?"

The door opened. A doctor entered, smiling brightly. His white coat was snug on his belly, two of the buttons looking strained. A stethoscope hung around his neck. He wore a name badge too, but his was decorated with a cartoon elephant.

"Ar-y-a-na," he said, his eyebrows raised as he carefully enunciated the syllables of my name. He looked back at the paper the receptionist had left on the counter. "Welcome, Aryana."

He shook Ann's hand and sat on a chair facing me. He squinted as he looked at me, as if he couldn't decide where to begin.

"Do you know why you are here?" he asked.

I didn't.

"I want to see how strong and healthy you are. And if there's something we can do to help you, then that's what we'll do."

This did not sound terrible. Not yet anyway.

The doctor asked me many of the same questions. I told my story again. It was mechanical at this point. I'd found ways to distill it to its most important parts, the ones that drew the long, mournful looks from the Americans. The doctor let out a heavy sigh.

He was kind, his voice soft and feathery. I imagined happy grandchildren at his feet, delighting in his affection. I began to relax. Ann checked her watch. He asked me whether I took any medications or if I'd ever had surgery on any part of my body. He asked if I'd broken any bones or stayed in the hospital for long periods of time, if I'd ever fainted or had nosebleeds or felt my heart racing when I was sitting perfectly still. He asked if I suffered from headaches and wanted a detailed description of my most recent bowel movement. When I did not understand his words, he used his own body to demonstrate. It would have been comical under different circumstances.

"When was your last menstrual cycle?"

I had no idea what he was asking.

"Your period. Blood," he said pointing to his own crotch, hidden beneath a white coat. At the mention of blood, all of mine rushed to my face and I lowered my head.

"I'm sorry," he said, but I was still mortified. "I have to ask."

I wish it could have ended there. Stripped bare by a barrage of questions, I was then handed a thin cotton gown and told to undress. The doctor left the room. Ann motioned for me to remove my clothing. When I hesitated, she stood up. Reluctantly, I did as I was told, knowing that only Ann could get me to Tilly.

The doctor returned and began his examination. He placed the cold bell of his stethoscope on my chest and my back and peered into my ears and mouth with a scope. He tapped on my knees and elbows with a rubber hammer and then instructed me to lie down.

I looked to Ann. She pointed first to my head and then to one end of the exam table. The doctor put two hands on my belly, one on top of the other, and pressed down, moving a couple of inches at a time. I wondered if he thought I'd hidden something inside my abdomen. Then he moved to the end of the bed and said he needed to look at something.

I was almost certain he'd said the word "gentle," so I thought everything would be okay. He lifted my gown and I brought it back down with my two hands, pulling my knees up to my chest and trying to sit on the table. I looked to Ann, who hadn't moved from her seat, as if she'd known all along what this doctor was going to do.

"Has anyone hurt you there?" he asked.

"You, no!" I shouted, hot and angry that he would dare to look down there. I could not bear it. "You, no!"

You know, he had heard. *You know.*

He looked at Ann, who pressed her lips together in the first display of real sympathy I'd seen from her. They looked unsurprised, as if they'd been hoping for a different answer.

I was told to dress, but then made to urinate into a cup. They tied a rubber band around my arm and drew blood. The doctor handed me a lollipop and patted my shoulder. I jerked away from him, and he and Ann exchanged another resigned look.

"At least she's safe now," the doctor said once I was dressed. She thanked the doctor and led me back into the twist of hallways.

"Tilly. Where Tilly is?" I said when I realized we were exiting the hospital.

"Not here," Ann said, and my amorphous feelings about her gelled into something very close to hate.

She drove for twenty minutes. I saw buildings higher than I'd ever seen before and others that looked like they could be blown over by a strong wind. We passed a leafy park and bountiful store windows. I tried to read the road signs, but there were so many and my eyes were blurred with tears. I saw women pushing strollers and middle-aged men jogging down sidewalks.

Ann turned onto a street with two-story homes sitting shoulder to shoulder. Their front doors and windows were in full view, with no privacy wall to guard them from passersby. I remember my parents telling me that in some ways, parts of America were like Kabul. But nothing I'd seen thus far looked like home. Ann parked in front of a dark red building with a rusted tricycle in the small front yard.

The front door opened, and a neatly dressed man with red hair stepped onto the front porch. He came down the steps and stood on the walkway with his hands on his hips, a touch of triumph to his posture. A moment later, a woman in a long flowing dress emerged and stood next to him. She put her hand over her eyes to block the sun's glare. Her golden hair hung loose around her shoulders. I saw their lips move, though they did not turn to face each other.

"Aryana," Ann said, as if she were handing me a most precious gift, "this family has agreed to take you in . . . for now."

I saw a curtain flutter in a first-floor window. I couldn't tell what had made it flutter, nor could I see anything in the other windows. I did not understand why I'd been brought to this home. I looked up and down the street, looking for options or a way to get to Tilly. The curtain fluttered again. Still, I saw no one.

Even without the tall clay walls of Kabul, these American houses could still hold secrets.

CHAPTER 29

THE WOMAN'S NAME WAS JANET. HER HUSBAND'S NAME WAS EV-
erett. Ann introduced us as we sat in their kitchen. Janet stood with
her back to us, opening a cabinet door. A pop, a hiss, and three cups of
orange soda appeared on the wooden table. She'd placed the cups in the
center, just beyond everyone's reach. Small bubbles climbed the insides of
the glasses and a saccharine smell filled the room.

"Where are the others?" Ann asked.

"All the neighborhood kids love to play together, especially when the
weather's so nice," Janet replied, her voice melodic.

Ann laughed lightly.

"It is beautiful outside, isn't it? I need a day off so I can enjoy it. This
week has been rough."

While Everett nodded in agreement, Ann slid a paperclipped stack of
papers across the table toward him.

"I do want to thank you both for rising to the occasion and helping
us with another child," she said.

"We're always happy to do what we can in a pinch," Everett said.

"God's blessed us with a roof over our heads, a full table, and His guidance—all of it meant to be shared."

Everett pointed at a cross-stitched sign hanging on the kitchen wall, just beneath a clock with hands that did not seem to move. Each word was stitched in a different color so that, from afar, the rectangular frame looked like it contained a rainbow. But the letters were uneven and boxy and would have earned poor marks from my sewing teacher.

Whoever receives One such child in My Name receives Me, and whoever receives Me, receives not Me but Him who sent Me.

"Isn't that beautiful?" Ann said admiringly. She looked at Janet with an expectant smile on her face. "Is that your handiwork?"

"It is," Janet admitted. "I find it relaxing to work with my hands."

Everett leaned back in his chair, beaming at his wife.

"Really lovely," Ann said. "Well, let's just get back to Aryana here. As I mentioned on the phone, this situation came up urgently and suddenly. She's just arrived from Pakistan. She speaks English, but I can't tell how much. Doesn't eat a heck of a lot and has just that bag you see at her feet. She was medically cleared, though it does seem she has a history of sexual abuse."

I wanted to object but didn't know where to begin. Everything was wrong.

Everett clapped his hands so loudly that I jumped.

"We're going to take excellent care of her," he said, looking at me with great confidence. "We'll get her speaking English and maybe even learn a little Pakistani from her."

And then I was alone with Janet and Everett. When Ann left, Janet opened an empty bottle and drained all four cups of orange soda into it before placing it in the fridge. At the sound of footsteps overhead, Janet took a broom from a corner closet and rapped the hard end of it against the ceiling. The footsteps stopped.

Janet instructed me to leave my shoes in a closet by the front door.

She and Everett led me upstairs, shaking their heads at the way I used the railing to steady myself. I clutched my bag tightly, though they didn't seem the least bit interested in it.

There were four doors upstairs, one bathroom and three bedrooms. Janet and Everett had the room at the end of the hallway. Janet pulled a key out of her dress pocket and unlocked the second bedroom, on the front side of the house. Inside was a room with two twin beds. The walls were painted a pale green that reminded me of Tilly's eyes. The beds were neatly made, with thin quilts tucked in on all four sides. On the wall hung a framed painting of a single stemmed flower with layers of long, yellow petals and a dark eye at its center. The room was clean and bright.

"You'll stay in this bedroom," Janet announced. "No marks on the walls, please, and keep it tidy. Do you understand 'tidy'?"

Janet pretended to throw handfuls of something all over the room, her face in a pout. Then she turned to me and wagged her finger in my face.

"Clean. No mess," she repeated and pointed at a closet. "Put your bag in there."

I did not move. Janet frowned and tried to take the bag from me, but I pulled back, clutching it on my lap.

Janet withdrew. She pulled her shoulders back and cleared her throat.

"Everett," she called out, though her eyes stayed on me. Everett appeared in the doorway, a look of concern on his face.

"Is everything all right?" he asked.

"She may be deaf or dumb. She won't even put her bag in the closet." Everett shook his head.

"Maybe she just needs to adjust," he said gently. He put an arm around his wife and corralled her out of the room. "Let's give her time alone to meditate on her new surroundings."

I was relieved to see them pull the door closed as they left, though my stomach knotted to hear the scrape and click of a key inserted into a lock. When their footsteps faded, I crossed the room and pressed my ear to the wood. Hearing nothing, I tried to turn the knob. I was locked in. I looked out the window. I was on the second floor with a view of the front yard and the curb that had tripped me on my way out of Ann's car.

I went back to the bed and sat down, wondering if I would ever be let out of this room.

The room did not have a clock, but after a while I gauged by the sun's shift in the sky that two or three hours had passed. I was thirsty and a bit hungry too, but I could have slept that off. It was my full bladder that demanded attention. I started to knock on the door, gently at first and then a bit louder when no one responded.

"Hello," I called. "Please, I need something."

I crossed my legs and tightened every muscle of my body. The way Janet had warned me about keeping the room clean, I was terrified of what she might do if I soiled the room with urine. I knocked louder and yelled with urgency.

"Please! Hello? I need bathroom."

Janet unlocked the door and pointed toward the bathroom just down the hall. I raced into it and closed the door behind me, fumbling with the lock but giving up because I was hit by a sharp cramp in my lower belly.

I was sitting on the toilet when Janet opened the door and peered in. I closed my legs and pulled the edge of my shirt toward my knees. My body clamped down. Despite my urgency, I could not go with her staring at me.

"I just want to remind you to be neat in here too. Not a drop on the floor and wipe down the sink when you're done. No wasting toilet paper or dropping anything unusual into the commode," Janet said. When she stopped speaking, her eyes drifted down toward the pants collected around my ankles and my bare legs. She moved in closer and stared at my scalp. She parted my hair with one hooked finger. "No lice. That's good. You do need a good shampooing, though."

She retreated and started to close the door behind her.

"There is no lock on the bathroom, by the way," she said, flashing me a smile that was short one tooth. She looked so perfectly assembled otherwise. "For your own safety, of course."

Was I wrong to wish for privacy in this moment? Why had Antonia and Tilly seemed so different from this woman?

I finished hurriedly and, while washing up, drank water from my cupped hands. I made sure the sink was dry before I stepped out. The bedroom door was open. I slipped back in and saw that my bag was still on the floor where I'd left it but unzipped and empty of all my clothes. The bag held only a hairbrush and my notebook, into which I'd tucked my copy of *Eastern Bound*.

I raced down the stairs, feeling robbed. The kitchen was empty, but a small screen door was half open. I walked toward it slowly and saw Janet standing in the backyard, bent over a bucket wide enough for a child's bath. She was holding a broomstick upside down, the handle submerged in the water.

I stepped outside barefoot and walked toward her.

"Your belongings needed a good washing. I'm only doing it today because you're new," she said. "And it needs to be done right at least once."

With blades of grass between my toes, I stood beside Janet. Round and round, she pumped the broomstick up and down, as if trying to keep my shirts and pants from escaping. The water smelled of something so harsh that it stung my eyes and nostrils worse than raw onions. I could not bring myself to look away and stood there as she drowned my clothes, watching my shirt bleed red pigment into the milky water.

CHAPTER 30

I WALKED BACK TO THE HOUSE, MY EYES BURNING WITH TEARS. I was lucky Janet hadn't taken the clothes off my back or she might have found the ring in my pocket. I needed to find a new place to hide it for now. From the corner of my eye, I thought I saw Everett walk past the opening between the kitchen and the living room. I stayed back to avoid him and moved toward the stairs when I didn't hear footsteps.

Just as I opened the door to the bedroom, I heard a click behind me. I whirled around to see a boy and a girl watching me from the half-open door across the hall. The girl looked to be a couple of years older than me and had sharply cut bangs. The boy was younger, perhaps in his first or second year of school. These were the children Janet had said were playing in the neighborhood. It must have been their footsteps I'd heard when Ann had left.

"What's your name?" the boy whispered. He had freckles across his cheeks and nose and hair the color of a setting sun. When I didn't answer, he repeated his question. He looked harmless, and I was desperate to feel a little less alone.

"Sita—" I paused, then righted myself. "Aryana."

"Aryana," he said. "That's a funny name. My name is Gabriel. This is Shawna."

As if he were crossing a busy road, Gabriel looked both ways before stepping into the hallway.

"I'll be your friend," Gabriel said. "But only if you're nice. Are you nice?"

It felt like a thousand years since I'd spoken to another child. I nodded, hoping that Gabriel would keep talking. Shawna lingered in the doorway, pinching her bottom lip between two fingers.

"Don't get in trouble," Gabriel wasted no time in warning me. "They don't like noise or a mess. I heard her tell you that already. Everett doesn't like it if you talk about baseball or fish. He likes you if you pray to God a lot. Can you do that?"

I nodded.

"That's good. Is this your first foster home?"

I didn't know what a foster home was, but this was my first of anything in America so I nodded again.

"Can't you talk?" he said, his head cocked.

"Yes, I can speak English," I said, but careful as I was with my pronunciation, Gabriel's face twisted in confusion.

"You talk strange."

I looked at a spot on the floor. He was half my age so his criticism embarrassed me into silence. Lucky for me, he seemed content to do most of the talking—or, more accurately, whispering. We could hear the applause, soft laughter, and dings of a television program playing in the living room and Janet's humming in the kitchen. By the clink of pots and pans, I guessed she was cooking. The aromas were light, smelling more like a garden than any food I recognized.

Shawna walked across the hall and, with feline ease, slipped past me, entered the bedroom, and slid onto a folding chair in the corner of the room. She wore her hair in two braids that just reached her shoulders and had on a lilac-colored dress with a hem of ivory lace.

"I sleep here," she said. Her eyes flittered from the shaggy carpet to the quilts on the beds. Her eyes were round as coins, her cheekbones high and regal.

I spoke quietly. "This is bed for you?"

"You can have it if you want," she offered meekly. "Or you can take the other one. I'm glad I'll have a roommate. I'm not mad at all."

I didn't want either bed.

Shawna checked the ends of a braid, fanning the strands of hair as she watched me. Gabriel had entered by then and looked up at me with such unabashed curiosity that a red heat crept up my neck.

"How old are you?" Shawna asked.

"Twelve year old," I replied, translating the age my sister would have been into English. Answering simple questions took extra time and effort, making me feel like I was moving through water.

"Oh, me too," she said. "But I'll be thirteen in two months."

We hadn't heard Janet tread up the stairs. She stood in the doorway, drying her hands on a towel and smiling brightly.

"Rayna," she said, which I realized was her attempt at pronouncing my name, "you need a bath. Shawna, get her a towel and teach her how to properly wash up, please. She can't join us for dinner like that."

Janet was wrong about my name but right that I needed a bath. Still, I was terrified of getting undressed in this new house with strangers, even behind closed doors. I looked at Shawna, but she had pulled a towel out of a dresser drawer and was walking out of the room. Janet motioned for me to follow her.

Gabriel retreated to the room across the hallway, slipping past Janet without looking up at her. I took in every glance, every interaction. No one shouted or lashed out or threatened me. I could survive this, I thought, and soon Tilly would come for me. I wanted nothing more than to run into her arms.

Shawna turned the faucet on and let a stream of water bubble over her fingers and into the tub.

"Only as deep as your hand," she said, measuring her own hand against the edge of the tub to demonstrate the amount of water allowed. Then she pointed at the bar of soap on a ceramic dish on the corner of the tub. She had her hand on the door to step out when I stopped her.

"Please, how can I lock door?" I asked in a hushed voice. Shawna shook her head apologetically.

"Don't worry, he's not going to come in here," she said as she walked away, leaving me to wonder if she was talking about Gabriel or Everett.

I stripped down to my underwear in the corner of the bathroom just behind the door. If anyone were to barge in, they would not have seen me. I turned my pants pocket inside out and gnawed with my teeth to free the ring I'd sewn there. The medicine cabinet door opened with a creak. It was empty and not a good place to hide anything. The sink stood on a pedestal with a soap dispenser on one side of the faucets and a glass jar of big cotton puffs on the other. I tucked the ring amid the balls and checked to be sure it wasn't visible.

I pressed my ear to the door. Hearing no steps in the hallway, I darted into the bathtub and pulled the white shower curtain closed. I slipped into the cool water and began to rub soap on my arms and legs. I was washing my shoulders when the bathroom door opened.

"Let's get you cleaned up," Janet said cheerfully.

I wrapped my arms around my knees. Janet pulled the shower curtain back and saw that I'd not removed my underwear.

"Well, modesty is a good thing but not practical in a bathtub." The draft coming in through the open bathroom door sent a shiver down my body and the water seemed to be getting colder by the minute.

"Yarenna," Janet said, then tried again. "Mm . . . Aryayna? Such a tongue twister! How about we call you Anna? That's a lot easier."

My skin prickled.

"Now, a warm bath and a good scrubbing will make you a whole new person."

She smiled sweetly, her head tilted to the side. But her transfixed eyes and set jaw warned me not to disobey. She poured shampoo onto the top of my head and watched as I washed my hair. With a huff, she pushed my hands out of the way and dug her fingers into my hair, scratching at my scalp. Then she handed me a washcloth similar to the ones my mother would crochet and told me to scrub hard, then harder, at my skin. Not since I was an infant had anyone but my mother seen me naked.

"It should go without saying, but you need to clean your girl parts too," she said, pointing one finger in the general direction of my body.

I emerged from the bathroom, reddened and chafed by more than the scrubbing. I slipped into a dress that she had brought me, one that looked just like the one Shawna wore. She'd taken the clothes I'd just shed, as I thought she might.

We were summoned for dinner around the time the sky had started to turn a dusky orange. I followed Shawna and Gabriel down the steps and into the kitchen, where the table had a setting for each of us, silverware, plates, and cups arranged as perfectly as the features on a face.

"Let us bow our heads and say grace," Everett said with his hands clasped together, his voice deepening. "Bless us, Oh Lord . . ."

Gabriel fidgeted in his seat. He shot a quick glance my way, wiggling the fingers of his clasped hands. Shawna kept her head bent, her shoulders pulled primly back. I followed suit, recognizing the posture of prayer. My family had prayed at meals too, though we held our hands cupped instead of clasped, as if Allah's blessings would fall from the heavens like snowflakes.

The meal was a colorful one—slices of red tomatoes and green peppers arranged in a circle, chicken breast the color of honey, corn on the cob, and a bowl of pasta. Everett helped himself, as did Janet. I waited, noticing but not caring that the food looked raw or at least undercooked.

"Now the children," Janet said. Children always ate last at my aunt's house as well. She worried that my uncles would find picked-apart platters devoid of meat and think her a terrible host.

I reached for the corn, but yelped when I felt a hard thwap across the back of my hand. Janet held a metal spatula in the air like a scepter, one that seemed to have appeared out of thin air.

"The macaroni is for the children. A child is a simple creature and needs simple foods. We don't want you to fall ill your first day here," she said, glancing at Everett, who nodded approvingly.

I lowered my gaze to hide the tears rimming my eyes. I felt a tap against my shin and realized it was Gabriel. He held out the serving spoon for the pasta, his eyes darting to his own plate so that I might see the scoop he had served himself and realize that Shawna had taken the same amount. I accepted the spoon with a trembling hand and served myself the exact amount that he and Shawna had taken. The dull glow of the ceiling light cast shadows beneath Shawna's eyes. Where before I'd seen high cheekbones, I now saw sunken cheeks. Her lips were thin. She had edges I'd not noticed at first.

I chewed slowly, surrounded by strangers with their own peculiar haunts and habits. I wondered why this place of salvation felt suffocating.

I prayed for a moonless night, for a chance to be visited in the dark by the distant twinkle of gathered stars.

CHAPTER 31

WHEN I WAS EIGHT YEARS OLD, I'D CHALLENGED NEELAB TO A
race around the palace gardens. She was always reluctant to run against
me. I loved to run, enthralled by the feeling of lightness. It was also a skill
born of necessity, for otherwise my mother would have known that I had
dawdled on my way home from school and Boba would have realized his
binoculars were missing before I could return them to his office.

You were born with bird bones and that's unfair, my friend had declared.

That's ridiculous. Birds are terrible runners, I'd retorted, though I reveled in
the supernatural idea that my bones might carry the gift of flight.

We were a couple of days away from the spring solstice. I had marked
a circuitous path, and learning it was part of the game. The course ran
past a long rectangular pool and an acre of green grass. It cut through the
pocket of fruit trees and followed the far western border, looping around
one of the buildings that once served as army barracks and coming back
to the starting point.

The palace was distracted as everyone inside prepared for the
Nowruz celebrations, either at home or with loved ones. Soaked in water,
dried apricots and the mealy oleaster fruit grew plumper than they'd been

before they were plucked from the trees. Bright green and black raisins simmered in tall pots, their sugars steeping the water of the *haft mewa*, the seven-fruit compote. It was so labor-intensive that the medley was made only for the occasion of the new year. Mounds of shelled pistachios, walnuts, and blanched almonds soaked in wide bowls to soften their skins and make them easier to peel. The walnuts were the most difficult, and every year it was the walnuts that made my mother swear she would never make *haft mewa* again.

Despite the festive air, Neelab was reluctant to play. In our games and contests, winners weren't rewarded with trophies or prizes. Instead, the winner had the chance to assign the loser a punishment. When I'd claimed victory, I'd restricted Neelab to moving around by hopping on one foot for an entire day. She thought she'd secured her revenge when she made me walk an entire day with orange peels stuffed in my shoes, but to her dismay, I'd ended up with soft, citrus-scented heels.

Neelab finally agreed to the race, maybe because she'd designed some clever retribution for me. We began at the starting point, on her count. I put my all into my start, but Neelab paced herself. She wasn't on my heels but kept respectably close. I wanted to put more distance between us, wanting to win by more than a few strides. I pumped my arms at my sides and leaned into the wind. When I had passed the green acre, I stole a glance over my shoulder. Neelab was smiling, closer to me than I would have guessed.

As I looped around the building, Neelab was briefly out of view. I made a hasty decision to leap over a row of shrubs instead of circling around them. They were barely waist high, and I was certain I could clear them.

I was wrong.

Neelab stood over me, panting and terrified to see me bleeding. My shirt had been smeared red. I had a gash across my left eyebrow where my face had met a rock. Boba took me to the hospital, where a doctor stitched my gaping wound closed.

It is so big! I cried to Boba while we waited for the doctor to see me. I had seen my reflection on a glass door.

The wound is where the light enters you, Boba said softly.

I did remember the verse from Rumi, but did not admit I hadn't quite grasped the meaning. I didn't want my father to think I was dense.

When pain retreats, when skin repairs, when a broken bone becomes whole again, it is a miracle. It is grace, he explained. *But you would never feel this without the hurt. I would never wish the wound for you, sweet, mischievous Sitara. But I certainly wish you the light.*

SHAWNA FELL ASLEEP BEFORE ME. ON PARALLEL BEDS A FEW FEET apart, we lay curled on our sides, my back to her. Her breaths stretched long and slow as winter nights. I hoped the rhythm would lull me to sleep too. But flickering headlights came through the bedroom window, and my eyelids, heavy as they were, kept fluttering open. When I did drift off, I fell into a terrifying nightmare in which someone was searching me out in the palace basement with a flashlight. I rolled over so that I was facing Shawna and watched lights play against the striped wallpaper like a movie projected onto a screen.

I heard the television switch off and then the sound of footsteps plodding up the stairs. A distant door creaked open, and I heard Everett's voice.

"I'm going to check on them. They've probably kicked their blankets off, restless sleepers."

Everett entered the room and sat on the edge of Shawna's bed. I watched through the mesh of my eyelashes, not wanting him to know I was still awake. His hand hovered above the subtle curve of her hip, moved down toward her feet, and then back upward, as if he were tracing her form in the air. He leaned in and I heard him inhale deeply. His fingers touched her hair ever so lightly.

He pulled her blanket up and smoothed it over her shoulders. I saw her eyelids squeeze tight then, though she did not stir. Lines formed across her forehead. His hands moved out of view, disappearing as he straightened the four corners of the blanket that had been perfectly in place before he entered the room.

Shawna let out a soft whimper and he hushed her. My muscles had turned to stone. Was he hurting her or soothing her? I felt stupid not to know the difference, to feel uncertain about something as important as this.

Shawna's eyes opened for a flash, the single beat of a bird's wings. They closed again, a flight stymied, before I could even tell if she'd seen me. I closed my eyes too, as Faheem did when he played hide-and-seek.

But I didn't feel like a child. I felt like a coward.

Shawna did not scream. She did not cry. She did not kick or bite or utter a single word of protest. Maybe I'd been waiting for her to do something to make me certain. My head spun.

In the morning, Shawna avoided my eyes and I avoided hers. She spoke brightly, but her voice quavered like a plucked string. As she pulled her bedsheets over her mattress, arranging the pillow and quilt so evenly that it seemed impossible a body, much less two, had ever rested on it, she filled the silence with chatter about the beehive they had once found under the rafters. She picked out clothes from a dresser drawer and held them close to her chest as she walked to the bathroom.

"You better wash and dress too," Shawna said. "It's Sunday and Miss Janet likes to go to church early. I'm to get breakfast ready for everyone by seven-thirty. If you want to help, you can."

Adults shake their heads and shine flashlights into dark corners when children insist that there's a monster lurking in the closet. But irrational fears are a training ground. That drop in the stomach, that quickening of the pulse, those prickling bumps on the skin—all are electrical impulses that teach a child to recognize peril. They stop short of teaching the child to run.

I followed Shawna's lead in the kitchen. She cracked eggs into a bowl and showed me where the plates were kept. Janet came down the stairs, wearing a pale green dress with a dark green vine print.

"Good morning, Miss Janet," Shawna said.

Janet looked at me expectantly.

"Good morning, Miss Janet," I parroted.

"Good," she said, without returning the greeting. Her hair was smoothed back in a knot, and she wore a pearl bracelet on her wrist. Because I'd tried on my mother's pearl necklace more often than my mother knew, I recognized that the beads on Janet's wrist had likely never seen the sea. I wanted to say so out loud but held my tongue.

"Miss Janet," I said instead, approaching her timidly.

"Yes, Anna?" she replied. I didn't bother correcting her.

"I want to see Ms. Tilly. Please. She is in hospital." I would have explained more if Janet hadn't turned her attention back to the calendar on the wall.

"I don't know who Ms. Tilly is, dear. I'm sorry to hear she's in the hospital. I think it would be wonderful to pray for her in church this morning."

I was trying to find more persuasive words when Everett descended the stairs wearing a green tie and a white short-sleeved dress shirt. A crease sharp as a blade ran down the length of his slacks. His hair was parted on the side and had a remarkable sheen to it. He must have taken great care to pat every rogue strand into place. I could picture him lingering in front of a mirror to take in his carefully arranged image.

Shawna greeted him as she had Janet. He barely looked at her when he replied. I followed suit, as did Gabriel, who had burst into the kitchen with his shirt on inside out.

"Good morning, family," Everett said, breathing in deeply. "Nothing like a good breakfast to begin our Sunday."

I knew what to expect by then. Janet and Everett enjoyed fried eggs, orange slices, and toast and jam while we ate slices of white bread that might have stuck to the roof of my mouth all day had I not had a glass of water to wash it loose.

Once we children had washed the breakfast dishes, they piled us into their car. I did not bother telling them I was not Christian because I worried that they might make me stay behind with Everett or punish me for disobedience. I was also curious. My mother had said that the church she'd visited in Oklahoma had the most beautiful glass windows she had ever seen, as colorful and intricate as the painted mosques we attended on holidays.

Everett's cologne filled the car, musky and overwhelming. Janet looked over her shoulder at us.

"Gabriel, roll up your window. The wind's blown your hair every which way. You're looking more like a sheepdog than a young man."

Gabriel did as he was told, and the smell of cologne intensified. My head ached, and I thought how terribly untidy it would be if I were to vomit in the backseat of Everett's car.

The church was a brick building with white trim and a sloped roof. It had a single spire with small windows toward the rear and an enormous metal cross planted in the front lawn. Janet and Everett, who knew a lot of people in the church, shook hands and hugged other worshippers just outside the heavy, wooden doors. Intrigued, I found myself moving toward the entrance ahead of Shawna and Gabriel.

We slid onto a long bench three rows from the front. The church had a smell much milder than cologne but distinct—like flowers pressed into the pages of an old book. A hundred lit candles in short glasses were arranged at the front. These drops of fire unnerved me, and I found my-self looking away.

A painted glass window drew my attention. It looked like a rainbow had crystallized and shattered and someone had arranged the pieces in the shape of a cross. I couldn't understand a word the gowned priest was saying. I didn't understand the Arabic of our prayers either. We stayed there for hours. The priest raised a hand, and like the tipping of candle flames by a draft, the heads of all the worshippers bowed forward.

I kept my gaze on the window for the entire service, tracing the bor-ders of each of the colors and counting the number of shades of blue and then losing myself in the task of counting how many fragments had come together to form this marvel.

When the priest called Everett's name, Janet's expression was one of composed surprise. She squeezed Everett's hand gently. Everett looked almost embarrassed, and I wondered what the priest had said about him. He stood, reluctantly, suppressing a smile. He kept his head bowed. The church clapped politely. *Amen,* I heard people say, and it reminded me of our *Ameen.* Janet whispered sugared words of gratitude to the people seated closest to us.

Outside, under the late morning sun, Shawna, Gabriel, and I waited while Janet and Everett lingered to shake hands and ask after people's children. They pointed toward us and beamed with pride, as if they'd just carved the three of us from a single block of wood.

"This is what every Sunday looks like," Shawna whispered to me, answering a question I hadn't yet asked.

"I have to pee," Gabriel said, as he shifted his weight.

"I told you not to drink water this morning," Shawna chastised.

"I was thirsty," he pouted. "And you drank water. I saw you."

"But I can hold it. You can't."

Gabriel took a step forward, inching toward Janet. Shawna muttered something under her breath.

"What is problem?" I asked Shawna.

Shawna shook her head, just as Gabriel tugged on the sleeve of Janet's jacket. Janet's mouth pulled tight at the corners and her eyes narrowed as she looked down at Gabriel.

"They do not like to be interrupted," Shawna sighed.

Janet brought her lips close to Gabriel's left ear. She cupped a hand over his right ear, as if to prevent her message from floating out the other side of his head. Gabriel nodded stiffly. He took a step back and fell back into line. Shawna didn't bother to ask what Janet had said. Gabriel chewed his lip. When I looked down, I could see his small hands clench at his sides. I turned to Shawna, but before I could speak, she silenced me.

"It will be worse."

Gabriel looked like he might burst, his face flushing as we clamored into the backseat of the car again to head home. Janet walked so serenely that I was certain Gabriel must not have told her of his urgent need for a bathroom.

But once all four tires were on the road and the church was shrinking in the rearview mirror, Janet flipped the sun visor down. It had a small mirror in it so that we could see her seething.

"Why is it that we cannot get through a church service without you threatening to wet your pants?" she asked, exasperated.

"But I really need to go," Gabriel cried.

"How many hours do you sleep at night? Ten? Twelve?" Everett yelled. His voice exploded in the small space of the car. I looked to Shawna, who had one hand on Gabriel's leg. Her head was lowered as if she were in prayer still. "If you can hold it all night long, how is it possible that you can't hold it for a simple service?"

Everett whipped a sharp left turn, crossing two lanes and spinning into a graveled parking lot of a long brick building. Shawna fell against my left shoulder until the car righted itself and came to a sudden stop. Though the road was busy, the parking lot was empty.

Gabriel's cheeks were streaked with tears by then. He sniffled, his leg tapping furiously as he held both hands over his groin.

"Go on. Get out of the car if you need to go so bad," Everett said coolly. He kept his hands on the wheel. "But stand where we can see you."

Gabriel unlocked the door and stepped out. He started to run toward the edge of the parking lot when Everett rolled his window down and called out to him.

"Stand where we can see you, I said!" He jabbed his finger toward the hood of the car. Gabriel ran back. It was painful to watch him struggle but hard to look away too. I felt bad about it, but later realized all people are terrible in that way—ready to cause a car accident just to get a good look at the one that's already happened.

Gabriel stood in front of the car, his hands fumbling with the buttons of his pants. Between his tears and trembling fingers, he was struggling.

"I thought he was in a hurry to go," Everett sighed. He looked off into the distance for a second, as if contemplating this matter. Then, without another word, he clapped the heel of his hand against the steering wheel and the blare of the car horn made Shawna and me jump in our seats. Even Janet looked startled.

Gabriel let out a wail. His sniffles turned to tears then, and I saw a dark spot bloom on the front of his pants, even as his fingers continued to work on the zipper. He relieved himself of whatever urine was left in his bladder and then returned to the car. He was crying, quietly but for the sniffles.

"That's just filthy," Everett said when Gabriel started to climb back into the backseat.

"Shawna," Janet said. "Let Gabriel sit on your cardigan. We don't need piss on the seats. If I'd known we'd have to be potty training when we agreed to take him in . . ."

Gabriel sat on Shawna's sweater, his eyes bleary and repentant.

Everett's cologne masked the smell of urine and was more offensive anyway. When we arrived at the house, Janet instructed us to change out of our church clothes. Gabriel brought his soiled pants to the sink in the mudroom. He stood on a stool and scrubbed powdered detergent on his pants, dunked them into hot water, and scrubbed some more. He'd leaned so far into the deep sink that it seemed he might fall into it. And, in fact, he looked like he wouldn't mind disappearing into the murky water.

We were sent to the backyard, where Shawna showed me how to pull weeds from the soil so that none of the root was left behind. Janet had on a pair of gardening gloves and was weeding the flower beds in front of the house. We'd been tasked with the backyard.

The early afternoon sun warmed my skin. Beads of sweat gathered down the middle of my back and along my forehead. We were on our knees, listening to the faint sounds of birds chirping and children playing somewhere out of view. Gabriel worked between us, Shawna filling the silence with small conversations about subjects she seemed to pluck from the sky.

"Do you think rabbits live back here? I've never seen one, but that doesn't mean that they don't. I did see a groundhog once."

Gabriel said nothing. I wished I could do something to lift his spirits.

"You are fast," I told him, looking at the pile of uprooted weeds in front of his feet. He wiped his nose with the back of his hand. He was so young and yet still older than my brother would ever be.

"No, I'm not," he muttered. "She'll probably get mad at me for this too."

I looked at the three piles of weeds we'd collected, at the troubling inequality of them. I took some of my pile and added it to his, evening them in size. Shawna paused, a strangled weed in her right hand. She tossed it onto Gabriel's heap, then added some more from hers in a moment of complicity.

"She thinks her flowers don't grow because deer eat them. But I think the flowers don't grow because they don't want to look at her," Shawna said. Her voice sharpened in mockery. "Oh, roses! Please come out! Tulips, where are you?"

Gabriel's eyes crinkled at the corners. His tiny, pearly teeth shone as he laughed.

In that hour, even as we toiled, each of us reverted to our disparate origins. The deeper we dug, the closer we got to our true selves. We unearthed worms and beetles and a dozen other defenseless creatures. Grass stained our knees. The sun warmed our scalps. Thorny wildflowers pricked our fingers, and yet we did not bleed because, in that brilliant hour, we believed we were God's children.

CHAPTER 32

MY BACK ACHED FROM AN HOUR OF HUNCHING OVER IN THE GAR-
den. I tossed and turned in bed but couldn't find a comfortable position.
Shawna and Gabriel would be off to school in the morning. I missed
them already. More than anything, I didn't want to fall asleep in a dark
bedroom. But when Janet passed the room, she reached in and flicked the
light off.

"Shawna?" I whispered.

"Yes?"

"You are not sleep?"

"No."

I wasn't sure what I wanted to ask her. I was afraid of questions, unsure if my asking some would end in more questions being asked of me.

"How long you are here?"

"You mean in this house?"

"Yes."

"One year," Shawna said, her voice resigned. "It is not a good place.
But I haven't been in a good place in a long time."

This frightened me. What if it took Tilly a very long time to get better? Would they move me to some other place that was worse than this? Would Everett sit on the edge of my bed while I tried to sleep too?

Before I could ask any more, Shawna rolled over and turned her back to me. I listened to the quiet, trying to imagine where Janet and Everett were in the house and what they were doing. I could make out their voices coming from the kitchen.

I thought back to the church and understood that I'd lost myself in that stained-glass window because I was thinking of my mother. I'd wanted to feel what she'd felt when she had sat in an American church for the first time, watching color and light radiate over people looking for God. Had she prayed in church? Why hadn't I asked her this?

I fell asleep crying, wondering if I was right or wrong to have bowed my head during the service. I'd prayed to the only God I'd ever prayed to. I'd prayed for Tilly to get better and Antonia to come for me and for God to take good care of my parents and brother. But I'd felt nothing, not the tiny comfort that came from praying beside my mother or hearing the familiar song of the Qur'an being read. Maybe, I'd wondered, I'd gone too far from home for God to hear me.

In the morning, Shawna and Gabriel readied themselves for school. I stayed in bed until Shawna came back upstairs.

"It's very late. I told Janet you were washing up and changing your clothes, so please hurry."

I pulled the blanket over my face, not wanting her to see my face.

"Aryana?" she said gently. "Aren't you going to get up? They'll be upset."

I could hear the concern in her voice, even if I couldn't feel particularly moved by it this morning.

"Please. You still . . . you still have to get up."

Maybe because of her, I shuffled my way to the bathroom, where I washed up and changed into a fresh pair of clothes. We ate breakfast together, dry cereal with one slice of apple for each of us. Hungry as I'd been when I'd gone to bed the night before, I barely touched a flake.

"Why aren't you eating, Anna?" Janet asked, standing over me with her hands on her hips. "We will not allow wastefulness here. Surely you can understand that, coming from the kind of place you come from."

I forced half a spoon of cereal into my mouth.

Gabriel gave me a hug before he left. He looked up at me with eyes round with hope, urging me to remember the earthworm he had dangled in front of me while we were in the garden and the rock Shawna had found that glittered with flecks of gold and silver. She'd slipped it into her pocket to ask her science teacher to confirm the treasure.

But that had been before last night. That seemed so long ago.

"Look under my bed. I have something special there. You can have one if you want," Shawna whispered to me once she made sure Janet wasn't close enough to hear.

I nodded and mumbled something in response. They were gone. I watched them from the living room window, their backpacks bouncing with every step, as they turned the corner. I was left alone with Janet. Everett had left early in the morning to assist with something at the church. I wondered if he would wear a short-sleeved shirt, as he had on Sunday, or if he would wear something to conceal the scratches I hoped I'd left on his forearms. I wondered if the God in the church would know where the scratches had come from.

Janet poured herself a cup of coffee and cream, the metal spoon scraping the inside of the cup as she swirled dark and light into one.

"I'm waiting on word from Ann," she said, as if I'd asked her a question. "We'll get you into school soon enough. I have some lovely books you can read until then to help guide you."

I plodded back up the stairs, feeling as heavy and out of place as an elephant in this house.

I sat on the corner of my bed, looking at the bed where Shawna had slept, her quilt now perfectly tucked in at the corners. I knelt on the floor and looked under the bed, where I spied a small metallic cylinder.

I pulled it into the light and saw that it was a roll of round candies, the same ones Everett kept in his jacket pocket and sucked on as we drove to church the previous morning.

I let the roll drop from my fingers and tumble back under the bed. I pulled my knees to my chest and leaned against the nightstand, watching dust motes float in the sunlight. Janet hummed downstairs, a tune that didn't seem to have a melody.

I thought I had felt every shade of dark in the weeks since the coup, but I'd been wrong.

Boba had read me the epic *Shahnameh* in parcels, reciting couplets about kings and queens and mythical winged creatures. On my fortieth day of life, my father had held me in his arms. Milk-drunk and dressed in a pink crocheted sweater knitted by my grandmother, I had seemed to him to bear a striking resemblance to Rudabeh, daughter to the king of Kabul in the *Shahnameh*. Like her, I had eyelashes like a raven's wings and a face that glowed like the moon.

Does that make you a king, Boba?

A crown wouldn't fit a square head like mine, he had replied, rapping his knuckles against his head. I'd laughed, because Boba made the funniest faces when he talked about himself. *And besides, crowns come and go despite men's best efforts.* He had cleared his throat and recited a verse from the *Shahnameh*:

> *Luxury and caresses, one's fortune had been*
> *Before cast into an abyss he'd never seen;*
> *Another lifted from the pit and placed on a throne*
> *Upon his head, a crown of glittering stone*
> *In the turning of tides, the world takes no shame*
> *It is prompt to dole out both pleasure and pain.*

I was standing. I felt fresh air on my face. With the window open, nothing stood between me and the sky. I tilted my head back and inhaled sharply, the air tasting as sweet as the roses in the palace gardens and as liberating as the first breath I'd taken coming out of the hatch at the Islamabad embassy.

I've come so far, I thought. But maybe I hadn't gone far enough. I slid one leg over the window ledge, then the other, and sat perched on the narrow sill.

My heels tapped against the side of the house. I felt a tingle on the sole of my foot where the skin had thickened. It wasn't pain—just a new somatic awareness. My body was conscious in a way it had never been before. My hands seemed impossibly small. My breathing felt labored, my bones porous and brittle. I felt a thousand years old and longed for rest.

I didn't hear the doorbell ring or Janet's insincere greeting. I didn't notice the footsteps coming up the stairs. I didn't even hear my sister's name called, with all its syllables intact.

I had come so far. Perhaps I needed only to go a little further.

I teetered, as if I were on a Kabul rooftop while the room filled with the bitter smoke of desire and dissent, while sin and solitude dragged their talons across my flesh, while my flailing arms sought both refuge and revenge.

I longed for the crystalline prophesies of my father and released my hands from the window ledge.

Catch me, I cried to the wind, to the freedom in its current. *Catch me!*

PART II

November 2008

CHAPTER 33

NIA COULD HAVE FILED SOME REPORTS WITH HER HIGHER-UPS IN the State Department and gone back to Kabul or moved on to a new post. She could have believed the foster care system was better equipped to raise a child than a woman who had already decided family life wasn't for her.

But she didn't walk away. She's the type to run toward a fire, after all. Antonia claimed me, with all my scars and fears and outbursts.

Our years together have been anything but easy.

We started off in Tilly's cottage outside of Annapolis with pictures of her and Nia as a child framed against the floral wallpaper. She had pictures of Nia's father too, teaching Nia how to hold a fishing line, or sitting at a desk, fingers hovering over a typewriter. Sometimes, when she didn't know I was watching, I'd spot Nia staring at the photographs too. Most of the time, Nia pored over paperwork and went back and forth on the phone with a lawyer. She tried to hide her red-rimmed eyes. She took calls on the phone in another room. She kept a steady rotation of library books on parenting and loss in her nightstand drawer. But the walls of Tilly's home were thin. We could hear each other crying. We watched each other pick at food.

Whether by blood, by fire, or by default, to become a mother is no easy feat.

And I don't think I ever thought of Nia as my mother. I certainly never called her Madar. But somewhere along the line she became Mom, a distinct and hard-earned title.

About a year after I'd arrived in the U.S., Mom took me to a therapist. It was only in that small, wood-paneled room with a set of building blocks and two blond-haired dolls in the corner that anyone talked to me about what had happened the year I turned ten. In that space, with Antonia on the other side of a plywood door, I was asked to talk about the specific events that had me grinding my teeth in my sleep and vomiting at the sight of a uniform.

After the fifth visit, I begged Mom not to take me anymore. My headaches were coming twice as often and hitting me twice as hard. My appetite had shriveled, and my concentration was shot. I was a taut string, vibrating at the lightest touch.

Mom stopped the appointments. She could hardly afford them anyway. She had been forced to take a leave from work until they could figure out where to place her. Just ten years earlier, women officers were made to resign if they got married. A single mother was a hard sell. Mom's superiors suggested she leave the Foreign Service and focus on finding a husband.

But even had she wanted to, Mom could hardly search for love and marriage when I needed so much.

Grief is a tarry substance, and I was covered in it, head to toe. Everything stuck to me—a sideways glance, a phrase beyond my grasp, the sight of a girl running into her mother's arms. And if I had tried to strip myself of it, I would have lost flesh in the process.

I had much to figure out. In my head, I was ten-year-old Sitara. To this new world, I was twelve-year-old Aryana. And in truth, I wasn't strong enough to shoulder two identities and two nationalities. I survived by letting Sitara go, adding her to the body count of the palace coup. I tucked away the family I'd lost, the childhood I'd had.

I became Aryana. We told the world that Mom had adopted me and we knew little about my background. As soon as I said those words, people usually remembered something they needed to do or told me about an adopted cousin who was so beloved by all their family. Few asked any more questions.

I learned to eat new foods. I learned to speak new words. I learned to (mostly) sleep through the night and survive the brutal headaches.

I took on Mom's last name and officially became Aryana Shephard, the girl who fell from the sky.

Mom became my therapist, my teacher, and my parent. She bought pads of paper and watercolor paints. We would sit on a bench and try to re-create the fleet of white sails in the sparkling Chesapeake Bay. We hiked in the fall and pressed sunset-colored leaves into the pages of books. We made a fire and dug through Tilly's scrapbooks, filled with newspaper clippings, programs, and pictures of her in various costumes.

I felt less alone. I began to wake feeling better rested. I spent less time in a dark room waiting for the pills to loosen the vise on my head.

Mom noticed the difference too. When we couldn't hike, she would still insist on a long walk.

"Want to race?" she asked playfully one day. The sidewalk stretched long and clear ahead of us. When I laughed, she put her hands on her hips and issued a challenge. "Do you think I'm too fast for you?"

She broke into a jog.

I broke into a run.

I ran daily after that, despite the pain I felt when the knobby flesh on the sole of my foot pounded against concrete. I ran to feel like the girl who used to think the world was hers to run through. I ran to confirm that nothing was holding me by my ankles. After every run, I would lean over with my hands on my thighs and take long, heaving gulps of air until the burn in my lungs dissipated. I'd lived until then not realizing what a privilege it was to be able to catch my breath.

One day Mom sat me down and told me she'd been offered a post in Turkey.

I ran right out the front door and down the street. I ran with my chest on fire, with tears streaming down my cheeks. I ran past the school where kids mocked me when I slipped and said *al-jabr* instead of algebra in math class. They thought I was too dumb to pronounce it correctly.

"Al-jabr" means the reunion of broken parts, Boba had taught me. *It was a term first used for broken bones, then later to describe a mathematical equation.*

I was still a floating variable, the x that stood alone and undefined. If Mom left me now, I didn't see how I could survive. I certainly wouldn't go back to Everett and Janet. I pressed the heels of my hands against my temples trying to hold myself together.

"Aryana!" Mom cried, breathless and flushed. She had caught up with me.

"You want to leave me!" I'd shouted. I watched her closely, without her noticing. I'd seen the exhaustion, the frustration, the resentment in her face. I knew there were moments she regretted making me her problem. I had long wondered if I might one day find that social worker sitting in our living room ready to cart me off to a new home.

"No, no. Not at all! I will not leave you!" she said, kneeling in the grass. "I will only go if you go with me. That's what I wanted to ask you."

I leaned against her. When we could breathe, we stood and walked home.

Two months later, we packed our bags and boarded a plane with our American passports. We spent the next four years in three different countries, with side excursions on different continents. In the moments when my heart opened to God, I thanked Him for designing this way for me to disappear and exist, this chance to become an American without living under an American microscope.

My world had swerved from beautiful to punishing and back again.

I have run along the turquoise Bosphorus and with my back to the snowcapped Dolomites. I have circled the Mitad del Mundo and explored the streets of Cairo. It was on the banks of the Nile, realizing that a river must flow in one direction if it wants to reunite with the sea, that I decided I would leave my old name and my old world behind me.

I run because of all I have seen. I run despite all I have seen. I run against the wind, and sometimes I run with it. I run planned and unplanned routes. I measure my distance and run full miles, whether four or five or eight, never leaving a fraction on the ground.

I check my phone once more. No messages, which means the woman I operated on today is doing well—as well as can be expected for a kindergarten teacher whose body has become home to a cancer.

When we reviewed her imaging, swirling shapes and patterns on a black-and-white screen, she was trying hard not to appear overwhelmed.

This is a lot to take in. What are you most worried about? I asked, as I always do.

She hesitated, looking down before she asked what had been roiling in her mind.

I can still have kids, right? I mean, down the road. At some point.

We spent twenty minutes discussing fertility options. We did not discuss the chances of her being alive in five years.

I hope we won't one day sit here for that other conversation, the one in which I admit that anything more I do is just as likely to harm as it is to help. Those discussions are like handing someone a ball of brown clay and telling them they are free to shape it to their liking. Some people stare at the lump a good long while because they don't know what to make of it. Others can't seem to pinch or pull the ball in any way that gets it at all close to what they've imagined. Eventually, everyone realizes the clay is actually a ball of excrement that will never turn into something they want to hold in their hands.

I want to fight, some say. That means I cut wider, deeper, taking bigger risks to keep them alive for one last visit from a sister coming from their homeland, for the birth of a first grandchild, or maybe just one more

Super Bowl. Finish lines are arbitrary inventions. Others listen to the options I offer, thank me for my time, and ask their misty-eyed children or spouses to take them home.

Just as I slip my phone into my armband, I hear a chime. It's a text message.

It's been three days, Aryana. Please say yes. I promise it won't even be the biggest decision you'll make today.

My fingers hover over the screen. I want to reply, but I can't think of what I want to say. And that's the problem. I tuck the phone back into my armband and begin to jog. The evening air is still, making hardly a whisper as it slips through the leaves.

I know it's been three days.

I reach the half-mile marker. The signs are small red squares nailed into the wood post fence. Green would have been a better choice. It's so basic that even preschoolers know it. Green means go. Red means stop.

Go.

Stop.

If life came with road signs or mile markers, Adam would have his answer by now and I could run without these thoughts knocking around in my head.

But life doesn't come with road signs or mile markers.

I reach the one-mile mark and pull my ponytail tighter. I don't deliberate in the operating room, even in the hairiest of situations. There's a fine line between being cautious and being hesitant. Caution means I've done my homework but hesitation means I haven't.

Adam's cousin issued a late invitation to her wedding, which is just a couple of weeks from now. It is the week I've planned to spend at a lake house, surrounded by trees stripped of leaves and catching the magic of moonlight on water. Adam thinks we should reschedule and join the family in celebrating at a restaurant in Connecticut.

I don't know how to tell him that I've had an uneasiness lately, something I haven't felt in a while. It makes me seek out quiet spaces and comforting rhythms until this wave passes.

I run my second, third, and fourth miles as dusk gives way to night. Headlights cut through the ring of trees that surround the path, casting eerie shadows on the ground. But I run at night because that's when it becomes impossible to tell if the salt on my face is from tears or sweat. Because that's when I confirm that I am no longer cowed by what might be lurking in the bushes. I don't look over my shoulder. I just run faster, harder.

Eager to prove myself to the dark.

CHAPTER 34

THE TEAM IS TURNING OVER THE ROOM FOR THE NEXT PATIENT so I pour myself a cup of coffee in the empty physician lounge where, for once, the television is not set to a twenty-four-hour news channel.

How do you do it? the talk show host asks her guest, a rock singer I've never heard of who suffered horrific physical abuse at the hands of his father growing up. His father took great care to strike only the parts of his body that would be covered by clothes. Even after his father died, he kept the years of abuse a secret.

I fall into an office chair and whirl myself to face the television.

After surviving something so ugly, how do you manage to wake up every day and create music? How do you step on a stage?

He bows his head.

I just keep all that in a box, I suppose. Don't let it get in the way of more important stuff.

I give my coffee a stir. Clumps of creamer refuse to dissolve.

Some of your fans might be survivors as well. Some might be wondering how you cope with the trauma.

He talks about the nonprofit he has started to foster healing through art programs. Not everyone can do that, of course. Some people can barely open a bottle of Klonopin.

Do you get nightmares or flashbacks? the host asks, and the musician draws a long sip of water from his glass.

My pager buzzes on my hip before he can answer. My patient, the kindergarten teacher, has been moved to the recovery unit.

She is still asleep and hooked up to monitors, but within the next half hour the sedation will wear off and I can tell her the good news, that her operation went well and her wound will heal without much scarring.

When she has had time to recover, I will tell her the bad news.

The mass I removed from her gallbladder is on its way to the pathology lab, where it will be sliced thin, stained, and examined under a microscope. In a few days, I'll get a report from a pathologist confirming my suspicion that the tumor has already sent tentacles into an otherwise healthy liver.

"How are you feeling?" I ask her later in the day, when I stop by the recovery room. She is pale and bleary-eyed from the anesthesia.

"Tired," she says, though she manages a smile. "Like I just ran a marathon."

Her mother is at her side now. She flew in from Chicago and looks duly grateful that her daughter can find lightness in the moment. I leave them to the inimitable comfort they bring each other. They'll need me more later.

I leave the hospital and take the train to Manhattan to meet Mom for dinner. She is in town for a luncheon. I can't recall which of her many causes this one is for, or which of her many connected friends invited her. I check my watch and hop on a train to Midtown to meet her at her favorite Indian restaurant. Mom is craving spice tonight.

"HEY, SUGAR!" MOM SAYS, THE DOOR CHIME RINGING IN MY WAKE
as I enter the restaurant. We hug, and she gives my hand a squeeze, like
I'm still a little girl.

"Have you been here long?" I ask.

"Just got in, but I ordered us some *pakora* to start. Figured you'd be
hungry."

"You figured right. I'm famished."

Mom dotes on me with the same precision and focus she always
brought to her work.

"How's Dayo? I haven't heard you talk about her in a while," Mom
says. She's always relieved to know I'm spending time with my best friend.
She's waited a long time to see me with people in my life. And apart from
Mom, Dayo is the only person who knows anything about my past.

"She's good, thanks. Busy as ever. How was the luncheon?" I ask once
we place our orders. When the *pakoras* arrive, we waste no time digging
into them.

"Mmm," she says, dabbing a napkin to her lips to catch the tamarind
sauce. "Remarkable. The vaccination program has been very successful in
parts of rural Pakistan."

Normally, I wouldn't let the mention of Pakistan dredge up the past
for me. But today, breathing in the cumin-infused air of the restaurant, I
drift to those wild days with Tilly.

"Pakistan," I repeat.

Mom looks up at me. She raises an eyebrow and waits.

"I can't believe it's been thirty years since Pakistan," I say, fully recognizing how cliché I sound marveling at the passage of time.

"It is hard to believe," Mom says. She sets her napkin on her lap.
"Tilly would have been so proud to see all you've done since then."

Tilly. I can't imagine what Mom went through from the moment
she discovered that we'd left with Indigo and his van full of travelers
to the moment she got the phone call from Washington that Tilly had

stopped breathing. Though they'd shuttled her directly from the tarmac to the hospital, she hadn't survived. She'd been diagnosed with cancer a few months before she went to Afghanistan, Mom told me when I was in high school.

Once I started to think back on those days with Tilly, I realized I'd known she wasn't well even then.

It wasn't until my third year of medical school, when I spent more time in the hospital than anywhere else, that I learned how many diseases have their own distinct smells. I also learned that I had the rare ability to sense them. Some were obvious, overwhelming even, like the rancid fish smell of bacterial vaginosis. Others, like the fruity ketones of diabetic breath, were more subtle. I had detected a handful of pregnancies, in patients and nurses, well before bellies had rounded. I would sniff urine samples before they went to the lab and stand an extra moment at a patient's bedside to hone my skills.

I was an intern taking care of a patient who had just had a broken foot casted when I smelled something organic and slightly spoiled, a mixture of moss and mildew. I only needed to check that her toes were pink and perfused, but I asked her if I could do a more thorough examination instead.

Rolling her eyes, she'd taken deep breaths so I could assess her lungs. Go ahead, she'd said. *But be careful with my ankle or you'll owe me an extra dose of morphine.*

Moments later, my fingers rolled across a small knot on the underbelly of her left breast. I felt again, to be sure.

A flash of understanding passed between us.

I'm getting married in three months, she'd said, as if in protest.

I hadn't yet learned the right combination of words to use in those heavy moments.

The ticking of the clock is constant, but time has an elasticity too.

The short weeks I spent with Tilly were a lifetime of songs, solidarity, and regrets.

"I think about Tilly a lot," I say. "I wish I could have done something to help her."

"There's nothing you could have done. You know very well how serious meningitis is."

The crash on the mountain on our way to Jalalabad.

The runny nose Tilly had in Islamabad.

I was in my first year of medical school, learning the anatomy of the head and neck, when I put the clues together. Tilly must have sustained a skull fracture in the car accident, opening a tiny crack in the wall meant to keep microbes out. While we hid in the embassy vault, surrounded by flames, those microbes were setting fire to the lining surrounding Tilly's brain and spine. She must have felt awful long before we boarded the plane to leave Pakistan.

I'd been afraid to tell Mom my theory because I'd thought I'd break her heart all over again but she'd been relieved. But I know unanswered questions about those we love can torment us and sometimes get in the way of good grieving.

Antonia had been frantic from the moment she'd heard about the riot in the Islamabad embassy. She'd been about to board a bus to meet us there when she learned of the evacuation plans. She'd come home and, while arranging Tilly's funeral, had also tracked me down.

"She shouldn't have been on that road," I say.

"Aryana," she says, a chastising edge to her voice. "Mom and I were adults. We each made decisions. Mom wanted to get you out of the country. It was almost as much for her as it was for you. And if she hadn't gotten on that plane with you, God knows how long it would have taken me to get you out of Pakistan, even with my contacts."

Mom purses her lips.

"You looked like you were going to jump," she says softly. "When I walked into that room and saw you standing at an open window, I was terrified. And that woman, nice as she seemed, was just fussing around her kitchen with a cup of coffee. A goddamned cup of coffee."

I flinch at the memory.

"We all end up where we were always meant to be, Aryana," she says.

On that day, I hadn't heard the door open. Antonia had managed to slip her arms around me before I realized she was there. I fell backward, into her embrace. I don't know how long we stayed on the floor of that room or if Janet stuck around to watch.

It had taken two whole days for Antonia to have me placed with her. Janet and Everett had protested after they learned that Antonia was unmarried but were quick to let me go.

I had been with Mom for a month before I went to her crying, begging her to bring Gabriel and Shawna to live with us. She thought I missed them at first, until I managed to tell her what had happened in that house. I remember the long interval before her face went slack with understanding. She didn't bring them to live with us, but she did raise hell with the foster care system and made sure they were removed from Janet and Everett's home. It wasn't until years later that it occurred to me that there was no real guarantee that Shawna and Gabriel had ultimately wound up in a better place.

"It still haunts me to think," Mom says, her voice thin as a butterfly's wing, "what was going through your mind while you were standing there that day."

Even now I'm not sure. I know I craved escape—from that room and that house and maybe even from the dark cave my head had become. I'd wanted to fly, to feel weightless in the infinite sky, even if only for an instant.

CHAPTER 35

ADAM PAUSES TO ADMIRE A PASSING FRENCH BULLDOG AS WE walk down a transformed street in my neighborhood. Since I moved in, much has happened here. The thrift shop is now a juice bar with wheatgrass growing in pots on a marble countertop. Two women took over the corner bodega and turned it into a yoga studio, where women in pink camo leggings salute the sun. The Jamaican restaurant has given way to a coffee shop outfitted with a fireplace, free Wi-Fi, and a water bowl for thirsty dogs.

Adam knows I miss the feel of the old neighborhood. The thrift shop felt like an old-world bazaar, its shelves mixed with necessities and handcrafts. Every time I entered the bodega, the owner called out, *Doctora!* and clutched his chest in mock pain. I went into his shop more often than I needed to, but not enough to make his lease affordable.

Adam and I have settled into this new world order, though, and decided that the coffee shop is our favorite addition to the block, especially when the two armchairs by the front window are up for grabs.

I've been dating Adam for almost a year, but we live on opposite ends of the city and work the kind of hours that don't leave much time for play, so a year is not really a year. Adam is in finance, having followed in his father's footsteps. I find his admiration for his dad endearing. Their conversations remind me of my father sharing his work with me as if I were a young apprentice.

I met Adam at an airport bookstore in Chicago. I was standing with a beach read in one hand and an exposé of Big Pharma in the other when he approached me.

The pimps of the medical world, he said, tapping on the orange pill bottle on the book's cover.

I turned to meet his eye.

Well, then. I cringe to think of what that makes me.

Adam let his hands drop to his sides then. He closed his eyes for a beat and then looked at me, head tilted.

You wouldn't happen to be a—

Forgiving person?

I was going to say surgeon. See, he said, pointing to his mouth, *I've got this foot I need removed.*

He asked what time my flight was and if I had time for him to buy me a cup of coffee. I said no, but later saw him standing at my gate. We were boarding the same flight, both of us headed home to New York City. Adam was returning from a college reunion, and I had just given a presentation at a conference.

Adam made easy conversation. He was smart and witty. He made me laugh and seemed genuinely embarrassed about the bookstore comment. He was impressed with my job but didn't feel the need to tell me he could've gotten into medical school if he'd wanted to or talk up the rigors of his profession. He seemed comfortable.

We boarded the plane, and Adam took his seat five rows behind me. I could feel his eyes on the back of my head. Just before the doors closed, Adam walked up the aisle and asked the man seated next to me if he would mind switching seats.

We're old classmates and haven't seen each other in years, he said to the man, who shrugged and accepted Adam's aisle seat. Adam and I sat shoulder to shoulder, thousands of feet above the ground, chatting about our favorite places in New York City, the sorry state of health care, and the likelihood of finding life on other planets in the next few decades.

Aryana, he said as we walked through the passageways of LaGuardia Airport, *got any other trips coming up?*

BEFORE ADAM, I'D DATED ONLY A HANDFUL OF GUYS. SCHOOL AND residency didn't leave much time or energy. I rarely made it past three dates with anyone. Usually about halfway through the second date, I would find myself making a mental list of everything I would be happier doing instead of forcing small talk over fajitas.

Adam caught me by surprise. He suggested we go bowling on our second date even though he's a terrible bowler. Two dates turned into four, then eight. He didn't need to know everything about me all at once. I told Adam that Mom had adopted me when I was very young. I told him about her work at the State Department and all the many places I'd been with her. He liked hearing about her job, and I liked that he found her impressive.

Adam's apartment is on the Upper West Side of Manhattan. My condo is in Queens. The fifteen miles between us easily take an hour to travel, and a minimum of three subway trains. And then we've got our schedules to contend with—the battle of working hours. I am in clinic or the hospital about sixty hours a week. Adam works around fifty hours each week and often has happy hours or dinner meetings to attend. But we have found our relationship groove and make the most out of what we can offer each other.

Sometimes what we offer each other is patience. I've told Adam I never imagined myself getting married, which is true. I blame my job, though it is much more than that. He thinks I'm going to come around because that's what people our age do. And while most of his friends are now fathers, he doesn't want to have children. That's fine with me. I've never thought it was safe for me to bring a child into this world, not with all my sharp edges and dark corners. I accepted long ago that I would be an endling, the last of my kind.

"I want to talk to you about something," Adam says after the barista has set our coffees on the refurbished chess table between us.

"The wedding, I know."

I hate that I've kept him waiting on an answer for so long. We've gone away together just once so far, on a long weekend getaway to the Bahamas, where Adam convinced me to try scuba diving. He's been going since he was a teenager and said that I looked like I'd be a natural. I took long breaths, slow and steady, through my mouth, but still felt like I was suffocating. Everything moved in slow motion underwater. It took forever to see who or what was behind me, or if I was alone. Back on the deck, Adam chuckled and told me it might have taken him a couple of times to get the hang of it too.

"It's not about the wedding," Adam says. "You've got to come for the wedding. You missed the deadline to answer, and the default response is yes. So there we go."

"There's no such thing as a default response for a wedding invitation," I groan.

This trip doesn't involve an oxygen tank, but it does require immersing myself in his family for a long weekend in Connecticut. It's safe to assume I'll be hearing a whole lot about his father's tennis elbow and having my hand squeezed by his mother while she tells me I work harder than any other young woman she knows.

"My cousin's marrying a woman who had to be talked out of an all-black Goth wedding. You are going to make me look amazing, and everyone will love you. But we can talk about that later. I wanted to talk to you about something else."

I curl my hands around my mug and lean back in my seat.

"I'm ready. What's the big news?"

"So," he says. "You know I've been working on getting some of the General Assembly folks to see the light on some of the banking legislation our office helped draft last year. I can't get anyone to introduce anything in session."

I nod.

"I've realized I don't want to ask people to do something. I want to be in the seat to get it done. I'm going to run."

I blink twice before I find my voice.

"What do you mean 'run'?"

"I mean run for office. Get my name on the ballot."

"Elections were a month ago. You mean for two years from now?"

Adam nods, as if I've said something encouraging.

"Exactly. The current assemblyman won his last term by the skin of his teeth. And he's got a couple of small-time challengers, but no one serious. I talked it over with a few of my dad's friends, some politicos, and they think that if I make my rounds in the right circles, I can get that seat."

"Adam," I say slowly, "this is really big . . . and exciting."

He begins to outline the next steps for me. He's already had a call with someone who might help run his campaign. I am stunned by how much has happened since I last saw him, just a week ago.

"It's wild. I mean, I've had this in the back of my mind for a while now, but waiting isn't going to change anything. I think this is the right time."

I am at a loss for words, which is strange for me.

Adam talks about signatures. Fundraisers. Brochures. Party nominations. Kingmakers.

A small knot forms in my stomach, no bigger than a pebble. I shift in my seat and try to focus on what he is saying.

"I can be that guy," Adam insists.

I look at Adam as if for the first time and try to imagine him as a politician. I'm surprised I didn't see it earlier. He is comfortable in a suit and can certainly work a room with his personality. He'll meet someone once and remember the person's name and alma mater and preferred beverage. He makes people feel important for the few minutes they chat with him.

"Of course you can. You'd be great. You will be great. I don't know why I'm surprised."

"I know politics isn't your thing, Ary, but it'll still be fun for you to have a front-row seat to it all," he says, putting his hands over mine and landing a kiss on my lips. I touch his cheek and laugh with him because I want to get this moment right.

Adam asks me about my week, checking in on the status of patients I'd described to him. He's so caring that way, remembering details I've relayed. He hears everything I say. He doesn't tune out while I complain about the new electronic charts at the hospital, or when I tell him the neighbor's cat crawled through the torn screen of my bedroom window for the third time this month.

We leave the coffee shop. Adam is buzzing with a new energy, an excitement he wants to share, and yet I can't help feeling blindsided. We're not married, and even if we were, I wouldn't dream of stopping him. We thrive this way. I have a one-bedroom apartment to my name, and Adam has a place his father passed down to him. We let each other keep our ambitions and independence, even if it keeps us in two different boroughs.

I've carved the life I have out of stone, and stones are not easily carved.

It is Saturday night and neither of us is working tomorrow, so Adam stays over. He has Thai food delivered while I slip away for a quick run. We watch a movie together, and I can see his eyes trained on the car chase on the television screen. His feet are propped on the coffee table, and mine are curled under me, the scar on my sole hidden from him just like the box in my closet.

Though I want to reveal it all to him, it will not be tonight. I envy the look on his face, the ability to focus all his attention in a single direction. I only feel that way in the operating room. Anywhere else, my thoughts are restless and fleeting.

I fall asleep with my head resting on Adam's shoulder, tilted toward him, though I sense we will spend the night dreaming in opposite directions.

CHAPTER 36

"AND THAT'S WITH ONLY ONE GIRLS' SCHOOL. IF THIS MODEL were to be replicated, well, I don't have to do the math for you."

Mom is the least retired retiree there is, which is why I can call her at seven in the morning and chat with her as I'm getting ready for clinic. She doesn't play bridge or watch game shows. She might not be able to keep a plant alive for more than forty-eight hours, but she can get a hundred families to keep their girls in school after they get their periods. She volunteers and serves on boards and still finds time to check in on me.

"Anyway, that's what's on my plate. How are things going on your end?"

"Good enough," I reply. I slip into a pair of black pants and a Kelly green blouse. "Work has been busy. Adam was over this weekend. He had some pretty big news for me."

I see sparks of light in the periphery of my vision. I find an orange bottle in my bag and throw back two white tablets with a swig of water. I don't have time for a migraine today.

"Oh, really? What kind of big news?"

Mom likes Adam, but certainly doesn't fawn over him. I think she's waiting for me to declare that I will love him forever before she vows to do the same, but I worry sometimes that without Mom's explicit approval, I might never take that step.

"He wants to run for a seat in the General Assembly. By the end of next week, it should be official."

"Well, that shouldn't come as much of a surprise," Mom says.

"What do you mean?" I put Mom on speakerphone and tie my hair up in a bun, taming the strays with a touch of hairspray.

"Because he can knock off every box on the politician checklist. Legal background, family connections, friends with money. Not to mention the way he parts his hair. He's got candidate hair."

It's easy to picture Adam shaking hands and kissing babies, standing before a podium and flashing a winning smile to a crowd. If I'd let myself, I would have seen this coming too.

"Candidate hair? Mom, you're terrible. Any other premonitions you care to share with me?"

"I'll check my crystal ball later and get back to you. But tell me, Aryana, how do you feel about this?"

"I don't know. I mean, it's his decision and his career."

I slip into a pair of black patent leather shoes with a low heel. I check my bag for my ID badge.

"Aryana," Mom says. "This is more than just his decision. If he's running for office, that means you'll be involved too. People will want to know everything about him first, but then they'll want to meet his very lovely and accomplished significant other. Did he talk to you about that at all?"

I am silent, which answers Mom's question. I didn't think Adam's run would affect me beyond cutting into our time together.

"Just think about it. Figure out where you stand and discuss it with him," Mom advises. "And if this isn't a good time for me to come down and stay with you, let me know. I can make other arrangements."

Mom lives two hours outside the city, in a quaint town where kids can go on hayrides in the fall and strawberry picking in the summer. There's a main street and a sandwich shop where people know each other by name. She moved there for the quiet nights, the deer that graze in her backyard, and the icicles that form along the eaves of her house in winter.

And it's only a quick train ride away, which gives us both comfort.

"Mom, don't be silly. I can't wait for you to come. I've already made plans for us for that Thursday night."

She's coming into town for her friend's retirement party, but it will also be Mom's birthday. I've bought us tickets to see a revival of *Oklahoma!*, which surprised her. She's noticed that I've been wading further and further away from shore lately, revisiting some moments I haven't thought about in years. The relief in her voice makes me wonder if she'd been thinking I wasn't okay until I volunteered to sit in a theater and watch a musical that reminds me of the night I snuck into my parents' empty home in Kabul.

Mom has reason to worry.

When I was fourteen years old, we lived in Istanbul. Antonia had befriended a circle of English-speaking friends with a few children among them. Even though being around people my own age only made me feel more awkward, I forced myself to engage for Mom's sake. I didn't want her friends wondering what was wrong with her adopted daughter. So I laughed at jokes, traded bracelets, and sang happy birthday—all of which consumed massive amounts of energy.

One night I was one of four girls invited to a birthday celebration by a British girl named Katie. It was a Friday night, and we were holed up in her room listening to Nirvana. Katie and the friends she had invited over from our international school were the good girls, satisfied by a bottle of iridescent nail polish. I had mostly lost my accent by then and looked and spoke like an ordinary American girl, even if I did struggle a bit with slang.

Katie's mom called us downstairs for homemade pizza. We came down the carpeted steps on our heels, our freshly lacquered toes flared. Katie's father, a British businessman, was stretched out on the sofa in the adjoining room watching an old film. We each took a slice and sauntered into the living room.

The actress was dainty and blond, her hair tied back with a black ribbon. She wore an eggshell blouse with a frilly neck and buttons running the length of her back. Her long black skirt swished as she walked. She spoke with a Russian accent, which caught my ear.

What's this movie about, Mr. Shipman? one of the girls had asked.

Anastasia Romanov, he'd said, keeping his voice low and his eyes on the screen. *A Russian princess.*

But Dad, I thought you hated the Russians, Katie had teased, as she descended to the floor cross-legged, a curled slice of pizza in her hand. The rest of us followed the birthday girl's lead.

Mr. Shipman explained that the film was about a woman pretending to be Princess Anastasia, the sole survivor of the execution of the Romanov family during the Russian revolution. No one could confirm her identity because the entire Romanov family had been taken to the depths of a palace and murdered after months of captivity.

I made sure no one noticed that my hands had begun to tremble, that I hadn't taken a second bite of my slice. I slipped away to the bathroom, ran the faucet, and pressed a towel over my mouth to muffle my cries.

Before the girls noticed I was gone, I had already run across two neighborhoods of Istanbul and back into Antonia's arms. Mom fixed it all with a phone call. She'd become very good at explaining my curious behaviors by then.

Anastasia Romanov's story tortured me. I needed to know everything about her. The more I read, the more obsessed I became with her story.

In 1918, after months of being held captive in a palace by the Bol-

sheviks, all members of the Romanov family were executed. Rumors cir-
culated that seventeen-year-old Grand Duchess Anastasia managed to
survive the firing squad and had escaped from the palace. Over the years
several women had come forward claiming to be Anastasia. A suicidal
woman pulled from a Berlin canal lived in an asylum for two years before
declaring that she was the grand duchess and had arrived in New York
City in 1928. She submitted the scars on her body as proof, claiming they
were from wounds inflicted on her by the Bolsheviks.

I remember looking down at my own body when I'd read that, thinking there wasn't a single mark on me, not even the one on my foot, that
could prove my identity. And if I told anyone my story, they might think
me insane as well.

A year after I'd lost my family, a determined geologist, following a
series of clues, found the remains of the Romanov family. The bodies
had been buried, unburied, burned, and doused with sulfuric acid before
being buried again. But instead of broadcasting his discovery, the geologist ran a few secret tests on the bones and buried them once more. There
was still fear, even six decades later, that revealing the truth about the
executions would invite punishment.

It wasn't until 1991, after the fall of the Soviet Union, that the
government allowed an investigation of the remains of the Romanovs.
I was training to become a surgeon when their remains were exhumed
one final time. I showed up at the pathology laboratory to evaluate
thin slices of tumors after reading that the Romanovs had been buried
in the Peter and Paul Cathedral and declared saints. No matter how I
adjusted the dials of the microscope, I could not bring the slides into
focus.

Though two Romanov bodies were still unaccounted for, the world
finally knew what had been done to them.

I was happy for the dead Romanovs—and envious too.

I wish I could say I stopped chasing their story then. But the internet had become my private sandbox where I could go digging into the past—both Anastasia's and mine.

There wasn't much to find on what had happened in Arg that night. Most of it was speculation and didn't offer names of those assumed dead except President Daoud and his brother. I searched for my parents' names, my brother's name, and my own. I found nothing. No one was looking for me, nor had anyone written about my father. And though I was sure someone knew where they'd been buried, I couldn't find a scrap of information about it.

The only news I found was a single line in an online discussion thread stating that my uncle had been killed after the Soviet invasion. There were no other mentions of my extended family.

But I didn't just search for news of my family. I scoured newspapers and the internet for any updates on my homeland. I'd been doing it even when I was still adjusting to life with Mom. Without fail, every tidbit of information I read made me wish I could turn around and share it with my parents, to see their reactions and thoughts.

I cried when I read about the Soviet invasion. A Communist government took over in Kabul. I recognized the man who led the committee. I'd seen him at some events and remember my father saying it was a shame he kept such poor company. He and the Communist committee didn't last. People cried for God's return, for an Afghanistan free of Soviets. The mujahideen answered the call—as did Hollywood. Rambo, with his oiled biceps and oiled machine gun, stood side by side with freedom fighters.

It didn't end when the last weary Russian soldier limped out of Afghanistan. The country was tattered and overrun with militias. From that morass emerged the Taliban with their extreme prescriptions.

The news coming out of the country was gut-wrenching but didn't get much ink. No one seemed to care anymore. The Cold War had been a phenomenon of the eighties and not as interesting after the fall of the Soviet Union. Rambo had gone home, mission accomplished.

It wasn't until the 9/11 attacks that Americans turned their attention back to Afghanistan's caves. I couldn't get away from the country's news then—a manhunt in the caves of Tora Bora, airstrikes on remote villages, girls liberated. Sure, some civilians were dying, but it probably wasn't that many. Who had time for that math? More important were the grandmothers who had walked miles to choose their next president with an inked finger.

When I read about the bags of cash the CIA delivered to the new president of the country, I almost heard my father's voice—*corruption doesn't happen without cooperation.*

My homeland, my story, overwhelms me. Some nights turn into morning and I realize I've been surfing the web for hours trying to make sense of war and politics.

It had seemed safer to focus my energies on a fairy tale, and so I turned to Anastasia Romanov as a healthier option, like snacking on celery sticks instead of fries. But eventually, my obsession waned. I'd read all there was to read about the fate of the Romanovs, and new breadcrumbs appeared only rarely. I had stopped poking around altogether—until last summer. I'd finished dictating the last of my operating reports over the phone in the physician lounge and, on a whim, typed "Anastasia Romanov" into the search box of the internet browser.

They had uncovered more bodies, those of the missing. The DNA tests confirmed that they were the final two missing Romanov children, one set of remains representing each child. Anastasia had not escaped.

I'd stepped out of the physician lounge and called Mom.

She didn't survive, I blurted out. *They found more bodies.*

What bodies? Who are you talking about?

Anastasia.

Mom was silent.

Romanov. Anastasia Romanov.

Mom still said nothing.

Did you hear me? It's confirmed now. She never made it out. All this time, people have been wondering—

Aryana, listen to me. Mom's voice had been steely and low. She sounded like she was trying to reach through the phone line and reset me. *You are not Anastasia. You are you, and you are here.*

Of course, I had said, suddenly understanding how unhinged I sounded. I'd felt a heat creep up my neck as I tried to regain my composure. *I know. I just thought it was interesting.*

If I leave the house now, I can be there in—

Mom, I'm really fine, I'd said to her in a voice I'd perfected—bright enough to reassure but not so saccharine as to alarm her. *And anyway, I'm getting together with Dayo tonight.*

Anastasia Romanov had inspired books, movies, conspiracy theorists, and imposters. People put time and money into investigating her fate. But were they hoping to find Anastasia alive or hoping to prove bullets and blades had ended her too? What titillating truth did people want to hear?

And then there was the darker question, one I was certain I was alone in pondering. And one that I pondered only when I was alone. Had Anastasia lived, would she have wished that she hadn't?

CHAPTER 37

My patient's daughter speaks in a conspiratorial voice, even as she tries to keep her expression neutral. I've just asked her to translate for her mother that her pancreatic cancer is spreading quickly.

Her mother, cachectic and slightly hunched, watches us with minimal interest.

"It's unethical for me to lie to her," I say.

"But she's not *asking* if it's gone into other organs. So you wouldn't be lying," pleads the daughter, a woman in her early twenties. People become experts at finding loopholes when they face losing someone they love.

"It is a lot for you to take this all in and then to translate it for your mother as well. I really do think we should bring in an official interpreter," I say gently. But the daughter hadn't wanted a stranger in the room for this conversation. She hadn't realized that would mean she'd be the one who had to describe to her mother the mechanics of her demise, the brevity of daylight left to her. At the young woman's side was a tote bag heavy with her mother's medical records and bottles of supplements, antioxidants and turmeric and an oil of some rare tree more common back home, where no one seemed to get this kind of cancer.

The daughter took off from work to be here. She has taken many days off work to be with her mother, who cleaned houses so that she would have clothes like her classmates, a pair of roller skates, and the expensive calculator she needed for math class.

My patient puts a hand on her daughter's shoulder. She says a few words to her daughter. Her daughter shakes her head and smiles. The mother looks at me and then back at her daughter. They exchange a few more words, and slowly the daughter's face is transformed.

My patient didn't come here today to find out something she didn't know. She came so that her daughter could hear, from me, the truth behind the ache in her bones, the drag in her step.

She is wearing a paper gown and looking at me imploringly, the thin skin of her hand wrinkling as she comforts her daughter.

"I can see how much you love your mother," I say.

"She . . . she has done everything for me," she replies, her voice breaking with frustration.

Finding the right words is like plucking wildflowers from a tangled brush.

"She put your needs first. Let's work on understanding her needs and wishes now."

The extra time I spend with them sets me back, making me a few minutes late for the next appointment. It is a domino effect, one that happens more often than I'd like because compassion is not easily rationed. I bounce from room to room, checking wounds and scans, charting treatment courses, offering surgery to one patient and a hug to another.

I fall into my office chair to sign off on orders and see a sticky note on my computer screen. It's a web address with my assistant Lacey's signature smiley face on the bottom.

Curious, I type the web address into the browser and see that one of my patients has transformed her food blog into one about her journey from diagnosis to treatment. She's written a post on her first visit with me, when I surprised her by asking about her work and family before asking about her symptoms. I remember her nodding and biting her lip in our last visit. It had taken time to get her talking. She's posted pictures of herself with her family, a tangle of limbs and grins on a scruffy sofa.

I close the browser. Clinic is messy enough as it is. The operating room is a theater sanitized of microbes and emotions. When I bring scalpel to skin, I am gloved and gowned, capped and masked. Patients are transformed too, draped in completely sterile blue sheets so that only the relevant square of skin is exposed.

My cell phone rings.

"What's up, Dayo?"

"My blood pressure," she replies. Dayo was two years ahead of me in residency, where we were the only women in the program. She chose to subspecialize in breast care while I chose oncology.

"What is it this time?" I say, glad to hear her voice. Dayo never gets angry without reason, nor does she ever not turn her anger into action.

"I just sent you something I got from an ER resident. She was intubating a critical patient, and some dude tells her that she looked hot doing it." I hear her greet someone cheerily, then pick up where she left off. "And this dude happened to be her supervising attending. Such bullshit."

"Completely. I'm sure you provided her with some sound advice already. When are you off next week? You owe me tacos."

"People are getting tired of my advice. Reporting this stuff doesn't give anyone satisfaction. Anyway, call me when the taco truck is on your block," she says before she hangs up.

Dayo, whose family had immigrated from Nigeria when she was sixteen, started off as my mentor but became so much more when the city imploded.

I was two months into my fellowship and one hour into a subtotal colectomy when a tech entered the operating room and announced that one of the towers at the World Trade Center was on fire. From then on, updates floated into the room every few minutes. At the news of a second plane striking the second tower, I saw Arg in my mind. The screech of fighter planes strafing the palace echoed in my ear. The smell of cauterized skin sent my heart pounding. If the team in that room could have seen my vital signs at that moment, they would have asked me to take a seat.

But I have trained myself to breathe my way through fire and ash. I focused on the procedure and didn't let my eyes go anywhere outside the surgical field, draped in blue. I made rounds on the floor, checking in on my patients and reviewing labs and doing my best not to look out the windows.

A man in a thin gray gown stood in the doorway of his hospital room, tethered to an IV pole. He looked over at the empty nurses' station. A young nurse emerged from the room next door, her scrubs stiff and her sneakers crisply white.

Please, the man had moaned. He held on to his IV pole with one hand and pressed his paunch with the other. *I haven't taken a shit in three days. Can't you give me something?*

Nothing changed on our unit. Infections and pain, life and death, all carried on as usual.

The city outside shut down, all eyes turned to the news. I stayed in the hospital, not only to care for our surgical patients upstairs but to be available to help. I wasn't the only one.

I walked through the emergency room, where doctors and nurses sat on gurneys or gathered around television screens to see what was happening just a few subway stops away. Rooms and equipment had been readied for the crush of patients that everyone believed would soon arrive. With the number of people working in those buildings, every hospital in New York City was on alert.

We didn't dress a single wound.

People in and around those towers either survived unscathed or died on the scene. There was nothing in between.

Once the wireless networks were working again, I got a call from Mom every two hours. It was a glimpse of what she must have been like in the field, assessing risks, gathering information, and disseminating plans.

Over the weeks that followed, the identities and nationalities of the hijackers were revealed. Fifteen of the nineteen were Saudi. Not one was Afghan, but rumor had it that the mastermind behind the attacks, Osama bin Laden, was hiding in the caves of Afghanistan. The collective heads of the world swiveled toward my homeland. The evening news showed women covered head to foot in bright blue burqas, cowering under the raised switch of a long-bearded man.

For years, I'd scoured newspapers for updates. Now, everywhere I looked, I saw the eleven letters of my country's name, the shape of it becoming as distinct and recognizable as her borders outlined on a map. It had become a country I didn't recognize, in both pictures and principles.

I wanted to shout. I wanted to hide. I wanted to tell people things had been different.

After one grueling fourteen-hour day in the hospital, most of it on my feet, I wanted nothing but a hot shower. Thick gray clouds cast a dreary mood on an already mourning city. I wore a quilted black jacket. I was at the revolving doors, about to exit the hospital, when I realized I'd forgotten my umbrella in the call room. I was so anxious to get home that I stuffed my hands in my pockets and pulled the hood of my jacket over my head to stay dry.

I took the train home. While standing at the crosswalk, I sent Dayo a quick text to ask if she wanted burritos, salads, or Thai. She lived only four blocks from my apartment, so we got together whenever our schedules aligned. I heard someone hollering across the street and glanced up just as I hit Send.

Three men stood on the opposite side of the road, their hair matted with rain. I felt their eyes on me and looked back down at my phone. Plenty of men behaved badly in the subway or on the streets, offering unsolicited opinions on my figure, suggesting I smile or asking for a sip of my coffee.

These men had something different to say.

We're going to bomb your people back to the Stone Age.

Get the hell out of this country.

I felt like my jacket had vaporized. I wanted to turn around but wondered if they would follow. And if I crossed to their side of the street—

The light changed.

They were coming toward me. I stood still, drops of rain cascading down my cheeks and soaking through my jacket. I stood rooted, but not out of bravery.

When they were close enough that I could see they were nothing but ordinary men, one of them made a gun of his fingers and pointed it directly at my head.

All of you.

I stumbled backward, colliding with a trash can full of upturned umbrellas. They were already half a block away when I grabbed the handle of one of the umbrellas and gripped it tightly. I looked around but couldn't tell if anyone had seen or heard anything.

With the broken umbrella still in my clutches, I jogged home, breaking into a run at times and looking over my shoulder.

I didn't realize I was shaking until I tried to slide the key into the front door of my apartment building. I took a deep breath and looked up, catching my reflection in the glass. My eyes were wide and my skin pale. The fleece hood was plastered to my head, making it look like I was wearing a hijab.

I knew why they'd targeted me.

They'd seen me for something I wasn't—a devout Muslim. But they'd also seen me for what I was.

My cell phone buzzed. It was Dayo, saying she would take care of the food. I texted her back that I needed to prep a lecture. Dinner another time, I promised.

I shoved my wet jacket into the front door closet and dropped the umbrella on the floor. I fell onto my sofa and then slowly slid to the floor. I was angry at myself for feeling so paralyzed.

I closed my eyes and saw the guns pointed at my family. The explosions, the smell of artillery, the thuds of their bodies crumpling to the floor. All of it, exhumed and sprawled across the floor in front of me.

I hadn't heard Dayo call my name. I jumped at her touch, shoving the sofa back as I scrambled. Dayo pulled away, as if her fingers had touched a hot stove.

Aryana! What's going on with you?

In all the years she'd known me, watching people live and die around us, Dayo had never seen me like this. She moved my coffee table aside and sat across from me.

I'm not going anywhere.

True to her word, Dayo stayed right there on the floor with me until I managed to right myself. Rummaging through her bag, she found a napkin and handed it to me so I could blow my nose. I told her about my hood looking like a hijab and the things the men had said to me.

Dayo sighed.

Such stupidity, she had said, incensed. *My family in Nigeria has been calling me nonstop. My aunt is telling my mother I should come home right away. This is the same woman who refused to leave her home during the civil war.*

I exhaled slowly and noticed a white plastic bag on the table. Dayo had ordered the food while I was still on the train and picked it up on her way over. It wasn't like me to cancel on her at the last minute, and she'd wanted to check on me.

They really got to you, she said as I rose to my feet. *Why do you think that is?*

I don't know, I said. I wasn't getting much sleep. The city smelled like char. I'd watched two patients die that week. I could have offered Dayo a thousand reasons for my sensitivity.

Dayo would have seen through it, even though, until then, I'd only told Dayo what I'd told everyone else about my past.

I'm going to sit here. You can talk to me or ignore me or go to sleep if you like, but I will not leave you alone like this, she'd said.

I knew her family had lived through a war as well. And now we'd both lived through the ugliest event in New York City's history. I wasn't going to shock her with what I'd seen. Curled on my couch, I told her I'd been dreaming of two soaring towers crashing down on my lost family while I watched from the rooftop of a vacant hospital. Then I told her the rest.

It was so long ago. I don't know why I'm crying about it today.

Lightning and thunder, Dayo said. *You know what happens in a storm? You see lightning before you hear thunder. After the flash, you hold your breath and count the seconds and listen for the bang. You don't hear the bang until later.*

We sat together, watching the news replay George Bush explaining to Americans what motivated the terrorists to attack. *They hate our freedoms,* he said.

Watch people believe him, Dayo scoffed. She turned the television off, went to my CD player, and filled the apartment with U2's music. It wasn't enough to drown out the sounds of the world outside.

Never forget, the city swore.

Never forget, the country echoed.

CHAPTER 38

"KNOCK KNOCK," MY ASSISTANT CHIRPS AS SHE POKES HER HEAD into my office. "I just put the chart in the holder. Room three is ready for you, Doc."

"Got it. Thanks, Lacey."

Lacey's ponytail swings as she half walks, half bounces down the hall. "Or it might be room four," she calls back.

She's a twenty-something-year-old with the personality of sunshine but none of its brightness. She's gone before I can complain.

I pick up the chart she's left for me and see that it's a patient I operated on two years ago. She's done remarkably well and only comes in every six months. Her imaging and bloodwork all continue to look clean, so this should be a pleasant visit.

I open the door with a smile but stop short when I see a man sitting in a chair, staring at the exam table. His face is drawn, and the scruff on his face is a mix of silver and black. He has olive skin and dark eyes. His collared shirt and charcoal slacks hang on him, and he's alone—both ominous signs.

When he sees me, he straightens his back and makes a motion to stand.

"Please," I say, gesturing for him to remain seated. I don't have his chart, so I cannot refer to him by his name. A mistake as simple as walking into the wrong room can knock a patient's confidence out completely and get us off on the wrong foot, so I sit on the wheeled stool and roll myself so that we're face to face. The edges of my white coat hang past my knees. "Thank you for your patience. How are you doing today?"

He meets my eyes.

"Fine, thank you," he says, his English accented. Iranian, I think. I once shocked a clinic nurse when I took one look into the waiting room and correctly guessed a patient was originally from Kyrgyzstan. She told me that if I ever quit medicine, I had a bright career in either the CIA or the circus.

"I'm Dr. Shephard. Tell me about yourself."

He looks at me then, as some people do, seeing something in my face that doesn't quite match my name.

"What do you do?" I ask to nudge the conversation along.

"I work in parking garage."

I picture him dressed in a uniform, sitting in a booth and reaching for credit cards from drivers. I picture him patrolling a dimly lit lot, and suddenly my heart skips a beat. But my eyes do this sometimes, seeing people I cannot possibly be seeing. Usually, I can talk quick sense into my mind, but not now. Not this time.

I roll the stool backward a few inches and take a long look at his face, his hands.

It cannot be.

He clears his throat to tell me more, but I stand. I mumble something that sounds like *Excuse me* and open the door, my hand fumbling on the handle as if it's too hot to touch, as if the office has been engulfed in flames. Red sparks explode in my periphery.

I don't draw a breath until I'm on the other side of that door. I scramble to get in front of a computer.

I could be wrong. Thirty years and thousands of miles stretch between then and now. And in those thirty years, though I am unrecognizable to anyone who knew me as a ten-year-old girl, I've never stopped looking over my shoulder. I arrived in this country disabused of happily-ever-after stories.

I log on and scan the list of names for today's clinic. And then I see it.

I sit back in the chair. An inexplicable laugh escapes my lips. I should not be surprised. Hormones rise and fall in cycles. The earth spins round and round on an axis and moves in an elliptical course around the sun. Nearly everything with momentum ends up back where it started.

I've imagined this moment. I've also feared this moment. I have even searched for him on the internet but didn't get far with only a first name. I have created a hundred different scenarios in which we would meet again, but none of them looked like this.

Abdul Shair Nabi. He's taken on a last name he didn't have in Kabul, but I have no doubt it's him. Shair, the guard who turned his gun on my family, is sitting in a small exam room, waiting for me to see him.

I am shaking, just slightly. The walls of the clinic look like they might fold.

I breathe deeply. I have prepared for this, not knowing when or if the moment would ever come. I can stand before him now as an adult, as a person he cannot silence at gunpoint. For three decades, I have wanted to hold him accountable. I have craved the chance to make him answer my simple questions.

Did you pull the trigger? Where did you take their bodies?

I stand, ready to march into the room and squeeze the answers out of him. But a flicker of doubt flashes across my mind. I can't make a mistake, especially not here. But just seeing his name on the computer screen, I can almost feel his hand clapped over my mouth.

I walk to the exam room, take a deep breath, and compose myself. I am here to ask questions.

"Sorry about that, Mr. Nabi," I say, careful to pronounce the name as if I weren't born with those vowels on my tongue. "I had to check on something rather urgently. Could you come to the exam table please?"

Shair rises and repositions himself at the end of the table. I remain standing.

"So you work in a parking garage?"

"Yes, I have ten years with same company," he says with a note of pride.

"That's a long time. What did you do before then?" I ask, throwing breadcrumbs.

"Before then, I am security guard. I work in office building. Thirty floors," he says. He draws a line from his lap to the ceiling to show the height of the building, and thereby the importance of his job. I nod in appreciation. "But now, I have pain every day," he says, pointing to his sternum. He tells me his doctor sent him for a CT scan that showed it wasn't simply heartburn.

"Have you lost weight?"

He nods.

"Before I am eighty kilos. Now I have seventy kilos."

The pain stops him from eating, not that he's feeling hungry anyway. He's been vomiting too. The mass growing inside him has sent molecules into the air of this room, a metallic and meaty scent.

"Who lives with you, Mr. Nabi?"

His heavy eyebrows form a steeple.

"My wife," he says. "And one daughter."

"Do you have any other children?"

"Two more," he says, then becomes tight-lipped, as if he will offer nothing more about them.

I picture the children staring at me, his son revolted by the blood on my clothes. That boy is a man now.

"Are any of them here with you today?"

He shakes his head.

"No, I'm driving no problem," he says, as if transportation is the issue.

Sons rarely accompany parents to their visits. Typically, it's daughters and spouses who help navigate appointments and medical care. Sometimes I find out a loved one has chosen to sit in the waiting room and needs to be invited in, because there's no way they won't be involved in the care.

It is highly unusual for a man with a family to come alone.

"Does your family know you are here?" I ask.

"I tell them I go for checkup," he says, which means he has kept this to himself.

I pause.

"Mr. Nabi," I say, doing my best to sound curious and not accusing. "Where are you originally from?"

"Afghanistan," he says. "But I am here long time. Fifteen years. I never have this problem before."

This problem is gastric cancer. It has spread beyond his stomach. Strange as it seems, cancers can be ranked, and this is one of the worst ones to have. I tell him he will need surgery, chemotherapy, and maybe radiation. I tell him we will need to take more pictures before surgery, and that he should bring his family in with him when he returns. We must move quickly. I watch for his reaction.

His face is serious, self-possessed. I can already tell he will not share this news with his wife or children because, if he cannot contain the cancer's spread in his body, he will at least control how news of it spreads through his family.

I will not confront him today. I want him to trust me, to come back to me ready to talk.

⁊

ADAM MEETS ME AT THE SUBWAY STATION. I WRAP MY ARMS around him. It's a simple show of affection, but it's taken me a long time to make it look like it comes easy.

"Rough day?" he asks, planting a kiss on my cheek.

"I've seen worse," I reply, taking in the scent of his cologne. I normally don't mind it, but today it tightens the vise on my head. I squeeze his hand before pulling away from him.

Once on an overnight shift in residency, I walked into a conference room where two of my fellow residents were ironing out the details for a website that would help define the rules of dating.

We use algorithms to make sound medical decisions. If we had algorithms for dating, we could create healthier relationships, Danny had said.

Relationships are all managed online now anyway. You find your person online and then click over to our site to not mess it up, Serj replied.

For example. Danny looked down at his notes. *Previous marriage should be date one. Previous engagement should be date three. But snoring?*

Date four, Serj replied.

Regular snoring or the noise your airways create? I had asked. *Having shared a call room with you, I say that needs to be bumped up.*

Damn, Aryana.

They don't call her the ice queen for nothing. Serj laughed. I let it slide. At least he hadn't called me hormonal. *But a child is date one for sure.*

What if you don't have custody?

First date, I insisted.

The list of disclosures had become long and complicated: a DUI, a history of cheating on an exam, a trust fund, car sickness, a personal history of addiction, undesirable recessive genes, cold sores, and a predilection for porn.

They never talked about at what point a person should reveal a history like mine. They didn't even get close.

There is never a right moment to bring up a dark past. It will ruin a good night. It will totally destroy a bad night. I was certain that knowing my history would scare Adam away before I could conquer my demons and let myself sink into this relationship with eyes wide open. I needed time.

At first, it was too early to tell him. In a blink, it became too late.

"Let's get something to eat and you can vent," Adam suggests. Before heading up to my apartment, we stop by two different shops to get our dinner: custom salads, organic brownies, and a bottle of wine. Adam sets the table, and I get a corkscrew out of a drawer. "So. What did you resect in the OR today?"

Adam gets a kick out of using the jargon. And he knows that my worst days are when something goes wrong. Sometimes, that happens during surgery. Tumors grow a lot of blood vessels. Months of chemo changes how organs function. Cancer cells hide in lymph vessels and nodes, out of sight. And even though the disease isn't my fault, I feel responsible for even the smallest complication.

"I have this speech therapist with colon cancer. She's been skipping her chemo because it's not fully covered by her insurance. Such BS. Now she's been having headaches on and off. We sent her to the ER for a head scan, and I have a really bad feeling about what we're going to find."

"That's criminal."

"Yeah. But good luck putting an insurance company behind bars."

"Does she have kids?" Adam asks.

"Two little girls. Of course. All three of them volunteer at the animal shelter together. Of course. Honestly, the best protection against cancer is to be a jerk. Jerks are totally immune."

"Is there any research to support this theory?" He unpacks the salad containers and digs forks out of a drawer.

"Who's going to give out that grant? There's no national jerk lobby."

Adam laughs out loud, and I feel a warmth I can't deny when I look at him, his midnight-blue shirt untucked and sleeves rolled up. He's already changed out of his slacks and into a pair of sweats. To be around him is to have a taste of a life that always seemed beyond reach—a life propelled by the future, not dragged by the past.

I could have a lovely life with Adam. But we cannot have that life if I don't come out of the shadows. I have told myself a thousand times that Adam will still love me even when he knows everything because it changes nothing about me.

And he deserves to know.

Adam sets two wineglasses on the table and watches me pour a rippling vermillion stream into each.

"You're the most amazing woman," he says tenderly. His raised glass shines like a chalice in the hands of a king.

"For not spilling a drop?" I demur.

He drops his head and I press my lips together. It's not the first time I've done this. I take a perfectly warm, loving moment and drop it into ice water.

Back in high school, Mom floated the idea of giving therapy a second try. I refused, but knew there was something wrong with me. In college, I took a couple of psychology classes that helped me name what I was feeling. In medical school, trauma and PTSD and treatment methods were covered in one lecture. For those of us not going into psychiatry, that was the end of it.

I could see my own pathology. I knew why I pushed men away and broke down at the sound of a *tabla* or the smell of my mother's perfume. I read about treatment too. I learned about cognitive behavioral therapy and desensitization and medications that were available. But I'd also heard that medical license applications asked about any history of mental health issues. If I stepped foot in a therapist's office or took a week of antidepressants, they might not license me. I couldn't risk my career to talk through my feelings with someone. I'd been doing the work myself and thought I was making good progress.

"Sorry, hon," I say, walking over to him to offer a kiss. "Forgive this sarcastic girlfriend?"

He looks at me, his face drawn.

"Why do you do this? I don't get it. I've asked you not to, but here we are again."

"It was a tiny joke," I contend.

"They're all tiny little jokes. Everything's a tiny little joke," he snaps.

"Adam, we were setting the table. It's not like we were in the middle of a candlelit dinner."

"Think of how long we've been together, and you still treat the L word like it's a nuclear bomb. It's three little words, Ary. Three little words that could change everything."

"You know I love you. You also know that I'm not the type to profess my love every five minutes."

Adam scoffs. He puts both hands on the kitchen counter and shakes his head.

"It's not a cashmere scarf, Aryana. If you only take it out on special occasions—"

"It'll be moth-eaten and I'll be alone and cold. I understand you're upset," I say, trying to figure out how to deescalate this situation.

"Don't patronize me," he warns. "Hell, it's supposed to be the other way around. I'm not supposed to be the nagging girlfriend."

I throw my hands up in frustration. Does that mean I'm supposed to be the nagging girlfriend? If I profess my love for him right now, he'll say it was forced. And if I don't, I'm still being emotionally frigid. He has boxed me into a corner.

"You win, Adam. You're the emotionally capable one here, and you've managed to prove beyond a reasonable doubt that I'm a callous wench. Point taken."

Just an hour ago, I was thinking it might be time to finally tell Adam the truth about my childhood and maybe even about seeing Shair. Just an hour ago, I loved him.

"This is on you. I've invested a lot into this, and I want to know I'm getting something in return. So don't confuse how we got here."

"We got here by you deciding to act more like a shareholder than a boyfriend," I reply.

He is quiet then, as am I. The furnace hisses, the steam summoned by the chill in the room. It's an argument we've had before, but somehow tonight feels different, heavier.

"We will not have this argument again," he says.

"No, we will not," I agree from the opposite side of the table, two untouched glasses of wine between us.

CHAPTER 39

BOOKS ARE A TINY STRING CONNECTING ME TO MY PARENTS. TO be a reader is to be like them. To be around books and readers has brought me comfort too.

In residency, I studied in a bookstore's coffee shop, which was where a clutch of women gathered monthly for book club. They would set their library books and blueberry scones on the table. I started eavesdropping and realized that the books they read were just an excuse to talk about their own lives. Every character, every broken heart, every twist of fate inspired a story about an unruly mother-in-law, a philandering father, or the cousin who came out to his unforgiving parents. Sometimes it sounded more like a therapy session than a book discussion.

I could never join a book club.

About a year ago, I started attending book talks. I could listen and offer an anonymous comment or none at all.

The bookstore I'm going to tonight is in the middle of a downtown block, between a nail salon and a dry cleaner. I walk past the tables of new releases and the bestseller shelf, picking up a copy of the book being discussed tonight along the way. At the far end of the shop, with the local authors shelf as their backdrop, I see the author and the bookseller sitting on a small dais. I slide into one of the folding chairs toward the back of the space.

Clay Porter is a war journalist who spent time embedded with troops in Afghanistan. I check the time on my phone. Adam is running late. I asked him to join me tonight because I'm hoping this talk will be a stepping-stone to a long-overdue conversation with him. We'll listen to Clay Porter share his experience in Afghanistan and then maybe grab some hot cocoa at the chocolatier at the end of the block, where I will tell Adam all he doesn't know.

The owner of the shop adjusts the ruby-red frames of her glasses and flashes a smile at the small audience. Clay Porter picks up his microphone and lets it hang between his knees while she recites his biography from an oversized index card.

"As any telling of war would be, this is a tough read," she begins. "But it's also a portrait of courage—the men and women in uniform and the civilians in the backdrop. And you as well. You willingly put yourself on the front lines. Did you feel fearless?"

Clay is thoughtful.

"Look, there were risks, but I was more protected than the civilians. I wasn't as much of a target as the soldiers," he says. "And I still wouldn't say I was fearless. I definitely felt fear. And I think all the people you mentioned felt fear too. That's what makes it courage, I guess. Now, courage without fear? That's just bravado."

The interviewer asks him about the people he got to know along the way. Some of the soldiers saw Clay as a confidant. One woman revealed that she'd been sexually assaulted by a superior. She reported the assault, but nothing happened, despite having a witness to back up her claims. Six months later, her superior was demoted—for stealing a cell phone. Another soldier on his second tour said he was almost glad to be back. He wasn't himself at home anymore, feeling too restless and anxious to be with his girlfriend. But he reported none of it, for fear of being classified as unfit to serve.

I'm pretty sure I'm unfit to do anything else, though, he had told Clay.

Adam slides into the empty chair beside me. He takes the book out of my hands, scans the back cover, and hands it back to me.

"Thank you for taking my question," a woman says, her mouth too close to the microphone. From where we're sitting, six rows back, I can see only a mop of curly hair. "Can you talk about what made you want to see this war up close?"

She lingers with the microphone in her hand until the interviewer signals for her to place it back into its stand.

"The thing is . . ." Clay says, shifting in his seat as he gathers his thoughts. He's wearing a black sports jacket over a heather-gray T-shirt. His angular face is shadowed with a two-day stubble. He has dark eyes, softened by lines. He looks old enough to be seasoned but young enough to have more to accomplish.

"I think there are some of us who can't look away. We keep trying to make sense of it all. Let's be real. History books are sanitized, abbreviated versions of the story. One guy assumes power, another guy loses it. But the soldiers and civilians are living this war and suffering the losses. I write about the husband who goes back to his wife in Michigan in a flag-draped casket and the Afghan children shot down during an American airstrike."

The room is chastened, uncomfortable. Adam shakes his head, and I'm not sure if he's taken umbrage with the child casualties or with Clay's cynicism.

"Don't you think we've done enough to clean up these third world countries?" a shaggy-haired man in a white T-shirt asks. I wonder if he came here for this talk or joined in on his way to browse the magazines. "We took the Taliban out for them. They should be responsible for fixing their own problems now."

Clay exhales slowly, as if he's answered this question a few times too many.

"I get the fatigue," he says. "I really do. But it's complicated."

I don't walk up to the mic. I don't even bother to raise my hand.

"We created the third world," I blurt.

Heads turn to follow my voice. Adam seems almost amused.

"Go on," Clay says.

"People say 'third world' and think it just means countries without internet or paved roads," I say. "But 'third world' is Cold War terminology. NATO countries are the first world and the Communist bloc is the second world. The third world was where those two clashed. So the mess in Afghanistan is actually a first and second world problem."

The man shakes his head.

"We didn't have soldiers before 9/11. We didn't make the Taliban. They were there already."

Adam notices I've moved forward in my seat. He puts a hand on my knee, his eyes are telling me to back down.

I seem completely incapable of biting my tongue today.

"The United States has always been willing to slip money and guns to anyone fighting the commies. Anyone. The U.S. didn't meet the Taliban after 9/11. That's just when they became the enemy."

The man in the white T-shirt grumbles and mutters. I lean back in the chair, my heart pounding. The space between Adam and me is tangible. He's shifted in his seat so that he's leaning away.

"What she said," Clay says, pointing at me and smiling.

"Indeed," the bookstore owner says. She flips to her next index card. "There are a lot of layers to the conflict in Afghanistan. Let's switch gears and talk about some of the surprises you found in Kabul. We never hear about lounges. Tell us about the Mirage."

Adam takes out his phone, which is glowing with two new messages.

"Gotta return this call. Shouldn't be long," he whispers as he ducks out of the store.

When the talk ends, Clay Porter sits at a table near the checkout desk to sign books. Three people have lined up to have their books personalized. A woman hovers behind Clay, thanking his interviewer for arranging the talk. I'm standing on line to pay for the hardcover in my hands when Clay approaches me.

"Thanks for kicking up the conversation a notch," he says. He tucks his book and pen into his messenger bag.

"I have a bad habit of saying what I'm thinking," I reply.

"Honesty? Yeah, that disqualifies you from a whole lot of jobs."

When I smile, Clay narrows his eyes slightly.

"Are you Afghan?" he asks. I'm taken aback. I thought he would ask me where I was from—not identify me.

"Does everyone look Afghan to you now?" I ask, with a laugh, a bit unnerved.

The woman speaking with the interviewer looks over at Clay without pausing in her conversation. She has long brown hair and is smartly dressed, like she fell out of a J.Crew catalog. She looks from me to Clay with curiosity.

"Anyway, thanks. This was great," I say and turn to hand my credit card to the cashier.

"What do you do, if you don't mind my asking?" His tone is casual.

"I'm a physician," I reply.

"What kind?"

"Surgeon," I say.

The long-haired woman, his wife or girlfriend, promptly joins our conversation.

"I hope you enjoyed the talk," she says to me, cheerily.

"Selena, this is . . ." Clay looks at me to fill in the blank.

"Aryana," I say. "And I'm very much looking forward to reading this. Good meeting both of you."

I stuff my receipt into my bag.

"Did you want him to sign your copy?" Selena asks. "You don't mind, do you, Clay?"

Since it would be awfully rude to decline the offer, I turn around. Clay pulls a pen out of his bag and takes the book from my hands. He flips it open and scribbles something on the title page.

"Did I hear you say you're a surgeon? I love that!" Selena says. She has Audrey Hepburn eyes, coquettish and warm. "My father was in a car accident three months ago. He woke up and found out a woman surgeon had stitched his liver back together. He's such a chauvinist that he actually asked if a male surgeon could redo it. That woman saved his life."

"I'm glad he did well," I say. I've met men like her father. I've also met quite a few women like her father. Turns out sexism doesn't discriminate.

Clay closes the cover and returns the book to me.

"Very good to meet you, Doc," he says.

As I push the door open, I hear Selena suggest a sushi restaurant to Clay. I hit the sidewalk and look for Adam. He is walking toward the corner, his phone pressed to his ear. He pivots on one heel and walks back toward me, and I can hear his conversation as he nears me.

"Not even close, bro. You need to bring me ten people and at least one corner-office big dog. Anyway, I gotta run. Yep, later," he says and ends the call.

"Sending Gavin your Christmas wish list?" I ask, trying to sound casual.

"The fundraiser's next week. And he owes me one anyway," he says, then suggests we go to the diner on the next block. He asks me when Mom's coming into town, although I'm sure he hasn't forgotten. We've both been tiptoeing around each other since our last night together, as if we're afraid to wake a sleeping argument. "Look, Aryana, I've been thinking. A lot actually."

I stop walking. His words are like a trumpet sounding before an announcement. Adam stands with his back to a nail salon. Hanging in the window is a poster of ten toes airbrushed into perfection, a red rose laid across the feet. It's such a saccharine backdrop that I almost ask if we can stand somewhere else.

"I think we're amazing and I love you. I just need you to tell me those walls aren't going to be up forever."

Adam isn't wrong to ask this of me. If I want this relationship, any relationship, to work, I'm going to have to figure out how to be more open. I cannot rely on a book talk to do the work for me, and I cannot choreograph the perfect moment.

"We are amazing," I tell him. "And walls are not. I get that. So I'll work on the walls."

I want to tell him his nagging girlfriend comment got under my skin, but decide against it. I don't want to be accused of being petty. I'm in new territory with this relationship, and it shows.

Adam smiles, satisfied.

"That's all I needed to hear, Ary," he says and resumes walking before I can wrap my arms around him for an embrace. "Tomorrow is big. We're officially announcing the campaign. I found a shark of a campaign manager. He's on a winning streak."

"That's incredible," I say, and I mean it.

When the waiter has jotted down our orders, I take a long sip of water and tell Adam I wish he could have heard more of the book talk.

"Yeah, you know me. I'd rather watch the movie. You went a little hard on that guy in there, though. No more documentaries for you, Ary."

Beads of condensation have collected on the outside of my glass. He doesn't know, I remind myself.

I think of the time I saw Adam give a best man's speech at his friend's wedding in New Jersey. I've given plenty of medical lectures to rooms of physicians without any qualms, but to speak on so important an occasion would have made me anxious. Adam was not. He walked the dance floor with a swagger I'd not seen before. Mic in hand, he talked about the time they'd gotten lost driving to Montreal and the time he'd been sick as a dog and his friend had brought him a can of expired chicken noodle soup. After a few claps on the back and a hug from the groom, Adam returned to his seat next to me, beaming.

All through dinner and as I walk home alone, I wonder why I struggle so to tell my story to a crowd of one, especially when that one is Adam.

CHAPTER 40

ADAM HAS JUST RETURNED TO THE TABLE. OUR SCHEDULES ARE so mismatched these days that we only meet up for food. He has been chatting up the owner of the restaurant, asking him what challenges he's been facing as a small-business owner and slipping him a freshly minted business card. He has a new energy about him, a little like a guy who tried to sell me disability insurance. I keep that observation to myself.

"I don't know how you do it," I tell him when he slips back into his seat and signals for the waiter to bring the check. "You can strike up a conversation with anyone."

"It's not magic. I told him my uncle ran a restaurant in Connecticut and I know how tough it is."

"Do you know how tough it is to run a restaurant?"

"Must be. My uncle never looked happy," Adam says. "I'm assuming it was the restaurant that was pissing him off."

"Makes good sense." I shrug. "So things are going well?"

"A week in and no major scandals," he says. "You should have seen the way Vigo grilled me before he joined the campaign. Made me swear on a Bible that I had no skeletons in the closet. I told him about that one college party and the weed, but he said that was forgivable."

"So nothing to worry about then."

"Yeah. They'll seek, but they shall not find."

"Do you really think they'll try to dig stuff up?"

"Depends on how tight the race gets. I've sworn everybody around me is clean too, so if you have any illegal side hustles, I don't want to know."

He's joking, but my stomach drops. I couldn't get my thoughts straight over dinner and need some quiet to figure out how to handle this. Adam suggests we go for a stroll. Outside, I tie my hair into a messy bun and tuck my long bangs behind my ears. The evening air feels good on my neck. Adam checks his phone and taps out a few quick replies. It's impressive to see what he's done in such a short time, how naturally this all comes to him.

We wander into Bryant Park, past two men playing chess and a mom chasing a giggling toddler. Adam stops and holds his phone at arm's length. He puts an arm around me and snaps a photo of us, him beaming and me with a surprised smile. He kisses my cheek and leads me to a vacant bench.

Squirrels bounce and run at our feet. A group of teenagers stands in a huddle. Two girls in thin jackets pretend not to feel the cold. A woman in a hijab walks past them with her husband.

Adam takes a deep breath.

"Aryana, I've been trying to figure out the best way to do this. I think we need some direction. We've been dancing around this for a while now, and maybe we should just take that next step."

He can't possibly mean what I think he means. We're facing each other, each of us with one foot on the ground. His arm hangs over the back of the bench.

"I'm not sure what you mean by 'next step,'" I say. I did not see this conversation coming.

"We're adults. We're professionals. I'm kicking off a really big next chapter in my life, and I want you to be there with me for it—officially. But before I get out here and make a big old fool of myself, I thought it might be smart to ask how you feel about that."

"Adam, right now? I mean, we just had a pretty rough conversation the other night."

"No need to go back there," he says firmly.

"Of course, but . . . wow. Babe, I'm so proud of what you're doing and excited for you. Yes, I want to be there for it all."

He leans in closer, puts a hand over mine, and speaks the warmest words I've ever heard from him.

"I want to wake up to you every day. I don't want to text you to find out what you're doing. I want to be more than your date. I know asking for more than this is a lot for you, but I think we deserve to give us a real shot. Officially."

Officially? I should be swooning. But I had so much I wanted to tell him tonight. I was going to leave nothing out.

But how can I tell him that I sometimes soak in my grief? That I dream of one day finding where my family is buried and laying flowers at their graves? That I have kept all this from him until now?

And if he's changed his feelings about marriage, then is he changing how he feels about children? Does he think I'm going to change how I feel about children? I already know I won't. I wouldn't wish myself as a mother on any child. I think of my mother and know that I could never be as present or as patient or as gentle as her. No child deserves any less.

I've thought a lot about how tightly my mother clung to us because she'd already lost my sister. Her scars were visible. And I know what I saw in her face in that final second of grief and that grief would have killed her if a bullet hadn't.

I am not as brave as my mother. I don't dare make myself as vulnerable as she was, taking a chance that might break me all over again.

"So, let me hear it, Ary. Are you ready for this? Do I renew my lease or not?"

I bring my face to his, hold my hand against his cheek. There is excitement in his eyes.

"I did not see this coming," I tell him. "My head is spinning a little, to be honest, but in a good way. Give me a little time to get my thoughts straight. Can you come over tonight?"

Adam shakes his head, but he looks encouraged.

"I have to be in the office early. What about tomorrow?"

I tell him if things move smoothly with my surgeries, I might get out at a reasonable hour. There's a frisson of excitement between us for the rest of the night as we make room for new possibilities.

I take the train home around nine o'clock. It's too late to get a run in. I need to be up early so I'll have time to review the scans before heading into the OR tomorrow morning. The subway car winds around a bend, torquing the passengers in one direction and then another.

The man to my left flips a newspaper open. I see a headline about a city council member with $2,000 of unpaid parking tickets.

What kind of world is Adam entering? Is it possible to steer clear of all that comes with public life? Will the spotlight fall on me too? I cross my legs and fold my arms over my bag. No one on the train notices my discomfort. People are too busy to notice me, I tell myself.

I cannot wait for the perfect moment to tell Adam what I've kept from him. I can start with my parents and my brother. I can begin in the years when tulips dotted the gardens and music floated from open windows. If I start there, maybe I can get through the rest.

But I already know I will leave out some details.

I cannot tell him that there are nights when I wish I hadn't crept into the basement of Arg alone but instead floated in sacred company to the stars above.

Antonia and I moved back to the United States for my last two years of high school. By then, girls already had best friends and social circles. When a girl named Martine befriended me, I was grateful. She was similarly an outsider, though in her case it was because she suffered from allergies so severe that to be around her came with balls of wadded tissues and constant sniffling. Martine said we didn't have to wait on a boy to give us permission to be part of prom and suggested we go together. I liked her reasoning and agreed to be her date.

We bought long, flowy dresses and heels we could barely walk in. Martine's mother was a hairdresser, lucky for us. She tried different hairstyles and eyeshadow shades on us for an entire month leading up to that May weekend. Antonia was going to drive us there, and Martine's father was going to pick us up. Three days before the prom, Martine walked up to my locker and told me that she'd been asked out to prom by a junior. When she didn't say anything more, I realized she was waiting for me to be excited for her.

It was small and frivolous and never should have sent me careening. I missed the next three days of school, staying home to brood about what a terrible person Martine was and wonder how I'd allowed myself to look forward to something as dumb as prom. I went back to school the Monday after prom weekend. Martine avoided me, put off by my sullen face and the way I clanged my locker shut between classes.

Antonia spent those evenings, and so many others, plucking thorns from my soul.

You miss them, she said. *That's grief, and grief is nothing but the far brink of love. Love is the sun, grief is the shadow it casts. Love is an opera, grief is its echo. You cannot have one without the other. But if you follow that grief, you'll find your way back to love. You haven't let yourself do that yet, and you need to—in your own way. So cry, scream, run, sleep, pray, or write love notes in the sand. But grieve, so you can get back to love, because love is a better place to be.*

I brush my teeth and slip into pajamas remembering Mom's words. She'd shocked me then, connecting my reaction to prom with the hole in my heart.

In the last decade, taking care of patients, I've learned more about grief.

Mothers lie on stretchers next to hospital beds, drinking in their children's faces while they can. Husbands sit in waiting rooms holding cups of coffee that went cold long ago. Brothers show up with gift-shop teddy bears, wishing they could rewind the years.

Grief starts before anyone has gone missing.

I roll onto my side and squeeze my eyes to shut out the light of the pale moon.

CHAPTER 41

I AM ON THE NUMBER 7 TRAIN GOING HOME, MY FINGER RUN-
ning over the edges of a square of paper on which I've written an address
while reviewing scans and upcoming appointments. Shair will return to
clinic in two days to hear me explain how best to keep him alive, a discussion I may be uniquely unqualified to lead in this case. I don't stand up
when the train reaches my station. Instead, I watch the doors slide closed
and watch the brick buildings blur as the train accelerates. The number
7 train rumbles deeper into the borough that is a compressed capsule of
the world.

I massage the angles of my jaw, feel the knotted muscles of my face. I
am grinding my teeth more. Adam has told me it sounds like nails dragging across a chalkboard. When I was younger, Mom tried rubbing my
back before bed, reading me soothing stories at bedtime, and even had me
treated for parasites. Nothing stopped it. After I fractured a tooth, Mom
had a custom guard made for me. It doesn't stop the grinding but has
saved me from breaking more teeth. I try not to let Adam see me wearing
it, which he thinks is vanity.

The doors open and I get off, jostled by people in a hurry to hit the gym or get home to a husband or to a teenager who favors television over homework. As I walk away from the station, the roar and clack of the train fades behind me. I did not pack an umbrella, which is enough to guarantee rain. The sky starts to drizzle. Cold droplets fall on my hair and stipple the concrete sidewalk. Though my wool coat is lined, I can almost feel the dampness through the layers. I move my nylon bag full of notes I still need to chart to my right shoulder.

I will get to them eventually.

My eyes stay on the rise and fall of the round toes of my flats.

Plenty of my colleagues live outside the city. They have cars and front yards and walk-in closets. I prefer the crowds, the small footprint. When I'm hungry for air and space, I take the train out of the city and visit Mom. We pick out zucchini and heirloom tomatoes at farm stands and stroll down the town's Main Street. From her balcony, the sky looks like a page out of an astronomy book. I've shared a lot with her, breathing in the clean air.

I have not yet told Mom about Shair. If I were to tell her, she would be rational and protective of me, and I am determined not to let rational thought get in my way right now. I'm keeping too much to myself these days. I'll fix this all soon.

I've been to this neighborhood before, once to find a sari for the wedding of a medical school classmate. As I wandered in and out of shops, Bollywood music floated into the streets, just as it had in Kabul. I peered into the window of a fried-chicken store and saw a man who was surely Afghan handing a white paper bag to a customer.

Decades ago, Horace Bullard, the son of a black plumber and a Puerto Rican mother, started the Kansas Fried Chicken franchise, one-upping the recipe of Kentucky Fried Chicken by adding a dash of Puerto Rican *sabor*. Rumor had it that he selectively sold his stores to Afghans because they'd taken up arms against the red flag of communism.

The Cold War, battered and deep-fried, played out in Harlem and

Flatbush. Afghans, their clothes splattered with cooking oil, became soldiers of capitalism and the American Dream. I watched the numbers of Afghans in the country multiply as more and more families fled the war and resettled in New York and northern Virginia and San Francisco.

The year we lived in Istanbul, Mom asked me if I wanted to attend a Kurdish Nowruz celebration. I couldn't resist the chance to revisit a holiday of my childhood. We watched heavy-bosomed grandmothers stand shoulder to shoulder in white dresses dotted with colorful pom-poms, kicking their feet in synchrony. I saw men leap over fires, cheered on by brothers and friends. A grandfather sang a ballad, his fingers plucking the strings of a tanbur.

It reminded me so much of home that I closed my eyes and listened, exchanging the Kurdish songs for ones stored in my heart. I felt the ground pulse with vibrations from the hundreds of people gathered to welcome a new year.

But when I opened my eyes, I saw a squadron of helmeted Turkish police officers closing in. I grabbed Mom's hand, and she followed my gaze. Batons struck the backs of silver-haired men and women wearing embroidered vests, and shrieks filled my ears as we ducked into a narrow alley, knocking over a stand of copper vases on our way. We did not speak until we were in the safety of a taxi on the other side of the neighborhood.

The government was seeking to stamp out Kurdish traditions, and Mom was furious at herself that she hadn't foreseen the crackdown. No one, though, had anticipated the Turkish reaction to the Nowruz celebration. We both steered clear of nostalgia after that. I told myself it would get easier with time.

But I am still drawn to my people. I have watched from afar as the country sank into civil war and then resurfaced with a new, fundamentalist face. I saw pictures of men with rockets on their shoulders and imagined the roofs falling, the barefoot survivors running toward a border. My ears perk up when I hear my mother tongue. I have dug up old songs on the internet and had small conversations with myself in Dari in the privacy of my apartment.

I look up at the apartment buildings on this block and wonder how many windows belong to people who used to be someone else too. Taking a seat on the low cement wall in front of one building, I look at the six-story structure across the street. Its glass-enclosed lobby holds two black armchairs and an artificial ficus plant.

The rain continues to come down gently while I wait.

My phone rings. If I answer Mom's call, I will lose my nerve. I text her that I'm still at work and return the phone to my pocket.

People enter and exit. I stare at their faces and try to rewind the years.

After an hour, I cross the street and enter the vestibule. I run my finger down the directory, a gray panel with dozens of slots. NABI is in apartment 5B. The outside door opens, and a woman enters, a cell phone pressed to her ear.

"Yes, yes. But no movie for the kids. Mom, that's not a good idea," she moans. I take a step back to give her room to get through.

"Do you need to get in?" the woman asks me, moving the phone away from her mouth as two bags of groceries dangle from the crook of her arm. A few inches shorter than me, she has the slightest hint of an accent. She tips back the hood of her rain jacket before fishing keys out of her pocket.

"No thanks," I say and flash a smile. "I'm waiting for someone to come down."

She nods, unlocks the door, and enters the lobby, where her voice echoes against the tiled floor and walls.

"Madar-*jan*," she says, shifting into Dari, "can we have this conversation face to face in one minute? I'm in the lobby."

I cannot stop my head from swiveling to have a second look at her. She must have sensed me watching, because she turns back too. I blink and look away. In a different life, I might have done exactly as she is doing right now—asking my mother if the matter can wait until I walk through the door.

But Shair's daughter and I have led two very different lives. I don't expect her to recognize me. I don't know what her parents told her about me once I left their apartment.

Facing the street, I pretend to check my phone. I hear a ding and imagine her disappearing behind the closing doors of the elevator, ascending to the fifth floor of the building, and making her way into an apartment that I imagine looks just like the one in Kabul's Macroyan apartment complex.

"This is not Kabul," I whisper, to stop myself from sliding headlong into the past. I leave the building and head back home.

As the train pulls into the station at my stop and the brakes screech to a halt, I think about the tracks that run directly between my home and Shair's apartment. Seeing him has reminded me of my early years here. Since the day he reappeared, my sleep has been fitful, conversations exhaust me, and running doesn't bring the relief it always has.

Whatever is about to come will either give me the answers I've been waiting for or unravel me completely.

CHAPTER 42

SHAIR RETURNS TO CLINIC TODAY, AND I HAVE METICULOUSLY
planned the details of our encounter. I have him scheduled as the last
patient of the day so that I can take my time and not worry about keeping anyone waiting on me. I have asked that he be brought into the room
farthest from the reception area so the staff does not overhear our conversation. I have pulled my hair into a high bun to stretch my height.

My phone buzzes with a text from Adam.

Morning. Sleep well?

Not at all, but I keep this to myself.

Morning to you too. You're up early.

Adam generally isn't up at this hour. He's a night owl, fueled by energy drinks and the rush of deadlines.

Not exactly. Pulled an all-nighter with my team. We came up with some great ideas.

That's good! I want to hear about it. You should get some sleep first, I reply.

I grab my bag and lock my apartment door behind me. The hallway
is dimly lit and quiet as I walk toward the elevator bank. The smell of
coffee tells me at least one of my neighbors is up.

I press the button and my breath catches in my throat when I see my hazy reflection in the elevator doors. I'm wearing an olive blouse tucked into a deep brown skirt. My cardigan has wooden buttons, and the gold of my necklace catches the light.

It shouldn't surprise me that I look like my mother. I buy clothes that remind me of her, dresses and skirts that I can hang in my closet to imagine I am a child peering into my mother's wardrobe. I have outfits that resemble each of the ones she is wearing in the photographs I snuck out of Kabul.

My chest tightens. I am sitting at the foot of a volcano, heat slithering toward me. I take a step to the side so I can no longer see my reflection and pull out my phone to distract myself. Adam hasn't fallen asleep yet it seems.

Met with my finance team yesterday. Things going well. Dollars rolling in but we need to widen the circle. Been meaning to talk to you about that. Maybe tonight?

I feel myself stiffen. It will take some effort to get used to Adam's new world, his priorities. Meet-and-greets and drinks with donors, interviews, and his face on flyers. I wonder what my father would make of this world, of the money and the spinning of stories. Once Adam knows everything, he'll understand why I've eschewed politics in any form until now.

Adam's also forgotten that Mom's coming into town today.

Taking Mom to see Oklahoma! *tonight, remember? Call me later. Congrats on the dollars!*

I roll my eyes. *Congrats on the dollars?* The longer I stare at the screen the more ridiculous the words look. I have never celebrated money. But I cannot unsend it, so I put the phone away and ready my metro card.

Clinic moves at a frantic pace. I check the schedule every chance I get to be sure Shair hasn't called in to cancel. Lacey's hair is faint pink at the ends. She is wearing glasses with lilac frames. When she hands me a chart, I look up and see that the glasses don't have lenses.

"Lacey, your glasses are . . . missing?" I say, baffled.

Lacey laughs and taps the hinge of her frames, then presses her fingers to her lips like we have some inside secret. I envy how lightly she moves through her day.

I do not eat lunch. I see one patient after another, one family after another. I'm on my third cup of coffee and feeling like my heart might pound out of my chest when I sit with a forty-year-old man diagnosed with a tumor that is choking off his small intestine. He works as a docent at a museum. His wife holds their one-month-old girl in her arms. The baby's mouth makes small sucking movements as she sleeps, and small as she is, she has filled the room with that newborn scent—talcum and milk. His wife looks like she hasn't slept in days. She rocks her child closer to her chest, as if cancer might jump off the counter and sink into her pink skin. I know this is the last time they'll bring the baby to clinic.

I see a woman in her fifties who is a sculptor and a dance teacher. There is less of her than at our last visit, as if she's wet clay on a pottery wheel, being reshaped into something new. I'd seen her three months ago, but on the day of surgery she called the office and said she was going to try homeopathic treatments recommended by her friend.

"I am glad to see you again."

"I don't know how this happened. I did a lot of research. I thought this would help more," she says, her voice small.

"It is not your fault. There's nothing you did wrong," I say. Even heavy smokers are shocked when they are diagnosed with cancer. Not one person I've ever cared for has seen it coming.

"I know. It's everywhere now," she says. "I think it's in our food. We're probably stuffing our mouths with it and wondering how it gets into us. Why aren't they researching this?"

"We don't have all the answers," I admit.

I manage to steer the conversation back to her disease and her treatment, conscious of the fact that she may not be wrong. And that my work is a little like trying to drain the ocean with a bucket.

All the while, I sense the ticking of the clock. Shair is my next patient.

Lacey hands me his chart when I come out of the room.

"In a gown, as you requested. Doubt you'll be in there long. He's not much of a talker," she says.

I stand outside the door for a beat. When I step into the room, Shair draws his shoulders back. He is perched on the exam table, his legs dangling over the side. His calves are thin, tendinous. The years have not been good to him. I picture him standing in the elevator of his building, breathing in the mixture of sweat and spices and car exhaust.

"Welcome back, Mr. Nabi," I say. As I shut the door behind me, I see that he is not alone. The woman I saw in the lobby of his building sits in the visitor's chair, legs crossed. She has placed her handbag and her father's neatly folded clothes on the chair beside her.

"Hello, I'm Dr. Shephard," I say. I do not reach out to shake her hand as I normally would. "How are you related to Mr. Nabi?"

"I'm his daughter," she says, looking over at her father. She does not recognize me from the lobby.

Shair mumbles something in greeting, but I cannot hear him over the roar of my own thoughts. I tuck the rolling stool under the sink. I will not sit today. I will not be diminished in any way.

"Your father mentioned you in his last visit," I say. I set his chart down on the counter. "It's good of you to be here with him today."

She nods.

"I would have come last time if I'd known. He doesn't tell us . . . didn't tell us about the appointment."

"This is not your fault," I tell her. "We've got a lot to talk about—good and bad. I've reviewed the imaging of his abdomen."

His jaw tightens, and he looks at his daughter from the corner of his eye. She fidgets in her seat, tries to find the right posture to receive what I am about to say.

"But he said his pain is in his back. Is this for the heartburn?"

I lean against the edge of the counter. I feel pity for his daughter, despite everything.

"Has he not discussed his diagnosis with you?"

She looks again at her father, but he raises an eyebrow in my direction. He wants me to tell her. I give her a moment to brace herself. Everyone deserves that much.

"He has stomach cancer," I explain, and she pales at my words. "It has spread beyond his stomach."

She plants both feet on the floor, blinks rapidly.

"Are you sure? I don't think . . . he quit smoking a long time ago," she says in an attempt to redeem him. "How many years has it been?"

"Not every cancer is caused by smoking," I reply. I am usually warmer with patients. I don't like that I'm a different doctor right now, but there is so much more happening in this room. "Mr. Nabi, you'll need surgery. I can remove most of the tumor."

I review the details, half of which they will forget. Words like "chemotherapy" and "radiation" sound more and more like "nuclear" and "apocalypse" in a room like this. I list the risks and benefits of treatment, which is like sitting two elephants on opposite ends of a seesaw.

"You can take time to think about this, but I wouldn't wait too long to decide. The sooner we act the better the results will be."

"You do the surgery?" he asks me.

"Yes," I say, though I've already decided I won't. Once I've had a real conversation with him, I will refer him to one of my colleagues.

Shair uses the palm of his hand to brush his hair to the side. He clears his throat.

"If I don't do this surgery," he says calmly, "what is happening?"

"*Boba!*" His daughter's eyes brim with tears. Her voice is a hoarse whisper as she makes a single plea to her father—*please.*

"It is a fair question. If you choose not to have surgery, the cancer will continue to spread. It will become more difficult for you to eat. You will continue to lose weight and become weaker. And it will continue to spread."

His daughter's eyes fill with tears. A small whimper escapes her lips.

"How much time? With surgery and without surgery?"

"It's hard to say. Without surgery, maybe three months. With surgery, perhaps a year or two. It really depends on how the tumor responds to chemotherapy and radiation as well."

His breathing fills the silence.

"What are you most worried about?" I ask automatically. I have not forgotten who I was when I first met Shair, nor can I forget who I am standing before him now. And I want to know everything about him, including the fears he harbors.

"I don't want," he says, then shakes his head and points to his open mouth, his stomach, the insides of his elbows. "I don't want tube, tube, tube, and machine."

His daughter mumbles something under her breath.

"I have pain," he admits. "Too much."

"I understand," I say. "We have several medications that can treat the kind of pain you have. Looks like you have a good understanding of what you want for treatment. Tell me, what kind of work did you do before you came to this country?"

Your Kabul is gone, he had said the night he took me to Antonia.

"He was a high-ranking general," his daughter manages to get out, her voice choked.

"A soldier," I say, knocking the stars off his epaulets with a single word. "I see. And where was this?"

"In Kabul. Afghanistan," his daughter replies, but I keep my eyes on Shair.

"Such a shame, what happened to that country," I say, shaking my head. "Were you in the army back when it all started?"

"You know my country," Shair says. He tilts his head, curious.

"Quite a history. Did you see the beginning of it all in '78?" I ask.

He lets out a long breath and nods.

Tinny music erupts from his daughter's purse. She pulls out her phone and answers it.

"Yes, Madar," she says, speaking in Dari. "We're talking to the doctor now. I can't talk to her now, Madar. Fine, but quickly."

She steps out of the room, the phone pressed to her ear.

I wonder if he will speak more freely with his daughter out of the room and if she knows what kind of man he really is. Shair shifts on the exam table. Paper crinkles under his thighs, making his every fidget obvious.

"Doctor, where you are from?" he asks me.

I respond with a tight smile. He doesn't get to ask me questions and certainly not ones about my family. I feel a small pulse of satisfaction at letting his question go unanswered.

"It was a beautiful country then, wasn't it?"

My voice nearly breaks. I focus on my breathing as I wait for him to answer.

"Yes, but people," he says, wistfully. "People make it for waste."

I have made fake profiles to enter chat rooms and join discussion boards to listen to people who remind me of my parents, people who share black-and-white pictures of Kabul fashion shows and laboratories with women holding test tubes. They post snapshots of hippies from the West and Indians on vacation in Kabul. They came for the pearly grapes, for the kebabs sprinkled with sumac, for the crystalline lakes and healing shrines.

He looks out the window of the exam room.

I remember the night he grabbed me by my neck and pressed my face to the car window.

Your people are gone.

"The coup must have been a very dangerous time, especially for you as a soldier."

Shair shrugs.

"It is gone now. Finish," he says.

I clear my throat.

"I read about what happened in the palace. There was a coup, right? What happened to all the people who were there that night?"

Shair is staring at the paper towel dispenser across from him. Or perhaps the diagram of the gastrointestinal system just beside it. Somewhere on the wall is a black hole that is slowly, steadily, sucking him in.

"And wasn't it a military coup? The army turned against the president. All those people in the palace thought the soldiers were there to protect them. Do I have it right?"

Shair's nostrils flare, his eyes shine. I am pulling at a loose thread.

"I am one man," he says. His voice teeters, then comes close to breaking.

"There were innocent people there. People who trusted you. People who treated you kindly."

His daughter steps back into the room. She takes one look at her father's face and becomes alarmed.

"*Padar?* What's going on? Is he okay?"

I don't turn away from Shair. He is crumbling, and I want to hear every word that comes out of him.

"What man can stop a river?" he asks, then slips into Dari. "What man can stop a river? This is God's river. I am nothing. God is God."

"Oh, *Padar*," Shair's daughter cries, thinking he is lamenting the future when his mind is on the past. "God is good. He will take care of you."

Shair's daughter wraps her arms around her father.

Tears slide down his cheeks, and he wipes them away with the pale palms of his hands.

His daughter stuffs her phone in her back pocket and sniffles loudly. She turns back to the chair and fishes in her purse until she finds a packet of tissues. In all my meticulous planning, I did not anticipate how it would feel to see his daughter with him. I wanted to loom over him and press him for answers. I wanted to pin him on the role he'd played that night as a traitor.

I step toward Shair, lean in close enough to him that I am reminded of the night he told me to play dead and carried me to a truck.

"You will tell me where they're buried," I whisper in his ear in Dari, my voice breaking. "You will tell me everything."

I slip out of the room and close the door behind me. Shair groans, and my throat threatens to close.

"So you've brought me here for this," he says, sounding almost amused. "Everyone waits on a darkening sky and the heavy fogs, but here is Judgment Day. I never expected to escape it. I never did."

"*Padar*, what are you saying?" his daughter cries.

I grab my bag from my office and sneak out the back door of the clinic before Lacey or anyone can see my wet cheeks. He is no longer a lion. And I am no longer a little girl.

I melt into the crowd outside, absorbed into the thrum of a city that has taught me never to forget.

CHAPTER 43

I DON'T KNOW HOW TO FEEL ABOUT THIS AFTERNOON'S ENCOUN-ter with Shair. I am rattled and triumphant and nervous and a bit ashamed too. I did not expect to feel like this.

But it doesn't matter. I have waited so long for this day, doubting it would ever come. I cannot lose control now, not when I finally have a chance to make him admit what he did.

I'm not looking for revenge. I've not fallen for the myth of closure either. I don't expect that whatever Shair admits to me will lessen my hurt. All I want is an accurate record of history. I want a truthful account of that night. I want something to mark the graves of my family so that the world can know for certain that they lived and died.

Truth matters.

I step into wide-leg pants and an emerald wrap top. I open my jewelry box to choose a necklace, maybe the one Adam gave me for my birthday. I hold it up against my neck and ignore the faint trembling of my hands as I examine myself in the mirror.

Something looks off, so I put the necklace back and try again. I try two other necklaces. Neither works.

I open the bottom drawer of the box and pull out the felt-wrapped ring. It's been nearly a year since I last looked at it. It's been decades since I've worn it. I'm not a child anymore and don't want to be responsible for destroying something that should be in a museum.

The turquoise and garnet are just as brilliant now as they were when I first saw them dazzle a room gathered to celebrate the treasures of Ai-Khanoum.

I was reading myself to sleep one night when I learned that Anastasia's mother, the Empress of Russia, had instructed her daughters to sew her collection of jewelry, an estimated twenty pounds of diamonds and gems, into their corsets. At the first attempt to execute the family, the bullets fired at the Romanov sisters ricocheted off those hidden stones. When the dust cleared and the girls, unharmed, stood before the assassins, there must have been a moment of divine confusion. I imagine the girls and the soldiers must have felt they'd just witnessed a miracle.

But the girls didn't evade death. The soldiers moved forward a few paces to kill the girls more directly, crushing their skulls and mangling their faces with the butts of their rifles, plunging their bayonets through their corsets and into their bodies. The jewels somehow landed in auctions and museums everywhere from Europe to Washington, DC. Gems often have curious journeys.

I have carried this ring across the world. When I was ten years old, I'd worn this ring like a shipwrecked person wears a life preserver. Maybe I'd made a mistake in doing so. Maybe it wasn't saving me at all.

Over the years I have felt its weight grow in my hands. It feels so heavy now that I wonder how I managed to lift my hand with it on as a child. At least a dozen times I made plans to turn the ring over to a museum, anonymously, like a desperate woman leaving a newborn baby at a fire station. But I couldn't bring myself to see it displayed in a house of plundered treasures. Statues and carvings and stonework float out of countries wrestling with genocide. Museums are more than willing to take them in, without asking the seller many questions.

Finders keepers, children shout on sunlit playgrounds.

Finders keepers, their parents whisper in halls of antiquities.

I know in my heart this ring belongs closer to where it was unearthed, closer to the remains of the woman who once wore it on her finger. But how can I entrust it to anyone?

Before the DNA tests concluded that the entire Romanov family had perished together on that night, dozens of women had claimed to be Anastasia or one of her sisters. If it weren't for the lure of a bejeweled inheritance, I doubt that anyone would have willingly assumed the identity of the ill-fated Romanovs. Two young women claiming to be grand duchesses were taken into a nunnery in the Ural Mountains. They died years later, their graves marked with tombstones bearing the names of the Romanov sisters—their lies etched into stone.

The name on my tombstone will be a lie as well.

This bothers me, and I haven't figured out how to fix it without turning my life inside out.

People wanted to believe Anastasia had survived somehow. She hadn't. And I can say with perverse certainty that it wouldn't have mattered if she had escaped alive. After her lungs had filled with gun smoke, after she'd seen the eyes of every member of her family go lifeless, there would have been little difference between living another five minutes and living five decades.

"Are you ready?" Mom asks, tapping on my bedroom door.

"Two minutes," I say, replacing the ring before Mom sees it and wonders why I've taken it out tonight.

On the way to the theater, we talk about Adam's campaign. Mom tells me she's been following him on Facebook, which Adam uses for networking and Mom uses to connect with friends and colleagues around the world. I've stayed away from all of it because even when I searched for Shair or members of my family, I was always too scared of being found.

My confrontation with Shair is at the tip of my tongue, but I hold back from telling Mom because I still worry she'll step in and I need to do this on my own. Shair had come undone when I left. Lacey called me, feeling compelled to let me know that he was trembling and emotional when he'd come out of the room.

I've never seen a patient so terrified of dying, Lacey had commented.

"Speaking of Adam," Mom says, prodding. "Is there anything you want to share with me about the two of you?"

"What do you mean?" I ask. The train comes to a stop. I scan the newcomers, wondering if I'll bump into any of Shair's family members and unsure whether I would recognize them if I did.

Mom purses her lips, then reaches into her purse and takes out her phone. In a few clicks, she's pulled up Adam's profile. She hands me her phone so I can take a closer look.

"I saw this earlier today," she says.

Adam has posted the picture of the two of us in Bryant Park. The way he's cropped the photo, my smile looks coy and playful. And he's used a filter that makes it look warm and nostalgic. Underneath is a caption that sounds nothing like Adam, the boyfriend, and everything like Adam, the politician.

Daytime date with my one and only. This woman knows the importance of health care and saves lives daily. Like the speech therapist with colon cancer who just wants to see her two little girls grow up. That mom is in a battle with her insurance company too, fighting to be able to afford the medications she needs to live.

Lucky for me, this doc doesn't need a scalpel to save my life. She just needs to say yes when that moment comes.

The post is followed with a slew of hashtags related to health care and the General Assembly, a couple for women doctors and surgeons, and even one that reads #sayyestoAdam.

I feel sick.

I can't believe he would violate my trust. I can't believe he would put a patient's private information out there and risk my job. I'm stunned because Adam knows about protected information and the law. And he knows I don't share my personal life online, where hospital administration or patients could find it.

"Why would he do this?"

Mom lets out a heavy sigh.

"The two of you will have to have a conversation about boundaries. Or maybe a new conversation about boundaries," she says. "But this is going to come up as the campaign progresses, and there's a long road between now and election day."

I bite my lip, then take out my phone and shoot a quick text to Adam.

I need you to take down that pic of us you posted on FB. It's a HIPAA violation.

"God, what is it about politics that makes people lose their heads?" I ask Mom.

Mom chuckles.

"They think the ends justify the means," she says.

I'm kicking myself for trusting Adam with small stories from my day. That's a HIPAA violation on my part too, I realize, but it's hard to keep everything I see at work bottled up.

Does this mean I can never trust Adam to keep something to himself? And has the campaign changed him, or is it revealing who he's been all along? I think of the cautionary hand on my knee in the bookshop, the rosy picture he's posted on Facebook, his sudden desire for commitment, or at least the appearance of it. I can't help but feel like he's staging a new reality.

Mom checks her watch, and I'm reminded how excited we've been to see this quirky, off-Broadway production of *Oklahoma!* I tell myself not to think about Adam's post or Shair and focus on the performance. We enter the dimmed theater and pick up our tickets from the plump woman in the box office. An inky-eyed Maltese dressed in a tuxedo sits on a director's chair next to her, overseeing ticket sales. Mom hoots with delight at the well-behaved dog and snaps a photograph.

Our seats are left of center stage. We settle in just as the lights flash on and off and the chime of a triangle signals the start of the show. Mom takes the armrest between us and smiles.

"I can't believe you did this, Ary. You really didn't have to," she says. She is looking more and more like Tilly these days, especially since she hasn't cut her hair in months. "But if, at any point, you don't want to be here, we'll go. You rise and I'll follow."

"I'm fine, Mom. It's just a show for me," I tell her truthfully. I'd only heard Tilly read scenes from the script. I don't know the music and never saw the performance in Kabul. But all those library books Mom checked out on grief and trauma have made her cautious about triggering experiences.

Through the opening act, Mom's lips move ever so slightly during the musical numbers, the lyrics ready on her tongue as if she's been in rehearsals all week. Music is miraculous in that way—songs wiggle their way into some black box in the corner of our hippocampi. Decades later, triggered by a word or an image or a few notes, they fly to the surface at warp speed.

I felt this rush when I discovered Afghan music on the internet. The soundtrack of my childhood flooded my room and swept me into the past. I found myself singing lines I didn't realize I knew, humming melodies I hadn't heard since before I lost my parents. I couldn't get enough. I clicked on the second and third song before the prior one had finished. I hopped from one memory to another—an Eid fete, a Nowruz celebration, a wedding. In the same way that my muscles ache if I run after a long hiatus, the music squeezed my heart if I let too much time pass since I'd last listened.

Mom looks like she's experiencing that same ache.

My phone buzzes. I open my purse to read Adam's text without taking my phone out of my bag.

I'll take it down. So am I even allowed to tell people you exist?

I tap out a reply.

If a tree falls in the forest, but no one posts about it on Facebook, is the tree even real?

My finger hovers over the Send icon, waiting for my better judgment to kick in. Maybe I'm being overly controlling when it comes to my privacy. No one will recognize me from my picture, and Adam has no idea why I'm so sensitive on the matter anyway.

I delete my message without sending it. Instead, I tap out a more tempered response.

Let's not discuss via text. At the show now. How's tomorrow?

I will tell Adam everything. That's the only way he'll understand.

Applause fills the theater. I close my bag and try to focus on the show. My mind races, though, replaying the afternoon with Shair and his daughter. I wonder if he's realized who I am or if he's shared anything with his family.

I watch the actors move about onstage in exaggerated movements. The songs are bright and infectious, sung in a western drawl that doesn't befuddle me as it did when I was a teenager. Cowboys in vests and chaps and women in corsets stomp their boots in celebration of a new frontier. With steer roping and butter churning, with a rifle at every corner, this is as American as a musical can get.

Why don't we all take a swim together? In Persia, where I come from, bathing is a so-cial event, sings a character with eyebrows that dance like Groucho Marx's. He is Ali Hakim, a flirtatious Persian peddler. He tells Laurey that in Persia women swim nude. Mom must sense my reaction. She leans in and waits for me to speak.

"I can't imagine there were a whole lot of Persian men in Oklahoma a hundred years ago," I whisper. "And why does he have to be such a perv?"

Mom opens her mouth to speak but stops short. Her brows come to-gether, and she takes a long hard look at the stage. She watches the rest of the show a bit flattened. I should have kept my remarks for the ride home.

During the intermission, we stand in the line for the bathroom. Mom shakes her head.

"I'll admit, the peddler is a curious character. I don't know how Rodgers and Hammerstein came up with him. Things are different now. When we did the show in Kabul, I honestly don't think anyone raised an eyebrow. It was just good fun."

"Did you get an Afghan to play the part of Ali Hakim?"

"No," Mom says as she tries to recall. "I remember trying to get my driver to do it. He came in for one rehearsal and read a few lines. But then he dropped out. Apparently his wife told him he should leave the stage for people who look more like movie stars."

"He would have choked on those lines about women swimming naked."

"I suppose he would have," Mom admits. "Mansour was a good man. A terrible singer, but a good man."

The door opens and there's finally enough room for Mom and me to step into the ladies' room. Two gray-haired women stand at the sinks. One touches up her lipstick while the other shakes drops of water from her fingertips. A toilet flushes.

Mom disappears into a stall while I wait for the next one. Somewhere behind me, I hear a woman speaking in Russian. I think of all the lemon candies my father gave me, and the chocolates with the fanciful wrappers, small treasures from the land of the hammer and scythe. I would eat them wearing my American denim.

I remember my father's amusement to see the Americans and the Russians investing competitively in Afghanistan's resources.

One dollar comes in, two rubles come in. One builds a university, another builds a tunnel. One day I told the Americans that the Russians were planning an irrigation project for one of the provinces. The next day the Americans asked for a meeting with me to discuss building a highway across the country. They fight like siblings and we are the favorite toy.

Years later I learned that this sibling rivalry was also called the Cold War and that everyone from Reagan to Rocky Balboa was involved.

I remember watching my mother dress the night of the Ai-Khanoum party and asking her about both the Russians and the Americans being present together.

They should know better than to have their schoolyard scuffle in our home. Our people have seen enough.

Mom and I are walking back to our seats when my phone buzzes. It's not Adam this time. It's the answering service. I show Mom my phone and sneak out of the theater as the lights dim.

"Hello, Dr. Shephard. I'm so sorry to disturb your evening." It is a man's voice on the line. He is so bright and chipper that I can be certain he is nowhere near the East Coast. "But I've got a gentleman patient of yours who says he needs to speak with you urgently. I'll be honest, I might not have understood exactly what he was saying. His last name is N-A—"

"Thanks for letting me know," I say, my tone clipped. I spin around to look behind me. This phone call has the effect of a home intrusion. "Have a good night."

"But, Doc," the man says just before I end the call. "Don't you need his name and number?"

CHAPTER 44

I WILL NOT CALL SHAIR BACK. I WANT TO BE ABLE TO LOOK INTO his eyes when we have our next conversation, to watch his pupils dilate and constrict, to see the muscles of his face arrange themselves into an expression I can judge for myself.

I am on the pullout couch. I've given Mom my bed, since I have my desk and computer in the living room. I log into the hospital system once more before I turn in for the night. I spot a low calcium level and give the nurse a call.

"I was just about to call you," he says. "He says he's not in pain but needs something to help him sleep."

It's not easy to sleep with IV lines and alarms and stiff bedsheets. I prescribe something to get him through the night, and then I crawl into bed. With my eyes closed, the day replays in my mind. I roll from my left side to my right and see Adam's post about my patient. I huff in frustration and take my phone out to read myself to exhaustion.

Around one in the morning, the answering service calls again. I answer quickly and keep my voice low so I don't wake Mom.

"It's the same gentleman, Doc. He won't tell me anything. Just says he really needs to talk to you."

He reads me Shair's phone number.

"You know, Doc, my aunt Regina wouldn't walk to her mailbox without making sure it was okay with her doctor. My mom used to joke that some people are called patients because that's what you need to care for them."

I smile in the dark and thank him for passing the message along.

I set my phone on the side table and close my eyes again, but I'd have better luck trying to catch a tadpole in a pond.

Shair is sleepless too. I wonder if his wife is watching him pace their apartment in the middle of the night or if she learned long ago to sleep through his midnight agitations. I don't care what she thinks or knows, really. Over the years I decided to focus my energies on the man who could have saved us but didn't.

It is three o'clock in the morning, far too early to go to the hospital, and I'm not in the mood for a run just now. I rake my fingers through my hair, furious with Shair for robbing me of sleep.

A glass of water sits on my coffee table, an industrial piece with a pop-up top. It is made of raw mango wood, stained a light golden brown that lets the grain tell its story. I see feathers and speckled waves, cheetah spots and wavy tresses. I open the top and pull out Clay Porter's book. I turn on the lamp and begin reading.

In the first chapter, Clay describes Afghanistan before the war. He writes about the jewel-tipped branches of her orange, pear, and apricot trees. He writes about the women with beehive coifs and European hippies in fringed vests and shearling coats searching for enlightenment in Afghan villages. Clay has created a window into a world that lives in my memories, but not anywhere on the news.

The images must have lulled me to sleep because when I open my eyes, I see that the pink light of dawn has given way to a crowning sun.

The book has slipped out of my hands, the open pages splayed across my chest as if my heart might have desired to read them too.

I take a quick shower, wrap a towel around myself, and slip into the bedroom quietly to get my clothes. Mom is awake, sitting on the side of the bed with her feet on the floor.

"Morning, love," she says, still sounding groggy.

"Sorry if I woke you. Get some more sleep. It's still early," I tell her.

She shakes her head, then stands and stretches her arms above her head.

"Didn't sound like you got much sleep last night," she says. "I heard your phone ring a couple of times. Everything all right?"

I pull a camisole over my head, then slip my arms into a cardigan.

"It's a new patient. He's very anxious," I say. I could tell her right now. I could tell her everything, and she could make sure I don't do anything wildly destructive. But I say nothing.

"Are you sure that's all, Aryana? You just seem a little . . ." She is careful with her words, as if navigating a minefield.

Mom can tell when my head starts spinning in that dangerous direction. I cannot hide from her completely. I step into my closet to finish dressing before I face her.

"I want to give the ring to a museum."

Mom is caught off guard. She sits on the edge of the bed and crosses her legs, the hem of her nightgown falling just past her knees.

"The ring?" she asks.

"Yes, the ring," I confirm. "I don't think it should be with me anymore. Maybe it never should have been with me."

"I don't know about that. But which museum?"

"The Kabul Museum," I reply. "I've been reading about it, and UNESCO has brought back hundreds of pieces from around the world. Stuff that traded on the black market. I think it's time for this ring to be returned."

Mom purses her lips, concern etched into her face.

"How long have you been thinking about this?" she asks. What she means to ask is how long I've kept this thought to myself.

"Not long. I don't even know how I would do it. Let's talk about it more later," I say, wanting to reassure her. "Though it'll be after dinner. Today's going to be a long one."

Mom's grown accustomed to my hours—workdays that start early and sometimes bleed into the next day. Mom's friends are gathering tonight for the retirement party. As I leave, I can feel her questions following me. I think about telling her once more that I'm fine, but I know that the harder I try to convince her, the more unconvinced she'll be. I really should be a better liar than I am.

I show up at the hospital and change into scrubs. I check out the board at the OR front desk to see if I'm in my regular room.

"Dr. Shephard. There's a patient who needs to talk to you," Inez, our charge nurse, says. Inez is one year away from retirement, and half the surgeons have vowed to retire with her. No one runs a tighter ship.

"I'm headed to pre-op now," I say, grabbing a bouffant cap.

"Not in pre-op. Out by registration. He's not a patient on today's schedule," she says. She rests a hand on her hip. "He's refusing to talk to anyone but you. And so you know, I went ahead and called security to be around. I don't want us to end up in the news."

Shair is here.

I head out to the registration area. Families sit in clusters, chatting or toying with their phones. A woman facing the window knits. Three patients occupy the registration cubicles to sign consent forms and have hospital bands placed on their wrists. They all fade to the background when I spot Shair standing in the corner of the room, a row of windows to his left. His shirt is buttoned askew, his collar lopsided. I stiffen but do not hesitate to walk out from behind a counter to face him. Thanks to the two-inch platform of my clogs and the hunch of his shoulders, we stand eye to eye.

"Having trouble sleeping?" I say in the sweetest Dari I can muster.

"Are you the girl?" he asks, his voice gruff but muted. He searches my face for an answer.

"I have very simple questions for you," I continue in the same language we spoke the night of the coup. "Who killed my family that night and where are the bodies of the murdered?"

His face softens, the lines melt away and the corners of his eyes crinkle with laughter. I do not flinch, not even as anger bubbles in me.

"You are the girl," he says in Dari. There is a buoyancy in the rasp of his voice. "I knew she could help me save you. You were so determined to—"

He is a shadow of who he was then, the man who held me captive in his home, pushed me around at gunpoint, and threatened me in the night. I am close enough to see the thin, slight twitching around his eyes, to smell the scent that comes as one inches toward a century of life, and the more distant scent of the cancer that will stop him from getting there.

"You didn't save me," I fire back with my hands on my hips. "You were a traitor. You turned your gun on the very people you were meant to protect. You turned your gun on your own government. People put their trust in you."

There is more I want to say, but my Dari is rusty and I don't want to stumble in front of him.

"I was given orders. And those orders were meant to give our country a better future," Shair insists. "You were a child. You couldn't possibly understand."

"I was a child. You most certainly were not," I say. Shair blinks slowly. "You were a cowardly man who, even now, is not man enough to admit his sins."

Spittle collects in the corners of Shair's mouth as he tries to find words. From the corner of my eye, I see a security guard approaching. He moves slowly, gauging the situation.

"This many years later, still . . ." Shair laments.

"This many years later, still you have not answered my question," I say, my voice controlled. People around us would be stunned if they understood our conversation. "Did you kill my family? My father and mother—the woman who showed you only kindness—and my brother who was barely old enough to be steady on his feet. What a threat he must have been to the future of the country! Did you kill him too?"

"What difference does it make?" Shair says quietly. His hands move to his belly and his eyes droop, forlorn. "The dead are dead. The dying will soon be dead. Only the living can stand and be counted."

"It makes all the difference in the world. It is the difference between heaven and hell," I say.

"Heaven and hell," Shair scoffs. "As if those are two separate places. As if you and I have not already stood in both!"

The security guard takes another two steps closer. His lips are compressed, his brow furrowed.

"Are you the nurse that called?" he asks me. He puffs his chest and positions himself so that his golden badge enters our conversation first. He reminds me of a boy in a superhero costume. "Everything all right here?"

Shair lets out a mournful chuckle. He ambles toward the door, not an ounce lighter than when he entered this room. He is almost at the door when he turns and points at me with one finger.

"She is not nurse. She is doctor," he says, punching out the words like letters on a typewriter. And then he is gone.

Curious eyes follow me as I retreat behind the heavy doors of the operating suites. They will make assumptions, I know. Some will guess that he is a desperate patient and I am a coldhearted surgeon. Others might think he is an old man who has dangerously lost his mind. Maybe they're all right.

I want to pound on his chest and demand answers. I want to scream to the world what a monster he is. I want to hold up the picture of my mother and father, of my three-year-old brother who lost his life to men grasping for power. Every day they have been absent from my life has been because Shair turned on us, because he didn't bother to warn my mother.

I scrub my hands raw in the deep sinks, digging the bristles into my skin. My scarred foot releases the pedal and I hold my hands up, arms bent. Water slides down my forearms and drips from the knobs of my elbows like teardrops.

Shair wants to count me among the living to ease his own conscience, but I am not certain that is where I belong.

CHAPTER 45

MY LAST CASE OF THE DAY IS CANCELED BECAUSE THE PATIENT forgot to stop taking her daily aspirin a week prior to surgery, as I'd asked. People are curious creatures. We forget to skip our medicine almost as often as we forget to take our medicine. We hate to exercise. We feel good when we exercise.

I want to move forward.

I keep looking back.

I'm on the train headed into Midtown to meet Adam for dinner. I've brought Clay Porter's book with me. His words have the richness of fiction. The people he portrays are flawed and hopeful. He writes about a seven-year-old boy who works in his father's tin shop, cutting sheets of tin into round discs with a chisel and hammer, and I can almost hear the clanging.

I wonder what Clay observed in Afghanistan. Maybe he walked past our family home, my elementary school, or the palace with its repaired buildings and grounds. I make a note to look for his articles when I get home, to read his observations from my homeland.

My secret homeland.

On reaching my stop, I slip the book back into my tote and pull on my gloves before I exit the train. The temperature has dropped about ten degrees since this morning. Storefronts twinkle with strings of white lights and sprigs of fir. We are meeting at a Peruvian restaurant just three blocks from here. It's one of our regular halfway spots and has a sparse menu, but the food is so good I haven't tired of it yet.

Adam wraps his arms around me and kisses me before we enter. The hostess seats us at a corner table. Two glasses of water appear, each with far too much ice. He is cheerful, almost surprisingly so given our text messages. I'm wondering if I read too much into the exchange.

"So tell me," he says. "What did you have going on today?"

"Are you in the mood to hear about small bowel?"

"Maybe not," Adam admits. He was once clearing some workspace on my desk and found one of my anatomy books, a photographic collection of dissected cadavers. He didn't eat meat for a month. "Just feel like we've got a lot of catching up to do every time I see you."

"I'm not going to end up in another social media post, am I?" I ask. Adam shakes his head.

"Look, I took it down. I put up a picture with my brother's dog."

"Why not a picture with his hamster?"

"Dogs poll better."

"And it's all about the polling," I say.

"It's all about the people," he insists. "That's why people liked the post with you. It was about people."

I take a deep breath. He needs to know my whole story, and this is the moment that makes the most sense. I feel a flutter in my stomach, an almost embarrassing tickle of nerves.

Our waiter comes over and flips a page in his memo pad. His hair is parted and gelled to perfection, not a strand out of place. He asks if he can start us off with some appetizers.

"We'll do the ceviche," Adam says. "You want anything else, Ary?"

"Ceviche is fine."

Adam still has his menu open.

"Why don't we just order now too? Do you know what you want?" he asks me.

We order entrées. Our waiter clicks his pen and drops it into his shirt pocket before moving on.

"I'm glad we could make tonight happen," Adam says. "It's a lot easier to talk in person than over text. Look, I should have cleared that post with you first, but you wouldn't believe how many likes it got."

"Likes," I repeat.

"It upped my following by forty-five percent. Some people thought you were Latina, which worked out well, given the demographics of the district. And then the health-care piece, that was golden too. Everybody's got someone affected by cancer. It was really effective."

I see so clearly now what he is doing. I should have seen it long ago.

"I'm just asking that you consider helping me win some points. It would be a shame not to use what we have, and we can do it without breaking HIPAA or whatever."

I take a long, slow sip of water and shake my head.

"It's not just HIPAA. You know I like my boundaries, Adam."

Adam exhales, his lips form a tight circle.

"All right, all right. Forget I asked," he says. Our waiter swirls a cocktail glass of ceviche in the space above the table and then sets it gingerly on the table. I take the first bite—lunch left me hungry.

"But I need you to be part of this. There are other ways to help. I've been working my contact list so I can show some good fundraising numbers, but I have to widen the circle."

"This is what you wanted to talk about the other day," I say, remembering the text about dollars.

"Right. So here's the thing," Adam says, with a sheepish grin. "Can you put me in touch with your colleagues? Hospital executives, star surgeons . . . I've got to pitch the campaign to them, and I'm sure I can win them over on health-care issues. I'm sure some of them would want to have a future assemblyman as a friend," Adam offers.

"You want me to ask my colleagues to give you money?" I ask, taken aback. "I can't ask them to do that."

"Why not? This is how it works, Ary. Some of them have probably already done this for other politicians. I could use your help finessing a pitch to them. What issue matters most to physicians, and how can I angle myself so that they'll be motivated to support my run?"

I put down my fork.

"Adam, I didn't ask for this, and I don't want to be part of it. No, I won't be the token demographic on your arm, and I'm not going to cold-call my colleagues for you."

Adam looks at me for a beat, then slides back in his chair. He has his hands on either side of the table, as if he'll be blown away if he doesn't hold on.

"Wow," he says finally. "That's incredibly supportive of you."

"Are you serious? You didn't want to come with me to our holiday party last year, but now you want to schmooze with my coworkers? You're asking me to do things that make me cringe, to put it mildly. That's a big deal, and it's too bad you can't see it."

"This would be good for both of us, Aryana. We could get in with the kind of people who make things move, the kind of people who matter in this city. To get there requires stepping out of our comfort zones. And it's not exactly sinister to try to get a leg up on my opponents."

"You're doing this for both of us but didn't bother to ask me if I wanted to be *in* with these special people. You didn't ask me if I wanted any of this."

Adam taps his fingers against the table. His ceviche sits untouched.

A long stretch of silence passes.

"Why did marriage just come up now? Did it really have anything to do with your lease or is it about the campaign?" I ask.

"C'mon, Aryana," Adam says. "Are you serious?"

By the look on my face, he can see that I am serious. And by the way he avoids answering, I can see that I'm right.

"Aryana, be smart," he says in a low voice. "Strategy isn't a sin. People vote for people they like. We are the kind of couple people would like. And we were headed that way, weren't we?"

My head drops. I can see now with such clarity that it feels like a cataract has been removed. Somewhere along the line, I became a pawn in a game I never wanted to play. I take my napkin off my lap and set it on the table. I open my tote and take out two $20 bills. I place them on the edge of the table and rise, slipping one arm and then another into the sleeves of my coat as Adam stares at the money I've left on the table.

"Maybe we were," I tell Adam. And with those three little words, I have changed everything.

CHAPTER 46

THE MIDDAY SUN IS WARM ON OUR FACES, EVEN IF WE ARE ONLY days away from Christmas. Over breakfast, Mom suggested we go to Randalls Island. It's my first Saturday off in two weeks, and I don't want to waste it indoors.

Mom's sunglasses are large and round, her cheekbones high. She walks with her hands stuffed in her pockets. She swears yoga has kept her posture upright, and I believe it. She's the reason I've been meaning to start yoga for the past five years.

"Hell Gate," Mom muses as we stroll the asphalt path. "That's what this stretch of water was called. Do you know why?"

"Probably sank a good number of ships trying to get through here."

"True, but that's not where its name came from," she replies. "It's Dutch for 'bright strait' or something like that." We follow the walkway along the water's edge, the brink of the island.

"Poor Hell Gate. An innocent waterway with a bad name."

"Not all that innocent. She was a watery grave for plenty." Wispy clouds drift away from the sun. Mom shields her eyes from the bright glare on the water. "They blasted the straits with a ridiculous amount of explosives over a hundred years ago. People all the way in Princeton, New Jersey, felt the blast. They used the rubble to make that little island right there."

In my second year in an American school, I learned the word "rubble." I'd mistaken it for the name of Russian currency, which made my ESL teacher laugh. She'd flipped through pages of a textbook until she found a grainy photograph of a tattered child standing on a pile of bricks in Poland during the Second World War.

Rubble, she'd said, so brightly she could have been revealing a birthday cake. *Not ruble! This is rubble.*

I'd gone home early that day, having spent half an hour on a cot in the nurse's office with a stomachache.

I'd like to think I'm less affected by words now.

"How was last night?" I ask instead.

Mom laughs.

"Speaking of misfits," she says slyly, then stuffs her hands in her pockets and curls her shoulders in. "So much reminiscing last night. A gaggle of women who can't sit back and watch the sunset. Do you remember Evelyn? She's the one who suggested Randalls Island for a walk. She told us stories of the insane asylums and orphanages they had here. They moved cemeteries from Bryant Park and Madison Square to this island. Thousands of bodies relocated."

I see heaps of upturned earth and tilted headstones in my mind. I doubt Shair will come back to clinic. I'm going to have to find another way to push him for answers.

Mom interrupts my wandering thoughts.

"Are you ever going to tell me what happened between you and Adam?" Her lips pull to the side as she slides her shades down just enough that I can see her eyes. "Honey, I've been gazing at this lovely face for years. I can tell when something's bugging you."

And like everyone at a retirement party watching a slide show, I'm struck by a wave of nostalgia, the sepia-toned moments of our lives to-gether, and the violent way we came to be mother and daughter. I cannot imagine where or what I would be if she'd not taken me in.

"I broke up with Adam," I say.

"I see," she replies, reserving judgment as she always does.

"I never wanted to be a politician's wife. I certainly don't want to be a worm on a hook," I explain.

"Oh, Ary. I'm so sorry."

"I hadn't gone to meet him with the intention of ending things. But the way he saw me fitting into his campaign, I just couldn't stomach it."

In the distance, I hear a child babbling. A family has come around the bend, a couple wearing puffer coats and pushing a stroller. I estimate it has taken no less than a million miracles to create this moment.

"And now that you've had a chance to sleep on it, do you still feel the same way?"

"Completely," I reply without hesitation. "But I also think I may not be built for relationships. Maybe I'm meant to be married to my work."

"It is one way to live," Mom says. "But I don't know if I'd recom-mend it."

Mom had a couple of relationships over the years, none that made it to matrimony. I've always thought I was somehow the reason for that.

"I'm sorry," I say. "If it weren't for me—"

"If it weren't for you, Aryana, I would be spinning in circles. You didn't keep me from some storybook romance. I never wanted to be re-sponsible for a husband and a family. Maybe I knew I was a little too much like Tilly. So I chose a career that I thought would ensure I never had a chance to screw up a marriage or a child."

It saddens me that Mom had such little faith in herself and that she felt so hurt by her mother. But she's also been my role model. I learned from her how to throw myself into my career.

"Aryana, I could never fill in the missing pieces of your life. I've always known that. The holes were just too big for me to even think I could come close. But you—you filled a giant hole in my life and made me the proudest mom. There's so much I got to do because of you, so much I had the chance to experience."

I feel a tightness in my chest. Tears blur my vision and turn the world into swirls of gray and blue.

I wrap my arms around Mom and catch the light scent of her perfume. Even in the middle of winter, she smells like crushed flowers and nectar.

"I love you, Mom," I say, through a clenched throat. Her arms hold me tight, as they always have. Over the years she's told me not to follow in her footsteps. She's hinted and said outright that I would be a great mother. Every time I've told Mom that I'm not suited for motherhood, she's looked like I've revealed a fresh tragedy to her. Even now, I can see she still holds out hope.

WE WALK SLOWLY, THE WEIGHT OF THE ISLAND'S HISTORY PULL-ing at my feet. Maybe it's the thousands of damaged people—the war veterans, the orphans, the mentally ill—wanting someone to hear their stories.

Mom clears her throat.

"There's something I want to share with you," she says. "The Afghan government formed a commission to search for the bodies of those killed in the revolution. They're officially searching, though they don't have a lot of information yet. Thirty years later, everyone who knew anything is either dead, gone, or scared."

I'm halted by this news. I've kept up my own searches and haven't seen an announcement about this government search.

"Where did you hear this?" I ask Mom. "And why didn't you tell me?"

"I didn't want this news to toy with you. I heard from someone I used to work with at the embassy. If they'd found anything, I would have let you know. I didn't want to get your hopes up."

"Who was it? Does he know if they've found anything?"

"No, he hasn't heard anything and wouldn't hear anything directly. It's people he knows passing info along. But maybe the investigation will turn something up. It's been long enough."

I look at her.

"Mom, who is 'he'?"

Mom looks from me to the choppy water and back.

"Leo."

Leo Harris, from the Islamabad embassy. Mom hasn't mentioned him in a while. I remember sitting across a desk from him with Tilly. He went from stalling our request for a passport to escorting us to the tarmac to board a diverted plane. I remember him watching us board, hands on his hips and shirt darkened with sweat.

"Leo was CIA, wasn't he?" I say. I don't know why I've asked that way, as if I already know the answer. It's never occurred to me that Leo was anything but a Foreign Service officer.

Mom nods.

"He couldn't tell me much then, but he's been able to share a bit more now."

"Was he involved? Did he know what was coming?" I ask.

"No. No, he didn't know. And he was not involved. Not then. Later," she says, her voice dropping. "Later, things changed. I think he helped get money and supplies to the mujahideen and rouse support from Uzbekistan."

Uzbekistan. The CIA had probably sent guns and Qur'ans to the Uzbeks. The director seemed to think that stirring up their religious fervor would inspire them to fight harder against the Communists.

From what I've seen, the CIA likes to be very secretive about the elections it rearranges, the dictators it seats or unseats, and the conflicts it fuels. But once a couple of decades have passed, they open their files, knowing there remains little energy for outrage or shock once that much time has gone by.

I've spent more time than I care to admit digging through declassified CIA reports on Afghanistan—summaries about President Daoud Khan's popular support and which ministry leaders might not have been loyal to him, briefings about air bases the Soviets hoped to build on Afghan soil, and newspaper articles about the coup. I recognized a couple of names in the documents but never found my father, which told me that the CIA hadn't figured out which advisers were closest to President Daoud Khan.

"I can't believe you never told me what he was," I say.

"I had my suspicions but wasn't sure," Mom replies heavily. "And I didn't want to cause him any trouble."

"No. Causing trouble was his job."

Mom presses her lips into a thin line. She shivers as a cool wind whips our hair into our eyes.

"It's complicated," she says.

I'm an American now, but one who sees clearly what the CIA's meddling has done across the globe. I am no less grateful that Antonia is my mom, and that here I can be the doctor my father dreamed I would become. Sure, I've been saved here. But maybe I wouldn't have needed saving if people like Leo hadn't been so anxious about the creep of communism.

"You're right," I repeat. "It is complicated."

Mom nods.

"There might be a way to help the investigation," I say. The cold has me sniffling. "I found him."

"You found who?" she asks, handing me a tissue from her pocket.

"Or he found me, actually. After all these years. He didn't even recognize me."

Mom stops walking and faces me.

"Aryana, what are you talking about?" she asks.

"The soldier, Shair. He came to see me in clinic as a patient. I confronted him." Mom's jaw goes slack. I don't know if she's more surprised that he reappeared or that I didn't tell her about this right away. I tell her every last detail about our encounters, even confessing that I'd gone to his apartment building. "That monster has just been living his life. He's never had to pay for what he did that night."

"Aryana, I don't think it's a good idea for you to be in contact with him. And you certainly can't be his doctor."

As expected, Mom is protective and rational.

"I know. But he might be my only chance to find my family, to know who killed them."

Mom looks conflicted.

"Look, I know it's hard to think of it this way, but he did get you out of there that night. And he took a lot of risks to get you to me."

This is not the first time Mom has tried to get me to see things this way.

I think of the way Shair looked at me in the hospital, the way he corrected the security guard who mistook me for a nurse. But I am still angry.

"I'm not interested in being his redemption," I say, my voice carried south in the breeze. "I'm going to make him tell me everything."

A congregation of ring-billed gulls skitters over the choppy waters, then returns to the ground in search of food.

"What if he doesn't have the answers you're looking for?"

"He does. He has to," I say resolutely. "Otherwise, why would he show up in my life now? The universe can't be that sadistic."

I dare not blame God, even though I am not a religious person. Sometimes I regret that the faith I was raised in slipped away from me like a silk robe. I hold on only to the core, the belief that there exists a Creator and that heaven and hell are real.

Necessity isn't just the mother of invention. She's the mother of faith too.

The rest of it, the fasting, prayers, and holidays, mean nothing without my family or even a community. Growing up, Mom opted for a Unitarian church, an institution that probably grew out of necessity too.

"What if I speak with him?" Mom suggests. "Maybe I can get him to open up. What do you think?"

She isn't surprised when I shake my head. I will make him answer me, even if I must go to dangerous lengths to do it.

There are people in this world who return to watery graveyards—weary doctors, shell-shocked journalists, children of war. These are the people willing to cross hell's gates to prove life and loss are intertwined currents, capsizing some ships and righting others.

CHAPTER 47

I DREAM IT IS WINTER. I'M STANDING ON THE SIDEWALK IN THE quiet of night watching lush, velvety flakes melt onto concrete steps, car windshields, and painted benches. I am a nine-year-old with happy bruises on my shins and silk ribbons in my hair. I catch the falling snow on my tongue because letting it fall to the ground seems the crazier thing to do.

I drift in and out of sleep all night. Awake at four o'clock in the morning, I decide to get up and go squeeze in a run. Overnight, rain has slicked the city.

When I return, I find Mom in the living room.

"You're up," I say. Her feet are in the air, her weight balanced on her shoulders. "Correction. You're upside down."

With a graceful scissoring motion, Mom's legs return to the floor. She sits cross-legged, her face flushed.

"You put the twenty-something-year-olds at the studio down the street to shame."

Her bangs cling to her moist forehead.

"Eh. I don't think I have much in common with those LaLaLime

gals," she says, wrapping a towel around her neck. She points to Clay
Porter's book on the coffee table. "Is this what you're reading now?"

"Yes, he did a talk downtown," I tell her. Pouring myself a glass of
water, I try to finish my thought before I take a sip. "The way he writes
about the people affected by the combat, the children racing to the top of
a heap of rubble, it's like . . . it's like he shows you the tiny flower growing
through cracked concrete."

Mom picks up the book and turns it over to look at the back cover.

"I'm going to look up his articles. I wonder if he heard anything
about the investigation or a grave while he was there," I say.

"Maybe," she mumbles.

I shower and step back into the living room to find her with her laptop open, the screen casting a white glow on her face.

"Well, it looks like Mr. Clay Porter doesn't sleep much either," she says.

Drops of water fall from the ends of my hair to the shag rug beneath
my feet. I take two steps toward Mom and see that Clay has replied to an
email she sent him moments ago.

I WALK THROUGH THE ONCOLOGY UNIT. IN MY HANDS IS A MUF-
fin from the cafeteria and two candles I found in the kitchen of our
clinic. Marilyn, an interior designer, was admitted early this morning for
abdominal pain. The admitting physician gives me an update and smiles
at the muffin and candles in my hand.

The hallway smells like aluminum foil and gravel, like plastic pack-
aging and a veterinarian's office. Sometimes the scent hits me so strong
that I spritz orange oil onto the inside of a face mask and keep it hanging
around my neck.

Some of the patients smell it too. I had one patient whose taste buds
had been decimated by chemo. Though she said everything tasted like
cardboard, she couldn't shake the metallic smell of the chemo coming

from her own body. She washed her clothes as soon as she returned home from the hospital and showered twice a day out of desperation. One man told me his wife had started sleeping in a separate bedroom. She'd come up with some excuse to avoid hurting his feelings, but he'd overheard her talking to their grown daughter on the phone about his "cancer stink."

"Knock, knock," I say, standing in the doorway. Marilyn smiles as I enter. There are deep circles under her eyes.

"Hey, Doc," she says.

"I heard you came in. How are you feeling?"

"Lousy," Marilyn admits. "But not as lousy as a few hours ago."

"That's a start. You're a little dehydrated too. But that bag of happy birthday fluids should fix that."

There's a linen tote bag on the chair, decorated with an image of a long-lashed woman wearing a bandanna on her head and boxing gloves for fists. WARRIOR is written in pink scrawl above the picture. She is a reinvented Rosie the Riveter, doing her part in this new war. I lift the bag and set it on the windowsill.

Marilyn's war is ramping up. She's just had a whole-body scan done, with positrons and electrons colliding in a crash of light. *The wound is where the light enters,* my father used to say, quoting Rumi. As if he knew about radioactive isotopes and imaging. Clouds of brightness on her images correspond precisely with spots where Marilyn has been having more pain—her left hip, the middle of her back, and her right shoulder.

She sighs and glances at her bag.

"Ah, what I would give not to have to be a warrior today," she says. "I never even wanted to play dodgeball."

"I don't trust anyone who enjoys dodgeball," I say, and she smiles weakly.

She looks wistful.

"Are you going to give me bad news today?" she asks.

"I'm going to tell you what your scan showed," I say.

She listens. She looks frightened and angry and exhausted. She takes a breath. What she says next surprises me.

"Two months before my daughter was born, I painted her room carnation pink. It turns out her favorite color is moss green. She's almost a teenager now, and I promised her I'd help her redo it how she wants," she said.

And I know she will. Because when people have a reason to live, through some alchemy of the spirit, they make it happen. Warriors don't wage war dreaming of immortality. They step into the fight assuming the posture in which they want to be remembered, like posing for a statue.

Even as Marilyn lies depleted on a stretcher, I can picture her stirring cans of paint and watching her daughter climb a ladder to reach the corners of her room. She wants to be her daughter's mother forever, the mom who handed her brushes dipped in her favorite color, the mom who stood back and let her dress the world to her liking.

"I'll talk to the rest of the team. Let's see what we can do to get you home soon," I say, and she nods.

I move mechanically through clinic, my head growing dense with pain as the hours pass. I shake another pill out of the little orange bottle and swallow it dry, wishing it were a different species of painkiller.

I sit at my desk and turn the computer on. The screen lights up, and I look away while I dim the monitor. My throat is parched, but I don't get up. I find the website I need.

Lacey walks past my door.

"Everything all right, Doc?" she asks.

"Good as it gets," I reply.

"All right. I'm headed out. I told you my idiot brother's getting married, right? Tonight the families are meeting for the first time. The girl's nice enough, but her parents think Obama is a closet Muslim and my boyfriend's an actual Muslim. Wish me luck," she says.

"Sounds like a good time," I say, my eyes still navigating the screen. Lacey's words hit me a second later and I look up.

"Wait, I mean, I didn't know that," I say. Why am I struggling to see Lacey dating anyone but a male version of herself? She must sense the regret in my voice.

"Of course you didn't," Lacey laughs. "You couldn't know if I never told you."

I wish her and her family good luck getting through this first dinner and watch her walk away, feeling embarrassed at the assumptions I've made.

I enter the numbers from my credit card into the website and submit payment. I print out a confirmation page and know there's no turning back from this point.

I push my chair away from the desk and breathe. The office is dark and still, everyone having left long ago. My phone is quiet. I've not heard from Adam since I walked out of the restaurant, and part of me misses him. But a more rational part of me remembers that what I'm feeling is dressed-up loneliness. This is what I felt before I met Adam, when the scent of his cologne didn't linger still on my sofa.

I cross avenues, feeling upside down, as if the earth has just flipped on its axis. My feet move quickly, buoyed by the momentum of the city. The heady scent of incense emanates from a man dressed in a red and yellow caftan. I walk past two women offering salvation in the form of a pamphlet and enter the dank train station. I close my eyes and travel in time.

When I was sixteen, Mom's work took us to Bangalore, a city of blooming gardens and growing industry. We spent two days there as tourists. The equatorial sun blazed hot on our backs, and our clothes clung to our damp skin. Mom's fingers stuck to the pages of the guidebook she'd purchased.

We ventured into a cave transformed into a Hindu temple guarded by monolithic pillars and enormous sun discs carved to honor Shiva.

Once a year, the guide had explained, *and for no more than one hour, the rays of the sun fall between the horns of the Nandi and illuminate Shiva.*

Did they design the temple that way? I asked the guide, a lanky man who seemed unfazed by the sweltering heat. *Or did they discover the light fell that way after this had been constructed?*

I'm not sure, madam. But I can tell you that it doesn't matter one bit to the thousands who come each year to witness it.

Mom and I entered, our bare feet touching the cool, wet ground. I followed Mom's footsteps, and strangers followed mine. We moved deeper into the dimly lit hollow, our backs hunched as the slope of the roof became more severe. I was bent in half, passing statues adorned with strings of marigolds and jasmine, when I felt my pulse quicken, my head grow light.

The guide's words echoed in my ears.

Sometimes Shiva is depicted with a neck tinged blue from holding in his throat a churning poison gas that threatened to destroy the world. He has powers of destruction, but re-creation as well, as one cannot happen without the other.

I want to get out, I told Mom. The space was so narrow that she could barely turn around to look at my face. Mom made herself into a drill bit, clearing a path for me through the crush of tourists between us and the mouth of the cave.

I fell onto a bench outside the temple. Mom paid someone to slash open a coconut, and she forced a straw to my lips. I drank, wondering if the deities had driven me out of their sacred space. I've wandered into houses of worship since then, but never found a home in any of them.

I feel the rumble of the approaching train in my feet before I hear it.

When it arrives, I slip through the sliding doors and find my way to a seat. I stay on the train as it passes my stop. My mind does not wander. I am locked into this moment as I descend the steps and navigate the side streets to make my way back to Shair's building.

I press the button next to his name. Nabi. I hold it down, my fingertip blanching.

A voice crackles over the intercom, a greeting I can't make out. It doesn't matter.

"Send Shair Nabi downstairs," I shout.

CHAPTER 48

THERE IS SILENCE. MY BREATHING IS SHALLOW AND RAPID. I DIG my fingernails into the palms of my hands. I press the button again, a series of staccato buzzes.

There is noise over the intercom. I take a step back and brush my hair from my face. I stare at the elevator, expecting Shair to come charging out of it. I expect to face off against a soldier or a criminal, but when the doors open, the figure ambling toward me in the lobby is neither.

I look away so that I do not watch the struggle in his step.

He opens the glass door and joins me in the atrium. He squares off and meets my eyes—but only for a beat.

"Not here," he says, then pushes open the outside door and steps onto the sidewalk. I hesitate, not wanting to follow a single command. I feel a hand on my elbow and jump back.

"What are you trying to do to him? Why didn't you say who you were?" Shair's daughter shrieks in Dari. Her eyes are puffy, as if she's been crying. Behind her, standing in the elevator, is her mother. Tahera has grown round, heavy. The elevator door starts to close, and she lifts one hand to stop it, never turning her eyes from me.

She says nothing, just looks at me with the same hollow expression she had the night Shair deposited me in her care.

"This has nothing to do with you," I tell his daughter in English, wresting my arm from her grip. I remember the moment I saw her wearing the clothes I'd outgrown, and my resentment bubbles up. She follows me out the door until she sees Shair standing with his hands on his hips.

"Go inside," he tells his daughter.

"But, *Padar*—" she protests, shooting me a daggered look.

"Go, *bachem*. It's me she needs, not you. Go be with your mother and your children. I didn't finish feeding Elias."

She slaps her arms against her sides, like a bird deciding whether to rise or retreat. Shair is right. I don't need her. I turn back in time to watch him make a left at the end of the block.

"Don't walk away from me!" I shout. He is already out of sight. I will not wait another day for my answers, even if it means chasing him down in the street. I catch up to him quickly, but he doesn't bother to look at me.

"We will talk. But not here," he says in Dari, his face stoic as stone. Fuming, I walk beside him. Because I cannot tolerate following his lead, I set my pace to be in step with his.

"Where are you going?" I demand to know.

"There is a place," he mutters.

We walk a few more blocks. An elderly woman with a terrier on a leash smiles at us as she approaches.

"Stop playing games!" I say. I want to grab him by his shoulder and make him stop, but I can't recruit my limbs to action. The woman pauses in her step, then frowns at me. She shoots Shair a look of pity before her dog pulls her away. "Just answer my questions. Did you kill them? Are you running from the truth? Why won't you admit what you did?"

He still doesn't pause. He crosses the bustling street, and a car horn blares.

"Stop!" I shout, to both him and the car careening toward him. The driver slams on his brakes, and Shair lifts one hand, a quiet apology. I am behind him then. I feel the heat radiating off the hood of the car, meet the bewildered gaze of the driver, and then jog to the opposite curb.

If I'm honest, I've probably dreamed of running him over.

We walk another two blocks. Shair's breaths are heavier, labored. I can hear a faint wheeze as I walk with him.

"You will answer me today," I warn.

Shair stops at wrought-iron gates, at a set of brick pillars that mark the entrance to a cemetery.

"Here," he says before he trudges onward, through the entry. Cemeteries are their most honest selves in winter, when the trees are skeletal and the grass is yellowed and flattened against the cold earth. When anything that blooms announces itself as fiction, plastic. When loved ones say prayers in double time, quickened by cold gusts of wind.

Still, I've always found cemeteries settling—seeing the souls tucked in with their families, the tombstones carved with nicknames and finite dates, and the mounds of earth ready to catch tears. I think of Randalls Island and the people lucky enough to have been buried twice. Or the lifeless man buried in fresh flowers on the back of a truck in India, the vehicle escorted by swaths of people singing and beating drums. My grandmother's *jenaaza* in Kabul had been a hushed, colorless affair, with whispered prayers and free-flowing tears blotted by handkerchiefs.

Just a hundred yards into the cemetery, the din of city traffic fades respectfully. The graves have all types of markers. We pass a memorial to the victims of the fallen towers, the tomb of Louis Armstrong, and a statue of a distraught woman in robes draped over a headstone. Other markers are far less conspicuous, barely an inch above the ground.

Shair cuts across the lawn and I stick with him, grass crunching beneath our feet. My low heels sink into the moist earth. He stops so abruptly that I almost walk into him. I immediately take two steps back and almost lose my balance.

The borders of this section are marked off with soaring trees. Standing a few feet ahead of a row of storied evergreens, Shair cups his hands in prayer. My eyes fall to the ground, to the stone pillow at the head of the plot.

KAREEM NABI.

From the dates carved beneath his name, I understand this is Shair's son. Here lies the boy who, as a teenager, had seen my first blood.

"*Aye, bachem,*" he sighs. "May God forgive you and me both."

He reaches over and brushes curled leaves away from the headstone. With a grunt, he gets on his knees and begins to pluck blades of grass around the edges of the stone.

"I kept him from war for as long as I could. I called in every favor. I begged. I threatened. I made promises I knew I couldn't keep," he says. My heart betrays me, pinching in my chest to hear a father mourn his son. I stuff my hands in my pockets and pull my shoulders back as Shair continues. "It was becoming impossible, and I was out of favors, out of money. I had to get him out."

Shair tells me that he paid a smuggler to take his son to Czechoslovakia. Kareem was alone there, a teenage boy. It was two years before the rest of the family joined him.

"He was in a youth home. No one to look after him. All kinds of kids around him, plenty of them bigger than him. Older than him. He never told me what he went through there, but it changed him."

These are the familiar stories of refugee families, who are sometimes driven piecemeal from their homelands.

"By the time we were together again, he barely spoke. My daughter, to this day, cannot bear to be away from her mother. My youngest," Shair says, shaking his head, "he is too busy with his friends to make something of himself."

A bird takes flight from an oak tree, soars above our heads, and lights on a nearby tombstone.

"What happened to Kareem?" I ask.

"When we came here," he says, pausing to blow on his pale fingers to warm them, "I was the son and Kareem was the father. He learned English quickly. He found odd jobs and impressed every man he ever worked for. He had the discipline of a soldier. He wanted to do more. He talked to a man who had a coffee truck. He was making good money. So Kareem used everything he'd saved to buy one.

"He woke at three o'clock in the morning, five days a week. Loaded his truck in the dark with doughnuts and whatever else people eat. He did this every day, until one day."

Shair puts his palms to the ground. His face flushes with exertion as he pushes himself to stand.

"A man shot him for the few dollars he had in his pocket. Gone," Shair says, his voice breaking. "They could not find his murderer. I couldn't even seek revenge. In the end, I did the best I could and buried him here, where it is green and peaceful and close enough that I can pray over him."

I fold my arms across my chest and watch my breath form a small cloud.

"May God forgive him," I say quietly.

Shair looks infinitely grateful to me for this prayer, this small act of mercy.

"Do you believe in the seven ranks of heaven?" he asks, then chuckles. "Do you know that as they ascend, their gems increase in value? The second has only pearls, but the fourth has white gold, the fifth has silver, and the sixth . . . ah, the sixth dazzles with gold, garnets, and rubies! Even heaven is divided. Maybe the spirits of the dead are all too drunk on milk and honey to revolt."

He lets out an exasperated breath that ends with a smoker's wheeze.

"What can I say that will free you?" he asks, looking at me.

"Did you kill them?"

Shair presses the heel of his right hand to his temple, as if he's suffered a direct blow to the head.

"You would be surprised how many fingers can fit on one trigger."

"I deserve to know."

"And a dying man should keep no secrets," Shair concedes. "But are you ready to go back to those days? To that place?"

"How dare you ask me that?" I say, freshly outraged that Shair continues to dodge my question, even as we stand over Kareem's grave. "You carved your son's name into stone so that anyone who walks this way today, tomorrow, or a hundred years from now can read it and know he lived. You come, you pray, you lay flowers. It is evil to deny me this."

He turns his back to me.

"When there is poison in the blood, do you need an aspirin or an antidote?" Shair asks enigmatically. A gust of wind tilts him. He takes a step and rights himself.

"And I'm asking for answers, not more questions."

He exhales through his nose, the skin beneath his eyes is thin and violet-hued. The silver in his stubble catches the light from a sodium lamp.

"My orders were to stay at Arg that night, after the dead had been loaded onto a truck. Another soldier was given the keys. He was young, barely old enough to shave. I thought he might vomit into his boots. They didn't give him driving orders until he left the grounds. They said nothing more about it to the rest of us."

"Liar," I accuse, my voice gravelly.

"Those who knew were sworn to secrecy. Threatened into secrecy. In those days, one unfortunate word could get a person thrown into Pol-e-charkhi prison. Or worse," he says. "I pulled that kid aside and told him that he'd better lay the martyred to rest in a fitting way. I told him there were good people among the dead and that he alone could grant them their final dignity. It was the best I could do for them. When I next saw him, he told me he'd done what he could. He said he'd laid them to rest among giants with a view of Paradise. He wanted to tell me more, but I stopped him. My family was already waist-deep in risk."

"Liar," I repeat. But something tells me Shair is telling the truth.

Shair stares at the shadows we cast, the way they fall onto the ground but not on his son's headstone.

"Your mother was a kind woman," he says.

"After thirty years, are you still not capable of being honest? Tell me what you did to them. Have you no decency?"

"Decency," he scoffs. "What will you do with this information? I am curious. If I were to tell you I did not kill them, would you hunt down the man who pulled the trigger? And if I said they died by my gun, would you claw my eyes out?"

"You want to believe I'm a vengeful monster? Go on. But that doesn't absolve you," I reply.

"Let me ask you, sweet girl, as our lives are like tangled chains hanging around a neck. Do you hear Kabul's whispers in your ear? Does she call you too?" he asks, and I wonder if he's losing his mind. But to me, he's still the gruff soldier who silenced me with a hand over my mouth. "If she does, do not listen. It's a siren's call."

I don't want his advice. Poison gathers in my throat.

"Why won't you say it?" I ask.

Shair stares at the empty space beside Kareem's grave. He gazes into his cupped hands, either filling them with prayer or cursing their emptiness.

"You might believe me, you might not. But I never could have harmed your mother or your brother. Not any child, for that matter. I wasn't the one who killed your father either. None of you were supposed to be there that night. But even that doesn't absolve me."

I cannot speak.

"How desperately we struggle for meaningless things—revolution, martyrdom, bricks of gold," he says. "When the only thing worth fighting for is a glimpse of heaven in this life."

The darkness beneath the skirts of the evergreens deepens. The soft glow of the sodium lamp falls upon the stoic letters of Kareem's name, a small miracle arranged by the architect of light.

CHAPTER 49

"YOU WHAT?" MOM SAYS, LOWERING HER COFFEE MUG. TWO MORE people step up to the barista and order without looking at the menu. I move my handbag to the empty chair beside me.

"If I don't go now," I explain, "it means I don't really want to know what happened."

"It most certainly does *not* mean that." Mom rejects my logic. She gives her coffee another stir, the spoon clinking against the ceramic. "You don't have anything to prove, Aryana. But I get it. I understand why you want to go. I just want to be sure you're prepared for whatever you might find there."

"You don't have to worry about me," I say, my words weightless.

Mom's eyes close for a beat, her face melts into an expression of intertwined angst and love.

"This day was always coming," she says, locking eyes with me. "I did think you'd talk to me before booking a flight, though."

She is trying not to feel hurt, but I can see that she is. I wasn't trying to keep her in the dark.

"I love you, Mom," I say, the words rolling easily off my tongue.

They didn't always. For years, loving Mom felt like a betrayal. I could hardly acknowledge it to myself without feeling stained. "I've waited decades. I can't wait another second."

Mom puts her hand over mine, and her eyes well with tears.

"Even if nothing comes of this search, I want to take the ring back," I say. The stones had grown heavier over the past few years. The ring felt less like a talisman and more like a rusted yoke.

The coffee shop's door opens again. Mom, facing the door, raises her hand. Clay nods and walks over to join us. I hang my bag on my chair to make room for him.

"Clay," he says, shaking Mom's hand. "Good to meet you."

"Antonia," she replies. "And I'm glad to meet you as well."

Clay slides into the wooden chair and sets his phone down on the table.

"It's good of you to make time for us," Mom says.

Clay grins.

"I make a living by chasing people down for a conversation. I figure if I make it easier on other people, maybe my next interview will be a little easier to land."

"You believe in karma," Mom observes.

"I believe in a lot of things that are real," he replies with a grin. "Let me grab a cup of coffee. Anything for you ladies while I'm up there?"

We shake our heads, and he makes his way to the counter.

"You're ready for this?" Mom looks at me, her eyes clouding with melancholy. I nod and smile tightly as Clay returns a moment later with a mug of steaming black coffee.

Mom notices my hesitation and clears her throat.

"Clay, as I mentioned in my email to you, I worked in Kabul. I was there until 1978."

"Hmm. A year before the Soviets invaded. Why'd you leave then?" he asks. I tense at the realization that Clay will ask many questions because that is his nature, and because it has been my nature to avoid people like him.

"The Saur Revolution occurred that spring," Mom says, and Clay nods. Mom pronounces Saur like "sour," which sounds wrong in one way but right in another.

"The mission didn't close down then, but some of us came home. Some stayed on a bit longer."

Clay turns his attention to me.

"Were you there with her?" he asks.

"I was," I say, then take a deep breath before I continue. "I lost my family around the time of the coup and came to the U.S. with Mom."

Clay's expression grows somber.

"I'm sorry to hear that."

I nod and press on. I cannot linger here.

"I really wanted to speak to you about what you saw in Kabul while you were there. I read your book. The conversation at the bookstore got a bit sidetracked."

"If I remember correctly, you had a lot to do with us getting side-tracked."

"Well, you know what they say. Keep biting your tongue and one day you won't have one," I say.

"Is that quotable medical advice?"

Mom takes a long, slow sip of her coffee. Her eyes twinkle over the rim of her mug.

I rest my elbows on the table and make sure Clay sees I'm completely serious.

"I wanted to ask you about the antiquities and the museum. With the Taliban still lurking and all that's happening, did it feel like the collections were safe there?"

"They were safer than they had been in the past," Clay offers, qualifying his comments. "Would they be safer in Midtown Manhattan or the Louvre? Maybe. But that's not where they belong. Can I ask what's inspired your interest in the returning of the antiquities?"

I don't immediately answer, and this time Mom does not step in. Clay leans back in his chair and tries a different approach.

"Let me tell you what I know, and then you can tell me more about why you're asking. I started in Kabul in 2001. I went to get a firsthand look at the Taliban. Had a friend who hated them from the moment they blew up the Bamiyan Buddhas, though he didn't seem to care about much else they did. By then, everyone in America knew how they treated women. They weren't all that great to men either, but that's another story."

Clay shakes his head.

"People didn't really know what the Taliban looked like, though. I knew I could cut my teeth in Afghanistan, so I found myself a fixer and went out to the front line."

Clay is one of those creatures in this world who run toward the fire, who feel pulled in by crisis. Mom nods, his words resonate with her. She would have done the same had it not been for me. She would have spent all her days stationed in places where cardboard governments ruled in name and warlords ruled in truth had I not fallen into her life.

"So we went north. I'd grown out a decent beard. We managed to slip by unnoticed until eventually we got to this spot along the Amu Darya, river water running cold and fast. I was standing on a sandy bank looking at the western advance line. There was a decrepit Soviet tank tipped over. Not much evidence of conflict on that side. There was just nothing there to shoot at."

Clay runs his fingers through his hair.

"I'd eaten something that hadn't agreed with me that morning, and I thought I was going to be sick. I told my fixer I needed to make some notes and took off for a little walk. So I walked away, looking for privacy, and came upon this Corinthian column lying on the ground in a shallow trench. I started looking down at my feet, and there were pieces of pottery scattered on the ground. I picked up a couple of pieces and felt them in my hand, and I just knew I was standing on history, real archaeological history."

"Had you heard of Ai-Khanoum before then?"

Clay shakes his head.

"Nope. And I didn't have much time to poke around there either. I heard some pops in the distance, and my fixer came running to find me. He pointed out some black clouds in the sky and said he'd taken me close enough. I started reading up when I got back to Kabul."

"Many of the relics from Ai-Khanoum had already been excavated, though," I say. "Any chance you heard about their whereabouts?"

Clay nods, while his eyes look carefully into mine, as if he's looking to untangle something.

"I'd heard people from the national museum hid stuff in the basement of the palace in Kabul. That's in the book too."

I press my feet to the floor of the coffee shop, anchoring myself. Boba had been preparing the treasures of Ai-Khanoum for transport to the museum. It is unlikely they ever made it out of the palace. Instead, they were joined by whatever else the guardians of the museum could manage to smuggle into the palace before the Taliban rolled through to cleanse the city of icons.

I take a deep breath. Since speaking with Shair, I have become even more determined to face my past.

"I have a ring from Ai-Khanoum. I've had it for years, but I don't think it should be with me anymore. It should be in the Kabul Museum."

Clay takes his second sip of coffee. I'm sure it is cold by now, but he seems like the type of person who is accustomed to consuming food and drink at the wrong temperature.

"But before I turn it over, I need to know it will be safe there."

"Can I ask how you came to be in possession of this ring?" Clay asks gently.

I feel Mom's eyes on me. I look out the window. Day has succumbed to dusk, and the city begins to twinkle.

Ai-Khanoum, city of the Lady Moon. How had she felt when men speaking in foreign tongues brushed the dust from her walls, when she saw her reflection in the glistening eyes of explorers eager to claim her?

So many nights I've dreamed of a woman whose figure ran the length of a city. I see her emerging from the khaki earth, a goddess waking from slumber. Sand slips away from her knees and forehead, moonlight fills in the slivers of space between her limbs and frames the skyline of her face, the arch of her spine, the contours of her breasts. She dips her toes into the tumbling waters of the Amu Darya, her movements graceful as in a fairy tale. It is a dream from which I am always eager to wake because I know, if I linger, I will only doom myself to see her fall again.

CHAPTER 50

FROM THIS DIZZYING HEIGHT, THE EARTH LOOKS LIKE A TOPO-graphical map, with contours implied by shifts in hue. From this height, the eye cannot discern road from river—or friend from foe.

A few months ago, an American airstrike went awry. Sixty children were among the dead. I didn't look at the pictures, but still my head swam with images of small, grayed lips and lifeless eyes. Of motionless angels wrapped in white sheets. I was struck with a migraine so severe I could hardly think straight as visions snapped through my head like shrapnel.

I cannot allow that to happen now. I open my bag and swallow two pills, washing them down with a sip of cranberry juice.

"What are you thinking?" Clay asks. He has the middle seat and Mom has the aisle. She's fallen asleep, as she always does, moments after takeoff. I knew I would one day return to Afghanistan but hadn't imagined what that voyage might look like.

Where do I begin?

"Nothing, really. Just haven't seen this view for a while," I say.

When we met in the coffee shop, I'd only meant to talk to Clay about the Ai-Khanoum ring. He didn't need to know how I'd come to be in possession of it, and I wasn't going to tell him if he asked. But sitting across from him, I had a change of heart. I was tired of holding everything in. I had asked him if, as a journalist, he was obligated to maintain confidentiality.

Well, as a journalist, I have an obligation to protect my sources. But I don't think I'm here as a journalist. I'll tell you what. I don't know where this conversation is going, but I do promise, as a person, to keep my lips sealed. I'm good at that.

I'd hoped for something closer to an oath but found myself reassured by his hand over his heart, a gesture I knew he'd picked up from his time in Afghanistan.

I had told Clay everything while Mom listened. There was no way around it. These were all details of one entangled story.

Clay's expression hadn't belied the least bit of surprise. He'd listened intently, but without reacting. He wasn't patronizing or disbelieving. I started with the coup and moved quickly through the moments that orphaned me. Though I kept my account skeletal, my escape from Arg and my homeland tumbled out of me so easily that I wondered why I'd hidden all of it from Adam for so long.

I didn't expect Clay to want to accompany us on this trip, and yet here we are. If I had known in the coffee shop that I'd be sitting next to Clay for a ten-hour flight, I don't know if I would have had the courage to tell him quite so much. Now I wonder if I look to him like another casualty of war, if he's imagining the scars on my psyche, or if he's going to ask questions that tilt me into dark thoughts. I am not accustomed to such insecurities. They are something between uncomfortable and painful, like shoes half a size too small.

"Aryana," he says, taking a book out of his bag and resting it on his tray. "What happens if this trip doesn't give you the answers you're looking for?"

I look at him to gauge his intent.

"Just making conversation," he says, putting his hands up defensively. "This isn't an interview."

Clay is here for a story, but not my story. When Mom told him about the search efforts for the remains of those killed in the coup, he let out a long, heavy breath. He called me the next day and asked if he could join us. I made him promise not to write anything about me, and he agreed. Though the coup had defined my life, it was barely a blip in the newspapers or history books, so I'm grateful he wants to write now about what happened in April 1978, even if his focus is on the antiquities lost that night.

"I'm not prepared to face that possibility," I admit.

"The search could go on for months or years. You don't plan on spending that much time in Kabul, do you?"

I shake my head.

"I can't. I have to get back to my practice."

"You enjoy what you do?"

"There's nothing else I imagine myself doing," I reply. "It's who I am."

"People talk about cancer like it's a war too. A different kind of war."

"I've never liked that, turning people into soldiers. It works for some people who win but others aren't up for the fight," I say. I flex my feet to keep my blood circulating in my calves. When Mom wakes up, I'm going to remind her to do the same so she doesn't develop a blood clot. "Surrender doesn't make them any less brave."

Clay flexes his feet as well, taking my cue. "What do you think it's going to feel like to be back there?"

I've asked myself that same question. I don't know how I'll feel when my feet hit the tarmac. I'm not sure how I feel about my motherland anymore, and I'm even less sure how she feels about me.

I'm nervous about the possibility that my country will find a way to reject me, or that I'll be overwhelmed at the sight of Arg or the discovery of the graves of my parents and brother.

Clay must sense that I can't organize an answer to his question. He fills in the silence.

"I grew up in Kansas, and not even Kansas City. Just a sleepy little town full of good people during the day and only the sound of crickets at night. They thought about shutting down the local prison once, but that would've left a third of the town out of a job. I couldn't wait to get out of there when I was a kid, so I only applied to colleges that were far from home."

"Where did you end up going?"

"Community college. Turned out that I didn't have the money for much more at that point, and my dad knew that, so he'd applied for me. I was probably the most resentful kid on that campus my first semester. I took a journalism class on a whim, and I've never looked back."

"How did your parents feel about your career choice?" I am always careful with the tenses, not wanting to sting anyone with an assumption that loved ones are living.

"They were just happy I'd stopped complaining about being stuck in our town. But the thing is, I wasn't all that angry at our town. It just didn't give me a way to see how I was going to fit into the world."

"And of all the ways to be a journalist, you chose war reporting."

"Did I mention I come from a sleepy little town?" he asks with his voice lowered.

"And how does it feel when you go back to your sleepy little town?" I ask.

Clay's smile fades. He runs his thumb along the edge of his foldout tray.

"The first time I went back," he begins, without looking my way, "I felt like I was walking onto a movie set. Everything looked so perfectly arranged. There was the grocery store with thirty different kinds of cereal, the boxes lined up perfectly on the shelves. A big yellow school bus stopped in front of our home at twenty minutes past seven in the morning, five days a week. People stopped at red lights and let moms with strollers cross the street. Sure, unexpected things happened here and there, but they were the kinds of unexpected things you expected to see. Someone died of pneumonia. A foreclosure sign went up on a house. And people . . . people just went bowling on Saturday nights and talked about the weather and walked their dogs."

I watch his hands as he talks, glad that we're sitting shoulder to shoulder instead of face to face.

"I'd seen too much while I was over there," he continues. "Home felt plastic, like a toy fresh out of its box."

"You're not the only one drawn to the thing that keeps you up at night," I say.

Clay chews his lower lip.

"But it can't go on like this. There's got to be a reset button," he says.

"If you found one, would you push it?" I ask.

Sitting next to Clay, I pick up a faint scent—a warm blend of teak, nutmeg, and apple. I become self-conscious that I've noticed and shift in my seat, trying to add an inch to the space between us. The scent is subtle, though, and doesn't cause my head to squeeze the way Adam's cologne often did. Clay's too busy digging for an answer to my question to notice my fidgeting.

"I don't know. But I am sure if my mom found that button, she'd be the first to push it. She thought I would end up writing for the *Kansas City Star*."

Mom groans, turning her head to the other side without opening her eyes. "People are always complaining about moms pushing their buttons," she says.

I stifle a laugh.

Clay looks impressed at Mom's ability to slide into a conversation half-asleep.

During my surgical residency, I'd scrubbed in for a difficult case. An eighty-nine-year-old man had suffered complication after complication in the treatment of his colon cancer. His physical deterioration seemed to accelerate his dementia, leaving his children to make decisions on his behalf. When he came into the hospital writhing in pain from yet another bowel obstruction, his children insisted that something—anything, everything—be done to save him.

But the man's cancer had robbed his blood of the elements it needed to form clots. He bled profusely. Bright red blood splattered onto my mask, my glasses, and my sterile gown. I cauterized and irrigated and cauterized some more, finally getting the bleeding under control.

At the close of the case, I left the recovery area and walked down a hospital corridor, heavy-footed in my clogs, to see an ailing patient in the intensive care unit. I noticed people looking at me askance. A woman's hand flitted to her mouth.

I looked down and cursed under my breath.

Blood had soaked through the sterile gown, painting scarlet splatters across my scrub top. I took a few papers out of my pocket, unfolded them, and used them to cover the stains.

The woman I passed probably thought I'd done my patient more harm than good. I didn't blame her for looking away. To wrest a body—or a country—from the grips of demise is a bloody affair.

CHAPTER 51

EVEN WITHOUT THE TURBULENCE IN THE SKIES, MY STOMACH would have been doing somersaults. I press my face to the glass and trace the jagged lines of the mountains.

"No city in the world makes a grander entrance," Mom whispers.

I hear the lift of pride in her voice too and remember that Kabul was much more than just another post for her.

This leg of the flight, from Dubai to Kabul, is just under three hours. There are only a handful of Westerners on the flight. Some toy with spreadsheets on their laptops, while others sleep with arms folded and heads tilted back. The rest are my countrymen, some dressed in loose-fitting tunics and pantaloons, some in suits, and a few in acid-washed jeans and slim-cut dress shirts. They are men with features as rugged as the mountains, with skin the color of the earth. They look as if they were bits of homeland shaped into people.

I have kept to my seat and avoided eye contact with them for the duration of the flight.

The cabin air is stale, and my limbs are stiff. I've only picked at the trays of food that have been placed before me, my appetite as thin as the atmosphere at this altitude. I reach over and touch Mom's hand.

"I'm really glad you're here with me."

"Me too," she says, a light rasp in her voice. She clears her throat and exhales slowly and for a second I wonder if this trip might be too much for her. The years are starting to show on Mom.

When the pilot announces that we'll be landing within twenty minutes, I squeeze the armrest. My mind is flooded with my parents' faces, with echoes of Faheem's giggles, with the feeling of sitting in green grass with Neelab and Rostam. As the plane descends, I plunge deeper into a sea of memories. Images I thought had faded bubble to the surface. By the time the plane touches down and rolls along the narrow tarmac, I can barely swallow.

I concentrate on the muscles of my throat, trying to reverse this feeling.

As a first-year medical student, I spent a lot of time in the anatomy lab, two large rooms in the basement of the school. The thick steel door did little to contain the smell of formaldehyde. We were doing head and neck dissections when I stayed back one day to ask our anatomy professor a question I hadn't wanted to ask in front of my classmates. We stood over my group's cadaver, an elderly woman with one replaced hip and a hint of mauve nail varnish on her fingers. My classmates kept her hands tucked under the drape so we wouldn't see them during dissections but I would lift the edge and let her fingers show when it was my turn to expose a new muscle or nerve. I thought she deserved to be known as a whole, not just the sum of her parts.

When people feel sad, they get a lump in their throats, I said. *But what does that mean anatomically? What's happening?*

My anatomy instructor, Dr. Sinks, was a wizened woman who looked to be in her late seventies. She had stark white hair cut in a severe bob and was nearly a foot shorter than me. She presided over the dissections in a rubber apron with her gloved hands clasped behind her back. When something noteworthy was discovered on any one cadaver, she would climb atop a stool and whistle between her teeth to capture our attention. She was surprisingly cheerful for someone who spent much of her day away from daylight and in a room with the deconstructed bodies of her contemporaries.

Ah, the physiology of globus hystericus, she'd said. She plucked a scalpel and a probe from a set of tools on a nearby table. With a touch that was at once delicate and determined, she peeled back the layers of the neck.

Not long ago, anything from fever to depression was attributed to the so-called roaming uterus, she explained. *Surgeons performed "hysterectomies" to remove the offending organ. But the globus sensation is caused by the autonomic nervous system activating a fight-or-flight response to stress. The glottis expands to take in more air while the muscles of swallowing press against it. It's almost as if the body were choking itself.*

I could have hugged Dr. Sinks, rubber apron and all. Once I knew the muscles, I could fight for control over them. It has been no small feat, but I have learned how to breathe through the feeling, to wrest the little fingers off my airway.

Passengers rise to their feet and pull bags and jackets from the overhead compartments. Bits of Dari and Pashto conversations swirl around me, filling my ears faster than I can process any of it. Mom and I arrange our headscarves, letting the ends fall over our shoulders and pulling the fabric down to our foreheads. A crush of bodies move toward the exit, down the stairs, and onto the tarmac. We're greeted by a bright but brisk day.

We find our luggage on the conveyor belt and pass through checkpoints. Clay hails a yellow taxi, and for a second it feels like we are back in New York. We ask the driver to take us to the Intercontinental Hotel. He is not the least bit flummoxed by his English-speaking passengers.

"Intercontinental. Yes, sir. Yes, madam. Very nice hotel," he says approvingly.

Mom and I slide into the backseat of the cab. Clay sits in the passenger seat up front with the driver. He sets his bag between his feet and looks back over his shoulder to ask us if we have a preferred route.

"Do you want to go through Wazir Akbar Khan?"

The driver glances in his rearview mirror, from which dangles a *tasbeh*, amber beads and a burgundy tassel. He looks back at Clay and smiles.

"You are many times in Kabul?" he asks.

"Many times, friend," Clay replies.

We head west, down the long road that leads out of the airport and into the city. My sleep-deprived eyes move slowly across the landscape, as if I'm submerged underwater. Billboards. A shopping center with sale signs in the windows. A braying donkey. The ding of a bicycle bell. Cars pressed bumper to bumper.

"You are businessman?" the driver asks Clay. I am grateful Clay is here to absorb the driver's attention, to distract him with conversation until I can collect myself. Clay tells the driver he's a journalist in a way that implies we're all journalists.

"Just look at this," Mom says softly. Kabul is a jungle of juxtapositions. An internet café practically shares a wall with a mosque. Men with mobile phones pressed to their ears buy vegetables from the back of a wooden wagon.

The Intercontinental Hotel comes into view, a vintage postcard come to life. The hotel, only five stories tall but wide, sits atop a high hill and boasts incredible views of the city. I have walked through the front doors in glossy Mary Janes for a family wedding and circled the pool in the back, my small hand fitting snugly in my father's, as men swam laps and women wearing round-rimmed sunglasses lounged in the sun.

We pass through multiple security checkpoints, pat-downs, and metal detectors to enter the hotel lobby, a grand room constructed of marble, boasting wide columns with gilded bases. Elaborate chandeliers brighten the long marble-tiled hallway, a regal floor designed with medallions and intricate borders to mark off sitting areas with tufted sofas and armchairs.

Men and women in dark blazers and brochure-worthy smiles greet us from behind the reception desk. Sparks of light dance at the far edges of my vision. I sense a migraine coming on, fueled by the recycled cabin air, the lack of sleep, the empty stomach, and more.

We turn our passports over to the woman behind the front desk counter. She has thick, perfectly shaped brows and is a decade younger than me, and still I surreptitiously search her face for any familiar features. Could she be a cousin? Maybe the sister of someone I knew? When she notices my stare, I turn my attention to my phone.

"I hope you will enjoy your rooms. They are on the second floor with a view of the pool, as you requested Ms. . . . Aryana," she says as she hands my passport back to me. Afghanistan was once named Ariana. I wonder if she can see through my documents and clothes to know that I am made of this earth too.

She points us in the direction of the elevators and assures us that the bellhop will bring our luggage to us shortly. Clay's room is down the hall from ours. We all need to rest and agree to meet in the hotel lobby in two hours for dinner, adjusting ourselves to local time. Our room is simple but thoughtfully decorated, the pattern on the blue carpet reminiscent of the patterns on the walls of the Alhambra in Spain. The plush bedspread and cushioned headboard are the same regal shade of blue. Our bathroom has steel fixtures against white marble, spotless top to bottom. Two bottles of water sit atop the wooden dresser.

I look out the window while Mom thanks the bellhop for setting our bags inside the room. When she closes the door, she joins me to check out the view.

"I swam in that pool a handful of times. Had plenty of dinners in the restaurant downstairs. It's strange to see it again, on the other side of a war," she says.

"This hotel is a five-star experience compared to some places we've stayed in, isn't it?" I add.

"It certainly is. Remember the stray cat that wandered in through the window in Turkey?" Mom laughs at the memory as she plops down on the bed, propping a pillow under her swollen feet.

Mom and I, in our travels, never sought out luxury. We were comfortable with the thrum of people and traffic outside the windows of our sparse rooms, which kept us exploring the world outside.

We have chosen this luxurious hotel for its security. The Taliban were ousted but not eradicated. Extremists continue to wreak havoc on the country by planting car bombs, suiting up in suicide vests, and exploding hand grenades at hotels, embassies, and the offices of nongovernmental organizations.

"I wish we could have stayed at the old apartment on Chicken Street," Mom says wistfully. Her eyes close almost against her will, and she drifts into a light sleep. I do not wake her. It would break her heart to see my rituals—my careful study of the hotel floor map on the back of the door, my testing of the windows to be sure they open, and my evaluation of the space beneath the beds to see how many people it will accommodate. I do not put my feet up until I have memorized the paths to the roof and to the stairwell and confirmed that a leap from this floor might allow us to escape with only broken bones.

CHAPTER 52

SINCE I LAST LOGGED IN, A HALF-DOZEN NEW IMAGING RESULTS have come in as well as a flurry of labs. I respond to messages left by oncologists and primary care doctors and answer a bullet-point list of questions from my office manager. I scroll through my inbox one more time and see a new message from Adam.

Aryana, please give me a call. I've been thinking about you.

I look up from the computer. Mom, her cheeks still pink with her yoga flush, stands over me with a towel wrapped around her. Her hair is wet from her shower and for a split second I see Tilly. I close my laptop without responding to Adam's email.

I have been thinking about him too, imagining what he might say if I told him I was in Kabul right now.

"Any fires?" Mom asks.

"All under control," I say. She knows how hard it is for me to unplug from my work because she's wired the same way.

We find Clay in the hotel café reading a local newspaper printed in English. Since today is Saturday, the embassy and the government offices won't be open until tomorrow. Clay has already called an old contact, a linguist named Waleed, and arranged for him to drive us around Kabul.

"Good morning, ladies," Clay says as he sets down his coffee cup. There is a basket of bread on the table, along with jam and a plate of cheeses.

Over breakfast, we make an ambitious list of places we want to see, pushpins on my personal map of Kabul. Clay takes notes, his gray eyes gauging and designing. We head to the lobby, where the hotel doorman signals us over and leads us out the doors to meet our escort. Leaving the hotel is easy. There are no X-rays or pat-downs for those headed into the city.

Waleed has arrived ahead of schedule, a sign that he's been working with foreigners. He is polite, articulate. In a Kabul full of Western contractors, aid workers, journalists, and military personnel, he has found his niche.

He could be anywhere between twenty-five and forty years old. Age is hard to guess since clocks and hearts seem to tick faster here, where lives are lived in urgency. He wears jeans and a pressed shirt, bowing forward as he shakes our hands. He has a fully charged mobile phone and a solid enough command of English that he can even crack some jokes.

"Good morning, friends. Mrs. Shephard and Dr. Shephard. Mr. Porter says this is not your first visit, so I will not say welcome. I will say welcome *back* to Kabul."

"We're happy to meet you," Mom says graciously. I can see the woman she was in her younger years, marching into unknown territory armed with diplomacy, an earnestness in her interactions with people, and a rooted belief that there is good in others. Were it not for me, Mom probably would have stayed in Afghanistan until the embassy shut its doors and called every last person home.

Waleed's eyes linger on my Eastern features, my Western dress. He looks at the three of us, and I can guess at the assumptions he is making about our relationships.

"Sir," Waleed says, turning to Clay, "where would you like to take these ladies today?"

I instinctively take a step forward, as if I'm coming out from behind a curtain to claim my spot on the stage.

"Waleed-*jan*, I was born in Kabul, but I've not been back here since before the Russians invaded. Let's start with a drive past Polytechnic University. It's closer than anything else."

He blinks back his surprise.

"Yes, Doctor," Waleed says, turning on his heel and extending his arm to invite us to follow. He pauses for a beat before he continues. "Doctor-*sahib*, you remind me of my dear sister. She is also a doctor, in the very busy maternity hospital. She would be very happy to meet you."

The pride in his eyes disarms me.

Waleed's Toyota is in decent shape. There is a bit of wear and tear on the body, but it seems reliable enough. He raises a hand to the armed security guard as he pulls away from the hotel.

"I will show you as much as I can," Waleed says. "Kabul is a city of high walls but higher flags."

We approach the university. The lecture halls and dormitories are mostly hidden from view, as are most buildings and offices. We weave through roads crowded with cars, taxis, buses, and bicycles carrying one to two passengers. A Coca-Cola sign hangs on a light post.

Today's sun is gentler than yesterday's. Waleed points out the Afghan Parliament building and, across the road, the hollowed-out Daru-laman Palace, which had been home to the Ministry of Defense when I was a child. Once stately as a New York City museum, the palace now has gaping holes in its walls, cratered interiors, and heaps of rubble in its halls.

"Waleed-*jan*," I say, as we stand on the edge of the grounds, "this is the view the members of Parliament have in their sessions."

"Yes, sister," Waleed replies in Dari. "But if they see it or not, everyone in Parliament knows what has happened here. You cannot hide the sun behind two fingers."

Mom and Clay watch me protectively as I step in and out of the car, as if I'm made of glass and at risk of shattering. They share quiet, concerned glances that I pretend not to see.

"I want to see my home," I say. Waleed nods. I describe my home's location by landmarks, which is how everyone, including Waleed, relays addresses in Kabul. He navigates the city expertly, and soon enough we are at the very place where the general had stopped his car and questioned Mom and me all those years ago.

Two boys come down the street, the taller one holding a soccer ball with frayed seams. The gutters on the side of the streets teem with waste. Waleed walks in step with Clay and two steps behind me.

The farther along the street we walk, the more disoriented I become. A third of the homes are gone. Another third are riddled with holes or look like the ground has shifted beneath them. Some are new constructions. We walk one block and another. I cannot remember.

"It should be here. This feels like the place," I say, imagining the rooftop my father had leapt upon and the balcony where my mother grew a small herb garden. I look carefully at each house. The shapes are all wrong, nothing fits my memory.

Mom has her hands on her hips.

"Gosh, just look at this," she whispers.

"This neighborhood suffered very much during the civil war," Waleed explains.

Clay bricks crumble beneath my boots. My throat tightens, and no amount of practiced breathing can release the tension.

I see a scrolled stone banister post, and the first step of a staircase that once led to a second floor. The spiral reminds me of the soft curls of my mother's hair, of the way her wrists twirled when she danced, and in a flash I know where I am. I take a sweeping look at the devastation, at the remains of my childhood home.

Mom puts an arm around me. Clay and Waleed have taken a respectful step back, recognizing in the hunch of my shoulders and the bow of my head the posture of grief.

I pinch my nose with the tissue Mom has slipped into my hand, then clear my throat.

Waleed takes two steps forward.

"When did you say your family left, sister?" he asks.

"Before the Russians came," I reply. I snap a few photos so I will have something to return to later. "I don't know if anyone lived here after we left."

I remember the general we'd seen sauntering out of my home so many years ago, as casually as if it were his brother's home.

I slip to the ground and scoop up clumps of debris with two hands. Sand falls through my fingers. A sliver of glass. A piece of splintered wood, maybe from a window frame.

Two curious women in burqas walk past me. The mesh window of their *chadoris* are turned toward me.

My Rodabeh, my princess of Kabul. My father's sweet words echo in my mind.

Your Kabul is gone, Shair had said to me all those years ago.

I rise, dust my hands off, and remind myself that even if the home had been in pristine condition, untouched by the onslaught of rockets this neighborhood suffered, it would not have brought me any peace.

I say a quick prayer under my breath.

I pray the rockets that destroyed this house did not claim the lives of innocents.

I pray a house will be erected on this land and children will experience the joy of waking up to the sound of their parents' voices.

I pray the rubble I have held in the palm of my hand will not haunt me.

"Aryana. Are you okay?" Mom asks quietly. I nod.

I turn my back to the dust and walk back to Waleed's car. I feel heavier and wonder what will become of me during this trip. But my father never averted his eyes, never walked out on meetings out of frustration.

"I want to see everything," I tell Waleed as we all return to our seats in the car. My headscarf has once again started to slide, so I pull it toward my forehead. "Where should we go next?"

Mom and Clay exchange a glance.

"Aryana," Clay says somberly, "we have time here. We can spread it out over the next few days."

"Clay's right, sweetheart," Mom says.

"We should be busy over the next few days," I reply. "I understand if you'd rather not, but I need to see exactly what I missed."

Mom looks like she's about to say something, then resists. She looks out her window, biting her lower lip.

"Then I suppose we have much to do. We will go to OMAR," Waleed says.

Clay lets out a long, slow breath. We are back on the road, my home falling away.

"Who is Omar?" I ask.

"OMAR is not a person, sister," Waleed replies, cutting the steering wheel sharply to the left to avoid a pothole.

The rest of the day is dizzying.

We see buildings buckled by rockets rained on the city from a distance, the mosque my father used to attend for *Jumaa* prayers, and a movie theater in the early stages of reconstruction.

Children selling bottles of soda or sticks of gum swarm our car at intersections. They are insistent, smiling through chapped lips. Spotting our cameras, they want their pictures taken.

"Hollywood," one calls out, as he puts a hand on his hip.

"*Titanic!*" yells another, sticking both his arms out like he's on the stern of the ship embracing an expanse of sea.

I am laughing.

I am crying.

I am thankful I am not alone.

Waleed takes us to a building on the outskirts of town. When the sign comes into view, I learn that OMAR is an acronym standing for Organization for Mine Clearance and Afghan Rehabilitation. We step out of the car and take a moment to fix our scarves and jackets before we walk to the entrance of the land-mine museum. A man in a hunter-green tunic and pantaloons runs over to us and announces that the museum is currently closed. In the field behind him are a couple of helicopters and a tank.

Waleed fishes a few bills out of his pocket, brightening the guard's face. He swings the door open and begins to give us a tour of the collection. We find mortars, AK-47s, a Molotov cocktail, bricks of TNT, and the weighted blue protective suit worn by de-miners. Mines of all shapes and sizes sit in glass display cases, like archaeological discoveries. Innocent items were booby-trapped so that when a child stooped to pick up a doll, her touch would trigger a blast that splintered her leg bones. The more casualties, the closer they were to winning the war.

Waleed tells us that plastic mines evade metal detectors, so de-miners must feel around for them, pluck each one painstakingly from the earth. Occasionally a wandering goat or nomad trips a wire and is pierced with ball bearings of nails. Small children have wandered into fields and disappeared in one clap of thunder.

Afghanistan does not have one million goats, Waleed tells us, nor one million chickens, nor one million schools—but the dead, the wounded, the missing, and the bombs can be counted in the millions.

Waleed's math has teeth. Clay makes notes on a small pad, and I take a few photos that I might later delete. When we leave, our next stop is the school I attended as a child. Girls with white headscarves pinned primly under their chins watch me from the corners of their eyes, whispering conspiratorially to one another and clutching books to their chests.

When I was a child, girls didn't have to cover their hair. My mother wore a headscarf only in a *masjid* or when visiting a family to offer her condolences and prayers. I cringe to see women sheathed head to toe in burqas, obscured from the world. I know that, for many, this cover is the least of their concerns, but it is one marker of how much has changed. I wonder what my mother would say if she were to see me wearing a headscarf now.

Waleed takes us to the maternity hospital. His sister meets us at the entrance, buttoning her white coat as she approaches us. A black stethoscope hangs around her neck.

Her name is Dr. Nazari. She wears not a drop of makeup, and the small gold hoops dangling from her ears are her only jewelry. Her hair is tied back at the nape of her neck. She looks to be about my age. She shakes my hand, her grip firm, her English accented.

Waleed and Clay stay back, out of respect for the laboring mothers who fill the halls and walk the grounds while they await their turn for a doctor's attention.

Mom asks how many patients they care for daily, and Dr. Nazari shakes her head.

"Too many. The answer to all your questions is 'too many.' How many mothers die of hemorrhage to bring a fourth or fifth child into this world? How many newborns take their last breath before they see a new moon?"

She leads us down a narrow hallway.

Round-bellied women lie on beds with metal frames, curtains pulled for privacy. Nurses wearing surgical face masks slip into rooms with IV poles and pans, with sheets and towels. Not since I was a medical student have I been in a hospital as an observer.

"What is your specialty, Doctor-*sahib*?" she asks me in Dari as she escorts us into the building.

When I tell her, she raises an eyebrow, impressed. I want to tell her she needn't be. Following her into this hospital, I feel humbled.

Before I can figure out how to tell her as much, a nurse runs up to Dr. Nazari. A baby has turned into the wrong position. She is needed urgently.

"I hope you will return, Doctor-*sahib*," she says as she squeezes my hands.

When Waleed returns us to the hotel, we are exhausted. The sole of my foot aches, like a fault line of pain. Clay wants to transcribe his notes while everything is fresh in his mind, and Mom wants to put her feet up.

I change into sneakers and my running pants. I find the hotel exercise room and feel like I am finally breathing when my feet pound against the treadmill belt. I turn the speed up, ignoring the throbbing in my foot and the stiffness in my legs. I wait for the release to come, the lift of hitting my rhythm. When it doesn't, I jab at the machine to turn up the speed.

But the belt catches, as if someone has thrown rocks into its gears, and in one hopeful stride I am tossed from the runway. I land in a crumpled heap with my back to the wall, wondering if I have what it takes to get through the miles ahead.

CHAPTER 53

WE STEP INTO THE TAXI THAT WILL TAKE US TO THE AMERICAN embassy. It's less than six miles away, but it is a weekday and the streets are as congested as Midtown Manhattan. Clay asks the driver if he is hopeful about any candidates in the upcoming presidential elections.

The driver's English is good enough to understand Clay, but he can't string together a reply.

"Who knows what we'll end up with? Donkeys look like stallions from a distance," he mutters in Dari as he adjusts the rearview mirror.

"How many television stations are there now?" Clay asks. The driver lets out a long whistle. There are more than he can count.

"Taliban here—one radio, one television, one mouth. Now, one thousand mouth," he laughs, pointing to his head. "One thousand head-ache. But I happy. You come my house, see my television."

"Ah, that would be great," Clay says earnestly. He looks perfectly at ease here, almost more than he did in the bookstore where I first met him. I find myself watching people we meet carve out space for him, as if this were his homecoming, not mine. Clay looks over the seat at me and grins. I look away, feeling revealed.

The cab hits a pothole deep enough to bounce us in our seats and send my stomach fluttering.

Mom is listening, though she's got her eyes on the world outside. She adjusts her headscarf and cranes her neck to see a sleek-lined building sitting next to a clay mosque. We pass a woman in a sun-faded *chadori* standing on the side of the road. She has a bundled child in her lap and one hand extended to passersby.

"Ariana TV. Very good," the driver says.

Aryana.

My name is everywhere. Emblazoned on airplanes, the movie theater, a television station, a soaring wedding hall, a congested intersection, and a host of restaurants. The country cannot let go of her historic name, my eponym.

Did the echo of my sister's name haunt or comfort my parents?

I listen, as if they might send an answer in the mountain breeze. Being in Kabul has sharpened my senses. I can see and hear my parents more clearly, as if I've tweaked a dial and caused the static to fall away.

Sitara! Come hold your brother's hand. I hear them call my name. I can smell the fried leeks my mother would stuff into dough to make savory flatbreads.

I see my father lift Faheem in his outstretched arms for a taste of flight. He tosses him into the air, and Madar watches her precious son become airborne for a heartbeat, then exhales to see him return safely to Boba's arms. Though nervous, she does not stop Boba, and I understand, because, like her, I can resist neither the pride on my father's face nor Faheem's elation to defy gravity.

Pieces of my father's midnight song return to me:

I lie in rest, and yet you travail
Your glimmering love set to prevail.

His voice pulls at my heart, like fingers on the string of a *rubab*. How silly I was to laugh at this song when I was a girl, to think he was chiding me for wanting to stay awake past my bedtime.

Another pothole.

They have named a road after the singer who died in a tunnel in a suspicious car crash not long after the coup. He had criticized the Communist regime at a time when dissidents were disappeared dozens at a time.

We are fast approaching the American embassy. The driver lets us out at the gates, where police officers eye us from a distance. They scan our faces and our clothes well before we move through the official security checkpoints and our bags are sent through an X-ray machine.

"It looks so different," Mom says, admiring the renovated structure. The pattern of glass panes on the facade reminds me of fish scales. Two flags, American and Afghan, fly high overhead.

We pass through another security checkpoint. Mom's connections and former position win her no special treatment here, her homecoming dulled by all that has happened since she served in this mission.

A woman with her hair in a youthful ponytail leads us to an office. She offers us water or juice, which we decline. Clay and I sit, but Mom paces the room, looks at the books on the shelf behind the desk, and then sighs and paces some more.

I shift in my chair. My back and hip are bruised from yesterday's treadmill mishap, but my legs still crave a run. I can't be still too long.

"Any idea who we're meeting?" Clay asks, taking a leather-bound notebook out of his bag.

Before Mom can answer, the door swings open and nearly hits her back.

"Oh no. I'm so very sorry," the woman exclaims. She's dressed in a long houndstooth blazer and black pants. "I didn't see you behind the door."

Mom waves away her concern, and a round of introductions and handshaking begins. Her name is Carla Stevens, and she's a political officer in the embassy. Mom takes a seat, and Carla offers us water or coffee.

"It's good to meet you. I can't imagine how this must feel for you," Carla says. Mom's face grows soft with nostalgia. "I've a great deal of respect for your work, Ms. Shephard."

I put a hand over Mom's. In the years when she had made waves at State, calling out the sexism and discrimination, many of her colleagues distanced themselves from her. Diplomats tend to be diplomatic, after all. If she hadn't pushed as hard as she had, she probably would have retired at a higher pay grade.

"I'm sure you'll do the same for those coming up behind you," Mom says. She looks at her pointedly, sweetly, as she transfers this obligation onto Carla's shoulders.

Carla nods and tucks a strand of her walnut-colored hair behind her ear. She extracts a pen and notepad from a desk drawer.

Mom signals for me to take over. I explain that we've heard about the government's commission to find the bodies of the assassinated. Then I tell her that I was orphaned the night of the coup and have been waiting decades for the chance to find answers. I'm even more concise with her than I was when I told my story to Clay. It's a bit like crossing a river after figuring out where the stepping-stones are. Carla allows me to finish before she speaks.

"First, let me offer my condolences. I can't imagine the pain this must have caused you," she says, her brows knitted with concern. "I must admit, I've not heard of any search efforts, but I'm going to make a few calls and I'll see if my contacts with this administration can shed some light."

"That would be wonderful," Mom says gratefully.

Carla stands then and waits for us to follow. But the three of us remain fixed in our seats. She blinks twice, slowly, before she flips her notebook open again.

"You mentioned you're staying at the Intercontinental. Let me get your room number and I'll be in touch just as soon as—"

"If you need your office to make the calls, we're happy to wait in the lobby area or an empty conference room or the cafeteria," I suggest.

Carla looks from me to Mom.

"You understand, of course, that it will take some time to even find the right person to talk to about this," she says.

Mom nods. She offers an understanding look but continues to sit back in her chair.

"And that's why Aryana suggested we step out and wait in another room. I know this disrupts your day, but our time here is limited. We need only to be put in touch with the search commission. We'll take it from there," she says brightly.

Carla doesn't look pleased. She sets her notebook on the desk and puts a hand on her hip. She looks through the office window as if hoping she might flag someone passing by for help removing us from her office.

She exhales sharply, then escorts us to the cafeteria. She reminds us that she can make no promises, but we three are already aware that no one can promise anything in this place. We opt for a corner table. Clay leans back and surveys the room.

"She's not going to get back to us anytime soon," he says grimly. "I think I'm going to make use of daylight while I can."

"She will get back to us," Mom insists. "We do have to understand that they're running an embassy here. We've just waltzed in with this request. We have to give her a chance."

Clay doesn't argue. None of us are inherently patient or passive. We're each accustomed to pushing—for the interview, for the allocation of funds, for the treatment a patient needs. We do not easily abide the inertia of sitting around a table.

"Where will you go?" I ask when Clay slips the strap of his bag over his shoulder.

"I've got a couple of stories I started on my last trip," he explains. He's going to stop by American University to see if he can reconnect with some contacts. Mom wraps her scarf around her neck as we watch him leave the cafeteria. The temperature has dropped significantly since we arrived.

"Mom, I think I want to tag along with Clay. Are you okay hanging out here on your own for a bit?" I ask.

Mom raises an eyebrow but doesn't say what I know she's thinking. She looks conflicted even as she reassures me that she doesn't mind waiting alone. She's never held me back and won't start now. I put on my coat and gloves, then my headscarf.

"I'll meet you back here in a couple of hours. Call me if anything comes up before then," I say and kiss her cheek. I walk quickly until I am out of the cafeteria, then my step slows. I spot Clay at the foot of the stairs, then pause while he makes a turn toward the exit.

Once he's out of view, I start to descend the stairs and make my way to the ground floor.

"Miss, your colleague is there. I will call him to wait for you," the guard says, recognizing me from when we entered. He opens the door a sliver just as Clay raises his hand to hail a passing taxi.

"No," I say cheerily. "No need to call him. We are going to different places. Excuse me while I check my messages."

I take my phone out of my bag and pretend to tap through messages. I give Clay's taxi ample time to drive away before I step outside. The guard watches me, more out of curiosity than obligation.

Though I am grateful not to have made this journey alone, I know that there are some things I need to do on my own. I adjust my headscarf once more, covering my ears and my hairline so I won't draw unwanted attention. The guard clears his throat. I open the door and step out into the cold homeland.

CHAPTER 54

IN OUR THIRD YEAR OF RESIDENCY, AFTER A PARTICULARLY HELL-
ish week in the hospital, I took Dayo out for sushi to celebrate her birthday. With half our training still to go, we were too far from the end to
see the light yet. We decompressed over cleverly named cocktails and an
assortment of rolls served in a wooden boat.

We were putting in eighty hours each week during a brutal flu season.

Half of our patients were placed in isolation, and we were donning
yellow gowns, blue gloves, and white masks just to enter their rooms and
ask how they were feeling. A construction worker had developed a rare
fungal infection in his bloodstream, and a jewelry maker had just returned from Mexico with a tumor in her lungs after paying for a therapy
we'd never heard of. The patient of the week award went to the man who
had been declared a VIP when he'd been admitted. I was paged urgently
to his room and walked in to find his wife holding tubing in her hand.
She was threatening to rip the urine catheter out of him while his mis-
tress stood on the other side of his bed, fuming.

We'd just repaired his abdominal hernia, and he seemed close to
incurring another hole in his body. I told his wife how many hours

I'd worked in the past week and how many more I'd have to work if I told my chief that I watched my patient's urethra get torn apart. She dropped the tubing, took out her phone, and snapped pictures of her husband and the other woman before storming out.

I predict his cause of death will not be old age, Dayo had said, her hands swirling over an imaginary crystal ball. Then she'd gone wide-eyed with inspiration and claimed to know just what we needed to take a break from reality. When we left the restaurant, Dayo led me two blocks over to meet someone named Everly.

Indulging my best friend, I followed her into a dimly lit store where we were greeted by a blue-eyed woman in her early twenties. She wore paisley-patterned pantaloons that tapered at her ankles and an ivory T-shirt. Her raven hair fell long on one side of her head but was buzzed short on the other, giving her a curious asymmetry. One wall of the shop held cracked geodes, fabric-covered pens, and incense. The other wall held one shelf of books and small statues of Buddha, peacocks, and Hindu deities. A glass case displayed chunky jewelry, including a few pieces of lapis lazuli set in silver.

With her hands pressed together, Everly said, *Welcome home,* in a voice as smooth as a river stone. If I had dared to look at Dayo at that moment, my eyeballs might have rolled irretrievably to the back of my head. Dayo told Everly we were both interested in getting a reading. Everly smiled as if she'd guessed as much and flipped the front door sign to CLOSED before picking a turmeric-colored scarf off a rack and hanging it loosely around her neck. Dayo motioned for me to go first, and I obliged, my joints loosened by the fizzy drinks we'd just consumed. I followed the woman to a carpeted nook in the back of the store, hidden behind a bookshelf. In the center of the cream carpet was the steel frame of a pyramid.

Everly motioned for me to join her in the square, and shooting another glance at Dayo, I did so. When she lit a bundle of sage, the burst of flame illuminated the peach undertones of her face.

I will expel the entities attached to you. Close your eyes and breathe it in, she instructed.

Through the mesh of my eyelashes, I watched her tap her nails and produce a deck of cards from a wooden box behind her.

When is your birth date?

I hesitated. I briefly considered daring her to guess but thought it would only drag this session out longer.

And her question gave me pause. For years I'd been using my sister's birthday. Though I was born in the month of Aqrab, a Scorpio, my sister had been born in the month of Jawza, making her a Gemini, clever and imaginative.

The first of November, I told her, which was the day my mother brought me into this world and named me Sitara.

I waited.

Everly closed her eyes and began tapping her nails against the crystal again.

You are passionate and stubborn and so very brave, she whispered. *You move with the force of waves and shape the earth around you.*

I felt a hairline crack in my skepticism and chided myself for it as she began to turn over tarot cards. The first was the King of Fire. She half-closed her eyes as she continued.

You are determined, impatient, and restless. Something makes you so very restless.

I felt my shoulders tense. I wanted to be back on the sidewalk. The next card she pulled out was the Knight of the Earth.

You will embark on a mission that will change your life.

My pulse quickened.

And the Six of Air, she said, withdrawing a third card. *You're struggling to climb out from under negativity. You're digging yourself out of a hole. You feel buried—*

I was on the sidewalk in a flash, Dayo following me and apologizing profusely. The buzz of the cocktails had dissipated.

I inhaled deeply, drinking in the gritty smells of exhaust and steel and anything else that lived aboveground. I managed to crack a joke.

I had to leave. She saw another six weeks of overnight shifts in my future.

Dayo didn't laugh. Instead, she squared her shoulders and fixed her glistening eyes on me.

I'm so sorry, Aryana. I didn't think . . . I'm so sorry, she whispered.

I WRAP MY SCARF AROUND MY MOUTH, BOTH TO WARM AND CONceal my face. I stand at one end of a long tree-lined road that leads to Arg, impassable to cars. I feel the uptick in my pulse, the adrenaline signaling my fight-or-flight response, and remind myself that I am an adult, an American, and that decades have passed since the day of the coup.

And yet.

The palace entrance, with its crenelated towers, does not reach as far into the sky as I remember. Objects in a child's rearview mirror are smaller than they appear, especially after that child has stood under the Eiffel Tower, walked through the Hagia Sofia in Turkey, and passed through the halls of the Vatican. I live in a city with a skyline to humble the world.

And yet.

Arg retains her stately grandeur, the lovely symmetry of her gates. I move the scarf away from my mouth and take long, refreshing breaths of cold air. The street is empty but for soldiers in their olive uniforms with red-and-gold trim. Rifles hang at their sides. Two of them step toward me, speaking to each other out of the corner of their mouths as they approach. A tank is parked meters away, just as it was on that day. In two hours, it will be noon, the very hour at which the tanks and guards of the citadel turned their guns on us all those years ago.

"Miss, where are you going?" one asks in English. I look foreign to him. He has a short beard. The skin around his eyes crinkles like he's spent his lifetime squinting against the sun. He and his partner assess me, hands on their rifles.

"I am passing by," I say calmly. "It is cold, and I wanted to take the shortest way."

The soldier's eyes graze over my heavy wool coat. I try not to think of the bullets sitting in the weapon at his side. I turn away from them and take two steps before they stop me again.

"Where have you come from?" the taller soldier asks.

I nod my head behind me, in the direction of the embassy.

"American embassy," he declares, as if he's solved a puzzle.

They ask where I am headed, and I tell them my plan, the one I came up with this morning when I saw Carla's polite smile, the one that inspired little confidence that she would manage to connect us to anyone of use.

"The Ministry of the Interior," I reply.

An eyebrow perks.

"What business do you have there?"

I cannot tell if he's asking me out of curiosity or protocol.

"With your permission, I'd like to pass," I say, pointing in the direction of the ministry.

"Do you know the way there?" he asks.

I tell them it is no more than five minutes away, a nearly direct walk from where I stand. They begin to laugh.

"Better take taxi. You lost here," one soldier advises. He gives me choppy directions to the Ministry of the Interior. It is not where it used to be, not in the place my father used to point out to me when we drove around Kabul.

I walk the length of Arg, wondering if any children race around the grounds as we once did, if they play history as we did, and if they storm into the president's office and fire imaginary bullets out of the tips of their fingers.

I slip into the congestion of Chicken Street as if drifting into a dream. The motley wares of shops spill out from their storefronts. Carpets hang on balcony railings, sacks of spices sit outside glass storefronts, and embroidered vests and dresses dangle from tattered awnings. Sunlight turns the kicked-up dust of foot traffic into a nostalgic haze.

A passing man raises an eyebrow at me, teasingly. Another blows cigarette smoke directly into my face—a lewd exhalation. I hold my breath and bite my tongue to avoid making matters worse as women have learned to do.

I look up at the apartment where I'd stayed with Mom and Tilly and imagine I see the pale pink curtain flutter. The store below is no longer a bakery. I step inside, and the shopkeeper, a long-faced man with a short beard, gives me a nod. He adjusts the wool cap on his head and points at the small carpets hanging from the wall, the shelves lined with metal handicrafts.

More folded carpets and woven decor are stacked on a rack along the wall. The store has a rich collection of war rugs, small tapestries of traditional colors depicting land mines, tanks, and Kalashnikov rifles. One has a helicopter motif around the border and fighter jets at the center. Some have USA woven into a border while others have Cyrillic lettering.

"Who makes these?" I ask in Dari.

"Women. Children. Small fingers, good weaving."

I think of the magazine article I read not long ago about opium's ugly hold on Afghans, how they smoke it to forget their poverty or to ease an ache. A traumatized country has self-medicated with the crop that grows heartily on this land and enables them to feed their families and appease the warlords. The piece included a photograph of a mother blowing tranquilizing smoke into her infant's face, the look on hers an expression of love. She did this, the writer explained, so she could sit in front of a loom for hours, tying thread after thread with cramped fingers stained with henna.

"Why do people weave war carpets?" I ask. He laughs, a joyless sound. "You don't like?"

I touch a woven tank and wonder if this trend started with the weavers or the customers. The shopkeeper does not wait on my reply.

"My customers like this very much. War, guns, history. If I put bullets on a chain, I can sell it as Afghan necklace."

I don't need to ask who his customers are. I can tell his shop is like one of the hundreds of souvenir shops in Times Square selling Statue of Liberty snow globes and place mats printed with the subway map—items no New Yorker would purchase.

The shopkeeper watches me with curiosity. He moves a bowl to the edge of the counter and invites me to look. The bowl jangles with pins of American and British flags and Russian and British military medals. I have no interest in this memorabilia. I thank him for his time and see the disappointment on his face.

I bow out of the store and nearly walk into two NATO soldiers. They are surrounded by a cluster of boys who have probably lived their entire lives in the shadows of soldiers.

I rub my hands together in the taxi, but they are still frigid when we arrive at the Ministry of the Interior. I'm trembling as I approach the glass doors at the front entrance, which is guarded by soldiers just as Arg was. They stop me before I come close. The world was so easy to navigate with my father at my side.

How will I present myself here?

I must choose between two conflicting rationales.

I will get nowhere if I admit who I am.

I will get nowhere unless I admit who I am.

By the time one of the guards approaches me and asks what business I have at the ministry, I've decided.

Moments later, I find myself sitting across the desk from a man with a thick mustache and thicker eyebrows. His spartan office has barely enough space for the two of us. A television set to a news show plays in the corner with the sound off.

Once upon a time, I was a little girl who wrote about the importance of recording history. I ask that little girl to send me some of her courage.

"I am the daughter of Sulaiman Zamani," I begin in Dari. "He had a position in this ministry until he and the rest of my family were killed in Arg along with President Daoud Khan."

The man listens, elbows on his desk. He considers me for a long moment before he speaks, and his face shows no hint of surprise. I wonder if many people have sat in this very chair claiming vital links to the past.

"I see. And you have been abroad for some time," he observes. He looks past me briefly and then continues. "Sister, what was it that you said to the guards outside?"

"I explained to them that I know about the mission to recover the bodies of those who were murdered," I say, my spine straight. "This is a personal matter for me, obviously. I would like to know what progress has been made."

"You would like for me to report our progress to you?" he says, with just the slightest hint of mockery.

His eyes drift up, past the top of my head. My skin prickles, and before I even turn around I know the doorway, the only way out of this room, is blocked. I turn my head and see three men standing behind me—two in uniform, and one in tunic and pantaloons.

"Boss," someone shouts from across the hall, "the Americans are on the phone again!"

"Sister, you tell an interesting tale," the mustached man says before looking to the men behind for affirmation. "Doesn't she, gentlemen?"

He leans back in his chair, his right elbow on the armrest.

"You are not the first to return from the comforts of faraway lands, now that the dust has cleared. Perhaps you've heard that the foreigners will pay $10,000 per month to rent your family home. Or maybe you have your eyes on a seat in this Parliament? Or an official appointment by the president? Our sisters and brothers return daily, holding up their skirts so their hems do not drag in our dusty roads, clogging our courts with documents older than the mountains. And oh, how they all sing of their love for this homeland!"

I am instantly aware of the men behind me.

"If all that you've described outrages you," I respond, "then please show some mercy on me. I'll leave Kabul soon enough with nothing but the grief that brought me here."

The mustached man says nothing. He purses his lips and looks over my head to the curious people listening in on our conversation.

"Be ready tomorrow," he says. "We'll send a car to your hotel. But be warned. You may think you've come only with grief, but that's not true. You've come with hope too. Don't blame me if you leave Kabul feeling robbed."

CHAPTER 55

WE'VE CHOSEN A RESTAURANT HIDDEN FROM THE STREET BY thick blast walls. Once I've scanned the room and located all the exits, I take a second survey of the restaurant's decor, which is nothing like the damask and rococo designs of the hotel dining hall. The chairs here are not lacquered. There are no chandeliers.

Our table is set against a wall of exposed brick, and our faces are illuminated in candlelight. We are in a restaurant named after Rumi, the Sufi poet. Expats gather around low-set tables, resting against merlot-colored pillows and cushions with arabesque motifs. Lanterns hang from the ceiling and cast a light as soothing as birdsong.

Mom and I sip saffron tea, liquid sunsets, from ceramic mugs with Sufi wisdom written into the glaze.

My soul is from elsewhere and I intend to end up there.

The weight of the poetry and the warmth of the drink help settle me. At least a dozen nationalities are represented in the room. Calligraphy in the Nastaliq style gilds the walls. Each word, each letter, creates shapes on the wall—a whirling dervish, a vessel, a mountain peak, a winged

bird. This restaurant would fit perfectly in my transforming neighborhood back home.

Books are arranged artistically on floating shelves with small signs
inviting customers to feed their souls while they feed their bodies. I reach
over and select a thin volume of poetry written by a woman who had been
murdered by her husband. I flip it open and my eyes fall on a line printed
neatly at the very center of the page.

Sparks rain from my sighs like stars

Our waiter sets down steaming plates before us. As if he's pushed
a rewind button, my head spools in reverse, back to the dinners of my
childhood. Seasoned *kofta* kebabs adorned with lemon wedges and perky
sprigs of cilantro and mounds of long-grain rice browned with caramel-
ized sugar and topped with sautéed and julienned carrots, plump raisins,
and pistachio slivers. Mom dips her fork into the fried eggplant drizzled
with tomato sauce, garlicked yogurt, and a dusting of dried mint.

"Well," Mom begins. Her headscarf, like mine, has fallen to her
shoulders.

"It's been a long day for us all."

When Carla came to the cafeteria and apologized that she hadn't yet
gotten the right person on the phone, Mom had asked if she could join
Carla on the calls and Carla had reluctantly agreed. Her call to the ministry came through while I'd been sitting across from the mustached man.

"And you didn't have to grease the wheels a little?" Clay asks me as
he tears off a piece of warm bread. I've filled them in on my visit to the
ministry and relayed the information I was able to obtain.

"Not at all. He just asked me to keep it quiet. Said he was breaking
all kinds of rules for me."

"And he didn't give any hint where this place might be?" Mom asks
again. She huffed a bit when I told her where I'd gone but bit her tongue.

She and I both know she would have done the same. Rather, she has done the same.

"Not at all," I reply. Clay's phone chimes with a message. Selena's name appears on the screen. Clay reads it, taps out a quick reply, and then sets his phone back on the table.

"There's a small kebab stand down in the market. I mean, literally a stand. The guy fries onions and tomatoes in this pan wide as this table. That kebab was *almost* worth two days of gastrointestinal hell."

Clay's willingness to dodge bullets and torture his bowels in his quest for the truth astounds me.

"Poor Selena. She's got to be wringing her hands every time you leave home," I say.

"Selena? Nah. The more danger I get into here, the happier she gets," Clay says.

I want to ask what he means, but bite my tongue so I don't risk offending a man in love. It occurs to me, though, that this is the first time Clay has mentioned Selena, and his eyes hardly lit up to see her name on his phone.

Is that how Adam and I acted toward each other? I had long ago stopped feeling the small thrill of his phone calls or text messages. Maybe walking through fire makes it hard to feel sparks.

Clay stabs a piece of kebab with his fork, inspects it, then brings it to his mouth. He chews thoughtfully, as if he's going to issue a final score for the chef. But when he's swallowed, he swipes his napkin across his mouth and looks at Mom.

"When you were here," he asks her, "did you have any idea of what was about to come?"

Mom pauses before answering, her face shadowed with regret.

"I was sent to Kabul as a reward for dealing with roadside militants and rampant crime in my two previous posts. Here, we were having soirees with Foreign Service officers from all over the world late into the night. For most of my time here, the biggest news was finding out an ambassador's wife had caught him in bed with a leggy economic officer from another embassy. We were having the time of our lives hanging out with each other in this beautiful country."

"What about the Russians?" Clay asks. "Were they part of the fun?"

"Sure," Mom recalls, adding a spoon of cilantro chutney to her plate. "It was before the war."

"But it was during the Cold War," Clay notes. "So part of the mission must have been about checking their presence."

"As officers of the U.S. Foreign Service, our mission was to build diplomatic relations between the United States and Afghanistan," Mom says in the carefully arranged language of a Foreign Service officer.

"Diplomatic relations with Afghanistan were one tactic in the Cold War strategy," Clay responds. "You've got the Russians and the Americans trying to be best buddies with the Afghan government. Two muscle-flexing superpowers playing tug-of-war, and they shredded this country to pieces."

Mom sets down her fork.

"That might seem like a neat little explanation for how things went down, but you fail to grasp that we were building real relationships with real people. I knew President Daoud. I'd met his family. We weren't here to battle Russians."

"Not militarily, no."

They seem to have forgotten that I am at the table as well. Mom's hands are clasped together primly, her head cocked to the side. Part of me thinks I should intervene now, but I also know that one way or another they will have this conversation, either tonight or another day. Part of me knows this is the conversation I have avoided having with Mom for much of my life, purely out of love.

I've felt a headache coming on since we sat down. Taking my pills on an empty stomach will be torture, so I focus on eating and try to ignore their debate.

"Look, I'm sorry. I don't mean to offend," Clay insists. "I'm just looking at it objectively."

"You're very critical of our work. But the Russians were probably the ones who masterminded the coup. And they poured millions and millions into this country and made sure people were grateful for their Polytechnic University—"

"And we did the same with American University," Clay adds.

"They built Salang Pass . . ." Mom continues.

"We started that dam . . ."

"And the Macroyan apartment complex . . ."

"While we sent in almost two thousand Peace Corps volunteers to teach English," Clay says softly. He's not cocky in his retorts, just insistent.

Mom leans back in her chair and folds her arms across her chest.

"Okay, smart-ass. Let's say we were going tit for tat. The coup changed everything. It was a Russian-orchestrated prelude to a kiss, the military invasion of this country, and the beginning of the end. You saw the Russian tanks with your own eyes, didn't you?"

"And I saw the Stinger missiles Reagan sent over like they were party favors."

I set my napkin beside my barely touched plate and push away from the table. When I stand, both Mom and Clay become still.

"I can't listen to this," I announce brusquely.

A waiter, a thick-browed man in his early twenties, pauses at our table to check in on us. Clay takes a sip of water and Mom purses her lips.

"Is there anything I can bring for you?" he asks in a deeply accented voice.

"A ceasefire would be great," I grumble.

The waiter looks bemused.

"Sorry, sister, this is not on our menu," he says. He turns his attention to a more tranquil table by the windows.

Mom is on her feet, her hand on my forearm.

"Ary, sweetheart," she starts, but I shake my head.

"It's okay, Mom. It's not your fault. It's no one's fault. You're right. Clay's right. But I didn't come here to do a postmortem on the Cold War. I came here to find my family."

Mom bites her lip. She looks pained, as if she might have absorbed my headache through her hand on my arm.

Clay exhales sharply.

"I need a walk," I say. They both rise to leave with me, remorse on their faces. "You guys should stay and finish eating . . . and talking."

I stand outside the restaurant for a few moments, letting their argument dissipate into the night air. I start walking in the direction of the hotel, though I know it is late and the air is thick with car exhaust and the smoke of burning wood, plastic, tires, and coal. I think of the six million people in this city and the scarcity of oxygen.

After two blocks, I pause.

Someone a few meters behind me has been walking at my pace and in the same direction since I left the restaurant. I glance over my shoulder. I cannot make out his features from this distance, but I can see he is wearing dark slacks and has his hands stuffed in his pockets. I cross the street and walk to the end of the block, past a furniture store and a print shop. I pause to look at the signs in the print shop window. The man stops walking again.

I spot a taxi a few feet ahead and make my way to it. I tap on the glass, and the driver looks up, surprised. He rolls down his window, and I tell him I need to get to my hotel quickly. He nods and I slip into the backseat.

As the driver pulls into the road, I turn. The man is standing in front of the print shop, where I stood only moments ago. I see the light of a cell phone in his hand, but he's not looking at the screen—he's watching the taxi.

At the hotel entrance, a female guard pats me down behind a curtain. If her hand lingered on my chest for a second, she would have felt my heart pounding. When my purse and body have passed through the security layers, I take the elevators up to the room and open the safe, my fingers trembling. The jewelry box sits alone and vulnerable in its small cell.

I open the box and touch the stones. Will the ring be protected here? Will it mean half as much to anyone as it has meant to me?

I tuck the box into the pocket of my cardigan, then leave the room and make my way down the hallway, into the elevator, and up to the empty rooftop balcony. The temperature has started to drop again. I peer out onto the swimming pool and the faint lights of cars approaching the hotel entrance.

From this humble summit, a hilltop set against mountains, I turn my gaze to the starlit night. The long tail of Draco still curls around Ursa Minor, as it did when I was a little girl. The sky is full of conquests and sorrow, heroes and villains, monsters and magic.

"Can you see me better from here?" I whisper to the still night, my cheeks tingling with cold. Below, the city is a pale reflection of the sky. I fill my lungs with the smoke of burning rue and grumbling generators, of freshly baked bread and a hint of gun smoke, of bright cardamom and heady hashish. The air intoxicates me, turns me foolish and honest as a drunk.

"Forgive me," I say, with my hand raised to the blanket of stars above, ashamed of how long it has taken me to return to the place I came from, to ascend into the elsewhere I'm intended to be.

CHAPTER 56

THE *AZAAN* ECHOES ACROSS THE DAWN SKY, THE HOPEFUL *MUEZZIN* singing that prayer is better than sleep. I have forgotten how to pray. The *surahs* I had learned to recite in my childhood in the sacred language of God were the first casualties in my private war. But the call wakens me, even if it doesn't waken something in me. I slide one leg and then the other out of bed. Mom is a few feet away on the second bed, curled on her side with her back to me.

I imagine Tilly here with us, listening to the *azaan*. I picture her whipping a comforter off the bed, spreading it on the floor, and prostrating herself to see what it is like to worship a foreign God. The image brightens my morning.

I open my laptop and see a new message from Adam in my inbox.

Hey. Your phone's going straight to voicemail. I left my thumb drive at your place. Stopped by to try to pick it up but your neighbor says you haven't been around in a few days. Hope you're enjoying your vacation. Kindly FedEx it to me or drop it off at my office.

I hear Adam's voice in my head. I hear him enunciate "vacation" and picture him tapping out one bitter letter at at time. There is a new email signature that links to a website. I click on it and see an image of Adam the candidate in a dress shirt, sleeves rolled up so his forearms are exposed. He's shaking hands with a Black man in a tan Carhartt jacket standing outside a subway stop. Adam's wearing his cocktail party smile.

It occurs to me that Adam's friends all look like him. His previous girlfriends all looked nothing like me. His website says he's running to stand up for the everyday people of his neighborhood, but I've never seen him spend more than a few moments with anyone that couldn't be mistaken for his brother. I look out the window, recall the Sufi-themed restaurant and the walk to the Ministry of the Interior. I try to imagine Adam dipping a toe into this world.

I'm equally concise in my reply.

Out of country. Will send it when I return.

"What time is it, sweetheart?" Mom mumbles.

"Too early," I whisper back.

She rests her head on her bent elbow and considers me.

"What were you just thinking about, Ary?" Her voice is throaty with slumber.

Everything. Nothing.

"The *azaan* reminded me that I've forgotten how to pray. And it made me think of Tilly," I confess, grinning. "I was thinking if she were here, she might have tried praying."

Mom's laughter is faint at first. Then it swells and pulls me in. A moment later, the sound of our laughter fills the quiet of our room. She sits up and wipes a tear from her eye.

"Let's do it," she says.

"Let's do what?" I ask.

"Pray."

"But I don't remember how."

Mom stands up in her flannel pajamas and walks to the window to take in the melting dawn sky. She parts the curtains and a pink glow spills into our room and onto the wrinkled bedsheets, the muddied boots by the door, and the headscarves hanging on the backs of chairs.

Mom surveys the room, taps her chin with her finger. I pull the comforter off my bed, spreading it out on the floor. I remember my father once telling me that whether prayers were made on a gold-threaded rug or on a straw mat, they carried the same weight with God.

Mom bends at the waist, her spine curving as she brings her face toward her knees in a yoga pose that is sister to a prayer posture. I do the same but less gracefully, touching my hands to my knees and drawing a deep breath. We rise and kneel in synchrony, then bring our heads to the floor. Mom's hands are stretched out in front of her in a child's pose, *balasana*. I touch my forehead to the comforter and hear my mother whisper the word for this spiritual submission—*sajada*.

The Arabic words float in my consciousness, but I don't reach for them. My head grows heavy, as if I am a tipped hourglass and it is filling with sand. I come up slowly into a kneeling position. The desert in me rearranges once more. Sands shift back into place and my chest lightens.

"There's a saying I heard once," Mom shares. "Prayer is you talking to God. But meditation is God talking to you."

The warbling of a bird blends into our thoughts.

"I remember Tilly sitting on the roof of the apartment one day with this wild glow on her face . . ." My words come out in a sputter. When I see Mom wipe a tear from her cheek, I stop. I could kick myself. "Oh, Mom. I'm so sorry. I didn't mean to upset you."

"Don't be sorry," Mom insists, her face pinched. She wraps an arm around me. "You know, we're so damned afraid that talking about the ones we've lost will hurt us as much as losing them did. So we just stop talking about them. But that's when we truly lose them."

She's right. I've stopped myself from thinking about my family because I'm afraid of spiraling into grief that has no bottom, into a place from which I cannot climb out.

"When I was a kid and I lost my dad, people told me I had to move on. They made me think grief was like a cold," she continues. "If you don't act sick, you'll get better. And if you don't get over it in a week, then you're weak or there's something really wrong with you. But I think it's okay to mourn people *out loud* for more than a few days. I never said that to you. I'm sorry, I didn't know better."

In that moment, I realize why I've lived my adult life feeling like my insides are made of sandpaper. I'm just as culpable as Shair in robbing myself of my family. I have not allowed them to be part of me, failing to understand that their light can be my dawn—that a good day begins with a good mourning.

"But Tilly," Mom says, touching the comforter with her fingertips, "my mother didn't brush feelings away. She sank into them, and sometimes so deeply that it scared me. I think that's why I made every effort not to be like her."

"She had regrets too," I tell Mom. "But she called you a superhero."

Mom looks at me, half her face in shadow.

"When you showed up," Mom says, her voice rocky, "you stole her heart. I remember talking to her while you slept one night. I was so afraid of making a mistake with you that I was just about paralyzed. But Mom grabbed me by the shoulders and said, 'Nia, when you find a child you can save, you don't overthink it. You save her or you lose yourself.'"

Mom once described Tilly as a roller-coaster mother. If what I saw were the highs, I can only imagine what the lows were like.

"I wonder if I should have asked you more about your parents, your brother. I thought I'd be pushing you into uncomfortable places, but now I think I might have been sparing myself."

I consider this. We both deserve more than coddling answers right now.

"You did the best you could. You're not to blame," I say. "I . . . I really hate the way I tried to keep them deep in me. It's my fault too that I couldn't hold on to them better."

"Sweetheart, you were just a child then."

We were all something different then—even Shair.

"Do you think I should forgive Shair?" I ask.

"That's not for me to decide," Mom replies. "And I'm more interested in you forgiving yourself. You have carried around this guilt because you made it out and they didn't. You did nothing wrong. You have held them in your heart and become an amazing person in their honor. I hope, no matter what happens on this trip, that you'll believe that and give yourself a break. You deserve to be happy and loved."

Mom rises and disappears into the bathroom. While the pipes whistle, then shirr with the flow of water, I take a moment to think about what I deserve.

I'll confess, I have craved romance, the kind I saw when my father would sing off-key love tunes to my mother and she would hide her smile, her flushing cheeks. There is a single quatrain from the *Shahnameh* embedded in my mind, as out of place there as a chandelier in a cave.

> *So tightly they embraced, before Zal left,*
> *Zal was the warp, and Rudabeh the weft*
> *Of one cloth, as with tears they said goodbye*
> *And cursed the sun for rising in the sky.*

I've always believed that if I just worked hard enough, practiced enough, insisted enough, anything would be possible—even some form of love.

But I've never believed I could have the bewildering passion of Rudabeh and Zal—one of the many things I lost in the fire. It is a petty thing to lament now, especially as I stand within kilometers of where I lost everyone.

Mom may be right about forgiving myself, but she does not know the abyss I see when I look inward. What if I forgive myself and nothing changes?

Chapter 57

THE DRIVER STILL HASN'T TOLD US WHERE WE ARE HEADED. We're stuck in traffic, feeling directionless. I scan the cars around us and the pedestrians along the road looking for the man I saw last night. I don't see anyone of the same height and build, no one with a khaki-colored jacket like his.

I haven't said anything about him to Clay or Mom. I don't want anyone to limit my movements or try to cut this trip short—not when I'm so close.

Right after the coup, I felt like all of Kabul was hunting me, but so much time has passed since then and so much has happened in those years that I can't possibly be of any interest. On the other hand, I've read that kidnappers prowl the country for foreigners in hopes of a hefty ransom. Judging by the comments I overhear, I know it's no secret I've come from abroad. *Maybe she's come to take a soldier back home,* one woman had muttered to her friend as I walked past.

My stomach growls. I didn't have much of an appetite this morning and didn't eat more than a square of toast.

"Clay, is this the block you were talking about?" Mom asks. As we got dressed this morning, she told me she and Clay ended up talking late into the night. Their conversation drifted from Afghan history to Beatles albums and the best way to brew a cup of coffee. Clay is interested in trying the coffee sock technique Mom learned in Malaysia. They seem downright chummy this morning.

"Yup, this is the one," Clay says. Holding his cell phone just below the car window, he snaps a photo. We are driving past a row of soaring mansions with elaborate balustrades, gilded columns, and second and third floors boasting wide balconies. "You know those pictures of drug kingpins wearing a dozen thick gold chains around their neck? You see that same flash in home construction too. It's called narcotecture."

"These are criminally ugly," Mom comments.

I catch the driver looking back in the rearview mirror. When our eyes meet, he glances at his cell phone. I wonder if we've been too trusting in getting into this car, then chide myself for being so paranoid.

"Agha," I ask, trying to sound casual, "we will need to stop along the way to pick up a couple of bottles of juice. We didn't have much breakfast."

The driver shakes his head.

"There is no need, sister. They will have something for you there," he says.

I swallow hard. Mom tries to read my face.

"I just asked if we could stop somewhere to get drinks," I say softly in English. I repeat the driver's response to Mom, who stiffens a bit. Clay, sitting in the passenger seat next to the driver, swivels his head to look back at Mom and me.

"How's everything going?" he asks.

"Good," I say, even as I run escape scenarios in my head. We could jump out at an intersection, press the driver for the truth, or send a distress message from my phone. I will not let us become three more ticks on the register of stolen lives.

We pass billboards advertising cell-phone companies and travel agencies. The road becomes wider, the buildings shorter and farther apart from their neighbors. The smoke gives way to dust. We are on the outskirts of Kabul, heading east. The city falls away and the driver's cell phone rings. He answers, telling the caller we will arrive shortly. Then he listens, nodding and looking at me in the rearview once more.

I search the backseat for anything that can be used as a weapon. I take a pen out of my purse and make a mental list of the places into which I can plunge its tip. When Mom sees my white-knuckled grip on the pen, her forehead wrinkles with worry.

"Ary . . ." she says. She means to reassure me, but I see a flicker of doubt cross her face. She looks at the back of the driver's head.

"My friend," Clay says, with his usual charm, "are we going where I think we're going?"

The driver looks at him briefly, then turns his eyes back to the road.

"He's asking if you're taking us to Pol-e-charkhi," I say in Dari.

The driver nods.

My father had advised President Daoud against the creation of a prison so large. *When you build a prison large enough to swallow all our schools, do not be surprised to see it do just that.*

The prison appears like a citadel in a desert. High stone walls topped with barbed wire. Corner towers with watch guards in position. It is ten blocks long and just as wide, with the central buildings laid out in the shape of a wheel. Clay looks over at me, his cell phone in his hand.

"No signal out here," he says. "How about you?"

I check my phone. Reception is faint for me as well. Still, I tap out a quick email to Carla at the U.S. embassy.

We're at Pol-e-charkhi. Brought here by people from Ministry of Interior after I met with them and inquired about recovered bodies. They are not saying much yet.

I click Send. The message goes into a queue, to be sent when a network becomes available.

Clay looks at me, his face shadowed with uncertainty too.

The driver pulls over and takes the keys out of the ignition. He points to a gate and tells us we can disembark.

"They are waiting for you inside," he tells us. One by one, we exit the vehicle and assemble by the passenger side. Mom adjusts her headscarf, pulling one end across her mouth to block the dust.

"I suppose we're going in," she says.

The driver walks to the gate, cups his hands around his mouth, and hollers for someone to open the door. A guard appears and eyes us slowly through the metal bars before turning a key. With a grating sound, the door swings open.

The guard motions with his head for us to follow him into a building smaller than the one beside it. It's an austere structure with windows a ten-year-old child couldn't fit through.

Inside, three uniformed men sit around a wooden table. One holds a cigarette between two fingers; he squints as he exhales a cloud of smoke into the room. The men eye us curiously while I take in the layout of the room. There isn't much to look at. There's a calendar on the wall, a desk with a shoebox on it, and a filing cabinet shoved into a corner of the room.

The men stand, and I note that each has a handgun holstered at his hip.

"Please sit," the smoking man says. The driver is gone. One of the soldiers opens three folding chairs and sets them at the table. We slide into the seats, positioned with our backs to the door. Not that it matters. If we were to run outside, we would run into an open dust bowl. "Tell us, please. We hear you have been asking about the bodies of President Daoud Khan and his family."

I sit with my legs crossed, my back straight. I imagine myself in an operating room and try to feel like I have some control.

"We've already discussed our situation with the Ministry of the

Interior. They arranged for the driver to bring us here, so surely they must have told you that my family was killed along with President Daoud Khan's family." I repeat my story, leaving out the detail of my presence at Arg the night of the coup. When I finish, there is a long pause.

The smoking soldier stubs his cigarette out in a glass ashtray.

"It is true," he says gruffly. "We have found a grave with bodies in it."

I feel my heart thumping. I sit forward in the chair.

"But this is nothing new. Every year at least one grave is found. Sometimes five, sometimes five hundred anonymous skeletons."

"And they all deserve a proper burial. Surely the remains of the people who died in the coup aren't only of interest to me."

"It was long ago," he says.

"There were many boots bloodied at Arg," I insist. "Surely someone has been willing to come forward and break his silence."

My voice rings with desperation. I fight to regain control.

The two soldiers look at the one who seems to be the superior of this trio.

"The investigation is ongoing," he says with an air of authority. "We are not yet confirming the identities of the bodies we have found."

"But you believe them to be the bodies of those killed in Arg?" I demand, a half-question, half-statement.

"You know, not everyone in Arg was killed that night. Some were brought to this prison and later exiled. The shah of Iran flew them to Europe. Perhaps your family has been living in exile?"

Having seen what I saw that night, I did not believe this. I'd read it online but saw no pictures to prove it had happened. Clay and Mom watch my face intently, struggling to track the conversation. They see my head drop, as if pulled to the ground by a force stronger than gravity. Finally, I muster the strength to continue.

"They were not exiled," I say softly. "They were not even given the mercy of prison. I am looking only for their bodies, brother. I was witness to their martyrdom."

Shahid. Witness.

Shaheed. Martyr.

So close. We were so close.

His expression softens.

"May their souls rest in heaven," he says, a small act of grace by a man who has likely seen little of it in his lifetime. I watch him reach for the shoebox on the desk.

"What I am about to tell you is not information for the public. I know your friend here is a journalist, but this is strictly confidential. Is that understood?"

"Absolutely," I say, looking at Clay and Mom and nodding. They follow my lead, sensing the direction of the conversation. I look at Clay's lap pointedly. He puts his pen down, closes his notebook, and sits back in his chair.

"We received word about the location of the bodies. We began digging. We found sixteen sets of remains and are currently working on confirming their identities."

"You've found them," I say. "They must be among the sixteen."

The soldier shakes his head.

"Sister, we believe the bodies we've found are all members of Daoud Khan's family."

"How can you know?"

He opens the shoebox and pulls out a clipped stack of photographs. He spreads the pictures across the table. I see a blue tarp and realize I'm looking at the site of the remains they found. In another photograph, small trinkets are arranged beside human remains and small placards. Among the skeletons, he explains, they had found clues left behind after decomposition. While I cannot read the names of the cards because my eyes have blurred, I can see metal suspender clips, a small golden Qur'an, and an orthopedic boot.

"He carried that in his pocket at all times," I say solemnly, recalling the time Neelab had asked her grandfather to show us the Qur'an that a Middle Eastern king had given him.

The president and his wife.

Their six children.

A brother.

A sister-in-law.

Four grandchildren, including a toddler.

My eyes close against the rush of memories. Neelab had learned to knit just so she could make that baby a hat for the winter. I see each of their faces—the furrowed brow of the president, Neelab's dimpled grin, and Rostam's ebullient smile—as if we have gathered in the dining hall of the palace. We were meant to spend our lives together.

It is so hard to breathe.

I clear my throat. I have had ample time to think of the artifacts I would look for in the dust.

"My father had a silver pocket watch engraved with a horse's head. My mother wore a gold pendant of God's name. My brother . . . my brother was three years old. His teeth . . . he had baby teeth . . ."

My throat constricts. No amount of meditation or concentration can release me from the choking feeling.

Mom wraps her arms around me. Clay lowers his head. I wait for the soldiers to speak.

"Sister, I'm sorry to inform you—"

I brace myself.

"But we have found none of the traces you mention."

I look up. That cannot be right. The bodies were all taken away that night. Surely they must have been buried in the same place. Then I remember the interaction in the Ministry of the Interior. I open my bag and pull out my wallet.

"How much do you want? Tell me. Fifty? One hundred? Two hundred?"

The soldiers look at one another.

"I want to give them a decent burial. You would want the same for your family."

"Aryana," Mom says sharply, as if trying to break me from a spell. A breath shudders through my chest.

The soldier in charge slowly collects the handful of bills I've tossed onto the table between us. He slides them back to me, and my stomach sinks.

"I have lost people I love too. With God as witness, I wish I could give you the peace you deserve this very moment.

"Come," he says. They lead us outside, and I expect him to ask us to leave now, but he does not. Instead, he points to something beyond another building and indicates that we should follow. We walk ten minutes from the walls of the prison to the far end of the land. There is little for the eyes to see out here. The looming mountains. A circle of thick branched trees between the grounds of Pol-e-charkhi and the neighboring farm. We ascend a small hill and see freshly upturned earth, a trench dug into the ground.

"The remains were here?" I ask.

He nods.

I lumber down the hill, stumbling at times. At the edge of the ditch, I fall to my knees and stare into the earth. Have they been too hasty? Maybe I will spot a remnant they've missed.

But there is nothing here.

I think of how far I've come, how long I've waited. My headscarf slips away, irreverent, as I press my head to the ground and grieve the last ounce of hope I'd managed to hold.

CHAPTER 58

THE RIDE BACK TO KABUL TAKES MUCH LONGER, AS IF THE CAR has become heavy with defeat.

"I'm so sorry, love," Mom says, trying to console me. I keep my head turned to the window. I cannot look at her now. I cannot look at anyone now. Clay hasn't said much, not after halting the soldiers who did not want me disturbing the excavation site.

Please. This is a lot. She needs a minute, he pleaded. He was right. The hurt was so raw that the coup might have been three days ago instead of three decades.

When we get back to the hotel, I take my migraine medication and sleep for the remainder of the afternoon. Mom tries to wake me for dinner, but I cannot drag myself out of bed. She rubs my back, caresses my hair. I hear her in the bathroom, trying to hide her heavy sighs and sniffles with the sound of running water. I want to tell her that my sorrow is enough for both of us, but I can't form the words.

In the middle of the night, a noise in the hallway wakens me. It's probably someone from the hotel collecting room service trays or dropping off newspapers. I shut my eyelids but cannot get back to sleep. I slide out from under the covers, open my laptop, and reconnect to the hotel Wi-Fi. I scan my email messages and, by force of habit, log in to the charting system to review any urgent messages from patients. My colleagues have been refilling prescriptions and following up on images. The staff have been making appointments and wrangling with the insurance companies for prior authorizations. There are only three unread messages. The first is a note that a patient's MRI was denied, the second is from a patient asking for a referral to an acupuncturist, and the third is a letter from a primary care doctor letting me know a mutual patient has passed away.

The patient is Shair Nabi.

I should not be surprised that he's gone. I recall his ragged appearance, the sallow color of his skin. I consider throwing my computer across the room.

I am furious with him for not telling me more before I left. I'm furious with myself for not pushing him harder, for tolerating his oblique answers and his evasiveness even in our final conversation.

Did he know he would not live to see me return?

So close. I was so close.

I press the heels of my hands against my eyes and see meteors burning out in space, violent flashes of light. Since the night of the coup, Shair has made me feel like the worst version of myself, and I have resented him for that too.

I put on my running clothes and lace up my sneakers. I slip out of the room without Mom noticing. The day must have exhausted her. When we get back home, I'll find ways to spend more time with her. No matter what happens during this trip, I don't want her to worry about me.

The exercise room is locked at this late hour. I should try to go back to sleep or read or look for snacks in our room, but instead I venture to the lobby and beg one of the front desk staff to open the gym door for me.

Whether out of pity or fear, a bleary-eyed man obliges. I thank him, the word coming out in Dari. He pauses just before he leaves, one foot in the hallway.

"Are you Afghan?" he asks in Dari as well. I nod. He presses his lips into a thin line. "Are you . . . are you all right, sister?"

I smile weakly.

"I'm as all right as any of us," I reply, and he lets out a long sigh.

"Then I'll pray for you too," he vows. I listen to the soft pad of his fading footsteps before I move to the treadmill.

And I run.

Within minutes, the leaden feeling around my head begins to lift. I drink in all the oxygen in the room and expunge the dust from my lungs. I feel the burn in my calves, my thighs. I run harder and the burn gives way.

It has taken them thirty years to find this site. And now that they've found the bodies of the president and his family, there will be no reason to search for a handful of his advisers whose names never made it into any of the history books.

Beads of sweat slide down my forehead, stinging my eyes.

I must let go. I cannot bring them back, nor can I have another conversation with Shair.

It is intolerable.

I will lose my sanity if I think of what I could have done differently, if I find all the permutations that could have led to a different outcome. I won't do it.

I will turn the ring over to the museum tomorrow and book an earlier flight home. Clay can stay and chase his stories. He is more at home here than I am anyway. I need to get back to my apartment, my patients, my life.

Six miles later, I slow the treadmill.

I return to the balcony and await the melodic beckoning of the *azaan*.

The dawn sky is a palette of pastels. I watch the apricot sun take her place against the whispers of clouds. When I have taken it all in, I slip back into the room and find Mom dressed but looking pale without her rouge and lipstick.

"Oh, thank God," she says, dropping her toothbrush on the dresser. "I thought you'd run off with some wild plan. . . ."

I sink into the bed and tell Mom that I do, in fact, have a plan. I lay out the agenda in my most matter-of-fact voice, as if I'm reviewing the results of a scan with a patient.

"Are you sure you want to leave?" she asks.

"I think I have to," I reply, then pause before continuing. "Shair is dead."

"Oh, Ary." Mom sinks into the bed next to me. I blink back tears. I'm willing to bet Mom is thinking of the very same moment I am recalling, when Shair pushed me into the safety of her arms. We are family because of him.

"Okay. All right," Mom says, righting herself and turning to the logistics of the task at hand, as she has done time and again over the last thirty years. She walks to the phone and calls Clay to break the news to him while I head for the shower.

We eat breakfast, our table draped in silence. I look from Clay to Mom.

"I'm all right," I tell them. "Truly I am."

They hardly look reassured.

"I'm going to get back to the hospital. Mom's going to get back to her work, and Clay is going to get back to Selena and his book talks," I insist.

"I don't need to rush back to my publicist," Clay says, his voice soft as velvet. "I'll go with you to the museum. And anywhere else you want to go, if you want company. I'm sticking around Kabul for a while. I've got a couple of weeks before my next string of book events."

Selena is his publicist. I blush, feeling dumb to have assumed she was so much more. I'm also a little surprised that this revelation stirs something in me.

Mom's eyebrow lifts in surprise. Ever my savior, she claps her hands and reiterates the day's plan.

"I'll go to the embassy," she begins. During our first visit there, she told a small circle of Carla's colleagues that she'd met most of the warlords and top-billed leaders of the mujahideen. They'd been firebrands at the local colleges while Mom was stationed in Kabul. Carla has asked Mom to come back and brief the team on what she remembers, since a handful of those men had returned to Kabul after years abroad. "I'm sure they're just indulging an old-timer. I can't be helpful now except to tell them not to make the same mistakes we made."

Her comment surprises me. Not wanting to see her and Clay embroiled in another long conversation about what mistakes she means, I review my plan for this morning.

"And I'm headed to the museum," I say, rising from my seat. Clay brushes crumbs from his lap and takes one last sip of water before joining me.

We part ways in front of the hotel. Our taxi heads south while Mom's goes east, toward the green zone. Clay sits in the backseat with me. I am exquisitely aware of the few centimeters of backseat between us. We are in Afghanistan and subject to judgmental eyes, but that's not the only reason.

"You should write about the remains that were found," I tell him. The cab rolls in and out of a deep pothole, jostling us in our seats. I recheck my seat belt and motion for Clay to buckle his. "They're holding back now, but they're going to have to go public with it soon. He was the president."

Clay grimaces.

"I don't know," he says.

"It's a worthy story," I insist.

"No question," he replies. He turns and looks straight into my eyes, holding my gaze steadily despite the uneven road. "But this story is too close to you, Aryana."

"It was the beginning of everything, Clay. People need to know how we got to all of this," I say, waving at the world outside. "You see that. I know you see it."

"It's too close to you," he repeats. "I came to write about the museum, the war. Not you."

"You can write about both. You don't have to make a choice," I insist. In the square set of his jaw, I see his resolve.

"Every article I write is a deliberate choice, Aryana. I go through a list of questions before I pick up my pen. Is it important enough to me? To other people? Can I do the story justice? Will I hurt anyone in telling this story? Will I find something I won't want to write about?"

I rest my forehead against the car window and take in the neighborhood, an adobe relief.

"And if it doesn't pass muster, then I don't do it. Because there are enough journalists swooping in here claiming they 'discovered' something that's been here forever. Or writing up poverty porn to get a byline."

Neither of us says another word until we pull up to the gates of the two-story museum, an elegant building of gray stucco and white architectural detail. The lawn in front, with its stone pathways and petite trees, is reminiscent of an English garden or a private school. I wouldn't be surprised to hear a bell toll and see a dozen boys in pressed uniforms come sauntering out the front door.

In stark contrast to the museum, the guards' station is a wooden shack with an uneven roof. Two men emerge wearing pigeon-colored uniforms. One has a rifle at his side.

"Do you think they're loaded?" I ask.

"It's never occurred to me that they might not be," Clay admits.

We walk through the gates topped with concertina wire. Through the front door, we enter the spacious atrium with freshly painted walls and bright lights. A man wearing a charcoal-colored turban and white tunic and pantaloons regards us with faint interest. He pauses in his polishing of a glass placard as we pass by, and I read the inscription: *A nation stays alive when its culture stays alive.*

He collects our admission fee and motions for us to proceed. Our footsteps pad softly against the tile floor. As far as I can tell, Clay and I are the only visitors here. Inside the purse I hold close to my side is the coveted ring that has traveled to the other side of the world and back again. This museum is a far cry from the ones I've visited in Europe or back home in New York City. I'm feeling torn.

I examine each room with a discerning eye, looking for signs to guide my decision. We are in a long, light-filled room looking at a glazed bowl painted with lapis pigments when we hear the clack of shoes echoing in the hall.

"Madam. Sir. Welcome." A bespectacled man with a thick thatch of hair crosses the room and greets us with a respectful bow. His face is young, and his pants and jacket are a size too big, as if he's dressed in hand-me-downs. "I am Nasrat, the head of the museum. Thank you for coming."

We exchange a few pleasantries with Nasrat and discover that he has personally curated the exhibits. He asks about our work and reason for being in Kabul. I tell him I'm a physician but here with Clay for research. My vague explanation doesn't trouble him. He walks with us, speaking breezily of arranging rooms while respecting chronology.

We pass an eighteenth-century horseman carved of wood. A stone vase with nude figures in relief. A traditional Kuchi-style Afghan dress. We turn a corner and come upon a slab of concrete carved with the letters of an ancient world.

"This is the Rabatak inscription from the rule of Emperor Kanishka," Nasrat explains. "The writing is Bactrian and Greek. It is from the second century."

Clay snaps a couple of pictures with his phone, testing different angles.

"Our history includes many rulers, many religions." Nasrat's brows lift in the direction of the doorway, and he speaks to Clay in a mock-conspiratorial tone. "But we speak this softly. No need to wake the Taliban."

"Do you have any pieces from Ai-Khanoum?" I ask.

"Doctor-*sahib*, thank you for asking about Ai-Khanoum," Nasrat says. He walks us to the end of the room and points to a row of empty glass cases.

"Most Bactrian pieces are not here," he laments softly. His accent is heavy, but his command of English remarkable. He goes on to tell us about the shell game played with relics of the ancient world—artifacts moved from the museum to the Serena Hotel, to vaults beneath the bank. Many were looted along the way and fell into the international black market.

"The Begram ivories were stolen and sold and are now in England's museum. Our antiquities are more welcome than refugees. But slowly, *inshallah*, we will bring them home. This is my work," Nasrat says with pride.

I get the feeling that an older man should be doing this work, one with gray hair and a wrinkled face and musty books on his shelves. But there are few old men in this country. This is a land of adolescence, pockmarked and developing, challenging authority and stepping into the shoes of ancestors.

Nasrat is a hopeful academic. He teaches at the university. He has a wife and two children, and he hopes his children will benefit from the teachings of history.

"This small corner of Kabul," he says, waving his arm to point to the carefully arranged artifacts in the room, "one day many people will come to see. Regime comes and goes. Alexander and his servant—both are dust. A bowl, a hairpin, a ring—only the things we create stay and tell our story."

Nasrat looks at me, his eyes well with conviction.

"Doctor-*sahib*, you save a person's life in this moment. A museum will save our lives after we are gone."

I thought I would be inspecting the museum's walls and fixtures to see if the building was secure enough to hold the ring. But it is Nasrat who makes me realize that the ring's fate is no less important than the museum's fate. This institution deserves this piece of history.

"I have something that should be here," I say. "Could we step into your office for a moment? I need you to promise to make it part of the collection."

Nasrat, intrigued, leads us to his windowless office, in which a two-shelf bookcase is crammed with texts and unbound manuscripts.

As Clay watches, I reach into my bag and pull out this most precious item. My voice does not break as I open the box and reveal the paired stones of the ring, as I tell the young curator that this piece was excavated by the French at Ai-Khanoum and should join the other treasures. Nasrat blinks slowly, looking from the ring to me to Clay—allowing plenty of time for me to have second thoughts, but I do not.

Nasrat rises, closes the door, and wipes his forehead with a handkerchief when he returns to his seat.

"As if this were just another day," he breathes. Nasrat pours us each a small glass of green tea from a thermos on his desk. Tendrils of cardamom-infused steam soothe my senses. He holds his cell phone, his finger hovering over the buttons for a long beat before he begins to dial.

Nasrat speaks to an official from the Ministry of Culture on the phone. A message goes out to a representative of UNESCO. The proper channels have been notified. The ring is in good hands. I stand and slide the strap of my bag over my shoulder, taking one last look at my talisman.

"You must tell me how you came to have this," Nasrat entreats. "You could not have been more than a child when Ai-Khanoum was excavated. Surely you did not dig this ring out of the earth yourself!"

"No," I reply, thinking of the way I'd clung to the ring, like a drowning girl holding on to a life preserver, and how we'd floated out of the castle together. "It was the other way around."

CHAPTER 59

"WE LEAVE IN THIRTY-SIX HOURS," I SAY, HANGING UP THE CALL. With the help of people at the embassy, Mom has booked new tickets for us. As much as I wanted to leave early, I do feel a bit disappointed to be turning away so soon.

But what more is there to do? I have seen the ruins of my family home and the gleaming new stores. I have walked through streets guarded by soldiers from a dozen countries and seen bright-eyed children chat up those soldiers like old friends. I've visited the triumphs of the many empires that ruled this land as well as the deadly munitions left behind. There are addicts shooting up in the desiccated bed of the Kabul River and women vying for seats in a resurrected Parliament. The shopping malls are new, the music is old. The people are paradoxes as well, wizened and doe-eyed, hopeful and traumatized.

"Will you come back?" Clay asks. He has brought me to a teahouse where young men and modestly dressed women congregate, a small rebellion against conservative traditions.

"I don't know," I reply. And I truly don't. "I would come back if they discovered another grave, but I can't really hold out hope for that. It's too consuming . . . and disappointing."

Clay takes a sip of his black tea, steeped to a deep mahogany color.

"Waleed just sent me a message. His sister wants to know if you'd come help train some of the surgeons here. They're eager to learn, from what he tells me."

I bring my cup of *kahweh* to my face and inhale the soft bouquet of scents. I detect minerals leached from the earth, cracked cardamom pods, a swirl of cinnamon, a hint of saffron dust, and a whisper of cloves. A single rose petal floats on the surface. My parents never served tea this way in our home.

"I'd like to. I just don't know if I can say yes right now."

Clay nods, understanding.

"You've got to do what's right for you."

"And what about you? What story will you be working on next?" I ask.

"I want to do a piece highlighting the impact of war on kids," he explains. "I mean, the impact our strikes have had here. I haven't gotten much interest in it, to be honest. People want to read about violent Afghan men. They don't want to hear about a kid who lost his parents in friendly fire."

"But you're still going to write it," I guess.

Clay looks down at the table.

"Have you heard of the napalm girl?" he asks. I've seen the picture but let Clay remind me of the backstory.

"This photographer snaps a shot of a nine-year-old Vietnamese girl running down the street without a stitch of clothes on her, not even socks. The skin on her arm is dripping off, and there are clouds high as mountains behind her, and it looks like she's come running from some dark hell. There are guys in helmets walking on the road too. You can tell from the look on her face and the way her ribs are showing, like she's using every bit of lung power she's got."

I set down my mug.

"It's a horrific picture but an incredible piece of photojournalism. I mean, it's the whole story in this black-and-white image. The truth it conveys is undeniable, but they still tried to come up with any excuse not to run it. Nixon thought it was 'fixed.' And then there was the issue of her *nudity*."

"People have an easier time kissing their elbows than believing war touches kids," I say, lifting the wilted rose petal from my cup, feeling its velvety skin between my fingers. When I look up, Clay is looking at me intently, as if I'm tea leaves at the bottom of the cup.

I look at him just a second more, just long enough to see him—one shoulder a smidge lower than the other from the backpack he keeps slung over it, the faint lines around his eyes from sun glare on Afghan plains, the perfectly mussed chestnut hair.

"Have you been to Bagh-e-Babur?" I ask.

"Not with you," he says.

I purse my lips and bury a smile.

The gardens are a mere ten minutes away. I can feel eyes on us as we step out of the taxi. I glance over my shoulder, but no one looks like the man who followed me outside the restaurant. I am certain by now that my anxieties got the best of me that night.

We stand just outside the high walls surrounding the gardens. I catch a few men looking at me. I'm dressed in a long skirt and a tunic with sleeves that fall to my wrists, like so many of the women here. And yet I exude an otherness that demands their attention. For a second, my neck warms with the heat of their curiosity, at the possibility that they are passing judgment on an Afghan woman walking with an American man.

But inside those high walls, the air clears and I feel my shoulders relax. We ascend stone steps and walk the avenue lined with maple trees. The Mughal gardens are rectilinear in design, laid out in sections with right angles and straight borders. Behind us, adobe homes adorn the skirt of a high hill.

"This was one of my father's favorite places to picnic," I recount. "I don't know how many biscuits I've eaten sitting on one of these tree branches. My mother would scold me and tell me to come down before I fell and broke a bone. But my father . . . my father made it seem like the trees had been planted a hundred years ago just so that I could climb them."

Clay walks beside me, loose-limbed and attentive.

"Your mom sounds like my mom. I lost my mom a year ago, out of the blue. She used to ask me why I couldn't write about sports or maybe even politics," he tells me. "I was here when she passed. I didn't get to say goodbye."

"I'm so sorry to hear that," I reply, and Clay clears his throat.

Three men in heavy coats sit on a blanket on the lawn, playing cards. A light wind rustles the leaves of the trees overhead. One man slaps down a card and lets out a triumphant shout. His friends shake their heads and accuse him, merrily, of cheating.

I am reminded of my parents playing, my father sitting cross-legged and my mother with her legs tucked to her side, her eyes hidden behind dark round lenses. I would peer over my father's shoulder as he arranged his fanned cards by suit, guarding them dramatically from my mother's eyes.

Padar, if you're not careful, you'll lose to her again!

Sitara, I'm prepared for it. She's won me over a thousand times already, my father would reply. He had a way of looking at my mother that made her look away and blush.

Sulaiman, please! Mom would chide, holding in her laughter behind a tight smile. *Stop or I'll not play with you at all.*

You see, Sitara. If you don't have the heart of a lion, do not travel the path of love.

We walk a flagstone path to the far end of the gardens. The swimming pool is empty of water, though that hasn't deterred a band of small boys from playing in the hollow. Two boys sit on the edge, their legs swinging. They turn their heads away and cheer, as if they've conjured the cool splash of water on a hot day.

"Sometimes I look at kids here and see ghosts from my childhood. I look for my friends and neighbors and cousins in their faces," I admit. "As if time might have stood still all the years I've been gone."

"Time isn't that courteous," Clay replies, his voice weighted with melancholy. "People keep living and growing and changing and dying whether we're there or not."

We pass a tree stump, thick and gray as an elephant's foot, and a marble *masjid* with scalloped archways. Men prostrate in prayer in the alcove of the structure, where slanted sunlight warms their devoted backs. We walk through wooden doors twice my height and enter another enclosure.

Babur ordered that this garden be constructed in the image of the gardens of Paradise. Clay and I circle his tomb, admiring the marble lattice of its exterior before stepping into the cool shade inside. The entire structure is a marble enterprise, with a tall, upright headstone.

"Do you believe in heaven?" Clay asks me. Stippled light falls through the latticework and creates the effect of waves on the tomb.

His question makes me think of what Shair said about the seven heavens as we stood over his son's grave. Whether I landed in the heaven with water or the one with white pearls, or brass, or gold, wouldn't matter to me. Nor would I care if I ascended to the heavens with the Angel of Death or Isa or stood in the shade of the enigmatic Lote tree with Moses. I only wanted to know whether God would spread a single family over its seven layers. Nothing beyond reunion mattered.

Shair would probably be buried today or tomorrow. I'd noticed an empty plot near his son's, in that cemetery designed to stay verdant all year long.

Then I remember something else Shair said, something another soldier had relayed to him about the martyred.

He said he'd laid them to rest among giants with a view of Paradise.

I grab Clay's arm.

"I need to go back to the prison," I say. I call Mom and tell her we'll be by soon to pick her up. I tell her I'll explain when we get there. It must take all the strength she has not to press me for details.

As I explain my theory to Clay, I realize how flimsy it sounds. It's just a few words remembered by a dying man. Still, I can't let this go unexplored.

Moments later, we are in a taxi outside the American embassy. Clay goes inside to get Mom. I'm too anxious to deal with going through security now. Instead, I take out my phone and call the officer we met at the prison. He doesn't sound surprised to hear from me.

"I have new information that I'd like to share with you," I tell him.

"I'm listening," he says.

"It's best we speak in person. I'm headed to you now. We won't be long," I say before hanging up the phone. I don't want to risk having him reject my theory over the phone.

I'm so distracted with what I might find at Pol-e-charkhi that I don't notice the man with the short beard and dark eyes coming toward me until he's closed the distance between us.

I look at him, my back pressed against the taxi.

I think about shouting or banging on the cab's window to get the driver's attention. But before I can do anything, the man is in front of me.

"Don't run," he says, as if he's read my thoughts.

CHAPTER 60

THE MAN IS WEARING A LOOSE BUTTON-DOWN SHIRT OVER GRAY slacks. He's close enough that he could grab my wrist, but he makes no move to touch me.

I know he is the man who followed me when I left the restaurant. Though it was too dark to make out his features then, I recognize the shape of him. The slight hunch of his shoulders, the tilt of his head as he regards me.

I square myself to him, though I don't feel threatened. Some other sensation pulses through me, one I cannot name.

"Who are you?" he asks me.

"Why do you ask?" I reply.

He comes a half-step closer and looks into my eyes, searching for something.

"Sitara?"

I cannot breathe.

"My God," he says, though I've not confirmed or denied anything. He shakes his head.

From the corner of my eye, I see a police officer watching us.

"Who . . . who . . ." I stumble as I begin to make sense of his face. I am looking at pieces of the past—the heavy-lidded eyes of a dead president, the dimpled chin of my best friend. I know before he says his name that I am as close as I can be to the halcyon days of my childhood, that I am standing before my co-conspirator and playmate Rostam.

"You're here," I say stupidly. I touch his forearm, and his eyebrows knit together. "How is this possible? You were in Arg that day!"

"As were you," he says, his voice tender. He looks older than he should, ragged as a wanderer. I want to embrace him but hesitate. Though I know him, we are far from the sanctuary of childhood.

"And Neelab?" I ask, hoping with every fiber of my being.

He shakes his head, and I am crushed anew.

WHEN MOM AND CLAY APPROACH, ROSTAM IS JUST BEGINNING TO tell his story. They both look concerned about the man standing so close to me that passersby take notice. Clay opens his mouth to say something but stops when he hears the crack in Rostam's voice.

"I never thought I'd see you again," he says. "How did you escape?"

We return to that day like warriors telling stories around a fire. I tell him how I slipped out of the bedroom to stare at the stars. I tell him about the soldier and the basement and two American women.

"We drove across the border," I say, looking over at Mom. "And then went to America. I used my dead sister's birth certificate to gain citizenship. She raised me."

I tell Mom and Clay that Rostam was a dear childhood friend and the grandson of President Daoud. They understand then, as best they can, what it means for us to see each other after so many years have passed.

Rostam and I return to the night of the coup and fill in the missing details.

Rostam and his family had been sequestered for hours. He and his grandparents, uncles, aunts, and cousins had played cards to pass the time. The children felt like they had stepped into a movie, something fictional and exciting.

That ended when shots broke out—first the indiscriminate strafing from above and then the deeply personal gunshots.

The family struggled with what to do. Someone wanted to raise a white flag. His grandfather and grandmother refused to leave, but urged the others to flee with the children. Cars had circled around to the palace entrance, ready to take them into the countryside.

It was too late.

A bullet struck Neelab in the chest. Rostam caught her, but the breath had already been knocked from her. The wounded moaned with pain. Blood streaked the floors. They tore curtains apart to make bandages and cried for help. In the middle of the night, soldiers caught Rostam attempting to escape and shoved him back into the room with the end of a rifle.

Kill me before they do, he heard his cousin beg. Rostam's uncle had only held his son tighter.

When the second round of gunshots erupted, Rostam's father had fallen but not before he told his son to try to get out through the gardens. Rostam had tried to do just that but slipped before he could get out of the room. He fell to the floor, a sharp pain in his leg. He touched his pants, wet over the wound. He couldn't tell how much blood was his and how much was Neelab's. When two soldiers approached him, he'd looked back at his father's dying face and waited for the bullets that would end his life.

But they didn't shoot him.

As they lifted him, Rostam's hands had slid over the wet floor. He realized the bullet had struck a nearby boiler and only grazed his leg. The wetness he felt was water, not his blood.

Rostam would never know why they had taken him to a hospital for treatment when they had executed so many of his family members. He spent a month and a half in the hospital, visited by the chief doctor and guarded over by soldiers. When he was deemed well enough, he was shackled and sent to Pol-e-charkhi, where he was reunited with other family members who had been spared—uncles, aunts, and cousins.

"We lived seven to a cell in that dungeon," he says. "We were allowed outside only to relieve ourselves. The rest of the time, we listened to the cries of the tortured through the stone walls. I hardly slept, wondering when it would be my turn to keep the others awake."

"How long were you there?" I ask.

"Six months. Then one day, it was over. The shah of Iran sent a plane and put us up in a hotel in Tehran for a month before we went to Switzerland."

Just before the coup, Rostam's mother had gone to Europe for treatment of a lung condition. News of the attack on Arg reached her, and she'd been warned not to return. From what she had been told, there was no one for her to return to anyway.

When Rostam reached Switzerland, he'd fallen into her arms and apologized profusely that he'd not been able to protect Neelab. She'd apologized for not being with them that night. They live in Germany now. Rostam returned to Kabul three months ago when he heard about the commission to locate the bodies.

Tears slide down my cheeks. Rostam rubs both eyes harshly, blotting his tears.

"The other night . . . was that you in the street? Were you following me?" I ask.

Rostam nods.

"I have become friendly with someone at the Ministry of the Interior," he says. "He told me someone named Zamani claimed to have lost her family in Arg. When he said your father's name, I nearly choked on my tea. I didn't know what to believe, or why you were using your sister's name. He told me you were staying at the Intercontinental. I'm embarrassed to say how much time I spent watching the hotel, but I needed to see with my own eyes if it was really you."

Rostam has come today to the American embassy to see if they would give him any information on who I might be. My heart soars to realize he had been looking for me and that I have been found.

"I'll be going home soon," Rostam says. "My mother wasn't well enough to make this trip, and I have to get back to her. Most days she does not recognize me."

I remember how his mother would gather Neelab and me in her arms and beg us not to get into any mischief around the palace. I hate to think of the suffering she's endured.

"I will be heading back home soon too," I tell Rostam. "But we're going back to Pol-e-charkhi first. I need to check once more."

Rostam nods. He doesn't need me to explain to him why it's so important to find them.

"May I join you?" he asks.

"Are you sure?" I want him to come with us but also realize that means returning to the place where he was held prisoner as a child and where many of his family members were buried.

"Yes," Rostam says, straightening his shoulders. "Staying away changes nothing."

We pile into the taxi. Mom sits in the backseat between Clay and me. Rostam slides in beside the driver. The drive to the prison is quiet. Rostam turns his head a few times to ask me about my work or if I've heard from anyone else we used to know. Clay asks him a few questions too. I suppose he can't help himself.

Hamburg is home. This is his third trip to Kabul. He used to work as a tech consultant but lately cares for his mother.

"Now that I have settled this matter, I can focus on getting back to work," he says in Dari to me, as if he owes me some explanation.

I catch his eyes falling on Clay and wonder if he assumes anything about us. A lifetime ago, Neelab teased that I could one day make us real sisters if I would just marry her brother. Seeing him now, I wonder what would have become of us if it hadn't been for the coup. If we'd been allowed to grow up as children with parents and siblings in a childhood unscathed, what would our relationship have grown into?

He scratches the back of his head, and I note that he's not wearing a wedding band. I wonder if his life has been a mirror image of mine. Now that he's exhumed and reburied his family, does he feel any lighter?

I fight back the urge to reach over the seat and hold on to him for fear of losing the one soul who knew me as Sitara, a girl who smiled for the stars.

CHAPTER 61

WHEN THE DRIVER PULLS UP TO THE OUTSIDE GATE OF THE POL-e-charkhi prison compound, I see his eyes skate over the long wall running the length of the compound and the guard towers. Though I've paid him handsomely for waiting outside the embassy and driving us this far out of town, he tells us we'll have to call another taxi to bring us back to the city. He's eager to get away from this place.

I try to see Rostam's face, but he keeps his eyes trained ahead. I don't think he's even looking at anything in particular. I touch his shoulder lightly.

"You can wait here," I say.

I am the first person out of the car. An armed officer approaches me, his posture alert until he recognizes me from our last visit.

"I called your supervisor on our way here," I explain. "He's expecting us."

The officer eyes me and the car with suspicion. He looks at the taxi driver, who shakes his head and points to us as if to say coming here was not his idea.

The officer walks to his station to make a call.

"Clay, can you work on him, please?" I say.

Clay nods, but then turns.

"Wait, what should I tell him?"

"Tell him to meet me out there," I say as I slip away from the car and head off on my own.

It is a stretch to think I might know why they have not yet found the rest of the bodies. Maybe I'm reading too much into what the soldier told Shair about his mission that night. Maybe I'm trusting Shair's memory more than I should. I won't know until I've looked in that circle of trees I saw the last time I came here, when I stood over the place where the bodies of the president and his family had been uncovered.

In Babur's gardens, I saw a grave for a king who was just as dead as any peasant. His tomb may have been built of marble, and it may have been more spacious than others, but it was still a grave. The gardens around it made it a place of beauty. Shair had chosen to bury his son in a place that was peaceful because of the evergreens and the flowers people laid on the tombstones. Even in life, we crave the green lush of heaven's gardens.

I wonder if the soldier who drove the last of the bodies away from Arg had seen that circle of giant trees. I wonder if he took Shair's words to heart and decided to lay those bodies to rest among woody giants with a view of Paradise in their green canopy.

I walk around the corner of the compound and head in the direction of the excavation site. I walk quickly, not wanting anyone to catch up to me right away. The closer I get to the site, the less explaining and convincing I'll have to do. I hear a car door slam behind me.

I look over my shoulder and see that Mom is watching me from a distance. Maybe she's staying back so she doesn't draw more attention to me crossing this dusty plain. Maybe she knows I need to make this small trek on my own.

I pull my headscarf across my mouth and nose. My throat already feels rough and parched.

As I approach the hill, I hear the echo of distant shouts. Up ahead, I can see the circle of soaring trees at the far end of the shooting range. I look over my shoulder once more and see two men peering out from a guard tower. I can't make out what they're saying. It's hard to hear with my pulse thrumming in my ears.

My step quickens. I break into a jog, wanting to be there already. I slip and fall onto my knees. I am back on my feet without stopping to dust myself off. I reach the circle of trees and rest my hand on the gnarled bark of a giant. The girth of their trunks testifies to the decades they have lived in this spot, this small community of sentries, witnessing and guarding Kabul's secrets.

The earth here is untouched, the circle twenty paces wide. I catch my breath, wondering where I should begin. I walk to the center and take a moment to absorb the tranquility. It is possible, from here, to ignore the prison beyond the berm. It is possible, in this remote copse, to feel a few beats of peace or hope. I fall to my knees, close my eyes, and wait for a sign, some spectral nod, that I am right.

"Doctor-*sahib!*" a voice calls out. I open my eyes and spot two men coming toward me.

"We must dig here," I command. I run my hands across the ground like a diving rod.

The two men stand over me.

"Why did you not bring shovels?"

They do not budge. Though they're not inclined to take orders from me, they leave me where I am.

Everyone arrives then. The officer we met last time. Rostam, Clay, and Mom. Two more guards, one looking more bewildered than the other.

"What are you doing out here?" the supervising officer asks me. "What's this information you claim to have?"

I take a deep breath and stand to face him.

"We must dig here," I command. "I was told this is where they were buried. Let's not waste time."

"You speak as if you have stars and stripes on your jacket," he mutters. "Who gave you this idea?"

"Please," I say. "The man who told me was a soldier at Arg that night. He knew. This must be the place."

I am leaning into what I believe in my heart. Shair may not have known the exact coordinates, but he brought me here.

"This is a small ask," Rostam adds. "Given the number of bodies found over the years, she's more likely to be right than wrong."

The officer huffs.

"There is a process to these matters," he says. "We don't just pick up shovels."

He turns his back on us and puts his hands on his hips.

"I'll have to answer for this," he mutters, then looks at two men waiting on his command. He shakes his head in the direction of the building.

Mom breathes an audible sigh of relief.

Heavy shovels and rusted picks are brought out in a wheelbarrow. The officer spreads the guards out within the circle. The earth in this patch is dry, every drop of moisture soaked up by thirsty roots. The surface does not want to be breached.

The officer walks to where Mom and I are standing.

"We shall see," he tells me. "But I suggest you take this time to ask yourself what you're hoping to find under this dirt."

I pick up an idle shovel and choose an area away from others. The guards look from me to their supervisor, wondering if he'll stop me from digging. He only shrugs and steps away to answer a call from the prison.

Rostam and Clay take turns too, giving the guards a break. Soon we are all sweating. My palms ache, but I do not pause. I toss small heaps of earth behind me, just past the trees.

The sun starts to set. I hear Rostam urge the guards to continue digging. One sets his shovel down and states that it's time for him to go home. The others, despite having unearthed nothing but stones, pick up where he left off. Mom sits with her back to a tree, watching the trench widen. A new guard appears with oil lamps and a thermos heavy with tea. They take turns drinking from a single cup. The sky darkens, steeped in night.

"Thank you," I tell the people around me. "Thank you for doing this. No matter what happens, I'll always remember I wasn't alone here."

I want to say so much more but choke up trying to find the words.

"Sister, we've all spent more energy on lesser tasks. No need to thank us," one says. I cannot make out his face in the dark. I turn and look at Rostam, whose eyes glisten in the lamplight. He turns his back and plunges a shovel into the ground.

Two hours after we should have given up, a shout cuts through the rhythmic toiling. The shovel falls from my hand and lands on the rutted earth with a clunk. Mom is at my side, and I lean my head on her shoulder as a circle of people gather around. Despite how I've longed for this moment, I am suddenly petrified to face it.

"My God," I hear Clay exclaim. He is at my side in a flash. Rostam follows, his face rough with sorrow. I look at him.

"Give them some time," Rostam advises. He leads me to a nearby tree, where I sit with my head resting on Mom's shoulder. The work resumes, shovels exchanged for brushes and hands. An unfurled sheet prepares to receive the unburied bones. Under a night sky twinkling with mythical creatures and parables, I do the same.

What will this change? I wonder. If I'm no less alone than I was yesterday, what is the difference? Will I feel released from this knotted grief? Will my dreams soften? Will I still be me?

I close my eyes and breathe in the scents of this night—mint on my mother's hands, the spice of my father's cologne, and Faheem's milky breath. It does not stop there. I sense my mother's spirit first, as if she's floated over and taken a seat beside me. I can almost feel her caress my head. My father comes next, smiling as if he were expecting me. His steps are slower because he's carrying my brother. Faheem's small arms are wrapped around my father's neck, his eyes bright with an eternal love.

I feel foolish then that I ever thought they might have resented me for surviving that night.

And so, when I'm summoned to see all that remains of my family, I walk steadily, I am ready, for I have already seen what I came to see.

EPILOGUE

THERE IS A JOKE I READ YEARS AGO IN AN ONLINE CHAT ROOM FOR Afghans. King Zahir Shah, who was monarch before Daoud Khan overthrew him and declared himself president, settled into a new life in Italy. He had gone from a gilded palace to a small apartment, from an exalted life to one of exile. He was a nobody living in a foreign land. Dejected, he went to see a psychiatrist. In the waiting room, an Italian man peered over the top of a magazine, curious how his malady ranked against those of others in the room. He leaned over and asked King Zahir Shah what affliction of the mind had prompted him to seek help.

King Zahir Shah explained that he had been, until recently, king of a sovereign nation. The Italian man said nothing.

When the door opened and the doctor's assistant asked who was next in line, the Italian man pointed to the bald man with a graying mustache seated beside him and said with great empathy: "Take him first."

Clay laughs when I tell him this story, at how much like delusion the histories of dispersed Afghans must sound to new neighbors. We are sitting on Mom's porch watching fireflies light up the nearby woods. Mom is inside, packing up the leftovers of tonight's dinner. Clay had offered to wash the dishes, but she shooed him away.

You're a guest in my home tonight, she'd said. *And only tonight. Tomorrow I'll expect all hands on deck for breakfast.*

This is our first weekend away at Mom's house. Clay spent our first hour here taking in all the pictures on the walls, the curio crowded with souvenirs from around the world, and the carefully arranged spines on the bookshelf. He looked hesitant about touching some pieces, leaning in with his hands behind his back.

My fingers float to my neck, a habit formed since I started wearing my mother's necklace. Clay bought me a glass dome for my father's pocket watch. It sits on my desk where I sometimes lose myself staring at it, watching time suspended. Dayo, my stoic friend, cried to see it. I showed her pictures of the three graves on a hilltop in Kabul. I told her about the burial I'd finally been able to arrange for my family. Though they hadn't been sent off with a twenty-one-gun salute like Rostam's grandfather, they had been laid to rest in dignity, with headstones to mark their existence.

"You're thinking about them," Clay observes.

I look down.

"Yeah, I am. It's just . . . it's just so different now. I used to only think of those last moments. It was so hard to think of anything else. But now I feel like I can have so much more back, and it's nothing like having them again, but it's something. It's a lot."

I think of Dayo and what she said about lightning and thunder, the flash and the bang. I think of the patients I've returned to and the storms they are enduring. I was wrong to think I could move on quickly. I expected so much more of myself than I expected from people I care for.

"That's a big step," Clay says as he takes my hand in his. I smile and lean toward him so our shoulders touch.

"I wonder what the little girl in the cemetery is doing now," I muse.

On our way to the airport in Kabul, I'd asked for one last stop at the cemetery. I'd walked up a hill with haphazardly arranged graves, some in protective metal enclosures that looked too much like cages for my taste.

As I'd approached the graves, a little girl carrying a bucket of water had appeared. She must have spotted me from a distance and scared off her competition. The cemetery had become a land of opportunity for children looking to help feed their families. She offered to sprinkle water on the graves of my loved ones to wash away their sins and maybe even inspire a patch of green to grow.

She'd been generous with the water, wetting the dirt as I said my silent goodbyes. I'd given her a bill that made her eyes go wide and asked her to look after their graves a few more times for me.

"She's probably wondering when you'll be back," Clay says.

I don't know the answer to that question yet. A lifetime ago, Shair had told me that Kabul was no longer my home. He'd been right, but only in a literal way. The city would always be a part of me, and I would always be a part of her. Our stories are intertwined.

I think of Rostam, wandering Kabul looking like a ghost of himself. He video-called me from Germany a week ago and introduced me to his wife and children. Though they were polite and even cracked a few jokes, the conversation quickly petered out. We were strangers, after all. Even Rostam struggled to come up with things to say, and after a few moments we promised to talk again soon. I take comfort in knowing he is surrounded by love. That might be all I can salvage from what we once were.

"Who knows? Maybe you and I will end up going back together," I say, thinking of Waleed's sister and the churning hospital. I'm surprised at how easily I talk about a future with Clay. Maybe that comes from having talked about so much of the past with him.

"Maybe. I've still got those stories to finish," Clay says. He managed to squeeze one article out of his trip to Kabul, but it was hardly the piece his chief had expected.

"Are you sure you don't want to write about . . ."

Clay shakes his head.

"That story is yours to tell, Aryana," he says. "I just hope I can be the first to read it."

I fill my lungs with the cool night air, the scent of evergreens and a distant fire. I wrap my arm around Clay's waist, and my head spins to think of how fast and far we've traveled together. There is so much more I want to learn about him. There is so much more of me I want to share with him.

And for the first time in my life, that thought does not daunt me.

AUTHOR'S NOTE

A few years back, I pinned a newspaper article by journalist Carlotta Gall to the corkboard above my desk. It was a short piece on the discovery of the remains of Afghanistan's first president, forty years after he and eighteen members of his family had been killed in a swift coup that forever changed the country's course. The youngest victim was only eighteen months old.

My parents were born and raised in a peaceful window of Afghan history that came just before that coup. When they speak of their childhoods, they speak of crisp melons, stern teachers, kites and bicycles, the indulgent hugs of a grandmother, and poetry-filled nights. The photographs they carried into their lives as refugees and immigrants, the pictures I've seen throughout my life, would surprise people who have only gotten to know Afghanistan in the past twenty years.

My previous novels about Afghanistan span the last century, from the time of kings and harems to the suffocating grip of the Taliban to a fledgling democracy. *Sparks Like Stars* is my exploration of how a country that inspired wanderlust could have tipped into decades of war and turmoil. I see Afghanistan as a survivor, victimized by colonialism, imperialism, the Cold War, and, at times, by her own people.

While Aryana, her family, Rostam, Neelab, Antonia, and Tilly are my own creation, many characters, details, and events in this story are factual. President Daoud Khan did drive around Kabul in a white Toyota Corolla. The Americans stationed in cosmopolitan Kabul did indeed put on a performance of the musical *Oklahoma!* around the time of the Saur Revolution. Before the coup, Afghanistan had been a desirable and exotic posting that promised good times for diplomats. I took liberties with the timing of the siege on the American embassy in Islamabad, shortening the time between the assassination of Afghanistan's president and the bubbling of anti-American tensions in neighboring Pakistan.

Afghans in the countryside were hospitable toward and likely intrigued by overlanders as well as bright-eyed Peace Corps volunteers from the sixties and seventies who still consider themselves "Friends of Afghanistan." They are some of the most inspiring people I've ever met and their Afghan students, people like my father, remember time spent with these Americans fondly.

My portrayal of President Daoud Khan and the coup itself was informed by many sources—friends and family, books like Tamim Ansary's *Games Without Rules*, Louis Dupree's *Afghanistan*, and the oral history collection maintained by the Association for Diplomatic Studies and Training (ADST). I read the interviews given by Americans who served in Kabul during the time of the coup, including Ambassador Theodore Eliot, political counselors, and officers of various positions. I reached out to Louise Taylor, who served as Director of the American Cultural Center in Kabul at the time of the coup and she was most generous with her time and memories, indulging my questions and enriching my story. The CIA's reading room also holds a trove of fascinating and carefully redacted documents and communications. Steve Coll's *Ghost Wars* is a worthy read for those looking for an easier to follow record of the CIA's contorted involvement in Afghanistan in the years prior to 9/11. President Daoud Khan's grandson, a survivor of the coup, shared his firsthand account with the Dari-speaking world. Mujib Mashal, and many of his journalist colleagues, have gifted us with compelling glimpses of life in Afghanistan today.

The low ceiling for women in the American foreign service is well described by many women who served and available on the ADST website as well as in Alison Palmer's memoir, *Diplomat and Priest.*

The *Head East* guidebook published in 1973 offered a wide range of travel tips to overlanders ranging from best post offices to cheap meals. My favorite section included a recommendation for travelers to wade through poppy fields dressed in a loin cloth to collect "pollen hash" that could then be pressed "against the warm sweating body of a fellow romantic field nymph or satyr." It's easy to lose an afternoon browsing posted photographs of hippies in eastern bazaars or picnicking with their packs to the Hindu Kush mountains.

Imperialism and colonialism are two-handed thieves, robbing nations of their destinies and their histories. The artifacts of Ai-Khanoum, like Afghans displaced by war, can be found around the world. The plunder of antiquities is receiving more thoughtful ink these days. I recommend *Afghanistan: Hidden Treasures from the National Museum, Kabul,* and *Afghan Art and Architecture through the Ages* by Hamid Naweed for those interested in the arts and civilizations unearthed by archaeologists.

Aryana's story is not my story, though I leaned into my personal experiences more for her than perhaps any other character I've written. Like me, she was an Afghan American physician in training in New York City on 9/11, when America's gaze swiveled back to Afghanistan and struggled to sort out friend from foe. And as physicians, both of us have had the privilege of sitting with families in their most vulnerable moments.

In the years since the coup, conflict in Afghanistan has claimed far too many lives. Those who survived plod forward bearing scars and trauma. Nadia Anjuman, a poet murdered by her husband, left behind verses that are fusions of hurt and hope. The title of this book comes from her stirring work, *The Night's Poetry*.

I hope I've done this sliver of history justice.

ACKNOWLEDGMENTS

My village came through for me again and I am more grateful than ever. To my husband, who wears a great many hats when it comes to my stories, your belief in me sustains me. Thank you to my beloved early readers and cheerleaders—Mom, Dad, and Uncle Isah. To my most precious book club—Zoran, Zayla, Kyrus, Cyra—may we always gather over stories. To my circles of friends and family, I can't imagine this journey without you. You know who you are.

Thank you to Louise Taylor, a former Foreign Service officer stationed in Kabul during the Saur Revolution, who provided invaluable insights. To those who collected and curated the oral histories at the Association for Diplomatic Studies and Training, I have spent hours delving into the past and enjoyed every bit of it. Thank you for making this available. A princess wave to Arzo Wardak, who helped nudge Anastasia into this story.

Helen Heller, you bring every manuscript I give you closer to its destined form. Your instincts are invaluable. Rachel Kahan, you are a true ally and make bookshelves adventurous, richer, and more honest reflections. Big hugs of gratitude to you both.

Many thanks to the team at William Morrow who have beautifully packaged this story and helped deliver it to readers—Mumtaz Mustafa, Cindy Buck, Jennifer Hart, Stephanie Vallejo, Allison Hargraves, Camille Collins, Kaitie Leary, and Liate Stehlik.

Dear readers, thank you for asking me when you can expect the next book, for inviting me into your living rooms, and for keeping me on my toes. Your personal notes give the work meaning. To organizers of book festivals, humanities organizations, librarians, teachers, bookshop champions, narrators, translators, journalists, and all who continue to uphold the importance of storytelling in its many forms, we are all forever in your debt.

Until next time.